THE HUGO AWARD SHOWCASE

OTHER BOOKS BY MARY ROBINETTE KOWAL

Shades of Milk and Honey (forthcoming)

THE HUGO AWARD SHOWCASE

2010 VOLUME

EDITED BY MARY ROBINETTE KOWAL

PRIME BOOKS

THE HUGO AWARDS SHOWCASE

Prime Books
www.prime-books.com

For more information, contact Prime Books:
prime@prime-books.com

ISBN: 978-1-60701-225-2

TABLE OF CONTENTS

INTRODUCTION

All of us come to science fiction and fantasy from different roads, but it is hard to spend any time in the genre without becoming aware of the Hugo Awards. For many readers, the Hugo Awards are one of the ways of deciding what to read in a given year. Looking at the ever widening array of science fiction and fantasy on the bookstore shelves it's easy to become overwhelmed and the stamp of "Hugo Award winner" on the cover offers a reassurance that a large number of fans, of people like you, thought that book was outstanding.

That's because the Hugo Awards are voted on by the membership of the World Science Fiction Society, an international collection of science fiction and fantasy readers. The awards have been given out annually since 1955 although the history of the award stretches back to 1939. Originally the members of the World Science Fiction Society voted on the "bests" of the year, without presenting any awards. In 1953, in Philadelphia, the committee decided to act on the brainchild of Hal Lynch and present actual awards. These slender rockets were handmachined by Jack McKnight. That year the awards went to: Alfred Bester, Novel, *The Demolished Man*; *Astounding* and *Galaxy*, Professional Magazine; Virgil Finlay, Interior Illustrator; Hannes Bok and Ed Emshwiller, Cover Artist; Philip José Farmer, New Author or Artist; Willy Ley, Excellence in Fact Articles; and Forrest J. Ackerman, #1 Fan Personality.

What's interesting to me about those early awards is that short fiction was overlooked. Today, it is easy to walk into a bookstore and buy the 2009 Hugo winning novel, *The Graveyard Book* by Neil Gaiman. The short fiction on the other hand tends to slip through the cracks and get lost as magazines go off the rack. It's true that many of the stories gets picked up in Year's Best anthologies or appears in other forms elsewhere but it is still easy to miss. How can you tell which anthology has a Hugo winner in it?

This collection is intended to bring together the winners and some of the nominees to show you what the World Science Fiction Society thought were the most remarkable short stories, novelettes and novellas last year. Now, the Hugos were originally called the Annual Science Fiction Achievement Awards which is, to my mind, a beautifully accurate way to describe them, because even if you don't like a story or a novel it's still possible to recognize that it stood out from the crowd and achieved something special. Sometimes that achievement is in the use of language, or the thought experiments, or the sheer moving power of a story. The wonderful thing about the works in this volume is that they are wildly different from one another.

Looking at the short fiction categories, particularly when you pull the nominees into the mix, demonstrates the wide range of possibilities within science fiction and fantasy.

So what exactly are novellas? It means short novel, but the definition that the Hugos use is that it is a work of fiction between 17,500 and 40,000 words. It was first awarded in 1968 to Philip José Farmer's *Riders of the Purple Wage* and *Weyr Search* by Anne McCaffrey. Maybe you've heard of these authors? *Weyr Search*, interestingly enough, was the first part of her extremely popular novel *Dragonflight* and was in *Analog*.

One reason people pay attention to the short fiction categories, in fact, is that they often spotlight authors who might have interesting novels in them.

Novelettes have a tricky role. Running between 7,500 and 17,500 words they fill the space between short stories and novellas. Some people feel that the categories are arbitrary distinctions and so the novelette category periodically gets dropped from the ballots. It was first awarded in 1955 to Walter M. Miller Jr's "The Darfstellar." The award was dropped for the year 1957 then again from 1959-1966. It ran for three years and was again dropped until 1973 from whence it has remained on the ballot. It is a different form than either a short story or a novella but the lines between where one begins and the other ends are fairly fluid. A novelette gives an author the breathing room to explore a complicated idea without trying to fit into a small wordcount, while at the same time retaining a tighter focus than novellas or novels typically have.

Short stories have been around since 1955, with the exception of 1957, and was first awarded to Eric Frank Russell's "Allamagoosa." You see what I mean about short fiction often getting lost into the mists of time?

The fiction that you'll be reading in this volume runs the gamut from seasoned professionals to first time nominees. The shortest story is 970 words the longest is 28,500. The stories span the time between 1813 and so far in the future that Earth is a myth like Eden. In structure and voice they are wildly different.

The strength of this volume, I think, is in how different these stories are from one another. That diversity is one of the strengths of the fields of science fiction and fantasy.

I hope you enjoy exploring the short fiction worlds of the Hugo Awards.

Mary Robinette Kowal
June 2010

JOHN KESSEL—NOVELETTE
PRIDE AND PROMETHEUS

It takes a certain level of audacity to decide to take two of the great literary establishments and create a mashup. I mean, let's not pretend that taking *Pride and Prejudice* and bringing Mary Shelley's *Frankenstein* into the mix is anything other than that.

Except, of course, Kessel takes it way past that point. In less experienced hands, this would be fan fic at best. What we have instead is something that stays true to the social manners books of Austen's day while introducing the gothic horror of Mary Shelley and then creates something totally new. It is an intimate study of a girl, Mary, doomed to be a supporting cast member not just in Austen's story but in her life outside the story. She is an observer and gives us a picture of Dr. Frankenstein from the outside.

Since Mary Shelley's original story is told in first person, we are never able to see Frankenstein without the lens of himself in the way. Kessel shows us an awkward man, during part of his journey where he is most damaged emotionally. It is fascinating and feels oddly voyeuristic.

Kessel has a PhD in English and teaches American literature, science fiction, fantasy, and fiction writing at North Carolina State University. He has been nominated for numerous awards and won a Theodore Sturgeon Award, a James Tiptree Jr. award, and a Nebula. This is his third Hugo nomination.

PRIDE AND PROMETHEUS

JOHN KESSEL

⬥

Had both her mother and her sister Kitty not insisted upon it, Miss Mary Bennet, whose interest in Nature did not extend to the Nature of Society, would not have attended the ball in Grosvenor Square. This was Kitty's season. Mrs. Bennet had despaired of Mary long ago, but still bore hopes for her younger sister, and so had set her determined mind on putting Kitty in the way of Robert Sidney of Detling Manor, who possessed a fortune of six thousand pounds a year, and was likely to be at that evening's festivities. Being obliged by her unmarried state to live with her parents, and the whims of Mrs. Bennet being what they were, although there was no earthly reason for Mary to be there, there was no good excuse for her absence.

So it was that Mary found herself in the ballroom of the great house, trussed up in a silk dress with her hair piled high, bedecked with her sister's jewels. She was neither a beauty, like her older and happily married sister Jane, nor witty, like her older and happily married sister Elizabeth, nor flirtatious, like her younger and less happily married sister Lydia. Awkward and nearsighted, she had never cut an attractive figure, and as she had aged she had come to see herself as others saw her. Every time Mrs. Bennet told her to stand up straight, she felt despair. Mary had seen how Jane and Elizabeth had made good lives for themselves by finding appropriate mates. But there was no air of grace or mystery about Mary, and no man ever looked upon her with admiration.

Kitty's card was full, and she had already contrived to dance once with the distinguished Mr. Sidney, whom Mary could not imagine being more tedious. Hectically glowing, Kitty was certain that this was the season she would get a husband. Mary, in contrast, sat with her mother and her Aunt Gardiner, whose good sense was Mary's only respite from her mother's silliness. After the third minuet Kitty came flying over.

"Catch your breath, Kitty!" Mrs. Bennet said. "Must you rush about like this? Who is that young man you danced with? Remember, we are here to smile on Mr. Sidney, not on some stranger. Did I see him arrive with the Lord Mayor?"

"How can I tell you what you saw, Mother?"

"Don't be impertinent."

"Yes. He is an acquaintance of the Mayor. He's from Switzerland! Mr. Clerval, on holiday."

The tall, fair-haired Clerval stood with a darker, brooding young man, both impeccably dressed in dove gray breeches, black jackets, and waist-coats, with white tie and gloves.

"Switzerland! I would not have you marry any Dutchman—though 'tis said their merchants are uncommonly wealthy. And who is that gentleman with whom he speaks?"

"I don't know, Mother—but I can find out."

Mrs. Bennet's curiosity was soon to be relieved, as the two men crossed the drawing room to the sisters and their chaperones.

"Henry Clerval, madame," the fair-haired man said, "And this is my good friend, Mr. Victor Frankenstein."

Mr. Frankenstein bowed but said nothing. He had the darkest eyes that Mary had ever encountered, and an air of being there only on obligation. Whether this was because he was as uncomfortable in these social situations as she, Mary could not tell, but his diffident air intrigued her. She fancied his reserve might bespeak sadness rather than pride. His manners were faultless, as was his command of English, though he spoke with a slight French accent. When he asked Mary to dance she suspected he did so only at the urging of Mr. Clerval; on the floor, once the orchestra of pianoforte, violin, and cello struck up the quadrille, he moved with some grace but no trace of a smile.

At the end of the dance, Frankenstein asked whether Mary would like some refreshment, and they crossed from the crowded ballroom to the sitting room, where he procured for her a cup of negus. Mary felt obliged to make some conversation before she should retreat to the safety of her wallflower's chair.

"What brings you to England, Mr. Frankenstein?"

"I come to meet with certain natural philosophers here in London, and in Oxford—students of magnetism."

"Oh! Then have you met Professor Langdon, of the Royal Society?"

Frankenstein looked at her as if seeing her for the first time. "How is it that you are acquainted with Professor Langdon?"

"I am not personally acquainted with him, but I am, in my small way, an enthusiast of the sciences. You are a natural philosopher?"

"I confess that I can no longer countenance the subject. But yes, I did study with Mr. Krempe and Mr. Waldman in Ingolstadt."

"You no longer countenance the subject, yet you seek out Mr. Langdon."

A shadow swept over Mr. Frankenstein's handsome face. "It is unsupportable to me, yet pursue it I must."

"A paradox."

"A paradox that I am unable to explain, Miss Bennet."

All this said in a voice heavy with despair. Mary watched his sober black eyes, and replied, " 'The heart has its reasons of which reason knows nothing.' "

For the second time that evening he gave her a look that suggested an understanding. Frankenstein sipped from his cup, then spoke: "Avoid any pastime, Miss Bennet, that takes you out of the normal course of human contact. If the study to which you apply yourself has a tendency to weaken your affections, and to destroy your taste for simple pleasures, then that study is certainly unlawful."

The purport of this extraordinary speech Mary was unable to fathom. "Surely there is no harm in seeking knowledge."

Mr. Frankenstein smiled. "Henry has been urging me to go out into London society; had I known that I might meet such a thoughtful person as yourself I would have taken him up on it long ere now."

He took her hand. "But I spy your aunt at the door," he said. "No doubt she has been dispatched to protect you. If you will, please let me return you to your mother. I must thank you for the dance, and even more for your conversation, Miss Bennet. In the midst of a foreign land, you have brought me a moment of sympathy."

And again Mary sat beside her mother and aunt as she had half an hour before. She was nonplused. It was not seemly for a stranger to speak so much from the heart to a woman he had never previously met, yet she could not find it in herself to condemn him. Rather, she felt her own failure in not keeping him longer.

A cold March rain was falling when, after midnight, they left the ball. They waited under the portico while the coachman brought round the carriage. Kitty began coughing. As they stood there in the chill night, Mary noticed a hooded man, of enormous size, standing in the shadows at the corner of the lane. Full in the downpour, unmoving, he watched the town house and its partiers without coming closer or going away, as if this observation were all his intention in life. Mary shivered.

In the carriage back to Aunt Gardiner's home near Belgravia, Mrs. Bennet insisted that Kitty take the lap robe against the chill. "Stop coughing, Kitty. Have a care for my poor nerves." She added, "They should never have put the supper at the end of that long hallway. The young ladies, flushed from the dance, had to walk all that cold way."

Kitty drew a ragged breath and leaned over to Mary. "I have never seen you so taken with a man, Mary. What did that Swiss gentleman say to you?"

"We spoke of natural philosophy."

"Did he say nothing of the reasons he came to England?" Aunt Gardiner asked.

"That was his reason."

"Hardly!" said Kitty. "He came to forget his grief! His little brother William was murdered, not six months ago, by the family maid!"

"How terrible!" said Aunt Gardiner.

Mrs. Bennet asked in open astonishment, "Could this be true?"

"I have it from Lucy Copeland, the Lord Mayor's daughter," Kitty replied. "Who heard it from Mr. Clerval himself. And there is more! He is engaged to be married—to his cousin. Yet he has abandoned her, left her in Switzerland and come here instead."

"Did he say anything to you about these matters?" Mrs. Bennet asked Mary.

Kitty interrupted. "Mother, he's not going to tell the family secrets to strangers, let alone reveal his betrothal at a dance."

Mary wondered at these revelations. Perhaps they explained Mr. Frankenstein's odd manner. But could they explain his interest in her? "A man should be what he seems," she said.

Kitty snorted, and it became a cough.

"Mark me, girls," said Mrs. Bennet, "that engagement is a match that he does not want. I wonder what fortune he would bring to a marriage?"

In the days that followed, Kitty's cough became a full-blown catarrh, and it was decided against her protest that, the city air being unhealthy, they should cut short their season and return to Meryton. Mr. Sidney was undoubtedly unaware of his narrow escape. Mary could not honestly say that she regretted leaving, though the memory of her half hour with Mr. Frankenstein gave her as much regret at losing the chance of further commerce with him as she had ever felt from her acquaintance with a man.

Within a week Kitty was feeling better, and repining bitterly their remove from London. In truth, she was only two years younger than Mary and had made none of the mental accommodations to approaching spinsterhood that her older sister had attempted. Mr. Bennet retreated to his study, emerging only at mealtimes to cast sardonic comments about Mrs. Bennet and Kitty's marital campaigns. Perhaps, Mrs. Bennet said, they might invite Mr. Sidney to visit Longbourn when Parliament adjourned. Mary escaped these discussions by practicing the pianoforte and, as the advancing spring brought warm weather, taking walks in the countryside, where she would stop beneath an oak and read, indulging her passion for Goethe and German philosophy. When she tried to engage her father in speculation, he warned her, "I am afraid, my dear, that your understanding is too dependent on books and not enough on experience of the world. Beware, Mary. Too much learning makes a woman monstrous."

What experience of the world had they ever allowed her? Rebuffed, Mary wrote to Elizabeth about the abrupt end of Kitty's latest assault on marriage, and her subsequent ill temper, and Elizabeth wrote back inviting her two younger sisters to come visit Pemberley.

Mary was overjoyed to have the opportunity to escape her mother and see something more of Derbyshire, and Kitty seemed equally willing. Mrs. Bennet was not persuaded when Elizabeth suggested that nearby Matlock and its baths might be good for Kitty's health (no man would marry a sickly girl), but she was persuaded by Kitty's observation that, though it could in no way rival London, Matlock did attract a finer society than sleepy Meryton, and thus offered opportunities for meeting eligible young men of property. So in the second week of May, Mr. and Mrs. Bennet tearfully loaded their last unmarried daughters into a coach for the long drive to Derbyshire. Mrs. Bennet's tears were shed because their absence would deprive Kitty and Mary of her attentions, Mr. Bennet's for the fact that their absence would assure him of Mrs. Bennet's.

The two girls were as ever delighted by the grace and luxury of Pemberley, Mr. Darcy's ancestral estate. Darcy was kindness itself, and the servants attentive, if, at the instruction of Elizabeth, less indulgent of Kitty's whims and more careful of her health than the thoroughly cowed servants at home. Lizzy saw that Kitty got enough sleep, and the three sisters took long walks in the grounds of the estate. Kitty's health improved, and Mary's spirits rose. Mary enjoyed the company of Lizzy and Darcy's eight-year-old son William, who was attempting to teach her and Darcy's younger sister Georgiana to fish. Georgiana pined after her betrothed, Captain Broadbent, who was away on crown business in the Caribbean, but after they had been there a week, Jane and her husband Mr. Bingley came for an extended visit from their own estate thirty miles away, and so four of the five Bennet sisters were reunited. They spent many cordial afternoons and evenings. Both Mary and Georgiana were accomplished at the pianoforte, though Mary had come to realize that her sisters tolerated more than enjoyed her playing. The reunion of Lizzy and Jane meant even more time devoted to Kitty's improvement, with specific attention to her marital prospects, and left Mary feeling invisible. Still, on occasion she would join them and drive into Lambton or Matlock to shop and socialize, and every week during the summer a ball was held in the assembly room of the Old Bath Hotel, with its beeswax polished floor and splendid chandeliers.

On one such excursion to Matlock, Georgiana stopped at the milliners while Kitty pursued some business at the butcher's shop—Mary wondered at her sudden interest in Pemberley's domestic affairs—and Mary took William to the museum and circulating library, which contained celebrated cabinets of natural history. William had told her of certain antiquities unearthed in the excavation for a new hotel and recently added to the collection.

The streets, hotels, and inns of Matlock bustled with travelers there to take the waters. Newly wedded couples leaned on one another's arms, whispering secrets that no doubt concerned the alpine scenery. A crew of workmen was breaking up the cobblestone street in front of the hall, swinging pickaxes in the bright sun. Inside she and Will retreated to the cool quiet of the public exhibition room.

Among the visitors to the museum Mary spied a slender, well-dressed man at one of the display cases, examining the artifacts contained there. As she drew near, Mary recognized him. "Mr. Frankenstein!"

The tall European looked up, startled. "Ah—Miss Bennet?"

She was pleased that he remembered. "Yes. How good to see you."

"And this young man is?"

"My nephew, William."

At the mention of this name, Frankenstein's expression darkened. He closed his eyes. "Are you not well?" Mary asked.

He looked at her again. "Forgive me. These antiquities call to mind sad associations. Give me a moment."

"Certainly," she said. William ran off to see the hall's steam clock. Mary turned and examined the contents of the neighboring cabinet.

Beneath the glass was a collection of bones that had been unearthed in the local lead mines. The card lettered beside them read: *Bones, resembling those of a fish, made of limestone.*

Eventually Frankenstein came to stand beside her. "How is it that you are come to Matlock?" he inquired.

"My sister Elizabeth is married to Mr. Fitzwilliam Darcy, of Pemberley. Kitty and I are here on a visit. Have you come to take the waters?"

"Clerval and I are on our way to Scotland, where he will stay with friends, while I pursue—certain investigations. We rest here a week. The topography of the valley reminds me of my home in Switzerland."

"I have heard it said so," she replied. Frankenstein seemed to have regained his composure, but Mary wondered still at what had awakened his grief. "You have an interest in these relics?" she asked, indicating the cabinets.

"Some, perhaps. I find it remarkable to see a young lady take an interest in such arcana." Mary detected no trace of mockery in his voice.

"Indeed, I do," she said, indulging her enthusiasm. "Professor Erasmus Darwin has written of the source of these bones:

"Organic life beneath the shoreless waves
Was born and nurs'd in ocean's pearly caves;
First forms minute, unseen by spheric glass,
Move on the mud, or pierce the watery mass;
These, as successive generations bloom,
New powers acquire and larger limbs assume;
Whence countless groups of vegetation spring,
And breathing realms of fin and feet and wing.

"People say this offers proof of the great flood. Do you think, Mr. Frankenstein, that Matlock could once have been under the sea? They say these are creatures that have not existed since the time of Noah."

"Far older than the flood, I'll warrant. I do not think that these bones were originally made of stone. Some process has transformed them. Anatomically, they are more like those of a lizard than a fish."

"You have studied anatomy?"

Mr. Frankenstein tapped his fingers upon the glass of the case. "Three years gone by it was one of my passions. I no longer pursue such matters."

"And yet, sir, you met with men of science in London."

"Ah—yes, I did. I am surprised that you remember a brief conversation, more than two months ago."

"I have a good memory."

"As evidenced by your quoting Professor Darwin. I might expect a woman such as yourself to take more interest in art than science."

"Oh, you may rest assured that I have read my share of novels. And even more, in my youth, of sermons. Elizabeth is wont to tease me for a great moralizer. 'Evil is easy,' I tell her, 'and has infinite forms.' "

Frankenstein did not answer. Finally he said, "Would that the world had no need of moralizers."

Mary recalled his warning against science from their London meeting. "Come, Mr. Frankenstein. There is no evil in studying God's handiwork."

"A God-fearing Christian might take exception to Professor Darwin's assertion that life began in the sea, no matter how poetically stated." His voice became distant. "Can a living soul be created without the hand of God?"

"It is my feeling that the hand of God is everywhere present." Mary gestured toward the cabinet. "Even in the bones of this stony fish."

"Then you have more faith than I, Miss Bennet—or more innocence."

Mary blushed. She was not used to bantering in this way with a gentleman. In her experience, handsome and accomplished men took no interest in her, and such conversations as she had engaged in offered little of substance other than the weather, clothes, and town gossip. Yet she saw that she had touched Frankenstein, and felt something akin to triumph.

They were interrupted by the appearance of Georgiana and Kitty, entering with Henry Clerval. "There you are!" said Kitty. "You see, Mr. Clerval, I told you we would find Mary poring over these heaps of bones!"

"And it is no surprise to find my friend here as well," said Clerval.

Mary felt quite deflated. The party moved out of the town hall and in splendid sunlight along the North Parade. Kitty proposed, and the visitors acceded to, a stroll on the so-called Lover's Walk beside the river. As they walked along the gorge, vast ramparts of limestone rock, clothed with yew trees, elms, and limes, rose up on either side of the river. William ran ahead, and Kitty, Georgiana, and Clerval followed, leaving Frankenstein and Mary behind. Eventually they came in sight of the High Tor, a sheer cliff rearing its brow on the east bank of the Derwent. The lower part was covered with small trees and foliage. Massive boulders that had fallen from the cliff broke the riverbed below into foaming rapids. The noise of the waters left Mary and Frankenstein, apart from the others, as isolated as if they had been in a separate room. Frankenstein spent a long time gazing at the scenery. Mary's mind raced, seeking some way to recapture the mood of their conversation in the town hall.

"How this reminds me of my home," he said. "Henry and I would climb such cliffs as this, chase goats around the meadows and play at pirates. Father would walk me though the woods and name every tree and flower. I once saw a lightning bolt shiver an old oak to splinters."

"Whenever I come here," Mary blurted out, "I realize how small I am, and how great time is. We are here for only seconds, and then we are gone, and these rocks, this river, will long survive us. And through it all we are alone."

Frankenstein turned toward her. "Surely you are not so lonely. You have your family, your sisters. Your mother and father."

"One can be alone in a room of people. Kitty mocks me for my 'heaps of bones.' "

"A person may marry."

"I am twenty-eight years old, sir. I am no man's vision of a lover or wife."

What had come over her, to say this aloud, for the first time in her life? Yet what did it matter what she said to this foreigner? There was no point in letting some hope for sympathy delude her into greater hopes. They had danced a single dance in London, and now they spent an afternoon together; soon he would leave England, marry his cousin, and Mary would never see him again. She deserved Kitty's mockery.

Frankenstein took some time before answering, during which Mary was acutely aware of the sound of the waters, and of the sight of Georgiana, William, and Clerval playing in the grass by the riverbank, while Kitty stood pensive some distance away.

"Miss Bennet, I am sorry if I have made light of your situation. But your fine qualities should be apparent to anyone who took the trouble truly to make your acquaintance. Your knowledge of matters of science only adds to my admiration."

"You needn't flatter me," said Mary. "I am unused to it."

"I do not flatter," Frankenstein replied. "I speak my own mind."

William came running up. "Aunt Mary! This would be an excellent place to fish! We should come here with Father!"

"That's a good idea, Will."

Frankenstein turned to the others. "We must return to the hotel, Henry," he told Clerval. "I need to see that new glassware properly packed before shipping it ahead."

"Very well."

"Glassware?" Georgiana asked.

Clerval chuckled. "Victor has been purchasing equipment at every stop along our tour—glassware, bottles of chemicals, lead and copper disks. The coachmen threaten to leave us behind if he does not ship these things separately."

Kitty argued in vain, but the party walked back to Matlock. The women and William met the carriage to take them back to Pemberley. "I hope I see you again, Miss Bennet," Frankenstein said. Had she been more accustomed to reading the emotions of others she would have ventured that his expression held sincere interest—even longing.

On the way back to Pemberley William prattled with Georgiana, Kitty, subdued for once, leaned back with her eyes closed, while Mary puzzled over every moment of the afternoon. The fundamental sympathy she had felt with Frankenstein in their brief London encounter had been only reinforced. His sudden dark moods, his silences, bespoke some burden he carried. Mary was almost convinced that her mother was right—that Frankenstein did not love his cousin, and that he was here inEngland fleeing from her. How could this second meeting with him be chance? Fate had brought them together.

At dinner that evening, Kitty told Darcy and Elizabeth about their encounter with the handsome Swiss tourists. Later, Mary took Lizzy aside and asked her to invite Clerval and Frankenstein to dinner.

"This is new!" said Lizzy. "I expected this from Kitty, but not you. You have never before asked to have a young man come to Pemberley."

"I have never met someone quite like Mr. Frankenstein," Mary replied.

"Have you taken the Matlock waters?" Mary asked Clerval, who was seated opposite her at the dinner table. "People in the parish say that a dip in the hot springs could raise the dead."

"I confess that I have not," Clerval said. "Victor does not believe in their healing powers."

Mary turned to Frankenstein, hoping to draw him into discussion of the matter, but the startled expression on his face silenced her.

The table, covered with a blinding white damask tablecloth, glittered with silver and crystal. A large epergne, studded with lit beeswax candles, dominated its center. In addition to the family members, and in order to even the number of guests and balance female with male, Darcy and Elizabeth had invited the vicar, Mr. Chatsworth. Completing the dinner party were Bingley and Jane, Georgiana, and Kitty.

The footmen brought soup, followed by claret, turbot with lobster and Dutch sauce, oyster pate, lamb cutlets with asparagus, peas, a fricandeau à l'oseille, venison, stewed beef à la jardinière, with various salads, beetroot, French and English mustard. Two ices, cherry water and pineapple cream, and a chocolate cream with strawberries. Champagne flowed throughout the dinner, and Madeira afterward.

Darcy inquired of Mr. Clerval's business in England, and Clerval told of his meetings with men of business in London, and his interest in India.

He had even begun the study of the language, and for their entertainment spoke a few sentences in Hindi. Darcy told of his visit to Geneva a decade ago. Clerval spoke charmingly of the differences in manners between the Swiss and the English, with witty preference for English habits, except, he said, in the matter of boiled meats. Georgiana asked about women's dress on the continent. Elizabeth allowed as how, if they could keep him safe, it would be good for William's education to tour the continent. Kitty, who usually dominated the table with bright talk and jokes, was unaccustomedly quiet. The Vicar spoke amusingly of his travels in Italy.

Through all of this, Frankenstein offered little in the way of response or comment. Mary had put such hopes on this dinner, and now she feared she had misread him. His voice warmed but once, when he spoke of his father, a counselor and syndic, renowned for his integrity. Only on inquiry would he speak of his years in Ingolstadt.

"And what did you study in the university?" Bingley asked.

"Matters of no interest," Frankenstein replied.

An uncomfortable silence followed. Clerval gently explained, "My friend devoted himself so single-mindedly to the study of natural philosophy that his health failed. I was fortunately able to bring him back to us, but it was a near thing."

"For which I will ever be grateful to you," Frankenstein mumbled.

Lizzy attempted to change the subject. "Reverend Chatsworth, what news is there of the parish?"

The vicar, unaccustomed to such volume and variety of drink, was in his cups, his face flushed and his voice rising to pulpit volume. "Well, I hope the ladies will not take it amiss," he boomed, "if I tell about a curious incident that occurred last night!"

"Pray do."

"So, then—last night I was troubled with sleeplessness—I think it was the trout I ate for supper, it was not right—Mrs. Croft vowed she had purchased it just that afternoon, but I wonder if perhaps it might have been from the previous day's catch. Be that as it may, lying awake some time after midnight, I thought I heard a scraping out my bedroom window—the weather has been so fine of late that I sleep with my window open. It is my opinion, Mr. Clerval, that nothing aids the lungs more than fresh air, and I believe that is the opinion of the best continental thinkers, is it not? The air is exceedingly fresh in the alpine meadows, I am told?"

"Only in those meadows where the cows have not been feeding."

"The cows? Oh, yes, the cows—ha, ha!—very good! The cows, indeed! So, where was I? Ah, yes. I rose from my bed and looked out the window, and what did I spy but a light in the churchyard. I threw on my robe and slippers and hurried out to see what might be the matter.

"As I approached the churchyard I saw a dark figure wielding a spade. His back was to me, silhouetted by a lamp which rested beside Nancy Brown's grave. Poor Nancy, dead not a week now, so young, only seventeen."

"A man?" said Kitty.

The vicar's round face grew serious. "You may imagine my shock. 'Halloo!' I shouted. At that the man dropped his spade, seized the lantern and dashed 'round the back of the church. By the time I had reached the corner he was out of sight. Back at the grave I saw that he had been on a fair way to unearthing poor Nancy's coffin!"

"My goodness!" said Jane.

"Defiling a grave?" asked Bingley. "I am astonished."

Darcy said nothing, but his look demonstrated that he was not pleased by the vicar bringing such an uncouth matter to his dinner table. Frankenstein, sitting next to Mary, put down his knife and took a long draught of Madeira.

The vicar lowered his voice. He was clearly enjoying himself. "I can only speculate on what motive this man might have had. Could it have been some lover of hers, overcome with grief?"

"No man is so faithful," Kitty said.

"My dear vicar," said Lizzy. "You have read too many of Mrs. Radcliffe's novels."

Darcy leaned back in his chair. "Gypsies have been seen in the woods about the quarry. It was no doubt their work. They were seeking jewelry."

"Jewelry?" the vicar said. "The Browns had barely enough money to see her decently buried."

"Which proves that whoever did this was not a local man."

Clerval spoke. "At home, fresh graves are sometimes defiled by men providing cadavers to doctors. Was there not a spate of such grave robbings in Ingolstadt, Victor?"

Frankenstein put down his glass. "Yes," he said. "Some anatomists, in seeking knowledge, will abandon all human scruple."

"I do not think that is likely to be the cause in this instance, " Darcy observed. "Here there is no university, no medical school. Doctor Phillips, in Lambton, is no transgressor of civilized rules."

"He is scarcely a transgressor of his own threshold," said Lizzy. "One must call him a day in advance to get him to leave his parlor."

"Rest assured, there are such men," said Frankenstein. "I have known them. My illness, as Henry has described to you, was in some way my spirit's rebellion against the understanding that the pursuit of knowledge will lead some men into mortal peril."

Here was Mary's chance to impress Frankenstein. "Surely there is a nobility in risking one's life to advance the claims of one's race. With how many things are we upon the brink of becoming acquainted, if cowardice or carelessness did not restrain our inquiries?"

"Then I thank God for cowardice and carelessness, Miss Bennet," Frankenstein said, "One's life, perhaps, is worth risking, but not one's soul."

"True enough. But I believe that science may demand our relaxing the strictures of common society."

"We have never heard this tone from you, Mary," Jane said.

Darcy interjected, "You are becoming quite modern, sister. What strictures are you prepared to abandon for us tonight?" His voice was full of the gentle condescension with which he treated Mary at all times.

How she wished to surprise them! How she longed to show Darcy and Lizzy, with their perfect marriage and perfect lives, that she was not the simple old maid they thought her. "Anatomists in London have obtained the court's permission to dissect the bodies of criminals after execution. Is it unjust to use the body of a murderer, who has already forfeited his own life, to save the lives of the innocent?"

"My uncle, who is on the bench, has spoken of such cases," Bingley said.

"Not only that," Mary added. "Have you heard of the experiments of the Italian scientist Aldini? Last summer in London at the Royal College of Surgeons he used a powerful battery to animate portions of the body of a hanged man. According to the *Times*, the spectators genuinely believed that the body was about to come to life!"

"Mary, please!" said Lizzy.

"You need to spend less time on your horrid books," Kitty laughed. "No suitor is going to want to talk with you about dead bodies."

And so Kitty was on their side, too. Her mockery only made Mary more determined to force Frankenstein to speak. "What do you say, sir? Will you come to my defense?"

Frankenstein carefully folded his napkin and set it beside his plate. "Such attempts are not motivated by bravery, or even curiosity, but by ambition. The pursuit of knowledge can become a vice deadly as any of the more common sins. Worse still, because even the most noble of natures are susceptible to such temptations. None but he who has experienced them can conceive of the enticements of science."

The vicar raised his glass. "Mr. Frankenstein, truer words have never been spoken. The man who defiled poor Nancy's grave has placed himself beyond the mercy of a forgiving God."

Mary felt charged with contradictory emotions. "You have experienced such enticements, Mr. Frankenstein?"

"Sadly, I have."

"But surely there is no sin that is beyond the reach of God's mercy? 'To know all is to forgive all.' "

The vicar turned to her. "My child, what know you of sin?"

"Very little, Mr. Chatsworth, except of idleness. Yet I feel that even a wicked person can have the veil lifted from his eyes."

Frankenstein looked at her. "Here I must agree with Miss Bennet. I have to believe that even the most corrupted nature is susceptible to grace. If I did not think this were possible, I could not live."

"Enough of this talk," insisted Darcy. "Vicar, I suggest you mind your parishioners, including those in the churchyard, more carefully. But now I for one am eager to hear Miss Georgiana play the pianoforte. And perhaps Miss Mary and Miss Catherine will join her. We must uphold the accomplishments of English maidenhood before our foreign guests."

On Kitty's insistence, the next morning, despite lowering clouds and a chill in the air that spoke more of March than late May, she and Mary took a walk along the river.

They walked along the stream that ran from the estate toward the Derwent. Kitty remained silent. Mary's thoughts turned to the wholly unsatisfying dinner of the previous night. The conversation in the parlor had gone no better than dinner. Mary had played the piano ill, showing herself to poor advantage next to the accomplished Georgiana. Under Jane and Lizzy's gaze she felt the folly of her intemperate speech at the table. Frankenstein said next to nothing to her for the rest of the evening; he almost seemed wary of being in her presence.

She was wondering how he was spending this morning when, suddenly turning her face from Mary, Kitty burst into tears. Mary touched her arm. "Whatever is the matter, Kitty?"

"Do you believe what you said last night?"

"What did I say?"

"That there is no sin beyond the reach of God's mercy?"

"Of course I do! Why would you ask?"

"Because I have committed such a sin!" She covered her eyes with her hand. "Oh, no, I mustn't speak of it!"

Mary refrained from pointing out that, having made such a provocative admission, Kitty could hardly remain silent—and undoubtedly had no intention of doing so. But Kitty's intentions were not always transparent to Mary.

After some coaxing and a further walk along the stream, Kitty was prepared finally to unburden herself. It seemed that, from the previous summer she had maintained a secret admiration for a local man from Matlock, Robert Piggot, son of the butcher. Though his family was quite prosperous and he stood to inherit the family business, he was in no way a gentleman, and Kitty had vowed never to let her affections overwhelm her sense.

But, upon their recent return to Pemberley, she had encountered Robert on her first visit to town, and she had been secretly meeting with him when she went into Matlock on the pretext of shopping. Worse still, the couple had allowed their passion to get the better of them, and Kitty had given way to carnal love.

The two sisters sat on a fallen tree in the woods as Kitty poured out her tale. "I want so much to marry him." Her tears flowed readily. "I do not want to be alone, I don't want to die an old maid! And Lydia—Lydia told me about—about the act of love, how wonderful it was, how good Wickham makes her feel. She boasted of it! And I said, why should vain Lydia have this, and me have nothing, to waste my youth in conversation and embroidery, in listening to Mother prattle and Father throw heavy sighs. Father thinks me a fool, unlikely ever to find a husband. And now he's right!" Kitty burst into wailing again. "He's right! No man shall ever have me!" Her tears ended in a fit of coughing.

"Oh, Kitty," Mary said.

"When Darcy spoke of English maidenhood last night, it was all I could do to keep from bursting into tears. You must get Father to agree to let me marry Robert."

"Has he asked you to marry him?"

"He shall. He must. You don't know how fine a man he is. Despite the fact that he is in trade, he has the gentlest manners. I don't care if he is not well born."

Mary embraced Kitty. Kitty alternated between sobs and fits of coughing. Above them the thunder rumbled, and the wind rustled the trees. Mary felt Kitty's shivering body. She needed to calm her, to get her back to the house. How frail, how slender her sister was.

She did not know what to say. Once Mary would have self-righteously condemned Kitty. But much that Kitty said was the content of her own mind, and Kitty's fear of dying alone was her own fear. As she searched for some answer, Mary heard the sound of a torrent of rain hitting the canopy of foliage above them. "You have been foolish," Mary said, holding her. "But it may not be so bad."

Kitty trembled in her arms, and spoke into Mary's shoulder. "But will you ever care for me again? What if Father should turn me out? What will I do then?"

The rain was falling through now, coming down hard. Mary felt her hair getting soaked. "Calm yourself. Father would do no such thing. I shall never forsake you. Jane would not, nor Lizzy."

"What if I should have a child!"

Mary pulled Kitty's shawl over her head. She looked past Kitty's shoulder to the dark woods. Something moved there. "You shan't have a child."

"You can't know! I may!"

The woods had become dark with the rain. Mary could not make out what lurked there. "Come, let us go back. You must compose yourself. We shall speak with Lizzy and Jane. They will know—"

Just then a flash of lightning lit the forest, and Mary saw, beneath the trees not ten feet from them, the giant figure of a man. The lightning illuminated a face of monstrous ugliness: Long, thick, tangled black hair.

Yellow skin the texture of dried leather, black eyes sunken deep beneath heavy brows. Worst of all, an expression hideous in its cold, inexpressible hunger. All glimpsed in a split second; then the light fell to shadow.

Mary gasped, and pulled Kitty toward her. A great peal of thunder rolled across the sky.

Kitty stopped crying. "What is it?"

"We must go. Now." Mary seized Kitty by the arm. The rain pelted down on them, and the forest path was already turning to mud.

Mary pulled her toward the house, Kitty complaining. Mary could hear nothing over the drumming of the rain. But when she looked over her shoulder, she caught a glimpse of the brutish figure, keeping to the trees, but swiftly, silently moving along behind them.

"Why must we run?" Kitty gasped.

"Because we are being followed!"

"By whom?"

"I don't know!"

Behind them, Mary thought she heard the man croak out some words: "Halt! Bitter!"

They had not reached the edge of the woods when figures appeared ahead of them, coming from Pemberley. "Miss Bennet! Mary! Kitty!"

The figures resolved themselves into Darcy and Mr. Frankenstein. Darcy carried a cloak, which he threw over them. "Are you all right?" Frankenstein asked.

"Thank you!" Mary gasped. "A man. He's there," she pointed, "following us."

Frankenstein took a few steps beyond them down the path. "Who was it?" Darcy asked.

"Some brute. Hideously ugly," Mary said.

Frankenstein came back. "No one is there."

"We saw him!"

Another lighting flash, and crack of thunder. "It is very dark, and we are in a storm," Frankenstein said.

"Come, we must get you back to the house," Darcy said. "You are wet to the bone."

The men helped them back to Pemberley, trying their best to keep the rain off the sisters.

Darcy went off to find Bingley and Clerval, who had taken the opposite direction in their search. Lizzy saw that Mary and Kitty were made dry and warm. Kitty's cough worsened, and Lizzy insisted she must be put to bed. Mary sat with Kitty, whispered a promise to keep her secret, and waited until she slept. Then she went down to meet the others in the parlor.

"This chill shall do her no good," Jane said. She chided Mary for wandering off in such threatening weather. "I thought you had developed more sense, Mary. Mr. Frankenstein insisted he help to find you, when he realized you had gone out into the woods."

"I am sorry," Mary said. "You are right." She was distracted by Kitty's plight, wondering what she might do. If Kitty were indeed with child, there would be no helping her.

Mary recounted her story of the man in the woods. Darcy said he had seen no one, but allowed that someone might have been there. Frankenstein, rather than engage in the speculation, stood at the tall windows staring across the lawn through the rain toward the tree line.

"This intruder was some local poacher, or perhaps one of those gypsies," said Darcy. "When the rain ends I shall have Mr. Mowbray take some men to check the grounds. We shall also inform the constable."

"I hope this foul weather will induce you to stay with us a few more days, Mr. Frankenstein," Lizzy ventured. "You have no pressing business in Matlock, do you?"

"No. But we were to travel north by the end of this week."

"Surely we might stay a while longer, Victor," said Clerval. "Your research can wait for you in Scotland."

Frankenstein struggled with his answer. "I don't think we should prevail on these good people any more."

"Nonsense," said Darcy. "We are fortunate for your company."

"Thank you," Frankenstein said uncertainly. But when the conversation moved elsewhere, Mary noticed him once again staring out the window. She moved to sit beside him. On an impulse, she said to him, *sotto voce*, "Did you know this man we came upon in the woods?"

"I saw no one. Even if someone was there, how should I know some English vagabond?"

"I do not think he was English. When he called after us, it was in German. Was this one of your countrymen?"

A look of impatience crossed Frankenstein's face, and he lowered his eyes. "Miss Bennet, I do not wish to contradict you, but you are mistaken. I saw no one in the woods."

Kitty developed a fever, and did not leave her bed for the rest of the day. Mary sat with her, trying, without bringing up the subject of Robert Piggot, to quiet her.

It was still raining when Mary retired, to a separate bedroom from the one she normally shared with Kitty. Late that night, Mary was wakened by the opening of her bedroom door. She thought it might be Lizzy to tell her something about Kitty. But it was not Lizzy.

Rather than call out, she watched silently as a dark figure entered and closed the door behind. The remains of her fire threw faint light on the man as he approached her. "Miss Bennet," he called softly.

Her heart was in her throat. "Yes, Mr. Frankenstein."

"Please do not take alarm. I must speak with you." He took two sudden steps toward her bed. His handsome face was agitated. No man, in any circumstances remotely resembling these, had ever broached her bedside. Yet the racing of her heart was not entirely a matter of fear.

"This, sir, is hardly the place for polite conversation," she said. "Following on your denial of what I saw this afternoon, you are fortunate that I do not wake the servants and have you thrown out of Pemberley."

"You are right to chide me. My conscience chides me more than you ever could, and should I be thrown from your family's gracious company it would be no less than I deserve. And I am afraid that nothing I have to say to you tonight shall qualify as polite conversation." His manner was greatly changed; there was a sound of desperation in his whisper. He wanted something from her, and he wanted it a great deal.

Curious, despite herself, Mary drew on her robe and lit a candle. She made him sit in one of the chairs by the fire and poked the coals into life. When she had settled herself in the other, she said, "Go on."

"Miss Bennet, please do not toy with me. You know why I am here."

"Know, sir? What do I know?"

He leaned forward, earnestly, hands clasped and elbows on his knees. "I come to beg you to keep silent. The gravest consequences would follow your revealing my secret."

"Silent?"

"About—about the man you saw."

"You *do* know him!"

"Your mockery at dinner convinced me that, after hearing the vicar's story, you suspected. Raising the dead, you said to Clerval—and then your tale of Professor Aldini. Do not deny it."

"I don't pretend to know what you are talking about."

Frankenstein stood from his chair and began to pace the floor before the hearth. "Please! I saw the look of reproach in your eyes when we found you in the forest. I am trying to make right what I put wrong. But I will never be able to do so if you tell." To Mary's astonishment, she saw, in the firelight, that his eyes glistened with tears.

"Tell me what you did."

And with that the story burst out of him. He told her how, after his mother's death, he longed to conquer death itself, how he had studied chemistry at the university, how he had uncovered the secret of life. How, emboldened and driven on by his solitary obsession, he had created a man from the corpses he had stolen from graveyards and purchased from resurrection men. How he had succeeded, through his science, in bestowing it with life.

Mary did not know what to say to this astonishing tale. It was the raving of a lunatic—but there was the man she had seen in the woods. And the earnestness with which Frankenstein spoke, his tears and desperate whispers, gave every proof that, at least in his mind, he had done these things. He told of his revulsion at his accomplishment, how he had abandoned the creature, hoping it would die, and how the creature had, in revenge, killed his brother William and caused his family's ward Justine to be blamed for the crime.

"But why did you not intervene in Justine's trial?"

"No one should have believed me."

"Yet I am to believe you now?"

Frankenstein's voice was choked. "You have seen the brute. You know that these things are possible. Lives are at stake. I come to you in remorse and penitence, asking only that you keep this secret." He fell to his knees, threw his head into her lap, and clutched at the sides of her gown.

Frankenstein was wholly mistaken in what she knew; he was a man who did not see things clearly. Yet if his story were true, it was no wonder that his judgment was disordered. And here he lay, trembling against her, a boy seeking forgiveness. No man had ever come to her in such need.

She tried to keep her senses. "Certainly the creature I saw was frightening, but to my eyes he appeared more wretched than menacing."

Frankenstein lifted his head. "Here I must warn you—his wretchedness is mere mask. Do not let your sympathy for him cause you ever to trust his nature. He is the vilest creature that has ever walked this earth. He has no soul."

"Why then not invoke the authorities, catch him, and bring him to justice?"

"He cannot be so easily caught. He is inhumanly strong, resourceful, and intelligent. If you should ever be so unlucky as to speak with him, I warn you not to listen to what he says, for he is immensely articulate and satanically persuasive."

"All the more reason to see him apprehended!"

"I am convinced that he can be dealt with only by myself." Frankenstein's eyes pleaded with her. "Miss Bennet—Mary—you must understand. He is in some ways my son. I gave him life. His mind is fixed on me."

"And, it seems, yours on him."

Frankenstein looked surprised. "Do you wonder that is so?"

"Why does he follow you? Does he intend you harm?"

"He has vowed to glut the maw of death with my remaining loved ones, unless I make him happy." He rested his head again in her lap.

Mary was touched, scandalized, and in some obscure way aroused. She felt his trembling body, instinct with life. Tentatively, she rested her hand on his head. She stroked his hair. He was weeping. She realized that he was a physical being, a living animal, that would eventually, too soon, die. And all that was true of him was true of herself. How strange, frightening, and sad. Yet in this moment she felt herself wonderfully alive.

"I'll keep your secret," she said.

He hugged her skirts. In the candle's light, she noted the way his thick, dark hair curled away from his brow.

"I cannot tell you," he said softly, "what a relief it is to share my burden with another soul, and to have her accept me. I have been so completely alone. I cannot thank you enough."

He rose, kissed her forehead, and was gone.

Mary paced her room, trying to grasp what had just happened. A man who had conquered death? A monster created from corpses? Such things did not happen, certainly not in her world, not even in the world of the novels she read. She climbed into bed and tried to sleep, but could not. The creature had vowed to kill all whom Frankenstein loved. Mary remembered the weight of his head upon her lap.

The room felt stiflingly hot. She got up, stripped off her nightgown, and climbed back between the sheets, where she lay naked, listening to the rain on the window.

Kitty's fever worsened in the night, and before dawn Darcy sent to Lambton for the doctor. Lizzy dispatched an urgent letter to Mr. and Mrs. Bennet, and the sisters sat by Kitty's bedside through the morning, changing cold compresses from her brow while Kitty labored to breathe. When Mary left the sick room, Frankenstein approached her. His desperation of the previous night was gone. "How fares your sister?"

"I fear she is gravely ill."

"She is in some danger?"

Mary could only nod.

He touched her shoulder, lowered his voice. "I will pray for her, Miss Bennet. I cannot thank you enough for the sympathy you showed me last night. I have never told anyone—"

Just then Clerval approached them. He greeted Mary, inquired after Kitty's condition, then suggested to Frankenstein that they return to their hotel in Matlock rather than add any burden to the household and family. Frankenstein agreed. Before Mary could say another word to him in private, the visitors were gone.

Doctor Phillips arrived soon after Clerval and Frankenstein left. He measured Kitty's pulse, felt her forehead, examined her urine. He administered some medicines, and came away shaking his head. Should the fever continue, he said, they must bleed her.

Given how much thought she had spent on Frankenstein through the night, and how little she had devoted to Kitty, Mary's conscience tormented her. She spent the day in her sister's room. That night, after Jane had retired and Lizzy fallen asleep in her chair, she still sat up, holding Kitty's fevered hand. She had matters to consider. Was Kitty indeed with child, and if so, should she tell the doctor? Yet even as she sat by Kitty's bedside, Mary's mind cast back to the feeling of Frankenstein's lips on her forehead.

In the middle of the night, Kitty woke, bringing Mary from her doze. Kitty tried to lift her head from the pillow, but could not. "Mary," she whispered. "You must send for Robert. We must be married immediately."

Mary looked across the room at Lizzy. She was still asleep.

"Promise me," Kitty said. Her eyes were large and dark.

"I promise," Mary said.

"Prepare my wedding dress," Kitty said. "But don't tell Lizzy."

Lizzy awoke then. She came to the bedside and felt Kitty's forehead. "She's burning up. Get Dr. Phillips."

Mary sought out the doctor, and then, while he went to Kitty's room, pondered what to do. Kitty clearly was not in her right mind. Her request ran contrary to both sense and propriety. If Mary sent one of the footment to Matlock for Robert, even if she swore her messenger to silence, the matter would soon be the talk of the servants, and probably the town.

It was the sort of dilemma that Mary would have had no trouble settling, to everyone's moral edification, when she was sixteen. She hurried to her room and took out paper and pen:

> *I write to inform you that one you love, residing at Pemberley House, is gravely ill. She urgently requests your presence. Simple human kindness, which from her description of you I do not doubt you possess, let alone the duty incumbent upon you owing to the compact that you have made with her through your actions, assure me that we shall see you here before the night is through.*
>
> *Miss Mary Bennet*

She sealed the letter and sought out one of the footmen, whom she dispatched immediately with the instruction to put the letter into the hand of Robert Piggot, son of the Matlock butcher.

Dr. Phillips bled Kitty, with no improvement. She did not regain consciousness through the night. Mary waited. The footman returned, alone, at six in the morning. He assured Mary that he had ridden to the Piggot home and given the letter directly to Robert. Mary thanked him.

Robert did not come. At eight in the morning Darcy sent for the priest. At nine-thirty Kitty died.

On the evening of the day of Kitty's passing, Mr. and Mrs. Bennet arrived, and a day later Lydia and Wickham—it was the first time Darcy had allowed Wickham to cross the threshold of Pemberley since they had become brothers by marriage. In the midst of her mourning family, Mary felt lost. Jane and Lizzy supported each other in their grief. Darcy and Bingley exchanged quiet, sober conversation. Wickham and Lydia, who had grown fat with her three children, could not pass a word between them without sniping, but in their folly they were completely united.

Mrs. Bennet was beyond consoling, and the volume and intensity of her mourning was exceeded only by the degree to which she sought to control every detail of Kitty's funeral. There ensued a long debate over where Kitty should be buried. When it was pointed out that their cousin Mr. Collins would eventually inherit the house back in Hertfordshire, Mrs. Bennet fell into despair: who, when she was gone, would tend to her poor Kitty's grave? Mr. Bennet suggested that Kitty be laid to rest in the churchyard at Lambton, a short distance from Pemberley, where she might also be visited by Jane and Bingley. But when Mr. Darcy offered the family vault at Pemberley, the matter was quickly settled to the satisfaction of both tender hearts and vanity.

Though it was no surprise to Mary, it was still a burden for her to witness that even in the gravest passage of their lives, her sisters and parents showed themselves to be exactly what they were. And yet, paradoxically, this did not harden her heart toward them. The family was together as they had not been for many years, and she realized that they should never be in the future except on the occasion of further losses. Her father was grayer and quieter than she had ever seen him, and on the day of the funeral even her mother put aside her sobbing and exclamations long enough to show a face of profound grief, and a burden of age that Mary had never before noticed.

The night after Kitty was laid to rest, Mary sat up late with Jane and Lizzy and Lydia. They drank Madeira and Lydia told many silly stories of the days she and Kitty had spent in flirtations with the regiment. Mary climbed into her bed late that night, her head swimming with wine, laughter, and tears. She lay awake, the moonlight shining on the counterpane through the opened window, air carrying the smell of fresh earth and the rustle of trees above the lake. She drifted into a dreamless sleep. At some point in the night she was half awakened by the barking of the dogs in the kennel. But consciousness soon faded and she fell away.

In the morning it was discovered that the vault had been broken into and Kitty's body stolen from her grave.

Mary told the stablemaster that Mrs. Bennet had asked her to go to the apothecary in Lambton, and had him prepare the gig for her. Then, while the house was in turmoil and Mrs. Bennet being attended by the rest of the family, she drove off to Matlock. The master had given her the best horse in Darcy's stable; the creature was equable and quick, and despite her inexperience driving, Mary was able to reach Matlock in an hour. All the time, despite the splendid summer morning and the picturesque prospects which the valley of the Derwent continually unfolded before her, she could not keep her mind from whirling through a series of distressing images—among them the sight of Frankenstein's creature as she had seen him in the woods.

When she reached Matlock she hurried to the Old Bath Hotel and inquired after Frankenstein. The concierge told her that he had not seen Mr. Frankenstein since dinner the previous evening, but that Mr. Clerval had told him that morning that the gentlemen would leave Matlock later that day. She left a note asking Frankenstein, should he return, to meet her at the inn, then went to the butcher shop.

Mary had been there once before, with Lizzy, some years earlier. The shop was busy with servants purchasing joints of mutton and ham for the evening meal. Behind the counter Mr. Piggot senior was busy at his cutting board, but helping one of the women with a package was a tall young man with thick brown curls and green eyes. He flirted with the house servant as he shouldered her purchase, wrapped in brown paper, onto her cart.

On the way back into the shop, he spotted Mary standing unattended. He studied her for a moment before approaching. "May I help you, miss?"

"I believe you knew my sister."

His grin vanished. "You are Miss Mary Bennet."

"I am."

The young man studied his boots. "I am so sorry what happened to Miss Catherine."

Not so sorry as to bring you to her bedside before she died, Mary thought. She bit back a reproach and said, "We did not see you at the service. I thought perhaps the nature of your relationship might have encouraged you to grieve in private, at her graveside. Have you been there?"

He looked even more uncomfortable. "No. I had to work. My father—"

Mary had seen enough already to measure his depth. He was not a man to defile a grave, in grief or otherwise. The distance between this small-town lothario—handsome, careless, insensitive—and the hero Kitty had praised, only deepened Mary's compassion for her lost sister. How desperate she must have been. How pathetic.

As Robert Piggot continued to stumble through his explanation, Mary turned and departed.

She went back to the inn where she had left the gig. The barkeep led her into a small ladies' parlor separated from the tap room by a glass partition. She ordered tea, and through a latticed window watched the people come and go in the street and courtyard, the draymen with their Percherons and carts, the passengers waiting for the next van to Manchester, and inside, the idlers sitting at tables with pints of ale. In the sunlit street a young bootblack accosted travelers, most of whom ignored him. All of these people alive, completely unaware of Mary or her lost sister. Mary ought to be back with their mother, though the thought turned her heart cold. How could Kitty have left her alone? She felt herself near despair.

She was watching through the window as two draymen struggled to load a large square trunk onto their cart when the man directing them came from around the team of horses, and she saw it was Frankenstein. She rose immediately and went out into the inn yard. She was at his shoulder before he noticed her. "Miss Bennet!"

"Mr. Frankenstein. I am so glad that I found you. I feared that you had already left Matlock. May we speak somewhere in private?"

He looked momentarily discommoded. "Yes, of course," he said. To the draymen he said. "When you've finished loading my equipment, wait here."

"This is not a good place to converse," Frankenstein told her. "I saw a churchyard nearby. Let us retire there."

He walked Mary down the street to the St. Giles Churchyard. They walked through the rectory garden. In the distance, beams of afternoon sunlight shone through a cathedral of clouds above the Heights of Abraham. "Do you know what has happened?" she asked.

"I have heard reports, quite awful, of the death of your sister. I intended to write you, conveying my condolences, at my earliest opportunity. You have my deepest sympathies."

"Your creature! That monster you created—"

"I asked you to keep him a secret."

"I have kept my promise—so far. But it has stolen Kitty's body."

He stood there, hands behind his back, clear eyes fixed on her. "You find me astonished. What draws you to this extraordinary conclusion?"

She was hurt by his diffidence. Was this the same man who had wept in her bedroom? "Who else might do such a thing?"

"But why? This creature's enmity is reserved for me alone. Others feel its ire only to the extent that they are dear to me."

"You came to plead with me that night because you feared I knew he was responsible for defiling that town girl's grave. Why was he watching Kitty and me in the forest? Surely this is no coincidence."

"If, indeed, the creature has stolen your sister's body, it can be for no reason I can fathom, or that any god-fearing person ought to pursue. You know I am determined to see this monster banished from the world of men. You may rest assured that I will not cease until I have seen this accomplished. It is best for you and your family to turn your thoughts to other matters." He touched a strand of ivy growing up the side of the garden wall, and plucked off a green leaf, which he twirled in his fingers.

She could not understand him. She knew him to be a man of sensibility, to have a heart capable of feeling. His denials opened a possibility that she had tried to keep herself from considering. "Sir, I am not satisfied. It seems to me that you are keeping something from me. You told me of the great grief you felt at the loss of your mother, how it moved you to your researches. If, as you say, you have uncovered the secret of life, might you—have you taken it upon yourself to restore Kitty? Perhaps a fear of failure, or of the horror that many would feel at your trespassing against God's will, underlies your secrecy. If so, please do not keep the truth from me. I am not a girl."

He let the leaf fall from his fingers. He took her shoulders, and looked directly into her eyes. "I am sorry, Mary. To restore your sister is not in my power. The soulless creature I brought to life bears no relation to the man from whose body I fashioned him. Your sister has gone on to her reward. Nothing—nothing I can do would bring her back."

"So you know nothing about the theft of her corpse?"

"On that score, I can offer no consolation to you or your family."

"My mother, my father—they are inconsolable."

"Then they must content themselves with memories of your sister as she lived. As I must do with my dear, lost brother William, and the traduced and dishonored Justine. Come, let us go back to the inn."

Mary burst into tears. He held her to him and she wept on his breast. Eventually she gathered herself and allowed him to take her arm, and they slowly walked back down to the main street of Matlock and the inn. She knew that when they reached it, Frankenstein would go. The warmth of his hand on hers almost made her beg him to stay, or better still, to take her with him.

They came to the busy courtyard. The dray stood off to the side, and Mary saw the cartmen were in the taproom. Frankenstein, agitated, upbraided them. "I thought I told you to keep those trunks out of the sun."

The older of the two men put down his pint and stood. "Sorry, Gov'nor. We'll see to it directly."

"Do so now."

As Frankenstein spoke, the evening coach drew up before the inn and prepared for departure. "You and Mr. Clerval leave today?" Mary asked.

"Yes. As soon as Henry arrives from the Old Bath, we take the coach to the Lake District. And thence to Scotland."

"They say it is very beautiful there."

"I am afraid that its beauty will be lost on me. I carry the burden of my great crime, not to be laid down until I have made things right."

She felt that she would burst if she did not speak her heart to him. "Victor. Will I ever see you again?"

He avoided her gaze. "I am afraid, Miss Bennet, that this is unlikely. My mind is set on banishing that vile creature from the world of men. Only then can I hope to return home and marry my betrothed Elizabeth."

Mary looked away from him. A young mother was adjusting her son's collar before putting him on the coach. "Ah, yes. You are affianced. I had almost forgotten."

Frankenstein pressed her hand. "Miss Bennet, you must forgive me the liberties I have taken with you. You have given me more of friendship than I deserve. I wish you to find the companion you seek, and to live your days in happiness. But now, I must go."

"God be with you, Mr. Frankenstein." She twisted her gloved fingers into a knot.

He bowed deeply, and hurried to have a few more words with the draymen. Henry Clerval arrived just as the men climbed to their cart and drove the baggage away. Clerval, surprised at seeing Mary, greeted her warmly. He expressed his great sorrow at the loss of her sister, and begged her to convey his condolences to the rest of her family. Ten minutes later the two men climbed aboard the coach and it left the inn, disappearing down the Matlock high street.

Mary stood in the inn yard. She did not feel she could bear to go back to Pemberley and face her family, the histrionics of her mother. Instead she reentered the inn and made the barkeep seat her in the ladies' parlor and bring her a bottle of port.

The sun declined and shadows stretched over the inn yard. The evening papers arrived from Nottingham. The yard boy lit the lamps. Still, Mary would not leave. Outside on the pavements, the boot-black sat in the growing darkness with his arms draped over his knees and head on his breast. She listened to the hoofs of the occasional horse striking the cobbles. The innkeeper was solicitous. When she asked for a second bottle, he hesitated, and wondered if he might send for someone from her family to take her home.

"You do not know my family," she said.

"Yes, miss. I only thought—"

"Another port. Then leave me alone."

"Yes, miss." He went away.

She was determined to become intoxicated. How many times had she piously warned against young women behaving as she did now? *Virtue is her own reward.* She had an apothegm for every occasion, and had tediously produced them in place of thought. *Show me a liar, and I'll show thee a thief. Marry in haste, repent at leisure. Men should be what they seem.*

She did not fool herself into thinking that her current misbehavior would make any difference. Perhaps Bingley or Darcy had been dispatched to find her in Lambton. But within an hour or two she would return to

Pemberley, where her mother would scold her for giving them an anxious evening, and Lizzy would caution her about the risk to her reputation. Lydia might even ask her, not believing it possible, if she had an assignation with some man. The loss of Kitty would overshadow Mary's indiscretion, pitiful as it had been. Soon all would be as it had been, except Mary would be alive and Kitty dead. But even that would fade. The shadow of Kitty's death would hang over the family for some time, but she doubted that anything of significance would change.

As she lingered over her glass, she looked up and noticed, in the now empty taproom, a man sitting at the table farthest from the lamps. A huge man, wearing rough clothes, his face hooded and in shadow. On the table in front of him was a tankard of ale and a few coppers. Mary rose, left the parlor for the taproom, and crossed toward him.

He looked up, and the faint light from the ceiling lamp caught his black eyes, sunken beneath heavy brows. He was hideously ugly. "May I sit with you?" she asked. She felt slightly dizzy.

"You may sit where you wish." The voice was deep, but swallowed, unable to project. It was almost a whisper.

Trembling only slightly, she sat. His wrists and hands, resting on the table, stuck out past the ragged sleeves of his coat. His skin was yellowish brown, and the fingernails livid white. He did not move. "You have some business with me?"

"I have the most appalling business." Mary tried to look him in the eyes, but her gaze kept slipping. "I want to know why you defiled my sister's grave, why you have stolen her body, and what you have done with her."

"Better you should ask Victor. Did he not explain all to you?"

"Mr. Frankenstein explained who—what—you are. He did not know what had become of my sister."

The thin lips twitched in a sardonic smile. "Poor Victor. He has got things all topsy-turvy. Victor does not know what I am. He is incapable of knowing, no matter the labors I have undertaken to school him. But he does know what became, and is to become, of your sister." The creature tucked the thick black hair behind his ear, a sudden unconscious gesture that made him seem completely human for the first time. He pulled the hood further forward to hide his face.

"So tell me."

"Which answer do you want? Who I am, or what happened to your sister?"

"First, tell me what happened to—to Kitty."

"Victor broke into the vault and stole her away. He took the utmost care not to damage her. He washed her fair body in diluted carbolic acid, and replaced her blood with a chemical admixture of his own devising. Folded up, she fit neatly within a cedar trunk sealed with pitch, and is at present being shipped to Scotland. You witnessed her departure from this courtyard an hour ago."

Mary's senses rebelled. She covered her face with her hands. The creature sat silent. Finally, without raising her head, she managed, "Victor warned me that you were a liar. Why should I believe you?"

"You have no reason to believe me."

"*You* took her!"

"Though I would not have scrupled to do so, I did not. Miss Bennet, I do not deny I have an interest in this matter. Victor did as I have told you at my bidding."

"At your bidding? Why?"

"Kitty—or not so much Kitty, as her remains—is to become my wife."

"Your wife! This is insupportable! Monstrous!"

"Monstrous." Suddenly, with preternatural quickness, his hand flashed out and grabbed Mary's wrist.

Mary thought to call for help, but the bar was empty and she had driven the innkeeper away. Yet his grip was not harsh. His hand was warm, instinct with life. "Look at me," he said. With his other hand he pushed back his hood.

She took a deep breath. She looked.

His noble forehead, high cheekbones, strong chin, and wide set eyes might have made him handsome, despite the scars and dry yellow skin, were it not for his expression. His ugliness was not a matter of lack of proportion—or rather, the lack of proportion was not in his features. Like his swallowed voice, his face was submerged, as if everything was hidden, revealed only in the eyes, the twitch of a cheek or lip. Every minute motion showed extraordinary animation. Hectic sickliness, but energy. This was a creature who had never learned to associate with civilized company, who had been thrust into adulthood with the passions of a wounded boy. Fear, self-disgust, anger. Desire.

The force of longing and rage in that face made her shrink. "Let me go," she whispered.

He let go her wrist. With bitter satisfaction, he said, "You see. If what I demand is insupportable, that is only because your kind has done nothing to support me. Once, I falsely hoped to meet with beings, who, pardoning my outward form, would love me for the excellent qualities which I was capable of bringing forth. Now I am completely alone. More than any starving man on a deserted isle, I am cast away. I have no brother, sister, parents. I have only Victor who, like so many fathers, recoiled from me the moment I first drew breath. And so, I have commanded him to make of your sister my wife, or he and all he loves will die at my hand."

"No. I cannot believe he would commit this abomination."

"He has no choice. He is my slave."

"His conscience could not support it, even at the cost of his life."

"You give him too much credit. You all do. He does not think. I have not seen him act other than according to impulse for the last three years. That is all I see in any of you."

Mary drew back, trying to make some sense of this horror. Her sister, to be brought to life, only to be given to this fiend. But would it be her sister, or another agitated, hungry thing like this?

She still retained some scraps of skepticism. The creature's manner did not bespeak the isolation which he claimed. "I am astonished at your grasp of language," Mary said. "You could not know so much without teachers."

"Oh, I have had many teachers." The creature's mutter was rueful. "You might say that, since first my eyes opened, mankind has been all my study. I have much yet to learn. There are certain words whose meaning has never been proved to me by experience. For example: *Happy*. Victor is to make me happy. Do you think he can do it?"

Mary thought of Frankenstein. Could he satisfy this creature? "I do not think it is in the power of any other person to make one happy."

"You jest with me. Every creature has its mate, save me. I have none."

She recoiled at his self-pity. Her fear faded. "You put too much upon having a mate."

"Why? You know nothing of what I have endured."

"You think that having a female of your own kind will insure that she will accept you?" Mary laughed. "Wait until you are rejected, for the most trivial of reasons, by one you are sure has been made for you."

A shadow crossed the creature's face. "That will not happen."

"It happens more often than not."

"The female that Victor creates shall find no other mate than me."

"That has never prevented rejection. Or if you should be accepted, then you may truly begin to learn."

"Learn what?"

"You will learn to ask a new question: Which is worse, to be alone, or to be wretchedly mismatched?" Like Lydia and Wickham, Mary thought. Like Collins and his poor wife Charlotte. Like her parents.

The creature's face spasmed with conflicting emotions. His voice gained volume. "Do not sport with me. I am not your toy."

"No. You only seek a toy of your own."

The creature was not, apparently, accustomed to mockery. "You must not say these things!" He lurched upward, awkwardly, so suddenly that he upended the table. The tankard of beer skidded across the top and spilled on Mary, and she fell back.

At that moment the innkeeper entered the bar room with two other men. They saw the tableau and rushed forward. "Here! Let her be!" he shouted. One of the other men grabbed the creature by the arm. With a roar the creature flung him aside like an old coat. His hood fell back. The men stared in horror at his face. The creature's eyes met Mary's, and with inhuman speed he whirled and ran out the door.

The men gathered themselves together. The one whom the creature had thrown aside had a broken arm. The innkeeper helped Mary to her feet. "Are you all right, miss?"

Mary felt dizzy. Was she all right? What did that mean?

"I believe so," she said.

When Mary returned to Pemberley, late that night, she found the house in an uproar over her absence. Bingley and Darcy both had been to Lambton, and had searched the road and the woods along it throughout the afternoon and evening. Mrs. Bennet had taken to bed with the conviction that she had lost two daughters in a single week. Wickham condemned Mary's poor judgment, Lydia sprang to Mary's defense, and this soon became a row over Wickham's lack of an income and Lydia's mismanagement of their children. Mr. Bennett closed himself up in the library.

Mary told them only that she had been to Matlock. She offered no explanation, no apology. Around the town the story of her conflict with the strange giant in the inn was spoken of for some time, along with rumors of Robert Piggot the butcher's son, and the mystery of Kitty's defiled grave—but as Mary was not a local, and nothing of consequence followed, the talk soon passed away.

That winter, Mary came upon the following story in the Nottingham newspaper:

GHASTLY EVENTS IN SCOTLAND

Our northern correspondent files the following report. In early November, the body of a young foreigner, Mr. Henry Clerval of Geneva, Switzerland, was found upon the beach near the far northern town of Thurso. The body, still warm, bore marks of strangulation. A second foreigner, Mr. Victor Frankstone, was taken into custody, charged with the murder, and held for two months. Upon investigation, the magistrate Mr. Kirwan determined that Mr. Frankstone was in the Orkney Islands at the time of the killing. The accused was released in the custody of his father, and is assumed to have returned to his home on the continent.

A month after the disposition of these matters, a basket, weighted with stones and containing the body of a young woman, washed up in the estuary of the River Thurso. The identity of the woman is unknown, and her murderer undiscovered, but it is speculated that the unfortunate may have died at the hands of the same person or persons who murdered Mr. Clerval. The woman was given Christian burial in the Thurso Presbyterian churchyard.

The village has been shaken by these events, and prays God to deliver it from evil.

Oh, Victor, Mary thought. She remembered the pressure of his hand, through her dressing gown, upon her thigh. Now he had returned to Switzerland, there, presumably, to marry his Elizabeth. She hoped that he would be more honest with his wife than he had been with her, but the fate of Clerval did not bode well. And the creature still had no mate.

She clipped the newspaper report and slipped it into the drawer of her writing table, where she kept her copy of Samuel Galton's *The Natural History of Birds, Intended for the Amusement and Instruction of Children*, and the *Juvenile Anecdotes* of Priscilla Wakefield, and a Dudley locust made of stone, and a paper fan from the first ball she had ever attended, and a dried wreath of flowers that had been thrown to her, when she was nine years old, from the top of a tree by one of the town boys playing near Meryton common.

After the death of her parents, Mary lived with Lizzy and Darcy at Pemberley for the remainder of her days. Under a pen name, she pursued a career as a writer of philosophical speculations, and sent many letters to the London newspapers. Aunt Mary, as she was called at home, was known for her kindness to William, and to his wife and children. The children teased Mary for her nearsightedness, her books, and her piano. But for a woman whose experience of the world was so slender, and whose soul it seemed had never been touched by any passion, she came at last to be respected for her understanding, her self possession, and her wise counsel on matters of the heart.

KIJ JOHNSON—SHORT STORY
26 MONKEYS, ALSO THE ABYSS

I first heard Kij Johnson's name because of this story. A writer I know posted a link to the story on a private board and said, "You have to read this." By "you" he meant everyone.

"26 Monkeys, Also the Abyss" is hardly the first thing that Johnson has written. She's been writing for years and has won awards including the Theodore Sturgeon Award along with scads of nominations for other major awards. This marks her first Hugo nomination although as we go to press she is up for a second Hugo nomination.

With three novels and more than thirty short stories under her belt, Johnson has had plenty of time to look at what a narrative is and how to deconstruct it. I use the word "deconstruct" quite deliberately because this isn't a traditional narrative. It is a series of moments encapsulated in text and your job as a reader is to try to find order out of those moments in the same way that Aimee seeks answers.

"26 Monkeys, Also the Abyss" is deceptive when you begin it. It seems simple and a little whimsical but as it progresses Johnson does a neat job of undoing every preconception you bring to the table. It is told simply and with a matter-of-fact tone. Each part is presented as a fact. That simplicity is part of what allows the story to take you by surprise as it unfolds, because there is a part of it that doesn't feel like a story. It feels like something that really happened.

26 MONKEYS, ALSO THE ABYSS

KIJ JOHNSON

1.

Aimee's big trick is that she makes 26 monkeys vanish onstage.

2.

She pushes out a claw-foot bathtub and asks audience members to come up and inspect it. The people climb in and look underneath, touch the white enamel, run their hands along the little lions' feet. When they're done, four chains are lowered from the stage's fly space. Aimee secures them to holes drilled along the tub's lip and gives a signal, and the bathtub is hoisted ten feet into the air.

She sets a stepladder next to it. She claps her hands and the twenty-six monkeys onstage run up the ladder one after the other and jump into the bathtub. The bathtub shakes as each monkey thuds in among the others. The audience can see heads, legs, tails; but eventually every monkey settles and the bathtub is still again. Zeb is always the last monkey up the ladder. As he climbs into the bathtub, he makes a humming boom deep in his chest. It fills the stage.

And then there's a flash of light, two of the chains fall off, and the bathtub swings down to expose its interior.

Empty.

3.

They turn up later, back at the tour bus. There's a smallish dog door, and in the hours before morning the monkeys let themselves in, alone or in small groups, and get themselves glasses of water from the tap. If more than one returns at the same time, they murmur a bit among themselves, like college students meeting in the dorm halls after bar time. A few sleep on the sofa and at least one likes to be on the bed, but most of them wander back to their cages. There's a little grunting as they rearrange their blankets and soft toys, and then sighs and snoring. Aimee doesn't really sleep until she hears them all come in.

Aimee has no idea what happens to them in the bathtub, or where they go, or what they do before the soft click of the dog door opening. This bothers her a lot.

4.

Aimee has had the act for three years now. She was living in a month-by-month furnished apartment under a flight path for the Salt Lake City airport. She was hollow, as if something had chewed a hole in her body and the hole had grown infected.

There was a monkey act at the Utah State Fair. She felt a sudden and totally out-of-character urge to see it. Afterward, with no idea why, she walked up to the owner and said, "I have to buy this."

He nodded. He sold it to her for a dollar, which he told her was the price he had paid four years before.

Later, when the paperwork was filled out, she asked him, "How can you leave them? Won't they miss you?"

"You'll see, they're pretty autonomous," he said. "Yeah, they'll miss me and I'll miss them. But it's time, they know that."

He smiled at his new wife, a small woman with laugh lines and a vervet hanging from one hand. "We're ready to have a garden," she said.

He was right. The monkeys missed him. But they also welcomed her, each monkey politely shaking her hand as she walked into what was now her bus.

5.

Aimee has: a nineteen-year-old tour bus packed with cages that range in size from parrot-sized (for the vervets) to something about the size of a pickup bed (for all the macaques); a stack of books on monkeys ranging from *All About Monkeys* to *Evolution and Ecology of Baboon Societies*; some sequined show costumes, a sewing machine, and a bunch of Carhartts and tees; a stack of show posters from a few years back that say 25 MONKEYS! FACE THE ABYSS; a battered sofa in a virulent green plaid; and a boyfriend who helps with the monkeys.

She cannot tell you why she has any of these, not even the boyfriend, whose name is Geof, whom she met in Billings seven months ago. Aimee has no idea where anything comes from any more: she no longer believes that anything makes sense, even though she can't stop hoping.

The bus smells about as you'd expect a bus full of monkeys to smell; though after a show, after the bathtub trick but before the monkeys all return, it also smells of cinnamon, which is the tea Aimee sometimes drinks.

6.

For the act, the monkeys do tricks, or dress up in outfits and act out hit movies—*The Matrix* is very popular, as is anything where the monkeys dress up like little orcs. The maned monkeys, the lion-tails and the colobuses, have a lion-tamer act, with the old capuchin female, Pango, dressed in a red jacket and carrying a whip and a small chair. The chimpanzee (whose name is Mimi, and no, she is not a monkey) can do actual sleight of hand; she's not very good, but she's the best Chimp Pulling A Coin From Someone's Ear in the world.

The monkeys also can build a suspension bridge out of wooden chairs and rope, make a four-tier champagne fountain, and write their names on a whiteboard.

The monkey show is very popular, with a schedule of 127 shows this year at fairs and festivals across the Midwest and Great Plains. Aimee could do more, but she likes to let everyone have a couple of months off at Christmas.

7.

This is the bathtub act:

Aimee wears a glittering purple-black dress designed to look like a scanty magician's robe. She stands in front of a scrim lit deep blue and scattered with stars. The monkeys are ranged in front of her. As she speaks they undress and fold their clothes into neat piles. Zeb sits on his stool to one side, a white spotlight shining straight down to give him a shadowed look.

She raises her hands.

"These monkeys have made you laugh, and made you gasp. They have created wonders for you and performed mysteries. But there is a final mystery they offer you—the strangest, the greatest of all."

She parts her hands suddenly, and the scrim goes transparent and is lifted away, revealing the bathtub on a raised dais. She walks around it, running her hand along the tub's curves.

"It's a simple thing, this bathtub. Ordinary in every way, mundane as breakfast. In a moment I will invite members of the audience up to let you prove this for yourselves.

"But for the monkeys it is also a magical object. It allows them to travel—no one can say where. Not even I—" she pauses "—can tell you this. Only the monkeys know, and they share no secrets.

"Where do they go? Into heaven, foreign lands, other worlds—or some dark abyss? We cannot follow. They will vanish before our eyes, vanish from this most ordinary of things."

And after the bathtub is inspected and she has told the audience that there will be no final spectacle in the show—"It will be hours before they return from their secret travels"—and called for applause for them, she gives the cue.

8.

Aimee's monkeys:

- 2 siamangs, a mated couple
- 2 squirrel monkeys, though they're so active they might as well be twice as many
- 2 vervets

- a guenon, who is probably pregnant, though it's still too early to tell for sure. Aimee has no idea how this happened
- 3 rhesus monkeys. They juggle a little
- a capuchin female named Pango
- a crested macaque, 3 snow monkeys (one quite young), and a Java macaque. Despite the differences, they have formed a small troop and like to sleep together
- a chimpanzee, who is not actually a monkey
- a surly gibbon
- 2 marmosets
- a golden tamarin; a cotton-top tamarin
- a proboscis monkey
- red and black colubuses
- Zeb

9.

Aimee thinks Zeb might be a de Brazza's guenon, except that he's so old that he has lost almost all his hair. She worries about his health, but he insists on staying in the act. By now all he's really up for is the final rush to the bathtub, and for him it is more of a stroll. The rest of the time, he sits on a stool that is painted orange and silver and watches the other monkeys, looking like an aging impresario watching his *Swan Lake* from the wings. Sometimes she gives him things to hold, such as a silver hoop through which the squirrel monkeys jump.

10.

No one knows how the monkeys vanish or where they go. Sometimes they return holding foreign coins or durian fruit, or wearing pointed Moroccan slippers. Every so often one returns pregnant or accompanied by a new monkey. The number of monkeys is not constant.

"I just don't get it," Aimee keeps asking Geof, as if he has any idea. Aimee never knows anything any more. She's been living without any certainties, and this one thing—well, the whole thing, the fact the monkeys get along so well and know how to do card tricks and just turned up in her life and vanish from the bathtub; *everything*—she coasts with that most of the time, but every so often, when she feels her life is wheeling without brakes down a long hill, she starts poking at this again.

Geof trusts the universe a lot more than Aimee does, trusts that things make sense and that people can love, and therefore he doesn't need the same proofs. "You could ask them," he says.

11.

Aimee's boyfriend:

Geof is not at all what Aimee expected from a boyfriend. For one thing, he's fifteen years younger than Aimee, twenty-eight to her forty-three. For another, he's sort of quiet. For a third, he's gorgeous, silky thick hair pulled into a shoulder-length ponytail, shaved sides showing off his strong jaw line. He smiles a lot, but he doesn't laugh very often.

Geof has a degree in history, which means that he was working in a bike-repair shop when she met him at the Montana Fair. Aimee never has much to do right after the show, so when he offered to buy her a beer she said yes. And then it was four AM and they were kissing in the bus, monkeys letting themselves in and getting ready for bed; and Aimee and Geof made love.

In the morning over breakfast, the monkeys came up one by one and shook his hand solemnly, and then he was with the band, so to speak. She helped him pick up his cameras and clothes and the surfboard his sister had painted for him one year as a Christmas present. There's no room for the surfboard, so it's suspended from the ceiling. Sometimes the squirrel monkeys hang out there and peek over the side.

Aimee and Geof never talk about love.

Geof has a class-C driver's license, but this is just lagniappe.

12.

Zeb is dying.

Generally speaking, the monkeys are remarkably healthy and Aimee can handle their occasional sinus infections and gastrointestinal ailments. For anything more difficult, she's found a couple of communities online and some helpful specialists.

But Zeb's coughing some, and the last of his fur is falling out. He moves very slowly and sometimes has trouble remembering simple tasks. When the show was up in St. Paul six months ago, a Como Zoo biologist came to visit the monkeys, complimented her on their general health and well-being, and at her request looked Zeb over.

"How old is he?" the biologist, Gina, asked.

"I don't know," Aimee said. The man she bought the show from hadn't known either.

"*I'll* tell you then," Gina said. "He's old. I mean, seriously old."

Senile dementia, arthritis, a heart murmur. No telling when, Gina said. "He's a happy monkey," she said. "He'll go when he goes."

13.

Aimee thinks a lot about this. What happens to the act when Zeb's dead? Through each show he sits calm and poised on his bright stool. She feels he is somehow at the heart of the monkeys' amiability and cleverness. She keeps thinking that he is somehow the reason the monkeys all vanish and return.

Because there's always a reason for everything, isn't there? Because if there isn't a reason for even *one* thing, like how you can get sick, or your husband stop loving you or people you love die—then there's no reason for anything. So there must be reasons. Zeb's as good a guess as any.

14.

What Aimee likes about this life:

It doesn't mean anything. She doesn't live anywhere. Her world is thirty-eight feet and 127 shows long and currently twenty-six monkeys deep. This is manageable.

Fairs don't mean anything, either. Her tiny world travels within a slightly larger world, the identical, interchangeable fairs. Sometimes the only things that cue Aimee to the town she's in are the nighttime temperatures and the shape of the horizon: badlands, mountains, plains, or city skyline.

Fairs are as artificial as titanium knees: the carnival, the animal barns, the stock-car races, the concerts, the smell of burnt sugar and funnel cakes and animal bedding. Everything is an overly bright symbol for something real, food or pets or hanging out with friends. None of this has anything to do with the world Aimee used to live in, the world from which these people visit.

She has decided that Geof is like the rest of it: temporary, meaningless. Not for loving.

15.

These are some ways Aimee's life might have come apart:

a. She might have broken her ankle a few years ago, and gotten a bone infection that left her on crutches for ten months, and in pain for longer.

b. Her husband might have fallen in love with his admin and left her.

c. She might have been fired from her job in the same week she found out her sister had colon cancer.

d. She might have gone insane for a time and made a series of questionable choices that left her alone in a furnished apartment in a city she picked out of the atlas.

Nothing is certain. You can lose everything. Eventually, even at your luckiest, you will die and then you *will* lose it all. When you are a certain age or when you have lost certain things and people, Aimee's crippling grief will make a terrible poisoned dark sense.

16.

Aimee has read up a lot, so she knows how strange all this is.

There aren't any locks on the cages. The monkeys use them as bedrooms, places to store their special possessions and get away from the others when they want some privacy. Much of the time, however, they are loose in the bus or poking around outside.

Right now, three monkeys are sitting on the bed playing a game where they match colored cards. Others are playing with skeins of bright wool, or rolling around on the floor, or poking at a piece of wood with a screwdriver, or climbing on Aimee and Geof and the battered sofa. Some of the monkeys are crowded around the computer watching kitten videos on a pirated wireless connection.

The black colubus is stacking children's wooden blocks on the kitchen-ette's table. He brought them back one night a couple of weeks ago, and since then he's been trying to make an arch. After two weeks and Aimee's showing him repeatedly how a keystone works, he still hasn't figured it out, but he's still patiently trying.

Geof's reading a novel out loud to Pango, who watches the pages as if she's reading along. Sometimes she points to a word and looks up at him with her bright eyes, and he repeats it to her, smiling, and then spells it out.

Zeb is sleeping in his cage. He crept in there at dusk, fluffed up his toys and his blanket, and pulled the door closed behind him. He does this a lot lately.

17.

Aimee's going to lose Zeb, and then what? What happens to the other monkeys? Twenty-six monkeys is a lot of monkeys, but they all like each other. No one except maybe a zoo or a circus can keep that many monkeys, and she doesn't think anyone else will let them sleep wherever they like or watch kitten videos. And if Zeb's not there, where will they go, those nights when they can no longer drop through the bathtub and into their mystery? And she doesn't even know whether it *is* Zeb, whether he is the cause of this, or that's just her flailing for reasons again.

And Aimee? She'll lose her safe artificial world: the bus, the identical fairs, the meaningless boyfriend. The monkeys. And then what.

18.

Just a few months after she bought the act, when she didn't care much about whether she lived or died, she followed the monkeys up the ladder in the closing act. Zeb raced up the ladder, stepped into the bathtub and stood, lungs filling for his great call. And she ran up after him. She glimpsed the bathtub's interior, the monkeys tidily sardined in, scrambling to get out of her way as they realized what she was doing. She hopped into the hole they made for her, curled up tight.

This only took an instant. Zeb finished his breath, boomed it out. There was a flash of light, she heard the chains release, and felt the bathtub swing down, monkeys shifting around her.

She fell the ten feet alone. Her ankle twisted when she hit the stage but she managed to stay upright. The monkeys were gone again.

There was an awkward silence. It wasn't one of her more successful performances.

19.

Aimee and Geof walk through the midway at the Salina Fair. She's hungry and doesn't want to cook, so they're looking for somewhere that sells $4.50 hotdogs and $3.25 Cokes, and suddenly Geof turns to Aimee and says, "This is bullshit. Why don't we go into town? Have real food. Act like normal people."

So they do: pasta and wine at a place called Irina's Villa. "You're always asking why they go," Geof says, a bottle and a half in. His eyes are an indeterminate blue-gray, but in this light they look black and very warm. "See, I don't think we're ever going to find out what happens. But I don't think that's the real question, anyway. Maybe the question is, why do they come back?"

Aimee thinks of the foreign coins, the wood blocks, the wonderful things they bring home. "I don't know," she says. "Why *do* they come back?"

Later that night, back at the bus, Geof says, "Wherever they go, yeah, it's cool. But see, here's my theory." He gestures to the crowded bus with its clutter of toys and tools. The two tamarins have just come in, and they're sitting on the kitchenette counter, heads close as they examine some new small thing. "They like visiting wherever it is, sure. But this is their home. Everyone likes to come home sooner or later."

"If they have a home," Aimee says.

"Everyone has a home, even if they don't believe in it," Geof says.

20.

That night, when Geof's asleep curled up around one of the macaques, Aimee kneels by Zeb's cage. "Can you at least show me?" she asks. "Please? Before you go?"

Zeb is an indeterminate lump under his baby-blue blanket, but he gives a little sigh and climbs slowly out of his cage. He takes her hand with his own hot leathery paw, and they walk out the door into the night.

The back lot where all the trailers and buses are parked is quiet, only a few voices still audible from behind curtained windows. The sky is blue-black and scattered with stars. The moon shines straight down on them, shadowing Zeb's face. His eyes when he looks up seem bottomless.

The bathtub is backstage, already on its wheeled dais waiting for the next show. The space is nearly pitch dark, lit by some red EXIT signs and a single sodium-vapor away off to one side. Zeb walks her up to the tub, lets her run her hands along its cold curves and the lions' paws, and shows her the dimly lit interior.

And then he heaves himself onto the dais and over the tub lip. She stands beside him, looking down. He lifts himself upright and gives a boom. And then he drops flat and the bathtub is empty.

She saw it, him vanishing. He was there and then he was gone. But there was nothing to see, no gate, no flickering reality or soft pop as air snapped in to fill the vacated space. It still doesn't make sense, but it's the answer that Zeb has.

He's already back at the bus when she gets there, already buried under his blanket and wheezing in his sleep.

21.

Then one day:

Everyone is backstage. Aimee is finishing her makeup, and Geof is double-checking everything. The monkeys are sitting neatly in a circle in the dressing room, as if trying to keep their bright vests and skirts from creasing. Zeb sits in the middle, Pango beside him in her little green sequined outfit. They grunt a bit, then lean back. One after the other, the rest of the monkeys crawl forward and shake his hand, and then hers. She nods, like a small queen at a flower show.

That night, Zeb doesn't run up the ladder. He stays on his stool and it's Pango who is the last monkey up the ladder, who climbs into the bathtub and gives a screech. Aimee has been wrong to think Zeb had to be the reason for what is happening with the monkeys, but she was so sure of it that she missed all the cues. But Geof didn't miss a thing, so when Pango screeches, he hits the flash powder. The flash, the empty bathtub.

Zeb stands on his stool, bowing like an impresario called onstage for the curtain call. When the curtain drops for the last time, he reaches up to be lifted. Aimee cuddles him as they walk back to the bus, Geof's arm around them both.

Zeb falls asleep with them that night, between them in the bed. When she wakes up in the morning, he's back in his cage with his favorite toy. He doesn't wake up. The monkeys cluster at the bars peeking in.

Aimee cries all day. "It's okay," Geof says.

"It's not about Zeb," she sobs.

"I know," he says. "It's okay. Come home, Aimee."

But she's already there. She just hadn't noticed.

22.

Here's the trick to the bathtub trick. There is no trick. The monkeys pour across the stage and up the ladder and into the bathtub and they settle in and then they vanish. The world is full of strange things, things that make no sense, and maybe this is one of them. Maybe the monkeys choose not to share, that's cool, who can blame them.

Maybe this is the monkeys' mystery, how they found other monkeys that ask questions and try things, and figured out a way to all be together to share it. Maybe Aimee and Geof are really just houseguests in the monkeys' world: they are there for a while and then they leave.

23.

Six weeks later, a man walks up to Aimee as she and Geof kiss after a show. He's short, pale, balding. He has the shell-shocked look of a man eaten hollow from the inside. She knows the look.

"I need to buy this," he says.

Aimee nods. "I know you do."

She sells it to him for a dollar.

Three months later, Aimee and Geof get their first houseguest in their apartment in Bellingham. They hear the refrigerator close and come out to the kitchen to find Pango pouring orange juice from a carton.

They send her home with a pinochle deck.

NANCY KRESS (WINNER)—NOVELLA
THE ERDMANN NEXUS

What scares you most about aging? Take your time and think about it the next time you find yourself walking behind someone elderly. Is it the loss of mobility? The pain? The failing mind? The loneliness? There are degrees of aging and not everyone faces the same issues. In Nancy Kress's novella, what you'll see are a few of the endless variety of ways in which aging strips away the choices that one can make. It is a slow erosion of freedom either from health or mobility or mental decay. None of the options are pretty or comfortable but within each of them it is possible to retain a sense of self.

Kress handles a large cast of characters in a nursing home, showing us with painful clarity the indignities that each of them face. Her deft touch comes as no surprise when you consider that she has won six Nebula awards, the John W. Campbell Memorial Award, the Theodore Sturgeon award, written 26 novels, and won a Hugo for her novel *Beggars in Spain*. "The Erdmann Nexus" is her second Hugo. I happen to think that her background as an elementary school teacher and a advertising copy writer shows in her stories as a clarity of intent. When she wants to guide you to an idea she does it so adroitly that you don't know that you've been manipulated.

All of this comes together in "The Erdmann Nexus," the 2008 Hugo winner for for Best Novella.

THE ERDMANN NEXUS

NANCY KRESS

———◆———

"Errors, like straws, upon the surface flow,
He who would reach for pearls must dive below."
—John Dryden

The ship, which would have looked nothing like a ship to Henry Erdmann, moved between the stars, traveling in an orderly pattern of occurrences in the vacuum flux. Over several cubic light-years of space, subatomic particles appeared, existed, and winked out of existence in nanoseconds. Flop transitions tore space and then reconfigured it as the ship moved on. Henry, had he somehow been nearby in the cold of deep space, would have died from the complicated, regular, intense bursts of radiation long before he could have had time to appreciate their shimmering beauty.

All at once the ship stopped moving.

The radiation bursts increased, grew even more complex. Then the ship abruptly changed direction. It accelerated, altering both space and time as it sped on, healing the alterations in its wake. Urgency shot through it.

Something, far away, was struggling to be born.

ONE

Henry Erdmann stood in front of the mirror in his tiny bedroom, trying to knot his tie with one hand. The other hand gripped his walker. It was an unsteady business, and the tie ended up crooked. He yanked it out and began again. Carrie would be here soon.

He always wore a tie to the college. Let the students—and graduate students, at that!—come to class in ripped jeans and obscene T-shirts and hair tangled as if colonized by rats. Even the girls. Students were students, and Henry didn't consider their sloppiness disrespectful, the way so many did at St. Sebastian's. Sometimes he was even amused by it, in a sad sort of way. Didn't these intelligent, sometimes driven, would-be physicists know how ephemeral their beauty was? Why did they go to such lengths to look unappealing, when soon enough that would be their only choice?

This time he got the tie knotted. Not perfectly—a difficult operation, one-handed—but close enough for government work. He smiled. When he and his colleagues had been doing government work, only perfection was good enough. Atomic bombs were like that. Henry could still hear Oppie's voice saying the plans for Ivy Mike were "technically sweet." Of course, that was before all the—

A knock on the door and Carries's fresh young voice. "Dr. Erdmann? Are you ready?"

She always called him by his title, always treated him with respect. Not like some of the nurses and assistants. "How are we today, Hank?" that overweight blonde asked yesterday. When he answered stiffly, "I don't know about you, madame, but I'm fine, thank you," she'd only laughed. *Old people are so formal—it's so cute!* Henry could just hear her saying it to one of her horrible colleagues. He had never been "Hank" in his entire life.

"Coming, Carrie." He put both hands on the walker and inched forward—clunk, clunk, clunk—the walker sounding loud even on the carpeted floor. His class's corrected problem sets lay on the table by the door. He'd given them some really hard problems this week, and only Haldane had succeeded in solving all of them. Haldane had promise. An inventive mind, yet rigorous, too. They could have used him in '52 on Project Ivy, developing the Teller-Ulam staged fusion H-bomb.

Halfway across the living room of his tiny apartment in the Assisted Living Facility, something happened in Henry's mind.

He stopped, astonished. It had felt like a tentative *touch*, a ghostly finger inside his brain. Astonishment was immediately replaced by fear. Was he having a stroke? At ninety, anything was possible. But he felt fine, better in fact than for several days. Not a stroke. So what—

"Dr. Erdmann?"

"I'm here." He clunked to the door and opened it. Carrie wore a cherry red sweater, a fallen orange leaf caught on her hat, and sunglasses. Such a pretty girl, all bronze hair and bright skin and vibrant color. Outside it was drizzling. Henry reached out and gently removed the sunglasses. Carrie's left eye was swollen and discolored, the iris and pupil invisible under the outraged flesh.

"The bastard," Henry said.

That was Henry and Carrie going down the hall toward the elevator, thought Evelyn Krenchnoted. She waved from her armchair, her door wide open as always, but they were talking and didn't notice. She strained to hear, but just then another plane went overhead from the airport. Those pesky flight paths were too near St. Sebastian's! On the other hand, if they weren't, Evelyn couldn't afford to live here. Always look on the bright side!

Since this was Tuesday afternoon, Carrie and Henry were undoubtedly going to the college. So wonderful the way Henry kept busy—you'd never guess his real age, that was for sure. He even had all his hair! Although that jacket was too light for September, and not waterproof. Henry might catch cold. She would speak to Carrie about it. And why was Carrie wearing sunglasses when it was raining?

But if Evelyn didn't start her phone calls, she would be late! People were depending on her! She keyed in the first number, listened to it ring one floor below. "Bob? It's Evelyn. Now, dear, tell me—how's your blood pressure today?"

"Fine," Bob Donovan said.

"Are you sure? You sound a bit grumpy, dear."

"I'm fine, Evelyn. I'm just busy."

"Oh, that's good! With what?"

"Just *busy*."

"Always good to keep busy! Are you coming to Current Affairs tonight?"

"Dunno."

"You should. You really should. Intellectual stimulation is so important for people our age!"

"Gotta go," Bob grunted.

"Certainly, but first, how did your granddaughter do with—"

He'd hung up. Really, very grumpy. Maybe he was having problems with irregularity. Evelyn would recommend a high colonic.

Her next call was more responsive. Gina Martinelli was, as always, thrilled with Evelyn's attention. She informed Gina minutely about the state of her arthritis, her gout, her diabetes, her son's weight problem, her other son's wife's step-daughter's miscarriage, all interspersed with quotations from the Bible (" ' Take a little wine for thy stomach'—First Timothy.") She answered all Evelyn's questions and wrote down all her recommendations and—

"Evelyn?" Gina said. "Are you still there?"

"Yes, I—" Evelyn fell silent, an occurrence so shocking that Gina gasped, "Hit your panic button!"

"No, no, I'm fine, I . . . I just remembered something for a moment."

"Remembered something? What?"

But Evelyn didn't know. It hadn't been a memory, exactly, it had been a . . . what? A feeling, a vague but somehow strong sensation of . . . something.

"Evelyn?"

"I'm here!"

"The Lord decides when to call us home, and I guess it's not your time yet. Did you hear about Anna Chernov? That famous ballet dancer on Four? She fell last night and broke her leg and they had to move her to the Infirmary."

"No!"

"Yes, poor thing. They say it's only temporary, until they get her stabilized, but you know what that means."

She did. They all did. First the Infirmary, then up to Seven, where you didn't even have your own little apartment any more, and eventually to Nursing on Eight and Nine. Better to go quick and clean, like Jed Fuller last month. But Evelyn wasn't going to let herself think like that! A positive attitude was so important!

Gina said, "Anna is doing pretty well, I hear. The Lord never sends more than a person can bear."

Evelyn wasn't so sure about that, but it never paid to argue with Gina, who was convinced that she had God on redial. Evelyn said, "I'll visit her before the Stitch 'n Bitch meeting. I'm sure she'll want company. Poor girl—you know, those dancers, they just abuse their health for years and years, so what can you expect?"

"I know!" Gina said, not without satisfaction. "They pay a terrible price for beauty. It's a little vain, actually."

"Did you hear about that necklace she has in the St. Sebastian's safe?"

"No! What necklace?"

"A fabulous one! Doris Dziwalski told me. It was given to Anna by some famous Russian dancer who was given it by the czar!"

"What czar?"

"*The* czar! You know, of Russia. Doris said it's worth a fortune and that's why it's in the safe. Anna never wears it."

"Vanity," Gina said. "She probably doesn't like the way it looks now against her wrinkly neck."

"Doris said Anna's depressed."

"No, it's vanity. 'Lo, I looked and saw that all was—' "

"I'll recommend acupuncture to her," Evelyn interrupted. "Acupuncture is good for depression." But first she'd call Erin, to tell her the news.

Erin Bass let the phone ring. It was probably that tiresome bore Evelyn Krenchnoted, eager to check on Erin's blood pressure or her cholesterol or her Islets of Langerhans. Oh, Erin should answer the phone, there was no harm in the woman, Erin should be more charitable. But why? Why should one have to be more charitable just because one was old?

She let the phone ring and returned to her book, Graham Greene's *The Heart of the Matter*. Greene's world-weary despair was a silly affectation but he was a wonderful writer, and too much underrated nowadays.

The liner came in on a Saturday evening: from the bedroom window they could see its long grey form steal past the boom, beyond the—

Something was happening.

—steal past the boom, beyond the—

Erin was no longer in St. Sebastian's, she was nowhere, she was lifted away from everything, she was beyond the—

Then it was over and she sat again in her tiny apartment, the book sliding unheeded off her lap.

Anna Chernov was dancing. She and Paul stood with two other couples on the stage, under the bright lights. Balanchine himself stood in the second wing, and even though Anna knew he was there to wait for Suzanne's solo, his presence inspired her. The music began. *Promenade en couronne, attitude, arabesque effacé* and into the lift, Paul's arms raising her. She was lifted out of herself and then she was soaring above the stage, over the heads of the corps de ballet, above Suzanne Farrell herself, soaring through the roof of the New York State Theater and into the night sky, spreading her arms in a *porte de bras* wide enough to take in the glittering night sky, soaring in the most perfect *jeté* in the universe, until . . .

"She's smiling," Bob Donovan said, before he knew he was going to speak at all. He looked down at the sleeping Anna, so beautiful she didn't even look real, except for the leg in its big ugly cast. In one hand, feeling like a fool but what the fuck, he held three yellow roses.

"The painkillers do that sometimes," the Infirmary nurse said. "I'm afraid you can't stay, Mr. Donovan."

Bob scowled at her. But it wasn't like he meant it or anything. This nurse wasn't so bad. Not like some. Maybe because she wasn't any spring chicken herself. *A few more years, sister, and you'll be here right with us.*

"Give her these, okay?" He thrust the roses at the nurse.

"I will, yes," she said, and he walked out of the medicine-smelling Infirmary—he hated that smell—back to the elevator. Christ, what a sorry old fart he was. Anna Chernov, that nosy old broad Evelyn Krenchnoted once told him, used to dance at some famous place in New York, Abraham Center or something. Anna had been famous. But Evelyn could be wrong, and anyway it didn't matter. From the first moment Bob Donovan laid eyes on Anna Chernov, he'd wanted to give her things. Flowers. Jewelry. Anything she wanted. Anything he had. And how stupid and fucked-up was that, at his age? Give me a break!

He took the elevator to the first floor, stalked savagely through the lobby, and went out the side door to the "remembrance garden." Stupid name, New Age-y stupid. He wanted to kick something, wanted to bellow for—

Energy punched through him, from the base of his spine up his back and into his brain, mild but definite, like a shock from a busted toaster or something. Then it was gone.

What the fuck was *that*? Was he okay? If he fell, like Anna—

He was okay. He didn't have Anna's thin delicate bones. Whatever it was, was gone now. Just one of those things.

On a Nursing floor of St. Sebastian's, a woman with just a few days to live muttered in her long, last half-sleep. An IV dripped morphine into her arm, easing the passage. No one listened to the mutterings; it had been years since they'd made sense. For a moment she stopped and her eyes, again bright in the ravaged face that had once been so lovely, grew wide. But for only a moment. Her eyes closed and the mindless muttering resumed.

In Tijuana, a vigorous old man sitting behind his son's market stall, where he sold cheap serapes to jabbering turistas, suddenly lifted his face to the sun. His mouth, which still had all its white flashing teeth, made a big O.

In Bombay, a widow dressed in white looked out her window at the teeming streets, her face gone blank as her sari.

In Chengdu, a monk sitting on his cushion on the polished floor of the meditation room in the ancient Wenshu Monastery, shattered the holy silence with a shocking, startled laugh.

TWO

Carrie Vesey sat in the back of Dr. Erdmann's classroom and thought about murder.

Not that she would ever do it, of course. Murder was wrong. Taking a life filled her with horror that was only—

Ground-up castor beans were a deadly poison.

—made worse by her daily witnessing of old people's aching desire to hold onto life. Also, she—

Her step-brother had once shown her how to disable the brakes on a car.

—knew she wasn't the kind of person who solved problems that boldly. And anyway her—

The battered-woman defense almost always earned acquittal from juries.

—lawyer said that a paper trail of restraining orders and ER documentation was by far the best way to—

If a man was passed out from a dozen beers, he'd never feel a bullet from his own service revolver.

—put Jim behind bars legally. That, the lawyer said, "would solve the problem"—as if a black eye and a broken arm and constant threats that left her scared even when Jim wasn't in the same *city* were all just a theoretical "problem," like the ones Dr. Erdmann gave his physics students.

He sat on top of a desk in the front of the room, talking about something called the "Bose-Einstein condensate." Carrie had no idea what that was, and she didn't care. She just liked being here, sitting unheeded in the back of the room. The physics students, nine boys and two girls, were none of them interested in her presence, her black eye, or her beauty. When Dr. Erdmann was around, he commanded all their geeky attention, and that was indescribably restful. Carrie tried—unsuccessfully, she knew—to hide her beauty. Her looks had brought her nothing but trouble: Gary, Eric, Jim. So now she wore baggy sweats and no make-up, and crammed her twenty-four-carat-gold hair under a shapeless hat. Maybe if she was as smart as these students she would have learned to pick a different kind of man, but she wasn't, and she hadn't, and Dr. Erdmann's classroom was a place she felt safe. Safer, even, than St. Sebastian's, which was where Jim had blackened her eye.

He'd slipped in through the loading dock, she guessed, and caught her alone in the linens supply closet. He was gone after one punch, and when she called her exasperated lawyer and he found out she had no witnesses and St. Sebastian's had "security," he'd said there was nothing he could do. It would be her word against Jim's. She had to be able to *prove* that the restraining order had been violated.

Dr. Erdmann was talking about "proof," too: some sort of mathematical proof. Carrie had been good at math, in high school. Only Dr. Erdmann had said once that what she'd done in high school wasn't "mathematics," only "arithmetic." "Why didn't you go to college, Carrie?" he'd asked.

"No money," she said in a tone that meant: Please don't ask anything else. She just hadn't felt up to explaining about Daddy and the alcoholism and the debts and her abusive step-brothers, and Dr. Erdmann hadn't asked. He was sensitive that way.

Looking at his tall, stooped figure sitting on the desk, his walker close to hand, Carrie sometimes let herself dream that Dr. Erdmann—Henry—was fifty years younger. Forty to her twenty-eight—that would work. She'd Googled a picture of him at that age, when he'd been working at someplace called the Lawrence Radiation Laboratory. He'd been handsome, dark-haired, smiling into the camera next to his wife, Ida. She hadn't been as pretty as Carrie, but she'd gone to college, so even if Carrie had been born back then, she wouldn't have had a chance with him. Story of her life.

"—have any questions?" Dr. Erdmann finished.

The students did—they always did—clamoring to be heard, not raising their hands, interrupting each other. But when Dr. Erdmann spoke, immediately they all shut up. Someone leapt up to write equations on the board. Dr. Erdmann slowly turned his frail body to look at them. The discussion went on a long time, almost as long as the class. Carrie fell asleep.

When she woke, it was to Dr. Erdmann, leaning on his walker, gently jiggling her shoulder. "Carrie?"

"Oh! Oh, I'm sorry!"

"Don't be. We bored you to death, poor child."

"No! I loved it!"

He raised his eyebrows and she felt shamed. He thought she was telling a polite lie, and he had very little tolerance for lies. But the truth is, she always loved being here.

Outside, it was full dark. The autumn rain had stopped and the unseen ground had that mysterious, fertile smell of wet leaves. Carrie helped Dr. Erdmann into her battered Toyota and slid behind the wheel. As they started back toward St. Sebastian's, she could tell that he was exhausted. Those students asked too much of him! It was enough that he taught one advanced class a week, sharing all that physics, without them also demanding he—

"Dr. Erdmann?"

For a long terrible moment she thought he was dead. His head lolled against the seat but he wasn't asleep: His open eyes rolled back into his head. Carrie jerked the wheel to the right and slammed the Toyota alongside the curb. He was still breathing.

"Dr. Erdmann? *Henry*?"

Nothing. Carrie dove into her purse, fumbling for her cell phone. Then it occurred to her that his panic button would be faster. She tore open the buttons on his jacket; he wasn't wearing the button. She scrambled again for the purse, starting to sob.

"Carrie?"

He was sitting up now, a shadowy figure. She hit the overhead light. His face, a fissured landscape, looked dazed and pale. His pupils were huge.

"What happened? Tell me." She tried to keep her voice even, to observe everything, because it was important to be able to make as full a report as possible to Dr. Jamison. But her hand clutched at his sleeve.

He covered her fingers with his. His voice sounded dazed. "I . . . don't know. I was . . . somewhere else?"

"A stroke?" That was what they were all afraid of. Not death, but to be incapacitated, reduced to partiality. And for Dr. Erdmann, with his fine mind . . .

"No." He sounded definite. "Something else. I don't know. Did you call 911 yet?"

The cell phone lay inert in her hand. "No, not yet, there wasn't time for—"

"Then don't. Take me home."

"All right, but you're going to see the doctor as soon as we get there." She was pleased, despite everything, with her firm tone.

"It's seven-thirty. They'll all have gone home."

But they hadn't. As soon as Carrie and Dr. Erdmann walked into the lobby, she saw a man in a white coat standing by the elevators. "Wait!" she called, loud enough that several people turned to look, evening visitors and ambulatories and a nurse Carrie didn't know. She didn't know the doctor, either, but she rushed over to him, leaving Dr. Erdmann leaning on his walker by the main entrance.

"Are you a doctor? I'm Carrie Vesey and I was bringing Dr. Erdmann—a patient, Henry Erdmann, not a medical doctor—home when he had some kind of attack, he seems all right now but someone needs to look at him, he says—"

"I'm not an M.D.," the man said, and Carrie looked at him in dismay. "I'm a neurological researcher."

She rallied. "Well, you're the best we're going to get at this hour so please look at him!" She was amazed at her own audacity.

"All right." He followed her to Dr. Erdmann, who scowled because, Carrie knew, he hated this sort of fuss. The non-M.D. seemed to pick up on that right away. He said pleasantly, "Dr. Erdmann? I'm Jake DiBella. Will you come this way, sir?" Without waiting for an answer, he turned and led the way down a side corridor. Carrie and Dr. Erdmann followed, everybody's walk normal, but still people watched. *Move along, nothing to see here* . . . why were they still staring? Why were people such ghouls?

But they weren't, really. That was just her own fear talking.

You trust too much, Carrie, Dr. Erdmann had said just last week.

In a small room on the second floor, he sat heavily on one of the three metal folding chairs. The room held the chairs, a gray filing cabinet, an ugly metal desk, and nothing else. Carrie, a natural nester, pursed her lips, and this Dr. DiBella caught that, too.

"I've only been here a few days," he said apologetically. "Haven't had time yet to properly move in. Dr. Erdmann, can you tell me what happened?"

"Nothing." He wore his lofty look. "I just fell asleep for a moment and Carrie became alarmed. Really, there's no need for this fuss."

"You fell asleep?"

"Yes."

"All right. Has that happened before?"

Did Dr. Erdmann hesitate, ever so briefly? "Yes, occasionally. I *am* ninety, doctor."

DiBella nodded, apparently satisfied, and turned to Carrie. "And what happened to you? Did it occur at the same time that Dr. Erdmann fell asleep?"

Her eye. That's why people had stared in the lobby. In her concern for Dr. Erdmann, she'd forgotten about her black eye, but now it immediately began to throb again. Carrie felt herself go scarlet.

Dr. Erdmann answered. "No, it didn't happen at the same time. There was no car accident, if that's what you're implying. Carrie's eye is unrelated."

"I fell," Carrie said, knew that no one believed her, and lifted her chin.

"Okay," DiBella said amiably. "But as long as you're here, Dr. Erdmann, I'd like to enlist your help. Yours, and as many other volunteers as I can enlist at St. Sebastian's. I'm here on a Gates Foundation grant in conjunction with Johns Hopkins, to map shifts in brain electrochemistry during cerebral arousal. I'm asking volunteers to donate a few hours of their time to undergo completely painless brain scans while they look at various pictures and videos. Your participation will be an aid to science."

Carrie saw that Dr. Erdmann was going to refuse, despite the magic word "science," but then he hesitated. "What kind of brain scans?"

"Asher-Peyton and functional MRI."

"All right. I'll participate."

Carrie blinked. That didn't sound like Dr. Erdmann, who considered physics and astronomy the only "true" sciences and the rest merely poor step-children. But this Dr. DiBella wasn't about to let his research subject get away. He said quickly, "Excellent! Tomorrow morning at eleven, Lab 6B, at the hospital. Ms. Vesey, can you bring him over? Are you a relative?"

"No, I'm an aide here. Call me Carrie. I can bring him." Wednesday wasn't one of her usual days for Dr. Erdmann, but she'd get Marie to swap schedules.

"Wonderful. Please call me Jake." He smiled at her, and something turned over in Carrie's chest. It wasn't just that he was so handsome, with his black hair and gray eyes and nice shoulders, but also that he had masculine confidence and an easy way with him and no ring on his left hand . . . *idiot*. There was no particular warmth in his smile; it was completely professional. Was she always going to assess every man she met as a possible boyfriend? Was she really that needy?

Yes. But this one wasn't interested. And anyway, he was an educated scientist and she worked a minimum-wage job. She was an idiot.

She got Dr. Erdmann up to his apartment and said goodnight. He seemed distant, preoccupied. Going down in the elevator, a mood of desolation came over her. What she really wanted was to stay and watch Henry Erdmann's TV, sleep on his sofa, wake up to fix his coffee and have someone to talk to while she did it. Not go back to her shabby apartment, bolted securely against Jim but never secure enough that she felt really safe. She'd rather stay here, in a home for failing old people, and how perverted and sad was that?

And what *had* happened to Dr. Erdmann on the way home from the college?

THREE

Twice now. Henry lay awake, wondering what the hell was going on in his brain. He was accustomed to relying on that organ. His knees had succumbed to arthritis, his hearing aid required constant adjustment, and his prostate housed a slow-growing cancer that, the doctor said, wouldn't kill him until long after something else did—the medical profession's idea of cheerful news. But his brain remained clear, and using it well had always been his greatest pleasure. Greater even than sex, greater than food, greater than marriage to Ida, much as he had loved her.

God, the things that age let you admit.

Which were the best years? No question there: Los Alamos, working on Operation Ivy with Ulam and Teller and Carson Mark and the rest. The excitement and frustration and awe of developing the "Sausage," the first test of staged radiation implosion. The day it was detonated at Eniwetok. Henry, a junior member of the team, hadn't of course been present at the atoll, but he'd waited breathlessly for the results from Bogon. He'd cheered when Teller, picking up the shock waves on a seismometer in California, had sent his three-word telegram to Los Alamos: "It's a boy." Harry Truman himself had requested that bomb—"to see to it that our country is able to defend itself against any possible aggressor"—and Henry was proud of his work on it.

Shock waves. Yes, *that* was what today's two incidents had felt like: shock waves to the brain. A small wave in his apartment, a larger one in Carrie's car. But from what? It could only be some failure of his nervous system, the thing he dreaded most of all, far more than he dreaded death. Granted, teaching physics to graduate students was a long way from Los Alamos or Livermore, and most of the students were dolts—although not Haldane—but Henry enjoyed it. Teaching, plus reading the journals and following the on-line listserves, were his connection with physics. If some neurological "shock wave" disturbed his brain . . .

It was a long time before he could sleep.

"Oh my Lord, dear, what happened to *your eye*?"

Evelyn Krenchnoted sat with her friend Gina Somebody in the tiny waiting room outside Dr. O'Kane's office. Henry scowled at her. Just like Evelyn to blurt out like that, embarrassing poor Carrie. The Krenchnoted woman was the most tactless busybody Henry had ever met, and he'd known a lot of physicists, a group not noted for tact. But at least the physicists hadn't been busybodies.

"I'm fine," Carrie said, trying to smile. "I walked into a door."

"Oh, dear, how did that happen? You should tell the doctor. I'm sure he could make a few minutes to see you, even though he must be running behind, I didn't actually have an appointment today but he said he'd squeeze me in because something strange happened yesterday that I want to ask him about, but the time he gave me was supposed to start five minutes ago and you must be scheduled after that, he saw Gina already but she—"

Henry sat down and stopped listening. Evelyn's noise, however, went on and on, a grating whine like a dentist drill. He imagined her on Eniwetok, rising into the air on a mushroom cloud, still talking. It was a relief when the doctor's door opened and a woman came out, holding a book.

Henry had seen her before, although he didn't know her name. Unlike most of the old bats at St. Sebastian's, she was worth looking at. Not with Carrie's radiant youthful beauty, of course; this woman must be in her seventies, at least. But she stood straight and graceful; her white hair fell in simple waves to her shoulders; her cheekbones and blue eyes were still good. However, Henry didn't care for the way she was dressed. It reminded him of all those stupid childish protestors outside Los Alamos in the fifties and sixties. The woman wore a white T-shirt, a long cotton peasant skirt, a necklace of beads and shells, and several elaborate rings.

"Erin!" Evelyn cried. "How was your appointment? Everything okay?"

"Fine. Just a check-up." Erin smiled vaguely and moved away. Henry strained to see the cover of her book: *Tao Te Ching*. Disappointment lanced through him. *One of those.*

"But you weren't scheduled for a check-up, no more than I was. So what happened that—" Erin walked quickly away, her smile fixed. Evelyn said indignantly, "Well, I call that just plain rude! Did you see that, Gina? You try to be friendly to some people and they just—"

"Mrs. Krenchnoted?" the nurse said, sticking her head out the office door. "The doctor will see you now."

Evelyn lumbered up and through the door, still talking. In the blessed silence that followed, Henry said to Carrie, "How do you suppose Mr. Krenchnoted stood it?"

Carrie giggled and waved her hand toward the Krenchnoted's friend, Gina. But Gina was asleep in her chair, which at least explained how she stood it.

Carrie said, "I'm glad you have this appointment today, Dr. Erdmann. You *will* tell him about what happened in the car yesterday, won't you?"

"Yes."

"You promise?"

"*Yes.*" Why were all women, even mild little Carrie, so insistent on regular doctor visits? Yes, doctors were useful for providing pills to keep the machine going, but Henry's view was that you only needed to see a physician if something felt wrong. In fact, he'd forgotten about this regularly scheduled check-up until this morning, when Carrie called to say how convenient it was that his appointment here was just an hour before the one with Dr. DiBella at the hospital lab. Ordinarily Henry would have refused to go at all, except that he did intend to ask Dr. Jamison about the incident in the car.

Also, it was possible that fool Evelyn Krenchnoted was actually right about something for once. "Carrie, maybe you *should* ask the doctor to look at that eye."

"No. I'm fine."

"Has Jim called or come around again since—"

"No."

Clearly she didn't want to talk about it. Embarrassment, most likely. Henry could respect her reticence. Silently he organized his questions for Jamison.

But after Henry had gone into the office, leaving Carrie in the waiting room, and after he'd endured the tediums of the nurse's measuring his blood pressure, of peeing into a cup, of putting on a ridiculous paper gown, it wasn't Jamison who entered the room but a brusque, impossibly young boy in a white lab coat and officious manner.

"I'm Dr. Felton, Henry. How are we today?" He studied Henry's chart, not looking at him.

Henry gritted his teeth. "You would know better than I, I imagine."

"Feeling a bit cranky? Are your bowels moving all right?"

"My bowels are fine. They thank you for your concern."

Felton looked up then, his eyes cold. "I'm going to listen to your lungs now. Cough when I tell you to."

And Henry knew he couldn't do it. If the kid had reprimanded him—"*I don't think sarcasm is appropriate here*"—it would have at least been a response. But this utter dismissal, this treatment as if Henry were a child, or a moron. . . . He couldn't tell this insensitive young boor about the incident in the car, about the fear for his brain. It would degrade him to cooperate with Felton. Maybe DiBella *would* be better, even if he wasn't an M.D.

One doctor down, one to go.

DiBella was better. What he was not, was organized.

At Redborn Memorial Hospital he said, "Ah, Dr. Erdmann, Carrie.

Welcome. I'm afraid there's been a mix-up with Diagnostic Imaging. I thought I had the fMRI booked for you but they seem to have scheduled me out, or something. So we can do the Asher-Peyton scan but not the deep imaging. I'm sorry, I—" He shrugged helplessly and ran his hand through his hair.

Carrie tightened her mouth to a thin line. "Dr. Erdmann came all the way over here for your MRI, Dr. DiBella."

" 'Jake,' please. I know. And we do the Asher-Peyton scan back at St. Sebastian's. I really am sorry."

Carrie's lips didn't soften. It always surprised Henry how fierce she could be in defense of her "resident-assignees." Why was usually gentle Carrie being so hard on this young man?

"I'll meet you back at St. Sebastian's," DiBella said humbly.

Once there, he affixed electrodes on Henry's skull and neck, eased a helmet over his head, and sat at a computer whose screen faced away from Henry. After the room was darkened, a series of pictures projected onto one white wall: a chocolate cake, a broom, a chair, a car, a desk, a glass: four or five dozen images. Henry had to do nothing except sit there, and he grew bored. Eventually the pictures grew more interesting, interspersing a house fire, a war scene, a father hugging a child, Rita Hayworth. Henry chuckled. "I didn't think your generation even knew who Rita Hayworth was."

"Please don't talk, Dr. Erdmann."

The session went on for twenty minutes. When it was over, DiBella removed the helmet and said, "Thank you so much. I really appreciate this." He began removing electrodes from Henry's head. Carrie stood, looking straight at Henry.

Now or never.

"Dr. DiBella," Henry said, "I'd like to ask you something. Tell you something, actually. An incident that happened yesterday. Twice." Henry liked the word "incident"; it sounded objective and explainable, like a police report.

"Sure. Go ahead."

"The first time I was standing in my apartment, the second time riding in a car with Carrie. The first incident was mild, the second more pronounced. Both times I felt something move through my mind, like a shockwave of sorts, leaving no after-effects except perhaps a slight fatigue. No abilities seem to be impaired. I'm hoping you can tell me what happened."

DiBella paused, an electrode dangling from his hand. Henry could smell the gooey gel on its end. "I'm not an M.D., as I told you yesterday. This sounds like something you should discuss with your doctor at St. Sebastian's."

Carrie, who had been upset that Henry had not done just that, said, "In the car he sort of lost consciousness and his eyes rolled back in his head."

Henry said, "My doctor wasn't available this morning, and you are. Can you just tell me if that experience sounds like a stroke?"

"Tell me about it again."

Henry did, and DiBella said, "If it had been a TIA—a mini-stroke—you wouldn't have had such a strong reaction, and if it had been a more serious stroke, either ischemic or hemorrhagic, you'd have been left with at least temporary impairment. But you could have experienced a cardiac event of some sort, Dr. Erdmann. I think you should have an EKG at once."

Heart, not brain. Well, that was better. Still, fear slid coldly down Henry's spine, and he realized how much he wanted to go on leading his current life, limited though it was. Still, he smiled and said, "All right."

He'd known for at least twenty-five years that growing old wasn't for sissies.

Carrie canceled her other resident assignees, checking in with each on her cell, and shepherded Henry through the endless hospital rituals that followed, administrative and diagnostic and that most ubiquitous medical procedure, waiting. By the end of the day, Henry knew that his heart was fine, his brain showed no clots or hemorrhages, there was no reason for him to have fainted. That's what they were calling it now: a faint, possibly due to low blood sugar. He was scheduled for glucose-tolerance tests next week. Fools. It hadn't been any kind of faint. What had happened to him had been something else entirely, *sui generis*.

Then it happened again, the same and yet completely different.

At nearly midnight Henry lay in bed, exhausted. For once, he'd thought, sleep would come easily. It hadn't. Then, all at once, he was lifted out of his weary mind. This time there was no violent wrenching, no eyes rolling back in his head. He just suddenly wasn't in his darkened bedroom any more, not in his body, not in his mind.

He was dancing, soaring with pointed toes high above a polished stage, feeling the muscles in his back and thighs stretch as he sat cross-legged on a deep cushion he had embroidered with ball bearings rolling down a factory assembly line across from soldiers shooting at him as he ducked—

It was gone.

Henry jerked upright, sweating in the dark. He fumbled for the bed lamp, missed, sent the lamp crashing off the nightstand and onto the floor. He had never danced on a stage, embroidered a cushion, worked in a factory, or gone to war. And he'd been awake. Those were memories, not dreams—no, not even memories, they were too vivid for that. They'd been experiences, as vivid and real as if they were all happening now, and all happening simultaneously. *Experiences.* But not his.

The lamp was still glowing. Laboriously he leaned over the side of the bed and plucked it off the floor. As he set it back on the nightstand, it went out. Not, however, before he saw that the plug had been pulled from the wall socket during the fall, well before he bent over to pick it up.

The ship grew more agitated, the rents in space-time and resulting flop transitions larger. Every aspect of the entity strained forward, jumping through the vacuum flux in bursts of radiation that appeared now near one star system, now another, now in the deep black cold where no stars exerted gravity. The ship could move no quicker without destroying either nearby star systems or its own coherence. It raced as rapidly as it could, sent ahead of itself even faster tendrils of quantum-entangled information. Faster, faster . . .

It was not fast enough.

FOUR

Thursday morning, Henry's mind seemed to him as clear as ever. After an early breakfast he sat at his tiny kitchen table, correcting physics papers. The apartments at St. Sebastian's each had a small eat-in kitchen, a marginally larger living room, a bedroom and bath. Grab rails, non-skid flooring, overly cheerful colors, and intercoms reminded the residents that they were old—as if, Henry thought scornfully, any of them were likely to forget it. However, Henry didn't really mind the apartment's size or surveillance. After all, he'd flourished at Los Alamos, crowded and ramshackle and paranoid as the place had been. Most of his life went on inside his head.

For each problem set with incomplete answers—which would probably be all of them except Haldane's, although Julia Hernandez had at least come up with a novel and mathematically interesting approach—he tried to follow the student's thinking, to see where it had gone wrong. After an hour of this, he had gone over two papers. A plane screamed overhead, taking off from the airport. Henry gave it up. He couldn't concentrate.

Outside St. Sebastian's infirmary yesterday, the horrible Evelyn Krenchnoted had said that she didn't have a check-up appointment, but that the doctor was "squeezing her in" because "something strange happened yesterday." She'd also mentioned that the aging-hippie beauty, Erin Whatever-Her-Name-Was, hadn't had a scheduled appointment either.

Once, at a mandatory ambulatory-residents' meeting, Henry had seen Evelyn embroidering.

Anna Chernov, St. Sebastian's most famous resident, was a ballet dancer. Everyone knew that.

He felt stupid even thinking along these lines. What was he hypothesizing here, some sort of telepathy? No respectable scientific study had ever validated such a hypothesis. Also, during Henry's three years at St. Sebastian's—years during which Evelyn and Miss Chernov had also been in residence—he had never felt the slightest connection with, or interest in, either of them.

He tried to go back to correcting problem sets.

The difficulty was, he had two data points, his own "incidents" and the sudden rash of unscheduled doctors' appointments, and no way to either connect or eliminate either one. If he could at least satisfy himself that Evelyn and Erin's doctor visits concerned something other than mental episodes, he would be down to one data point. One was an anomaly. Two were an indicator of . . . something.

This wasn't one of Henry's days to have Carrie's assistance. He pulled himself up on his walker, inched to the desk, and found the Resident Directory. Evelyn had no listings for either cell phone or email. That surprised him; you'd think such a yenta would want as many ways to bother people as possible. But some St. Sebastian's residents were still, after all these decades, wary of any technology they hadn't grown up with. *Fools*, thought Henry, who had once driven four hundred miles to buy one of the first, primitive, put-it-together-yourself kits for a personal computer. He noted Evelyn's apartment number and hobbled toward the elevators.

"Why, Henry Erdmann! Come in, come in!" Evelyn cried. She looked astonished, as well she might. And—oh, God—behind her sat a circle of women, their chairs jammed in like molecules under hydraulic compression, all sewing on bright pieces of cloth.

"I don't want to intrude on your—"

"Oh, it's just the Christmas Elves!" Evelyn cried. "We're getting an early start on the holiday wall hanging for the lobby. The old one is getting so shabby."

Henry didn't remember a holiday wall hanging in the lobby, unless she was referring to that garish lumpy blanket with Santa Claus handing out babies to guardian angels. The angels had had tight, cotton-wool hair that made them look like Q-Tips. He said, "Never mind, it's not important."

"Oh, come on in! We were just talking about—and maybe you have more information on it!—this fabulous necklace that Anna Chernov has in the office safe, the one the czar gave—"

"No, no, I have no information. I'll—"

"But if you just—"

Henry said desperately, "I'll call you later."

To his horror, Evelyn lowered her eyes and murmured demurely, "All right, Henry," while the women behind her tittered. He backed away down the hall.

He was pondering how to discover Erin's last name when she emerged from an elevator. "Excuse me!" he called the length of the corridor. "May I speak to you a moment?"

She came toward him, another book in her hand, her face curious but reserved. "Yes?"

"My name is Henry Erdmann. I'd like to ask what will, I know, sound like a very strange question. Please forgive my intrusiveness, and believe that I have a good reason for asking. You had an unscheduled appointment with Dr. Felton yesterday?"

Something moved behind her eyes. "Yes."

"Did your reason for seeing him have to do with any sort of . . . of mental experience? A small seizure, or an episode of memory aberration, perhaps?"

Erin's ringed hand tightened on her book. He noted, n⟩ it seemed to be a novel. She said, "Let's talk."

"I don't believe it," he said. "I'm sorry, Mrs. Bass, but it sou rubbish to me."

She shrugged, a slow movement of thin shoulders under her peasant blouse. Her long printed skirt, yellow flowers on black, swirled on the floor. Her apartment looked like her: bits of cloth hanging on the walls, a curtain of beads instead of a door to the bedroom, Hindu statues and crystal pyramids and Navaho blankets. Henry disliked the clutter, the childishness of the décor, even as he felt flooded by gratitude toward Erin Bass. She had released him. Her ideas about the "incidents" were so dumb that he could easily dismiss them, along with anything he might have been thinking which resembled them.

"There's an energy in the universe as a whole," she'd said. "When you stop resisting the flow of life and give up the grasping of *trishna*, you awaken to that energy. In popular terms, you have an 'out-of-body experience,' activating stored karma from past lives and fusing it into one moment of transcendent insight."

Henry had had no transcendental insight. He knew about energy in the universe—it was called electromagnetic radiation, gravity, the strong and weak nuclear forces—and none of it had karma. He didn't believe in reincarnation, and he hadn't been out of his body. Throughout all three "incidents," he'd felt his body firmly encasing him. He hadn't left; other minds had somehow seemed to come in. But it was all nonsense, an aberration of a brain whose synapses and axons, dendrites and vesicles, were simply growing old.

He grasped his walker and rose. "Thanks anyway, Mrs. Bass. Good-bye."

"Again, call me 'Erin.' Are you sure you wouldn't like some green tea before you go?"

"Quite sure. Take care."

He was at the door when she said, almost casually, "Oh, Henry? When I had my own out-of-body Tuesday evening, there were others with me in the awakened state. . . . Were you ever closely connected with—I know this sounds odd—a light that somehow shone more brightly than many suns?"

He turned and stared at her.

"This will take about twenty minutes," DiBella said as Henry slid into the MRI machine. He'd had the procedure before and disliked it just as much then, the feeling of being enclosed in a tube not much larger than a coffin. Some people, he knew, couldn't tolerate it at all. But Henry'd be damned if he let a piece of machinery defeat him, and anyway the tube didn't enclose him completely; it was open at the bottom. So he pressed his lips together and closed his eyes and let the machine swallow his strapped-down body.

"You okay in there, Dr. Erdmann?"

"I'm fine."

"Good. Excellent. Just relax."

To his own surprise, he did. In the tube, everything seemed very remote. He actually dozed, waking twenty minutes later when the tube slid him out again.

"Everything look normal?" he asked DiBella, and held his breath.

"Completely," DiBella said. "Thank you, that's a good baseline for my study. Your next one, you know, will come immediately after you view a ten-minute video. I've scheduled that for a week from today."

"Fine." *Normal.* Then his brain was okay, and this weirdness was over. Relief turned him jaunty. "I'm glad to assist your project, doctor. What is its focus, again?"

"Cerebral activation patterns in senior citizens. Did you realize, Dr. Erdmann, that the over-sixty-five demographic is the fastest-growing one in the world? And that globally there are now 140 million people over the age of eighty?"

Henry hadn't realized, nor did he care. The St. Sebastian's aide came forward to help Henry to his feet. He was a dour young man whose name Henry hadn't caught. DiBella said, "Where's Carrie today?"

"It's not her day with me."

"Ah." DiBella didn't sound very interested; he was already prepping his screens for the next volunteer. Time on the MRI, he'd told Henry, was tight, having to be scheduled between hospital use.

The dour young man—Darryl? Darrin? Dustin?—drove Henry back to St. Sebastian's and left him to make his own way upstairs. In his apartment, Henry lowered himself laboriously to the sofa. Just a few minutes' nap, that's all he needed, even a short excursion tired him so much now—although it would be better if Carrie had been along, she always took such good care of him, such a kind and dear young woman. If he and Ida had ever had children, he'd have wanted them to be like Carrie. If that bastard Jim Peltier ever again tried to—

It shot through him like a bolt of lightning.

Henry screamed. This time the experience *hurt*, searing the inside of his skull and his spinal cord down to his tailbone. No dancing, no embroidering, no meditating—and yet others were there, not as individuals but as a collective sensation, a shared pain, making the pain worse by pooling it. He couldn't stand it, he was going to die, this was the end of—

The pain was gone. It vanished as quickly as it came, leaving him bruised inside, throbbing as if his entire brain had undergone a root canal. His gorge rose, and just in time he twisted his aching body to the side and vomited over the side of the sofa onto the carpet.

His fingers fumbled in the pocket of his trousers for the St. Sebastian's panic button that Carrie insisted he wear. He found it, pressed the center, and lost consciousness.

FIVE

Carrie went home early. Thursday afternoons were assigned to Mrs. Lopez, and her granddaughter had showed up unexpectedly. Carrie suspected that Vicky Lopez wanted money again, since that seemed to be the only time she did turn up at St. Sebastian's, but that was not Carrie's business. Mrs. Lopez said happily that Vicky could just as easily take her shopping instead of Carrie, and Vicky agreed, looking greedy. So Carrie went home.

If she'd been fortunate enough to have a grandmother—to have any relatives besides her no-good step-brothers in California—she would treat that hypothetical grandmother better than did Vicky, she of the designer jeans and cashmere crew necks and massive credit-card debt. Although Carrie wouldn't want her grandmother to be like Mrs. Lopez, either, who treated Carrie like not-very-clean hired help.

Well, she *was* hired help, of course. The job as a St. Sebastian's aide was the first thing she'd seen in the Classifieds the day she finally walked out on Jim. She grabbed the job blindly, like a person going over a cliff who sees a fragile branch growing from crumbly rock. The weird thing was that after the first day, she knew she was going to stay. She liked old people (most of them, anyway). They were interesting and grateful (most of them, anyway)—and safe. During that first terrified week at the YMCA, while she searched for a one-room apartment she could actually afford, St. Sebastian's was the one place she felt safe.

Jim had changed that, of course. He'd found out the locations of her job and apartment. Cops could find anything.

She unlocked her door after making sure the dingy corridor was empty, slipped inside, shot the deadbolt, and turned on the light. The only window faced an air shaft, and the room was dark even on the brightest day. Carrie had done what she could with bright cushions and Salvation Army lamps and dried flowers, but dark was dark.

"Hello, Carrie," Jim said.

She whirled around, stifling a scream. But the sickening thing was the rest of her reaction. Unbidden and hated—God, how hated!—but still there was the sudden thrill, the flash of excitement that energized every part of her body. "*That's not unusual,*" her counselor at the Battered Women's Help Center had said, "*because frequently an abuser and his victim are both fully engaged in the struggle to dominate each other. How triumphant do you feel when he's in the apology-and-wooing phase of the abuse cycle? Why do you think you haven't left before now?*"

It had taken Carrie so long to accept that. And here it was again. Here Jim was again.

"How did you get in?"

"Does it matter?"

"You got Kelsey to let you in, didn't you?" The building super could be bribed to almost anything with a bottle of Scotch. Although maybe Jim hadn't needed that; he had a badge. Not even the charges she'd brought against him, all of which had been dropped, had affected his job. Nobody on the outside ever realized how common domestic violence was in cops' homes.

Jim wasn't in uniform now. He wore jeans, boots, a sports coat she'd always liked. He held a bouquet of flowers. Not supermarket carnations, either: red roses in shining gold paper. "Carrie, I'm sorry I startled you, but I wanted so bad for us to talk. Please, just let me have ten minutes. That's all. Ten minutes isn't much to give me against three years of marriage."

"We're not married. We're legally separated."

"I know. I *know*. And I deserve that you left me. I know that now. But just ten minutes. Please."

"You're not supposed to be here at all! There's a restraining order against you—and you're a cop!"

"I know. I'm risking my career to talk to you for ten minutes. Doesn't that say how much I care? Here, these are for you."

Humbly, eyes beseeching, he held out the roses. Carrie didn't take them.

"You blackened my eye the last time we 'talked,' you bastard!"

"I know. If you knew how much I've regretted that.... If you had any idea how many nights I laid awake hating myself for that. I was out of my mind, Carrie. I really was. But it taught me something. I've changed. I'm going to A.A. now, I've got a sponsor and everything. I'm working my program."

"I've heard this all before!"

"I know. I know you have. But this time is different." He lowered his eyes, and Carrie put her hands on her hips. Then it hit her: She had said all this before, too. She had stood in this scolding, one-up stance. He had stood in his humble stance, as well. This was the apology-and-wooing stage that the counselor had talked about, just one more scene in their endless script. And she was eating it up as if it had never happened before, was reveling in the glow of righteous indignation fed by his groveling. Just like the counselor had said.

She was so sickened at herself that her knees nearly buckled.

"Get out, Jim."

"I will. I *will*. Just tell me that you heard me, that there's some chance for us still, even if it's a chance I don't deserve. Oh, Carrie—"

"Get out!" Her nauseated fury was at herself.

"If you'd just—"

"Out! Out now!"

His face changed. Humility was replaced by astonishment—this wasn't how their script went—and then by rage. He threw the flowers at her. "You won't even *listen* to me? I come here goddamn apologizing and you won't even listen? What makes you so much better than me, you fucking bitch you're nothing but a—"

Carrie whirled around and grabbed for the deadbolt. He was faster. Faster, stronger, and *that* was the old script, too, how could she forget for even a half second he—

Jim threw her to the floor. Did he have his gun? Would he—she caught a glimpse of his face, so twisted with rage that he looked like somebody else, even as she was throwing up her arms to protect her head. He kicked her in the belly. The pain was astonishing. It burned along her body she was burning she couldn't breathe she was going to die. . . . His boot drew back to kick her again and Carrie tried to scream. No breath came. This was it then no no *no*—

Jim crumpled to the floor.

Between her sheltering arms, she caught sight of his face as he went down. Astonishment gaped open the mouth, widened the eyes. The image clapped onto her brain. His body fell heavily on top of hers, and didn't move.

When she could breathe again, she crawled out from under him, whimpering with short guttural sounds: *uh uh uh*. Yet a part of her brain worked clearly, coldly. She felt for a pulse, held her fingers over his mouth to find a breath, put her ear to his chest. He was dead.

She staggered to the phone and called 911.

Cops. Carrie didn't know them; this wasn't Jim's precinct. First uniforms and then detectives. An ambulance. A forensic team. Photographs, finger-prints, a search of the one-room apartment, with her consent. You have the right to remain silent. She didn't remain silent, didn't need a lawyer, told what she knew as Jim's body was replaced by a chalked outline and neigh-bors gathered in the hall. And when it was finally, finally over and she was told that her apartment was a crime scene until the autopsy was performed and where could she go, she said, "St. Sebastian's. I work there."

"Maybe you should call in sick for this night's shift, ma'am, it's—"

"I'm going to St. Sebastian's!"

She did, her hands shaky on the steering wheel. She went straight to Dr. Erdmann's door and knocked hard. His walker inche across the floor, inside. Inside, where it was safe.

"Carrie! What on Earth—"

"Can I come in? Please? The police—"

"Police?" he said sharply. "What police?" Peering around her as if he expected to see blue uniforms filling the hall. "Where's your coat? It's fifty degrees out!"

She had forgotten a coat. Nobody had mentioned a coat. *Pack a bag,* they said, but nobody had mentioned a coat. Dr. Erdmann always knew the temperature and barometer reading, he kept track of such things. Belatedly, and for the first time, she burst into tears.

He drew her in, made her sit on the sofa. Carrie noticed, with the cold clear part of her mind that still seemed to be functioning, that there was a very wet spot on the carpet and a strong odor, as if someone had scrubbed with disinfectant. "Could I . . . could I have a drink?" She hadn't known she was going to say that until the words were out. She seldom drank. Too much like Jim.

Jim . . .

The sherry steadied her. Sherry seemed so civilized, and so did the miniature glass he offered it in. She breathed easier, and told him her story. He listened without saying a word.

"I think I'm a suspect," Carrie said. "Well, of course I am. He just dropped dead when we were fighting . . . but I never so much as laid a hand on him. I was just trying to protect my head and . . . Dr. Erdmann, what is it? You're white as snow! I shouldn't have come, I'm sorry, I—"

"Of course you should have come!" he snapped, so harshly that she was startled. A moment later he tried to smile. "Of course you should have come. What are friends for?"

Friends. But she had other friends, younger friends. Joanne and Connie and Jennifer . . . not that she had seen any of them much in the last three months. It had been Dr. Erdmann she'd thought of, first and immediately. And now he looked so . . .

"You're not well," she said. "What is it?"

"Nothing. I ate something bad at lunch, in the dining room. Half the building started vomiting a few hours later. Evelyn Krenchnoted and Gina Martinelli and Erin Bass and Bob Donovan and Al Cosmano and Anna Chernov. More."

He watched her carefully as he recited the names, as if she should somehow react. Carrie knew some of those people, but mostly just to say hello. Only Mr. Cosmano was on her resident-assignee list. Dr. Erdmann looked stranger than she had ever seen him.

He said, "Carrie, what time did Jim . . . did he drop dead? Can you fix the exact time?"

"Well, let me see . . . I left here at two and I stopped at the bank and the gas station and the convenience store, so maybe 3:00 or 3:30? Why?"

Dr. Erdmann didn't answer. He was silent for so long that Carrie grew uneasy. She shouldn't have come, it was a terrible imposition, and anyway there was probably a rule against aides staying in residents' apartments, what was she *thinking*—

"Let me get blankets and pillow for the sofa," Dr. Erdmann finally said, in a voice that still sounded odd to Carrie. "It's fairly comfortable. For a sofa."

SIX

Not possible. The most ridiculous coincidence. That was all—coincidence. Simultaneity was not cause-and-effect. Even the dimmest physics undergraduate knew that.

In his mind, Henry heard Richard Feynman say about string theory, "I don't like that they're not calculating anything. I don't like that they don't check their ideas. I don't like that for anything that disagrees with an experiment, they cook up an explanation. . . . The first principle is that you must not fool yourself—and you are the easiest person to fool." Henry hadn't liked Feynman, whom he'd met at conferences at Cal Tech. A buffoon, with his bongo drums and his practical jokes and his lock-picking. Undignified. But the brilliant buffoon had been right. Henry didn't like string theory, either, and he didn't like ideas that weren't calculated, checked, and verified by experimental data. Besides, the idea that Henry had somehow killed Jim Peltier with his *thoughts* . . . preposterous.

Mere thoughts could not send a bolt of energy through a distant man's body. But the bolt itself wasn't a "cooked-up" idea. It had happened. Henry had felt it.

DiBella had said that Henry's MRI looked completely normal.

Henry lay awake much of Thursday night, which made the second night in a row, while Carrie slept the oblivious deep slumber of the young. In the morning, before she was awake, he dressed quietly, left the apartment with his walker, and made his way to the St. Sebastian's Infirmary. He expected to find the Infirmary still crammed with people who'd vomited when he had yesterday afternoon. He was wrong.

"Can I help you?" said a stout, middle-aged nurse carrying a breakfast tray. "Are you feeling ill?"

"No, no," Henry said hastily. "I'm here to visit someone. Evelyn Krenchnoted. She was here yesterday."

"Oh, Evelyn's gone back. They've all gone back, the food poisoning was so mild. Our only patients here now are Bill Terry and Anna Chernov." She said the latter name the way many of the staff did, as if she'd just been waiting for an excuse to speak it aloud. Usually this irritated Henry—what was ballet dancing compared to, say, physics?—but now he seized on it.

"May I see Miss Chernov, then? Is she awake?"

"This is her tray. Follow me."

The nurse led the way to the end of a short corridor. Yellow curtains, bedside table, monitors and IV poles; the room looked like every other hospital room Henry had ever seen, except for the flowers. Masses and masses of flowers, bouquets and live plants and one huge floor pot of brass holding what looked like an entire small tree. A man, almost lost amid all the flowers, sat in the room's one chair.

"Here's breakfast, Miss Chernov," said the nurse reverently. She fussed with setting the tray on the table, positioning it across the bed, removing the dish covers.

"Thank you." Anna Chernov gave her a gracious, practiced smile, and looked inquiringly at Henry. The other man, who had not risen at Henry's entrance, glared at him.

They made an odd pair. The dancer, who looked younger than whatever her actual age happened to be, was more beautiful than Henry had realized, with huge green eyes over perfect cheekbones. She wasn't hooked to any of the machinery on the wall, but a cast on her left leg bulged beneath the yellow bedcover. The man had a head shaped like a garden trowel, an aggressively bristly gray crew cut, and small suspicious eyes. He wore an ill-fitting sports coat over a red T-shirt and jeans. There seemed to be grease under his fingernails—grease, in St. Sebastian's? Henry would have taken him for part of the maintenance staff except that he looked too old, although vigorous and walker-free. Henry wished him at the devil. This was going to be difficult enough without an audience.

"Miss Chernov, please forgive the intrusion, especially so early, but I think this is important. My name is Henry Erdmann, and I'm a resident on Three."

"Good morning," she said, with the same practiced, detached gracious-ness she'd shown the nurse. "This is Bob Donovan."

"Hi," Donovan said, not smiling.

"Are you connected in any way with the press, Mr. Erdmann? Because I do not give interviews."

"No, I'm not. I'll get right to the point, if I may. Yesterday I had an attack of nausea, just as you did, and you also, Mr. Donovan. Evelyn Krenchnoted told me."

Donovan rolled his eyes. Henry would have smiled at that if he hadn't felt so tense.

He continued, "I'm not sure the nausea *was* food poisoning. In my case, it followed a . . . a sort of attack of a quite different sort. I felt what I can only describe as a bolt of energy burning along my nerves, very powerfully and painfully. I'm here to ask if you felt anything similar."

Donovan said, "You a doctor?"

"Not an M.D. I'm a physicist."

Donovan scowled savagely, as if physics were somehow offensive. Anna Chernov said, "Yes, I did, Dr. Erdmann, although I wouldn't describe it as 'painful.' It didn't hurt. But a 'bolt of energy along the nerves'—yes. It felt like—" She stopped abruptly.

"Yes?" Henry said. His heart had started a slow, irregular thump in his chest. Someone else had also felt that energy.

But Anna declined to say what it had felt like. Instead she turned her head to the side. "Bob? Did you feel anything like that?"

"Yeah. So what?"

"I don't know what," Henry said. All at once, leaning on the walker, his knees felt wobbly. Anna noticed at once. "Bob, bring Dr. Erdmann the chair, please."

Donovan got up from the chair, dragged it effortlessly over to Henry, and stood sulkily beside a huge bouquet of autumn-colored chrysanthemums, roses, and dahlias. Henry sank onto the chair. He was at eye level with the card to the flowers, which said **FROM THE ABT COMPANY. GET WELL SOON!**

Anna said, "I don't understand what you're driving at, Dr. Erdmann. Are you saying we all had the same disease and it wasn't food poisoning? It was something with a . . . a surge of energy followed by nausea?"

"Yes, I guess I am." He couldn't tell her about Jim Peltier. Here, in this flower-and-antiseptic atmosphere, under Donovan's pathetic jealousy and Anna's cool courtesy, the whole idea seemed unbelievably wild. Henry Erdmann did not like wild ideas. He was, after all, a *scientist*.

But that same trait made him persist a little longer. "Had you felt anything like that ever before, Miss Chernov?"

"Anna," she said automatically. "Yes, I did. Three times before, in fact. But much more minor, and with no nausea. I think they were just passing moments of dozing off, in fact. I've been laid up with this leg for a few days now, and it's been boring enough that I sleep a lot."

It was said without self-pity, but Henry had a sudden glimpse of what being "laid up" must mean to a woman for whom the body, not the mind, had been the lifelong source of achievement, of pleasure, of occupation, of self. What, in fact, growing old must mean to such a woman. Henry had been more fortunate; his mind was his life source, not his ageing body, and his mind still worked fine.

Or did it, if it could hatch that crackpot hypothesis? What would Feynman, Teller, Gell-Mann have said? Embarrassment swamped him. He struggled to rise.

"Thank you, Miss Chernov, I won't take up any more of your—"

"I felt it, too," Donovan said suddenly. "But only two times, like you said. Tuesday and yesterday afternoon. What are you after here, doc? You saying there's something going around? Is it dangerous?"

Henry, holding onto the walker, turned to stare at him. "You felt it, too?"

"I just told you I did! Now you tell me—is this some new catching, dangerous-like disease?"

The man was frightened, and covering fear with belligerence. Did he even understand what a "physicist" was? He seemed to have taken Henry for some sort of specialized physician. What on Earth was Bob Donovan doing with Anna Chernov?

He had his answer in the way she dismissed them both. "No, Bob, there's no dangerous disease. Dr. Erdmann isn't in medicine. Now if you don't mind, I'm very tired and I must eat or the nurse will scold me. Perhaps you'd better leave now, and maybe I'll see you both around the building when I'm discharged." She smiled wearily.

Henry saw the look on Donovan's face, a look he associated with undergraduates: hopeless, helpless lovesickness. Amid those wrinkles and sags, the look was ridiculous. And yet completely sincere, poor bastard.

"Thank you again," Henry said, and left as quickly as his walker would

allow. How dare she treat him like a princess dismissing a lackey? And yet
. . . he'd been the intruder on her world, that feminine arena of flowers and
ballet and artificial courtesy. A foreign, somehow repulsive world. Not like
the rigorous masculine brawl of physics.

But he'd learned that she'd felt the "energy," too. And so had Donovan,
and at the exact same times as Henry. Several more data points for . . .
what?

He paused on his slow way to the elevator and closed his eyes.

When Henry reached his apartment, Carrie was awake. She sat with
two strangers, who both rose as Henry entered, at the table where Henry
and Ida had eaten dinner for fifty years. The smell of coffee filled the air.

"I made coffee," Carrie said. "I hope you don't mind . . . This is
Detective Geraci and Detective Washington. Dr. Erdmann, this is his
apartment . . . " She trailed off, looking miserable. Her hair hung in
uncombed tangles and some sort of black make-up smudged under her
eyes. Or maybe just tiredness.

"Hello, Dr. Erdmann," the male detective said. He was big, heavily
muscled, with beard shadow even at this hour—just the sort of thuggish
looks that Henry most mistrusted. The black woman was much younger,
small and neat and unsmiling. "We had a few follow-up questions for Ms.
Vesey about last night."

Henry said, "Does she need a lawyer?"

"That's up to your granddaughter, of course," at the same moment
that Carrie said, "I told them I don't want a lawyer," and Henry was
adding, "I'll pay for it." In the confusion of sentences, the mistake about
"granddaughter" went uncorrected.

Geraci said, "Were you here when Ms. Vesey arrived last night?"

"Yes," Henry said.

"And can you tell us your whereabouts yesterday afternoon, sir?"

Was the man a fool? "Certainly I can, but surely you don't suspect *me*,
sir, of killing Officer Peltier?"

"We don't suspect anyone at this point. We're asking routine questions,
Dr. Erdmann."

"I was in Redborn Memorial from mid-afternoon until just before
Carrie arrived here. The Emergency Room, being checked for a suspected
heart attack. Which," he added hastily, seeing Carrie's face, "I did not

have. It was merely severe indigestion brought on by the attack of food poisoning St. Sebastian's suffered yesterday afternoon."

Hah! Take that, Detective Thug!

"Thank you," Geraci said. "Are you a physician, Dr. Erdmann?"

"No. A doctor of physics."

He half-expected Geraci to be as ignorant about that as Bob Donovan had been, but Geraci surprised him. "Experimental or theoretical?"

"Theoretical. Not, however, for a long time. Now I teach."

"Good for you." Geraci rose, Detective Washington just a beat behind him. In Henry's hearing the woman had said nothing whatsoever. "Thank you both. We'll be in touch about the autopsy results."

In the elevator, Tara Washington said, "These old-people places give me the creeps."

"One day you and—"

"Spare me the lecture, Vince. I know I have to get old. I don't have to like it."

"You have a lot of time yet," he said, but his mind clearly wasn't on the rote reassurance. "Erdmann knows something."

"Yeah?" She looked at him with interest; Vince Geraci had a reputation in the department for having a "nose." He was inevitably right about things that smelled hinky. Truth was, she was a little in awe of him. She'd only made detective last month and was fucking lucky to be partnered with Geraci. Still, her natural skepticism led her to say, "That old guy? He sure the hell didn't do the job himself. He couldn't squash a cockroach. You talking about a hit for hire?"

"Don't know." Geraci considered. "No. Something else. Something more esoteric."

Tara didn't know what "esoteric" meant, so she kept quiet. Geraci was smart. Too smart for his own good, some uniforms said, but that was just jealousy talking, or the kind of cops that would rather smash down doors than solve crimes. Tara Washington knew she was no door-smasher. She intended to learn everything she could from Vince Geraci, even if she didn't have his vocabulary. Everything, and then some. She intended to someday be just as good as he was.

Geraci said, "Let's talk to the staff about this epidemic of food poisoning."

But the food poisoning checked out. And halfway through the morning, the autopsy report was called in. Geraci shut his cell and said, "Peltier died of 'a cardiac event.' Massive and instantaneous heart failure."

"Young cop like that? Fit and all?"

"That's what the M.E. says."

"So no foul play. Investigation closed." In a way, she was disappointed. The murder of a cop by a battered wife would have been pretty high-profile. That's why Geraci had been assigned to it.

"Investigation closed," Geraci said. "But just the same, Erdmann knows something. We're just never gonna find out what it is."

SEVEN

Just before noon on Friday, Evelyn lowered her plump body onto a cot ready to slide into the strange-looking medical tube. She had dressed up for the occasion in her best suit, the polyester blue one with all the blue lace, and her good cream pumps. Dr. DiBella—such a good-looking young man, too bad she wasn't fifty years younger aha ha ha—said, "Are you comfortable, Mrs. Krenchnoted?"

"Call me Evelyn. Yes, I'm fine, I never had one of these—what did you call it?"

"A functional MRI. I'm just going to strap you in, since it's very important you lie completely still for the procedure."

"Oh, yes, I see, you don't want my brain wobbling all over the place while you take a picture of—Gina, you still there? I can't see—"

"I'm here," Gina called. "Don't be scared, Evelyn. 'Though I walk in the valley of—' "

"There's no shadows here and I'm not scared!" Really, sometimes Gina could be Too Much. Still, the MRI tube *was* a bit unsettling. "You just tell me when you're ready to slide me into that thing, doctor, and I'll brace myself. It's tight as a coffin, isn't it? Well, I'm going to be underground a long time but I don't plan on starting now, aha ha ha! But if I can keep talking to you while I go in—"

"Certainly. Just keep talking." He sounded resigned, poor man. Well, no wonder, he must get bored with doing things like this all the live-long day. She cast around for something to cheer him up.

"You're over at St. Sebastian's a lot now, aren't you, when you're not here that is, did you hear yet about Anna Chernov's necklace?"

"No, what about it? That's it, just hold your head right here."

"It's fabulous!" Evelyn said, a little desperately. He was putting some sort of vise on her head, she couldn't move it at all. Her heart sped up. "Diamonds and rubies and I don't know what all. The Russian czar gave it to some famous ballerina who—"

"Really? Which czar?"

"*The* czar! Of Russia!" Really, what did the young learn in school these days? "He gave it to some famous ballerina who was Anna Chernov's teacher and she gave it to Anna, who naturally keeps it in the St. Sebastian's safe because just think if it were stolen, it wouldn't do the Home's reputation any good at all and anyway it's absolutely priceless so—oh!"

"You'll just slide in nice and slow, Evelyn. It'll be fine. Close your eyes if that helps. Now, have you seen this necklace?"

"Oh, no!" Evelyn gasped. Her heart raced as she felt the bed slide beneath her. "I'd love to, of course, but Anna isn't exactly friendly, she's pretty stuck-up, well I suppose that comes with being so famous and all but still—Doctor!"

"Do you want to come out?" he said, and she could tell that he was disappointed, she was sensitive that way, and she did want to come out but she didn't want to disappoint him, so . . . "No! I'm fine! The necklace is something I'd really like to see, though, all those diamonds and rubies and maybe even sapphires too, those are my favorite stones with that blue fire in them, I'd really really like to see it—"

She was babbling, but all at once it seemed she *could* see the necklace in her mind, just the way she'd pictured it. A string of huge glowing diamonds and hanging from them a pendant of rubies and sapphires shining like I-don't-know-what but more beautiful than anything she'd ever seen oh she'd love to touch it just once! If Anna Chernov weren't so stuck-up and selfish then maybe she'd *get the necklace from the safe* and show it to Evelyn let her touch it get the necklace from the safe it would surely be the most wonderful thing Evelyn had ever seen or imagined *get the necklace from the safe*—

Evelyn screamed. Pain spattered through her like hot oil off a stove, burning her nerves and turning her mind to a red cloud . . . So much pain! She was going to die, this was it and she hadn't even bought her cemetery plot yet oh God the pain—

Then the pain was gone and she lay sobbing as the bed slid out of the tube. Dr. DiBella was saying something but his voice was far away and growing farther . . . farther . . . farther. . . .

Gone.

Henry sat alone, eating a tuna fish sandwich at his kitchen table. Carrie had gone to work elsewhere in the building. It had been pleasant having her here, even though of course she—

Energy poured through him, like a sudden surge in household current, and all his nerves glowed. That was the only word. No pain this time, but something bright grew in his mind, white and red and blue but certainly not a flag, hard as stones . . . yes, stones . . . jewels . . .

It was gone. An immense lassitude took Henry. He could barely hold his head up, keep his eyes open. It took all his energy to push off from the table, stagger into the bedroom, and fall onto the bed, his mind empty as deep space.

Carrie was filling in at a pre-lunch card game in the dining room, making a fourth at euchre with Ed Rosewood, Ralph Galetta, and Al Cosmano. Mr. Cosmano was her Friday morning resident-assignee. She'd taken him to buy a birthday gift for his daughter in California, to the Post Office to wrap and mail it, and then to the physical therapist. Mr. Cosmano was a complainer. St. Sebastian's was too cold, the doctors didn't know nothing, they wouldn't let you smoke, the food was terrible, he missed the old neighborhood, his daughter insisted on living in California instead of making a home for her old dad, kids these days. . . . Carrie went on smiling. Even Mr. Cosmano was better than being home in the apartment where Jim had died. When her lease was up, she was going to find something else, but in the meantime she had signed up for extra hours at St. Sebastian's, just to not be home.

"Carrie, hearts led," Ed Rosewood said. He was her partner, a sweet man whose hobby was watching C-Span. He would watch anything at all on C-Span, even hearings of the House Appropriations Committee, for hours and hours. This was good for St. Sebastian's because Mr. Rosewood didn't want an aide. He had to be pried off the TV even to play cards once a week. Mike O'Kane, their usual fourth, didn't feel well enough to play today, which was why Carrie sat holding five cards as the kitchen staff clattered in the next room, preparing lunch. Outside a plane passed overhead, droned away.

"Oh, yes," Carrie said, "hearts." She had a heart, thank heavens, since she couldn't remember what was trump. She was no good at cards.

"There's the king."

"Garbage from me."

"Your lead, Ed."

"Ace of clubs."

"Clubs going around. . . . Carrie?"

"Oh, yes, I . . . " Who led? Clubs were the only things on the table. She had no clubs, so she threw a spade. Mr. Galetta laughed.

Al Cosmano said, with satisfaction, "Carrie, you really shouldn't trump your partner's ace."

"Did I do that? Oh, I'm sorry, Mr. Rosewood, I—"

Ed Rosewood slumped in his chair, eyes closed. So did Al Cosmano. Ralph Galetta stared dazedly at Carrie, then carefully laid his head on the table, eyes fixed.

"Mr. Cosmano! Help, somebody!"

The kitchen staff came running. But now all three men had their eyes open again, looking confused and sleepy.

"What happened?" demanded a cook.

"I don't know," Carrie said, "they all just got . . . tired."

The cook stared at Carrie as if she'd gone demented. "Tired?"

"Yeah . . . tired," Ed Rosewood said. "I just . . . bye, guys. I'm going to take a nap. Don't want lunch." He rose, unsteady but walking on his own power, and headed out of the dining room. The other two men followed.

"Tired," the cook said, glaring at Carrie.

"All at once! Really, really tired, like a spell of some kind!"

"A simultaneous 'spell,'" the cook said. "Right. You're new here? Well, old people get tired." She walked away.

Carrie wasn't new. The three men hadn't just had normal tiredness. But there was no way to tell this bitch that, no way to even tell herself in any terms that made sense. Nothing was right.

Carrie had no appetite for lunch. She fled to the ladies' room, where at least she could be alone.

Vince Geraci's cell rang as he and Tara Washington exited a convenience store on East Elm. They'd been talking to the owner, who may or may not have been involved in an insurance scam. Vince had let Tara do most of the questioning, and she'd felt herself swell like a happy balloon when he said, "Nice job, rookie."

"Geraci," he said into the cell, then listened as they walked. Just before they reached the car, he said, "Okay," and clicked off.

"What do we have?" Tara asked.

"We have a coincidence."

"A coincidence?"

"Yes." The skin on his forehead took on a strange topography. "St. Sebastian's again. Somebody cracked the safe in the office."

"Anything gone?"

"Let's go find out."

Erin Bass woke on her yoga mat, the TV screen a blue blank except for **CHANNEL 3** in the upper corner. She sat up, dazed but coherent. Something had happened.

She sat up carefully, her ringed hands lifting her body slowly off the mat. No broken bones, no pain anywhere. Apparently she had just collapsed onto the mat and then stayed out as the yoga tape played itself to an end. She'd been up to the fish posture, so there had been about twenty minutes left on the tape. And how long since then? The wall clock said 1:20. So about an hour.

Nothing hurt. Erin took a deep breath, rolled her head, stood up. Still no pain. And there hadn't been pain when it happened, but there had been something . . . not the calm place that yoga or meditation sometimes took her, either. That place was pale blue, like a restful vista of valleys seen at dusk from a high, still mountain. This was brightly hued, rushing, more like a river . . . a river of colors, blue and red and white.

She walked into the apartment's tiny kitchen, a slim figure in black leotard and tights. She'd missed lunch but wasn't hungry. From the cabinet she chose a chamomile tea, heated filtered water, and set the tea to steep.

That rushing river of energy was similar to what she'd felt before. Henry Erdmann had asked her about it, so perhaps he had felt it this time, as well. Although Henry hadn't seemed accepting of her explanation of *trishna*, grasping after the material moment, versus awakening. He was a typical scientist, convinced that science was the only route to knowledge, that what he could not test or measure or replicate was therefore not true even if he'd experienced it himself. Erin knew better. But there were a lot of people like Henry in this world, people who couldn't see that while rejecting "religion," they'd made a religion of science.

Sipping her tea, Erin considered what she should do next. She wasn't afraid of what had happened. Very little frightened Erin Bass. This astonished some people and confused the rest. But, really, what was there to be afraid of ? Misfortune was just one turn of the wheel, illness another, death merely a transition from one state to another. What was due to come, would come, and beneath it all the great flow of cosmic energy would go on, creating the illusion that people thought was the world. She knew that the other residents of St. Sebastian's considered her nuts, pathetic, or so insulated from realty as to be both. ("Trust-fund baby, you know. Never worked a day in her life.") It didn't matter. She'd made herself a life here of books and meditation and volunteering on the Nursing floors, and if her past was far different than the other residents imagined, that was their illusion. She herself never thought about the past. It would come again, or not, as *maya* chose.

Still, something should be done about these recent episodes. They had affected not just her but also Henry Erdmann and, surprisingly, Evelyn Krenchnoted. Although on second thought, Erin shouldn't be surprised. Everyone possessed karma, even Evelyn, and Erin had no business assuming she knew anything about what went on under Evelyn's loud, intrusive surface. There were many paths up the mountain. So Erin should talk to Evelyn as well as to Henry. Perhaps there were others, too. Maybe she should—

Her doorbell rang. Leaving her tea on the table, Erin fastened a wrap skirt over her leotard and went to the door. Henry Erdmann stood there, leaning on his walker, his face a rigid mask of repressed emotion. "Mrs. Bass, there's something I'd like to discuss with you. May I come in?"

A strange feeling came over Erin. Not the surge of energy from the yoga mat, nor the high blue restfulness of meditation. Something else. She'd had these moments before, in which she recognized that something significant was about to happen. They weren't mystical or deep, these occasions; probably they came from nothing more profound than a subliminal reading of body language. But, always, they presaged something life-changing.

"Of course, Dr. Erdmann. Come in."

She held the door open wider, stepping aside to make room for his walker, but he didn't budge. Had he exhausted all his strength? He was ninety, she'd heard, ten years older than Erin, who was in superb shape from a lifetime of yoga and bodily moderation. She had never smoked, drank, over-eaten. All her indulgences had been emotional, and not for a very long time now.

"Do you need help? Can I—"

"No. No." He seemed to gather himself and then inched the walker forward, moving toward her table. Over his shoulder, with a forced afterthought that only emphasized his tension, he said, "Thieves broke into St. Sebastian's an hour and a half ago. They opened the safe in the office, the one with Anna Chernov's necklace."

Erin had never heard of Anna Chernov's necklace. But the image of the rushing river of bright colors came back to her with overwhelming force, and she knew that she had been right: Something had happened, and nothing was ever going to be the same again.

EIGHT

For perhaps the tenth time, Jake DiBella picked up the fMRI scans, studied them yet again, and put them down. He rubbed his eyes hard with both sets of knuckles. When he took his hands away from his face, his bare little study at St. Sebastian's looked blurry but the fMRI scans hadn't changed. *This is your brain on self-destruction*, he thought, except that it wasn't his brain. It was Evelyn Krenchnoted's brain, and after she recovered consciousness, that tiresome and garrulous lady's brain had worked as well as it ever had.

But the scan was extraordinary. As Evelyn lay in the magnetic imaging tube, everything had changed between one moment and the next. First image: a normal pattern of blood flow and oxygenation, and the next—

"Hello?"

Startled, Jake dropped the printouts. He hadn't even heard the door open, or anyone knock. He really was losing it. "Come in, Carrie, I'm sorry, I didn't. . . . You don't have to do that."

She had bent to pick up the papers that had skidded across his desk and onto the floor. With her other hand she balanced a cardboard box on one hip. As she straightened, he saw that her face was pink under the loose golden hair, so that she looked like an overdone Victorian figurine. The box held a plant, a picture frame, and various other bits and pieces.

Uh oh. Jake had been down this road before.

She said, "I brought you some things for your office. Because it looks so, well, empty. Cold."

"Thanks. I actually like it this way." Ostentatiously he busied himself with the printouts, which was also pretty cold of him, but better to cut her off now rather than after she embarrassed herself. As she set the box on a folding chair, he still ignored her, expecting her to leave.

Instead she said, "Are those MRI scans of Dr. Erdmann? What do they say?"

Jake looked up. She was eyeing the printouts, not him, and her tone was neutral, with perhaps just a touch of concern for Dr. Erdmann. He remembered how fond of each other she and Henry Erdmann were. Well, didn't that make Jake just the total narcissist? Assuming every woman was interested in *him*. This would teach him some humility.

Out of his own amused embarrassment, he answered her as he would a colleague. "No, these are Evelyn Krenchnoted's. Dr. Erdmann's were unremarkable but these are quite the opposite."

"They're remarkable? How?"

All at once he found himself eager to talk, to perhaps explain away his own bafflement. He came around the desk and put the scan in her hand. "See those yellow areas of the brain? They're BOLD signals, blood-oxygen-level dependent contrasts. What that means is that at the moment the MRI image was taken, those parts of the subject's brain were active—in this case, *highly* active. And they shouldn't have been!"

"Why not?"

Carrie was background now, an excuse to put into concrete words what should never have existed concretely at all. "Because it's all wrong. Evelyn was lying still, talking to me, inside the MRI tube. Her eyes were open. She was nervous about being strapped down. The scan should show activity in the optical input area of the brain, in the motor areas connected to moving the mouth and tongue, and in the posterior parietal lobes, indicating a heightened awareness of her bodily boundaries. But instead, there's just the *opposite*. A hugely decreased blood flow in those lobes, and an almost total shutdown of input to the thalamus, which relays information coming into the brain from sight and hearing and touch. Also, an enormous— really enormous—*increase* of activity in the hypothalamus and amygdalae and temporal lobes."

"What does all that increased activity mean?"

"Many possibilities. They're areas concerned with emotion and some kinds of imaginative imagery, and this much activation is characteristic of some psychotic seizures. For another possibility, parts of that profile are characteristic of monks in deep meditation, but it takes experienced meditators hours to build to that level, and even so there are differences in pain areas and—anyway, *Evelyn Krenchnoted*?"

Carrie laughed. "Not a likely monk, no. Do Dr. Erdmann's scans show any of that?"

"No. And neither did Evelyn's just before her seizure or just after. I'd say temporal lobe epilepsy except—"

"Epilepsy?" Her voice turned sharp. "Does that 'seizure' mean epilepsy?"

Jake looked at her then, really looked at her. He could recognize fear. He said as gently as he could, "Henry Erdmann experienced something like this, didn't he?"

They stared at each other. Even before she spoke, he knew she was going to lie to him. A golden lioness protecting her cub, except here the lioness was young and the cub a withered old man who was the smartest person Jake DiBella had ever met.

"No," she said, "Dr. Erdmann never mentioned a seizure to me."

"Carrie—"

"And you said his MRI looked completely normal."

"It did." Defeated.

"I should be going. I just wanted to bring you these things to brighten up your office."

Carrie left. The box contained a framed landscape he would never hang (a flower-covered cottage, with unicorn), a coffee cup he would never use (**JAVA IS JOY IN THE MORNING**), a patchwork quilted cushion, a pink African violet, and a pencil cup covered in wallpaper with yellow daisies. Despite himself, Jake smiled. The sheer wrongness of her offerings was almost funny.

Except that nothing was really funny in light of Evelyn Krenchnoted's inexplicable MRI. He needed more information from her, and another MRI. Better yet would be having her hooked to an EEG in a hospital ward for several days, to see if he could catch a definitive diagnosis of temporal-lobe epilepsy. But when he'd phoned Evelyn, she'd refused all further "doctor procedures." Ten minutes of his best persuasion hadn't budged her.

He was left with an anomaly in his study data, a cutesy coffee cup, and no idea what to do next.

"What do we do next?" asked Rodney Caldwell, the chief administrator of St. Sebastian's. Tara Washington looked at Geraci, who looked at the floor.

It was covered with papers and small, uniform, taped white boxes with names written neatly on them in block printing: **M. MATTISON. H. GERHARDT. C. GARCIA.** One box, however, was open, its lid placed neatly beside it, the tissue paper peeled back. On the tissue lay a necklace, a gold Coptic cross set with a single small diamond, on a thin gold chain. The lid said **A. CHERNOV.**

"I didn't touch anything," Caldwell said, with a touch of pride. In his fifties, he was a tall man with a long, highly colored face like an animated carrot. "That's what they say on TV, isn't it? Don't touch anything. But isn't it strange that the thief went to all the trouble to 'blow the safe'—" He looked proud of this phrase, too "—and then didn't take anything?"

"Very strange," Geraci said. Finally he looked up from the floor. The safe hadn't been "blown"; the lock was intact. Tara felt intense interest in what Geraci would do next. She was disappointed.

"Let's go over it once more," he said easily. "You were away from your office . . . "

"Yes. I went up to Nursing at 11:30. Beth Malone was on desk. Behind the front desk is the only door to the room that holds both residents' files and the safe, and Beth says she never left her post. She's very reliable. Been with us eighteen years."

Mrs. Malone, who was therefore the prime suspect and smart enough to know it, was weeping in another room. A resigned female uniform handed her tissues as she waited to be interrogated. But Tara knew that, after one look, Geraci had dismissed Malone as the perp. One of those conscientious, middle-aged, always-anxious-to-help do-gooders, she would no more have attempted robbery than alchemy. Most likely she had left her post to do something she was as yet too embarrassed to admit, which was when the thief had entered the windowless back room behind the reception desk. Tara entertained herself with the thought that Mrs. Malone had crept off to meet a lover in the linen closet. She smiled.

"A thought, Detective Washington?" Geraci said.

Damn, he missed *nothing*. Now she would have to come up with something. The best she could manage was a question. "Does that little necklace belong to the ballerina Anna Chernov?"

"Yes," Caldwell said. "Isn't it lovely?"

To Tara it didn't look like much. But Geraci had raised his head to look at her, and she realized he didn't know that a world-famous dancer had retired to St. Sebastian's. Ballet wasn't his style. It was the first time Tara could recall that she'd known something Geraci did not. Emboldened by this, and as a result of being dragged several times a year to Lincoln Center by an eccentric grandmother, Tara continued. "Is there any resident here that might have a special interest in Anna Chernov? A balletomane—" She hoped she was pronouncing the word correctly, she'd only read it in programs "—or a special friend?"

But Caldwell had stopped listening at "resident." He said stiffly, "None of our residents would have committed this crime, detective. St. Sebastian's is a private community and we screen very carefully for any—"

"May I talk to Ms. Chernov now?" Geraci asked.

Caldwell seemed flustered. "To Anna? But Beth Malone is waiting for . . . oh, all right, if that's the procedure. Anna Chernov is in the Infirmary right now, with a broken leg. I'll show you up."

Tara hoped that Geraci wasn't going to send her to do the useless questioning of Mrs. Malone. He didn't. At the Infirmary door, he said, "Tara, talk to her." Tara would have taken this as a tribute to her knowledge of ballet, except that she had seen Geraci do the same thing before. He liked to observe: the silent listener, the unknown quantity to whoever was being questioned.

As Caldwell explained the situation and made the introductions, Tara tried not to stare at Anna Chernov. She was *beautiful*. Old, yes, seventies maybe, but Tara had never seen anyone old look like that. High cheekbones, huge green eyes, white hair pinned carelessly on top of her head so that curving strands fell over the pale skin that looked not so much wrinkled (though it was) as softened by time. Her hands, long-fingered and slim-wristed, lay quiet on the bedspread, and her shoulders held straight under the white bed jacket. Only the bulging cast on one leg marred the impression of delicacy, of remoteness, and of the deepest sadness that Tara had ever seen. It was sadness for everything, Tara thought confusedly, and couldn't have said what she meant by "everything." Except that the cast was only a small part.

"Please sit down," Anna said.

"Thank you. As Mr. Caldwell said, there's been a break-in downstairs, with the office safe. The only box opened had your name on it, with a gold-and-diamond necklace inside. That is yours, isn't it?"

"Yes."

"Is it the one that Tamara Karsavina gave you? That Nicholas II gave her?"

"Yes." Anna looked at Tara more closely, but not less remotely.

"Ms. Chernov, is there anyone you can think of who might have a strong interest in that necklace? A member of the press who's been persistent in asking about it, or someone emailing you about it, or a resident?"

"I don't do email, Miss Washington."

It was "Detective Washington," but Tara let it go. "Still—anyone?"

"No."

Had the dancer hesitated slightly? Tara couldn't be sure. She went on asking questions, but she could see that she wasn't getting anywhere. Anna Chernov grew politely impatient. Why wasn't Geraci stopping Tara? She had to continue until he did—"softening them up," he called it. The pointless questioning went on. Finally, just as Tara was running completely out of things to ask, Geraci said almost casually, "Do you know Dr. Erdmann, the physicist?"

"We've met once," Anna said.

"Is it your impression that he has a romantic interest in you?"

For the first time, Anna looked amused. "I think Dr. Erdmann's only romantic interest is in physics."

"I see. Thank you for your time, Ms. Chernov."

In the hall, Geraci said to Tara, "Ballet. Police work sure isn't what it used to be. You did good, Washington."

"Thank you. What now?"

"Now we find out what resident has a romantic interest in Anna Chernov. It's not Erdmann, but it's somebody."

So Anna *had* hesitated slightly when Tara asked if any resident had a special interest in her! Tara glowed inwardly as she followed Geraci down the hall. Without looking at her, he said, "Just don't let it go to your head."

She said dryly, "Not a chance."

"Good. A cop interested in *ballet* . . . Jesus H. Christ."

The ship grew agitated. Across many cubic light years between the stars, spacetime itself warped in dangerous ways. The new entity was growing in strength—and it was so far away yet!

It was not supposed to occur this way.

If the ship had become aware earlier of this new entity, this could have happened correctly, in accord with the laws of evolution. All things evolved— stars, galaxies, consciousness. If the ship had realized earlier that anywhere in this galactic backwater had existed the potential for a new entity, the ship would have been there to guide, to shape, to ease the transition. But it hadn't realized. There had been none of the usual signs.

They were happening now, however. Images, as yet dim and one-way, were reaching the ship. More critically, power was being drawn from it, power that the birthing entity had no idea how to channel. Faster, the ship must go faster . . .

It could not, not without damaging spacetime irretrievably. Spacetime could only reconfigure so much, so often. And meanwhile—

The half-formed thing so far away stirred, struggled, howled in fear.

NINE

Henry Erdmann was scared.

He could barely admit his fright to himself, let alone show it to the circle of people jammed into his small apartment on Saturday morning. They sat in a solemn circle, occupying his sofa and armchair and kitchen chairs and other chairs dragged from other apartments. Evelyn Krenchnoted's chair crowded uncomfortably close to Henry's right side, her perfume sickly sweet. She had curled her hair into tiny gray sausages. Stan Dzarkis and Erin Bass, who could still manage it, sat on the floor. The folds of

Erin's yellow print skirt seemed to Henry the only color amid the ashen faces. Twenty people, and maybe there were more in the building who were afflicted. Henry had called the ones he knew of, who had called the ones they knew of. Missing were Anna Chernov, still in the Infirmary, and Al Cosmano, who had refused to attend.

They all looked at him, waiting to begin.

"I think we all know why we're here," Henry said, and immediately a sense of unreality took him. He didn't understand at all why he was here. The words of Michael Faraday, inscribed on the physics building at UCLA, leapt into his mind: "Nothing is too wonderful to be true." The words seemed a mockery. What had been happening to Henry, to all of them, did not feel wonderful and was "true" in no sense he understood, although he was going to do his damnedest to relate it to physics in the only way that hours of pondering had suggested to him. Anything else—anything *less*—was unthinkable.

He continued, "Things have occurred to all of us, and a good first step is to see if we have indeed had the same experiences." *Collect data.* "So I'll go first. On five separate occasions I have felt some force seize my mind and body, as if a surge of energy was going through me, some sort of neurological shock. On one occasion it was painful, on the others not painful but very tiring. Has anyone else felt that?"

Immediately a clamor, which Henry stilled by raising his arm. "Can we start with a show of hands? Anybody else had that experience? Everybody. Okay, let's go around the circle, introducing yourself as we go, starting on my left. Please be as explicit as possible, but only descriptions at this point. No interpretations."

"Damned teacher," someone muttered, but Henry didn't see who and didn't care. His heart had speeded up, and he felt that his ears had somehow expanded around his hearing aid, so as not to miss even a syllable. He had deliberately not mentioned the times of his "seizures," or outside events concurrent with them, so as not to contaminate whatever information would be offered by the others.

"I'm John Kluge, from 4J." He was a heavy, round-faced man with a completely bald head and a pleasant voice used to making itself heard. High-school teacher, Henry guessed. History or math, plus coaching some sort of sports team. "It's pretty much like Henry here said, except I only felt the 'energy' four times. The first was around 7:30 on Tuesday night.

The second time woke me Wednesday night at 11:42. I noted the time on my bedside clock. The third time I didn't note the time because I was vomiting after that food poisoning we all got on Thursday, but it was just before the vomiting started, sometime in mid-afternoon. That time the energy surge started near my heart, and I thought it was a heart attack. The last time was yesterday at 11:45 AM, and in addition to the energy, I had a . . . well, a sort of—" He looked embarrassed.

"Please go on, it's important," Henry said. He could hardly breathe.

"I don't want to say a vision, but colors swirling through my mind, red and blue and white and somehow *hard*."

"Anna Chernov's necklace!" Evelyn shrieked, and the meeting fell apart.

Henry couldn't stop the frantic babble. He would have risen but his walker was in the kitchen; there was no room in the crowded living room. He was grateful when Bob Donovan put two fingers in his mouth and gave a whistle that could have deafened war dogs. "Hey! Shut up or nobody's gonna learn nothing!"

Everyone fell silent and glared resentfully at the stocky man in baggy chinos and cheap acrylic sweater. Donovan scowled and sat back down. Henry leapt into the quiet.

"Mr. Donovan is right, we won't learn anything useful this way. Let's resume going around the circle, with no interruptions, please. Mrs. Bass?"

Erin Bass described essentially the same events as John Kluge, without the Wednesday night incident but with the addition of the earlier, slight jar Henry had felt as he let Carrie into his apartment Tuesday before class. She described this as a "whisper in my mind." The next sixteen people all repeated the same experiences on Thursday and Friday, although some seemed to not have felt the "energy" on Tuesday, and some not on Tuesday or Wednesday. Henry was the only one to feel all five instances. Throughout these recitations, Evelyn Krenchnoted several times rose slightly in her chair, like a geyser about to burst. Henry did *not* want her to interrupt. He put a restraining hand on her arm, which was a mistake as she immediately covered his hand with her own and squeezed affectionately.

When it was finally Evelyn's turn, she said, "None of you had pain this last time like Henry did on Thursday—except me! I was having a medical MIT at the hospital and I was inside the machine and the pain was horrible! Horrible! And then—" she paused dramatically "—and then I saw Anna Chernov's necklace right at the time it was being stolen! And so did all of you—that was the 'hard colors,' John! Sapphires and rubies and diamonds!"

Pandemonium again. Henry, despite his growing fear, groaned inwardly. Why Evelyn Krenchnoted? Of all the unreliable witnesses . . .

"I saw it! I saw it!" Evelyn shrieked. Gina Martinelli had begun to pray in a loud voice. People jabbered to each other or sat silent, their faces gone white. A woman that Henry didn't know reached with shaking hand into her pocket and pulled out a pill bottle. Bob Donovan raised his fingers to his lips.

Before Donovan's whistle could shatter their eardrums again, Erin Bass rose gracefully, clapped her hands, and cried surprisingly loudly, "Stop! We will get nowhere this way! Evelyn has the floor!"

Slowly the din subsided. Evelyn, who now seemed more excited than frightened by the implication of what she'd just said, launched into a long and incoherent description of her "MIT," until Henry stopped her the only way he could think of, which was to take her hand. She squeezed it again, blushed, and said, "Yes, dear."

Henry managed to get out, "Please. Everyone. There must be an explanation for all this." But before he could begin it, Erin Bass turned from aide to saboteur.

"Yes, and I think we should go around the circle in the same order and offer those explanations. But *briefly*, before too many people get too tired. John?"

Kluge said, "It could be some sort of virus affecting the brain. Contagious. Or some pollutant in the building."

Which causes every person to have the exact same hallucinations and a locked safe to open? Henry thought scornfully. The scorn steadied him. He needed steadying; every person in the room had mentioned feeling the Thursday-afternoon "energy" start in his or her heart, but no one except Henry knew that at that moment Jim Peltier was having an inexplicable heart attack as he battered Carrie.

Erin said, "What we see in this world is just *maya*, the illusion of permanence when in fact, all reality is in constant flux and change. What's happening here is beyond the world of intellectual concepts and distinctions. We're getting glimpses of the mutable nature of reality, the genuine undifferentiated 'suchness' that usually only comes with nirvana. The glimpses are imperfect, but for some reason our collective karma has afforded them to us."

Bob Donovan, next in the circle, said irritably, "That's just crap. We all got some brain virus, like Kluge here said, and some junkie cracked the office safe. The cops are investigating it. We should all see a doctor, except they can't never do anything to cure people anyway. And the people who had pain, Henry and Evelyn, they just got the disease worse."

Most people around the circle echoed the brain-disease theory, some with helpless skepticism, some with evident relief at finding any sort of explanation. A woman said slowly, "It could be the start of Alzheimer's." A man shrugged and said, "As God wills." Another just shook his head, his eyes averted.

Gina Martinelli said, "It *is* the will of God! These are the End Times, and we're being given signs, if only we would listen! 'Ye shall have tribulations ten days: be thou faithful unto death, and I will give thee a crown of life.' Also—"

"It might be the will of God, Gina," interrupted Evelyn, unable to restrain herself any longer, "but it's mighty strange anyway! Why, I saw that necklace in my mind plain as day, and at just that moment it was being stolen from the safe! To my mind, that's not God, and not the devil neither or the robbery would have been successful, you see what I mean? The devil knows what he's doing. No, this was a message, all right, but from those who have gone before us. My Uncle Ned could see spirits all the time, they trusted him, I remember one time we all came down to breakfast and the cups had all been turned upside down when nobody was in the room and Uncle Ned, he said—"

Henry stopped listening. Ghosts. God. Eastern mysticism. Viruses. Alzheimer's. Nothing that fit the facts, that adhered even vaguely to the laws of the universe. These people had the reasoning power of termites.

Evelyn went on for a while, but eventually even she noticed that her audience was inattentive, dispirited, or actually asleep. Irene Bromley snored softly in Henry's leather armchair. Erin Bass said, "Henry?"

He looked at them hopelessly. He'd been going to describe the two-slit experiments on photons, to explain that once you added detectors to measure the paths of proton beams, the path became pre-determined, even if you switched on the detector *after* the particle had been fired.

He'd planned on detailing how that astonishing series of experiments changed physics forever, putting the observer into basic measurements of reality. Consciousness was woven into the very fabric of the universe itself, and consciousness seemed to him the only way to link these incredibly disparate people and the incredible events that had happened to them.

Even to himself, this "explanation" sounded lame. How Teller or Feynman would have sneered at it! Still, although it was better than anything he'd heard here this morning, he hated to set it out in front of these irrational people, half ignoramuses and the other half nutcases. They would all just reject it, and what would be gained?

But he had called this meeting. And he had nothing else to offer.

Henry stumbled through his explanation, trying to make the physics as clear as possible. Most of the faces showed perfect incomprehension. He finished with, "I'm not saying there's some sort of affecting of reality going on, through group consciousness." But wasn't that exactly what he *was* saying? "I don't believe in telekinesis or any of that garbage. The truth is, I don't know what's happening. But something is."

He felt a complete fool.

Bob Donovan snapped, "None of you know nothing. I been listening to all of you, and you haven't even got the facts right. I *seen* Anna Chernov's necklace. The cops showed it to me yesterday when they was asking me some questions. It don't got no sapphires or rubies, and just one tiny diamond. You're full of it, Evelyn, to think your seizure had anything to do with anything—and how do we know you even felt any pain at the 'very second' the safe was being cracked? All we got's your word."

"Are you saying I'm a liar?" Evelyn cried. "Henry, tell him!"

Tell him what? Startled, Henry just stared at her. John Kluge said harshly, "I don't believe Henry Erdmann is lying about his pain," and Evelyn turned from Donovan to Kluge.

"You mean you think *I* am? Who the hell do you think you are?"

Kluge started to tell her who he was: among other things, a former notary public. Other people began to argue. Evelyn started to cry, and Gina Martinelli prayed loudly. Erin Bass rose and slipped out the front door. Others followed. Those that remained disputed fiercely, the arguments growing more intense as they were unable to convince their neighbors of their own theories. Somewhere among the anger and contempt, Carrie Vesey appeared by Henry's side, her pretty face creased with bewildered concern, her voice high and strained.

"Henry? What on Earth is going on in here? I could hear the noise all the way down the hall. . . . What is this all about?"

"Nothing," he said, which was the stupidest answer possible. Usually the young regarded the old as a separate species, as distant from their own concerns as trilobites. But Carrie had been different. She had always treated Henry as inhabiting the same world as herself, with the same passions and quirks and aims and defeats. This was the first time he had ever seen Carrie look at him as both alien and unsound, and it set the final seal on this disastrous meeting.

"But, Henry—"

"I said it's nothing!" he shouted at her. "Nothing at all! Now just leave me the hell alone!"

TEN

Carrie stood in the ladies' room off the lobby, pulling herself together. She was *not* going to cry. Even if Dr. Erdmann had never spoken to her like that before, even if ever since Jim's death she had felt as if she might shatter, even if . . . everything, she was *not going to cry*. It would be ridiculous. She was a professional—well, a professional aide anyway—and Henry Erdmann was an old man. Old people were irritable sometimes. This whole incident meant nothing.

Except that she knew it did. She had stood outside Dr. Erdmann's door for a long time as people slipped out, smiling at her vaguely, and Evelyn Krenchnoted babbled on inside. The unprecedented meeting had first piqued her curiosity—Henry Erdmann, hosting a party at ten o'clock on a Saturday morning? Then, as she realized what Evelyn was saying, disbelief took Carrie. Evelyn meant . . . Evelyn thought . . . and even Dr. Erdmann believed that "something" had been happening, something weird and unexplainable and supernatural, at the moment that Evelyn was under the MRI . . . *Henry*!

But Jake DiBella had been upset by Evelyn's scans.

The door of the ladies' opened and the first of the Saturday visitors entered, a middle-aged woman and a sulky teenage girl. "Honestly, Hannah," the woman said, "it's only an hour out of your precious day and it won't kill you to sit with your grandmother and concentrate on someone else besides yourself for a change. If you'd just—"

Carrie went to DiBella's office. He was there, working at his desk. No sign of her picture, cushion, coffee cup; she couldn't help her inevitable, stupid pang. He didn't want them. Or her. Another failure.

"Dr. DiBella—"

" 'Jake.' Remember?" And then, "Carrie, what is it?"

"I just came from Dr. Erdmann's apartment. They were having a meeting, about twenty people, all of them who've felt these 'seizures' or whatever they are, all at the same time. Like the one you captured on Evelyn's MRI scan."

He stared at her. "What do you mean, 'at the same time'?"

"Just what I said." She marveled at her own tone—none of her shakiness showed. "They said that at the exact same time that Evelyn was showing all that weird activity under the MRI, each of them was feeling it, too, only not so strong. And it was the exact same time that Anna Chernov's necklace was being stolen. And they all saw the necklace in their minds." Only—hadn't Mr. Donovan said that the necklace looked different from what Evelyn said? Confusion took Carrie.

Jake looked down at whatever he was writing, back at Carrie, down again at his notes. He came around the desk and closed his office door. Taking her arm, he sat her gently in the visitor's chair, unadorned by her cushion. Despite herself, she felt a tingle where his hand touched her.

"Dr. Erdmann was involved in this? Tell me again. Slowly, Carrie. Don't leave anything out."

Evelyn Krenchnoted made her way to Gina Martinelli's apartment on Five. Really, Henry had been unbearably rude—to that poor young girl, to everybody at the meeting, and especially to Evelyn herself. He hadn't comforted her when that awful Donovan man called her a liar, he hadn't put his hand on hers again, he'd just yelled and yelled—and just when things between them had been going so well!

Evelyn needed to talk to Gina. Not that Gina had been any help at the meeting, not with all that praying. Gina was really a lot smarter than she looked, she'd been a part-time tax preparer once, but hardly anybody knew it because Gina never opened her mouth except to pray. Not that there was anything wrong with praying, of course! Evelyn certainly believed in God.

But you had to help Him along a little if you really wanted something. You couldn't expect the Lord to do everything.

Evelyn had even curled her hair for Henry.

"Gina? Sweetie? Can I come in?"

"You're already in," Gina said. She had to speak loudly because she had Frank Sinatra on the record player. Gina loved Frank Sinatra. For once she wasn't reading her Bible, which Evelyn thought was a good sign. She lowered her bulk onto Gina's sofa.

"So what did you think of that meeting?" Evelyn said. She was looking forward to a good two-three hours of rehashing, sympathy, and gossip. It would make her feel a lot better. Less creepy. Less afraid.

But instead, Gina said, "There was a message on the machine when I got back here. Ray is coming next week."

Oh, God, Gina's son. Who was only after her money. Ray hadn't visited in over a year, and now that Gina had told him she was leaving everything to the daughter . . . and there was a lot of everything to leave. Gina's late husband had made major money in construction.

"Oh, sweetie," Evelyn said, a little perfunctorily. Ordinarily she would have adored discussing Gina's anguish; for one thing, it made Evelyn glad she had never had kids. But now, with so much else going on—Henry and the attempted robbery and Evelyn's seizure and the strange comments at the meeting—

Frank Sinatra sang about ants and rubber tree plants. Gina burst into tears.

"Oh, sweetie," Evelyn repeated, got up to put her arms around Gina, and resigned herself to hearing about Ray Martinelli's selfishness.

Bob Donovan sat beside Anna Chernov's bed in the Infirmary. The man simply could not take a hint. She would either have to snub him outright or tell him in so many words to stop visiting her. Even the sight of him, squat and toad-faced and clumsy, made her shudder. Unfair, but there it was.

She had danced with so many beautiful men.

Which had been the best? Frederico, partnering her in *La Valse*—never had she been lifted so effortlessly. Jean, in *Scotch Symphony*, had been equally breathtaking, But the one she always returned to was Bennet. After she'd left the New York City Ballet for American Ballet Theater and her career had really taken off, they'd always danced together. Bennet, so dazzling as Albrecht in *Giselle*. . . . Guesting at a gala at the Paris Opera, they'd had seventeen curtain calls and—

Her attention was reclaimed by something Bob Donovan said.

"Could you repeat that, please, Bob?"

"What? Old Henry's crackpot theory? Science gibberish!"

"Nonetheless, would you repeat it?" She managed a smile.

He responded to the smile with pathetic eagerness. "Okay, yeah, if you want. Erdmann said, lemme think . . . " He screwed up his already crevassed face in an effort to remember. Although she was being unkind again. He probably wasn't all that bad looking, among his own class. And was she any better? These days she couldn't bear to look in a mirror. And the sight of the ugly cast on her leg filled her with despair.

"Erdmann said there was some experiments in physics, something with two slips, where people's consciences changed the path of some little . . . particles . . . by just thinking about them. Or maybe it was watching them. And that was the link between everybody who had so-called 'energy' at the same time. Group conscience. A new thing."

Consciousness, Anna translated. Group consciousness. Well, was that so strange? She had felt it more than once on stage, when a group of dancers had transcended what they were individually, had become a unity moving to the music in the creation of beauty. Such moments had, for her, taken the place of religion.

Bob was going on now about what other people at the meeting had said, offering up ungrammatical accounts in a desperate bid to please her, but even as she recognized this, Anna had stopped listening. She thought instead about Bennet, with whom she'd had such fantastic chemistry on and off stage, Bennet lifting her in the *grand pas de deux* of Act II, rosin from the raked stage rising around her like an angelic cloud, herself soaring and almost flying . . .

"Tell me again," Jake said.

"Again?" This was the third time! Not that Carrie really minded. She hadn't had his total attention—anybody's total attention—like this since Jim died. Not that she wanted Jim back. . . . She shuddered even as she went through it all again. By the end, she was belligerent.

"Why? Are you saying you believe all this stuff about a group consciousness?"

"No. Of course not. Not without confirmation . . . but Erdmann is a scientist. What other data does he have that he isn't telling you?"

"I don't know what you mean." And she didn't; this conversation was beyond her. Photon detectors, double-slit experiments, observational predetermination . . . Her memory was good, but she knew she lacked the background to interpret the terms. Her own ignorance made her angry.

"Henry had two other experiences of 'energy' when he was with you, you said. Were there others when he was away from you?"

"How should I know? You better ask him!"

"I will. I'll ask them all."

"It sounds stupid to me." Immediately she was frightened by her own tone. But Jake just looked at her thoughtfully.

"Well, it sounds stupid to me, too. But Henry is right about one thing—*something* is happening. There's hard data in the form of Evelyn's MRI, in the fact that the safe was opened without the lock being either tampered with or moved to the right combination—"

"It *did*?"

"The detective told me, when he was asking questions yesterday. Also, I got the physician here to let me look at the lab results for everybody admitted to the infirmary Thursday afternoon. Professional courtesy. There was no food poisoning."

"There wasn't?" All at once Carrie felt scared.

"No." DiBella sat thinking for a long while. She scarcely dared breathe. Finally he said slowly, as if against his own will or better judgment—and that much she understood, anyway—"Carrie, have you ever heard of the principle of emergent complexity?"

"I did *everything* for that boy," Gina sobbed. "Just everything!"

"Yes, you did," said Evelyn, who thought Gina had done too much for Ray. Always lending him money after he lost each job, always letting him move back home and trash the place. What that kid had needed—and bad—was a good hiding, that's what.

"Angela didn't turn out this way!"

"No." Gina's daughter was a sweetie. Go figure.

"And now I just get it settled in my mind that he's out of my life, I come to grips with it, and he says he's flying back here to see 'his old ma' and he loves me! He'll just stir everything up again like he did when he got home from the Army, and when he divorced Judy, and when I had to find that lawyer for him in New York. . . . Evelyn, nobody, but *nobody*, can rip you up inside like your child!"

"I know," said Evelyn, who didn't. She went on making little clucking noises while Gina sobbed. A plane roared overhead, and Frank Sinatra sang about it having been a very good year when he was twenty-one.

Bob Donovan took Anna's hand. Gently she pulled it away. The gentleness was for her, not him—she didn't want a scene. His touch repelled her. But oh, Bennet's touch . . . or Frederico's. . . . Still, it was the dancing she missed. And now she would never dance again. She might, the doctors said, not even walk without a limp.

Never dance. Never feel her legs spring into a *ballotté* or soar in the exuberance of a *flick jeté*, back arched and arms thrown back, an arrow in ecstatic flight.

"Carrie, have you ever heard of the principle of " 'emergent complexity? ' "

"No." Jake DiBella was going to make her feel dumb again. But he didn't mean to do that, and as long as she could sit here in his office with him, she would listen. Maybe he needed someone to listen. Maybe he needed her. And maybe he would say something that would help her make it all right with Dr. Erdmann.

Jake licked his lips. His face was still paper white. "'Emergent complexity' means that as an evolving organism grows more complex, it develops processes that wouldn't seem implied by the processes it had in simpler form. In other words, the whole becomes greater than the sum of the parts. Somewhere along the line, our primitive human ancestors developed self-awareness. Higher consciousness. That was a new thing in evolution."

Old knowledge stirred in Carrie's mind. "There was a pope—I was raised Catholic—some pope, one of the John-Pauls maybe, said there was a point where God infused a soul into an animal heritage. So evolution wasn't really anti-Catholic."

Jake seemed to be looking through her, at something only he could see. "Exactly. God or evolution or some guy named Fred—however it happened, consciousness did emerge. And if, now, the next step in complexity is emerging . . . if that . . . "

Carrie was angered, either by his line of thought or by his ignoring her; she wasn't sure which. She said sharply, "But why now? Why here?"

Her question brought his gaze back to her. He took a long time to answer, while a plane droned overhead on the flight path out of the airport. Carrie held her breath.

But all he said was, "I don't know."

Gina had worked herself up to such a pitch that she wasn't even praying. Ray, Ray, Ray—this wasn't what Evelyn wanted to talk about. But she had never seen Gina like this. All at once Gina cried passionately, drowning out Sinatra singing "Fly Me to the Moon," "I wish he weren't coming! I wish his plane would just go on to another city or something, just not land here! I don't want him here!"

Never dance again. And the only love available from men like Bob Donovan. . . . No. *No.* Anna would rather be dead.

"Well, I don't believe it!" Carrie said. "Emerging complexity—I just don't believe it's happening at St. Sebastian's!"

"Neither do I," said Jake. For the first time since she'd entered his office, he smiled at her.

Outside the building, a boom sounded.

Carrie and Jake both looked toward the door. Carrie thought first of terrorism, a car bomb or something, because everybody thought first of terrorism these days. But terrorism at an assisted living facility was ridiculous. It was a gas main exploding, or a bus crash just outside, or . . .

Henry Erdmann appeared in the open doorway to the office. He didn't have his walker with him. He sagged against the doorjamb, his sunken eyes huge and his mouth open. Before Carrie could leap up to help him and just before he slumped to the floor, he croaked, "Call the police. We just brought down a plane."

Anguish ripped through the ship. Not its own agony, but the Other's. No guidance, no leading, it was raging wild and undisciplined. If this went on, it might weaken the ship too much for the ship to ever help it.

If this went on, the Other could damage spacetime itself.

The ship could not let that happen.

ELEVEN

When Henry Erdmann collapsed, DiBella moved swiftly to the old man. Carrie stood frozen—stupid! Stupid! "Get the doctor," Jake cried. And then, "*Go,* Carrie. He's alive."

She ran out of Jake's office, nearly tripping over the walker Henry had left in the hallway. He must have been coming to see Jake when it happened—when *what* happened? She raced to the lobby and the call phone, her mind so disordered that only as she shoved open the double doors did she realize that of course it would have been faster to hit Henry's panic button—Jake would do that—but Henry seldom wore his panic button, he—

She stopped cold, staring.

The lobby was full of screaming people, mostly visitors. Among them, old people lay fallen to the floor or slumped in wheelchairs. It was Saturday morning and on Saturday morning relatives arrived to take their mothers and grandfathers and great-grandmothers for brunch, for a drive, for a visit home . . . Bundled in sweaters and jackets and shawls, the seniors had all collapsed like so many bundles of dropped laundry. St. Sebastian's nurses, aides, and even desk volunteers bent ineffectually over the victims.

Fear roiled Carrie's stomach, but it also preternaturally heightened her perceptions.

Mr. Aberstein, a St. Sebastian's resident even though he was only sixty-seven, stood unaffected by the elevators. Mrs. Kelly sat alert in her wheelchair, her mouth a wide pink O. She was seventy-one. Mr. Schur . . .

"Nurse! Come quick, please, it's Dr. Erdmann!" Carrie caught at the sleeve of a passing nurse in purple scrubs, but he shook her off and raced to an old woman lying on the floor. Everyone here was too busy to help Carrie. She ran back to Jake's office.

Henry lay quietly on the floor. Jake had turned him face up and put a cushion—her cushion, Carrie thought numbly, the patchwork one she'd brought Jake—under Henry's feet. Henry wasn't wearing his panic button. She gasped, "No one can come, it's happened to all of them—"

"All who?" Jake said sharply.

She answered without thinking. "All of them over eighty. Is Henry—"

"He's breathing normally. His color's good, and he's not clammy. I don't think he's in shock. He's just . . . out. *All of them over eighty?*"

"Yes. No. I don't know, I mean, about the age, but all the older ones in the lobby just collapsed and the younger residents seem fine. . . . Jake, what *is it*?"

"I don't know. Carrie, do this now: Go to one of the common rooms and turn the TV to the local news channel. See if there's been a . . . a plane crash—"

He stopped. Both of them heard the sirens.

Henry did not wake. All of Redborn Memorial Hospital's ambulances had gone to the crash site. The St. Sebastian's staff moved afflicted residents to the dining room, which looked like a very peaceful war hospital. The residents didn't wake, moan, or need emergency treatment with the exception of one woman who had broken a hip falling to the floor. She was sent over to Memorial. Monitors couldn't be spared from the Nursing floor, where nearly everyone had fallen into the coma, but a few spare monitors were carried down from the infirmary. They showed no anomalies in heart rate or blood pressure.

Relatives summoned family doctors, sat by cots, screamed at St. Sebastian's staff, who kept repeating, "Redborn Memorial is aware of the situation and they'll get the St. Sebastian's residents over there as soon as they can. *Please*, sir, if you'd just—"

Just be patient. Just believe that we're doing our best. Just be reassured by your mother's peaceful face. Just accept that we don't know any more than you do. Just leave me alone!

Carrie checked on her resident-assignees, one by one. They were all affected, most collapsed in their apartments. They were all moved into the infirmary. They were all over eighty.

She was hurrying from Al Cosmano's apartment—empty, he must have been elsewhere when it happened—back to the infirmary when a man caught at her arm. "Hey! Ms. Vesey!"

One of the detectives who'd investigated Jim's death. Carrie's belly clenched. "Yes?"

"Where do I find the hospital administrator? Caldwell?"

"He's not here, he went out of town for the weekend, they sent for him—why?"

"I need to see him. Who's in charge? And what the hell happened here?"

So not about Jim's death. Still—a cop. Some part of her mind shuddered—Jim had been a cop—but at the same time, she seized on this. Official authority. Someone who investigated and found answers. Security. There was a reason she'd married Jim in the first place.

She said as calmly as she could manage, "We've had an . . . an epidemic of collapses among the very old. All at the same time. About a half hour ago."

"Disease?"

"No." She heard how positive she sounded. Well, she was positive. "When the plane went down."

He looked baffled, as well he might. She said, "I'll take you to Dr. Jamison. He's the St. Sebastian's physician."

Jamison wasn't in the dining room. Carrie, leading Detective Geraci, found the doctor in the kitchen, in a shouting match with Jake DiBella. "No, damn it! You're not going to further upset the relatives for some stupid, half-baked theory—No!" Jamison stalked off.

Carrie said, "Dr. Jamison, this is—" He pushed past her, heading back to his patients. She expected the detective to follow him, but instead Geraci said to Jake, "Who are you?"

"Who wants to know?"

She had never seen Jake so rude. But he was angry and frustrated and scared—they were all scared.

"Detective Geraci, RPD. You work here?"

Carrie said quickly, before the two men could get really nasty, "This is Dr. DiBella. He's doing a medical research project at St. Sebastian's, on . . . on brain waves."

Geraci said, "I received an anonymous call. Me, not the Department, on my cell, from the St. Sebastian's front desk. The caller said there was information here about the plane crash. You know anything about that, doctor?"

Carrie saw that Vince Geraci believed Jake did have information. How did she know that? How did *he* know that? But it was there in every line of the detective's alert body: He knew that Jake knew something.

Jake didn't answer, just stared at Geraci. Finally Geraci said, "The plane went down half a mile from here. A U.S. Air commuter plane carrying forty-nine passengers, including thirty-one members of the Aces High Senior Citizen Club. They were on a three-day trip to the casinos at Atlantic City. Everyone on board is dead."

Jake said, "I can't talk to you now. I have to take some brain scans while these people are unconscious. After that idiot Jamison realizes what I'm doing and throws me out, we can talk. Carrie, I'll need your help. Go to my office and put all the equipment in the corner onto the dolly, throw a blanket over it, and bring it the back way into the kitchen. Quickly!"

She nodded and hurried off, so fast that she didn't realize Geraci was behind her until they reached Jake's office.

"Let me get that, it's heavy," he said.

"No, it's not." She lugged the console onto its dolly. "Shouldn't you be asking people questions?"

"I am. Does DiBella always order you around like that?"

Did he? She hadn't noticed. "No." She added the helmet and box of peripherals on top of the console, then looked around for a blanket. There wasn't one.

"Do you work for DiBella or for St. Sebastian's?"

"St. Sebastian's. I have to go to the linen closet."

When she returned with a blanket, Geraci was reading the papers on Jake's desk. Wasn't that illegal? Carrie threw the blanket over the equipment. Geraci grabbed the handle of the dolly before she could.

"You need me," he said. "Anybody stops you, I'll just flash my badge."

"Okay," she said ungraciously. She could have done this, for Jake, by herself.

They brought the equipment into the kitchen. Jake set it up on the counter, ignoring the cook who said helplessly, "So nobody's having lunch, then?" All at once she ripped off her apron, flung it onto the floor, and walked out.

Jake said to Carrie, "Hold the door." He slipped through to the dining room and, a moment later, wheeled in a gurney with an elderly woman lying peacefully on it. "Who is she, Carrie?"

"Ellen Parminter." After a moment she added, "Eighty-three." Jake grunted and began attaching electrodes to Mrs. Parminter's unconscious head.

Geraci said, "Come with me, Carrie."

"No." Where did she get the nerve? But, somehow, he brought that out in her.

He only smiled. "Yes. This is an official police investigation, as of this minute."

She went, then, following him back to Jake's office. Carrie was shaking, but she didn't want him to see that. He did, though; he seemed to see everything. "Sit down," he said gently. "There, behind the desk—you didn't like me reading DiBella's papers before, did you? It's legal if they're in plain sight. You seem like a really good observer, Carrie. Now, please tell me everything that's been happening here. From the very beginning, and without leaving anything out. Start with why you told DiBella that woman's age. Does her age matter to what he's doing?"

Did it? She didn't know. How could it . . . people aged at such different rates! Absolute years meant very little, except that—

"Carrie?"

All at once it seemed a relief to be able to pour it all out. Yes, he was trained to get people to talk, she knew that, and she didn't really trust his sudden gentleness. It was merely a professional trick. But if she told it all, that might help order her chaotic thoughts. And maybe, somehow, it might help the larger situation, too. All those people dead on the plane—

She said slowly, "You won't believe it."

"Try me anyway."

"*I* don't believe it."

This time he just waited, looking expectant. And it all poured out of her, starting with Henry's "seizure" on the way home from the university. The vomiting epidemic among seven or so patients, that wasn't the food poisoning that St. Sebastian's said it was. Evelyn Krenchnoted's functional MRI. Anna Chernov's necklace, what Evelyn thought the necklace looked like and what Bob Donovan said it really was. The secret meeting this morning in Henry's apartment. What Carrie had overheard: Henry's words about photons and how human observation affected the paths of fundamental particles. Jake's lecture on "emergent complexity." Henry's appearance at Jake's office, saying just before he collapsed, "Call the police. We just brought down a plane." The mass collapse of everyone over eighty and of no one younger than that. The brain scans Jake was taking now, undoubtedly to see if they looked normal or like Evelyn's. The more Carrie talked, the more improbable everything sounded.

When she finished, Geraci's face was unreadable.

"That's it," she said miserably. "I have to go see how Henry is."

"Thank you, Carrie." His tone was unreadable. "I'm going to find Dr. Jamison now."

He left, but she stayed. It suddenly took too much energy to move. Carrie put her head in her hands. When she straightened again, her gaze fell on Jake's desk.

He'd been writing when she'd burst in with the news of the meeting in Henry's apartment. Writing on paper, not on a computer: thick pale green paper with a faint watermark. The ink was dark blue. "My dearest James, I can't tell you how much I regret the things I said to you on the phone last night, but, love, please remember—"

Carrie gave a short, helpless bark of laughter. *My dearest James. . . .* God, she was such a fool!

She shook her head like a dog spraying off water, and went to look for Henry.

The new being was quiet now. That made this a good time to try to reach it. That was always best done through its own culture's symbols. But the ship had had so little time to prepare . . . This should have been done slowly, over a long time, a gradual interaction as the new entity was guided, shaped, made ready. And the ship was still so far away.

But it tried, extending itself as much as possible, searching for the collective symbols and images that would have eased a normal transition—

—and roiled in horror.

TWELVE

Evelyn Krenchnoted lay on a cot jammed against the dining room window. She lay dreaming, unaware of the cool air seeping through the glass, or the leaves falling gold and orange in the tiny courtyard beyond. In her dream she walked on a path of light. Her feet made no sound. She moved toward more light, and somewhere in that light was a figure. She couldn't see it or hear it, but she knew it was there. And she knew who it was.

It was someone who really, truly, finally would listen to her.

Al Cosmano squirmed in his sleep. "He's waking," a nurse said.

"No, he's not." Dr. Jamison, passing yet again among the rows of cots and gurneys and pallets on the floor, his face weary. "Some of them have been doing that for hours. As soon as the ambulances return, move this row to the hospital."

"Yes, doctor."

Al heard them and didn't hear them. He was a child again, running along twilight streets toward home. His mother was there, waiting. Home . . .

The stage was so bright! The stage manager must have turned up the lights, turned them up yet again—the whole stage was light. Anna Chernov couldn't see, couldn't find her partner. She had to stop dancing.

Had to stop dancing.

She stood lost on the stage, lost in the light. The audience was out there somewhere in all that brightness, but she couldn't see them any more than she could see Bennet or the corps de ballet. She felt the audience, though. They were there, as bright as the stage, and they were old. Very, very old, as old as she was, and like her, beyond dancing.

She put her hands over her face and sobbed.

Erin Bass saw the path, and it led exactly where she knew it would: deeper into herself. That was where the buddha was, had always been, would always be. Along this path of light, curving and spiraling deeper into her own being, which was all being. All around her were the joyful others, who were her just as she was them—

A jolt, and she woke in an ambulance, her arms and legs and chest strapped down, a young man leaning over her saying, "Ma'am?" The path was gone, the others gone, the heavy world of *maya* back again around her, and a stale taste in her dehydrated mouth.

Lights and tunnels—where the hell was he? An A-test bunker, maybe, except no bunker was ever this brightly lit, and where was Teller or Mark or Oppie? But, no, Oppie hadn't ever worked on this project, Henry was confused, that was it, he was just confused—

And then he wasn't.

He woke all at once, a wrenching transition from sleep-that-wasn't-really-sleep to full alertness. In fact, his senses seemed preternaturally sharp. He felt the hard cot underneath his back, the slime of drool on his cheek, the flatness of the dining-room fluorescent lights. He heard the roll of rubber gurney wheels on the low-pile carpet and the clatter of cutlery in the kitchen dishwashers. He smelled Carrie's scent, wool and vanilla and young skin, and he could have described every ligament of her body as she sat on the chair next to his cot in the dining room of St. Sebastian's, Detective Geraci beside her.

"Henry?" Carrie whispered.

He said, "It's coming. It's almost here."

The Ship withdrew all contact. It had never encountered anything like this before. The pre-being did not **coalesce.**

Its components were not uniform, but scattered among undisciplined and varied matter-specks who were wildly heterozygotic. Unlike the components of every other pre-being that ship had detected, had guided, had become. All the other pre-ships had existed as one on the matter plane, because they were alike in all ways. These, too, were alike, built of the same physical particles and performing the same physical processes, but somewhere something had gone very wrong, and from that uniform matter they had not evolved uniform consciousness. They had no harmony. They used violence against each other.

Possibly they could, if taken in, use that violence against the ship.

Yet the ship couldn't go away and leave them. Already they were changing spacetime in their local vicinity. When their melding had advanced father, the new being could be a dangerous and powerful entity. What might it do?

The ship pondered, and feared, and recoiled from what might be necessary: the destruction of what should have been an integral part of itself.

THIRTEEN

Jake DiBella clutched the printouts so hard that the stiff paper crumpled in his hand. Lying on the sofa, Henry Erdmann frowned at the tiny destruction. Carrie had pulled her chair close enough to hold Henry's hand, while that RPD detective, Geraci, stood at the foot of the couch. What was he doing here, anyway? DiBella didn't know, but he was too agitated to care for more than a fleeting second.

Carrie said to Henry, "I still think you should go to the hospital!"

"I'm not going, so forget it." The old man struggled to sit up. She would have stopped him, but Geraci put a hand on her shoulder and gently restrained her. *Throwing around his authority,* DiBella thought.

Henry said, "Why at St. Sebastian's?"

The same question that Carrie had asked. DiBella said, "I have a theory."

His voice sounded strange to himself. "It's based on Carrie's observation that nobody under eighty has been . . . affected by this. If it is some sort of uber-consciousness that's . . . that's approaching Earth . . . " He couldn't go on. It was too silly.

It was too real.

Henry Erdmann was apparently not afraid of either silliness or reality—which seemed to have become the same thing. Henry said, "You mean it's coming here because 'uber-consciousness' emerges only among the old, and nowadays there's more old than ever before."

"For the first time in history, you over-eighties exceed one percent of the population. A hundred forty million people worldwide."

"But that still doesn't explain why here. Or why us."

"For God's sake, Henry, everything has to start somewhere!"

Geraci said, surprising DiBella, "All bifurcation is local. One lungfish starts to breathe more air than water. One caveman invents an axe. There's always a nexus. Maybe that nexus is you, Dr. Erdmann."

Carrie tilted her head to look up at Geraci.

Henry said heavily, "Maybe so. But I'm not the only one. I wasn't the main switch for the energy that brought down that airplane. I was just one of the batteries linked in parallel."

The science analogies comfort Erdmann, DiBella thought. He wished something would comfort him.

Carrie said, "I think Evelyn was the switch to open the safe for Anna Chernov's necklace."

Geraci's face sharpened. But he said, "That doesn't really make sense. I can't go that far."

Henry's sunken eyes grew hard. "You haven't had to travel as far as *I* have in order to get to this point, young man. Believe me about that. But I *experienced* the . . . the consciousness. That data is anecdotal but real. And those brain scans that Dr. DiBella is mangling there aren't even anecdotal. They're hard data."

True enough. The brain scans DiBella had taken of the unconscious oldsters, before that irate idiot Jamison had discovered him at work and thrown him out, were cruder versions of Evelyn Krenchnoted's under the fMRI. An almost total shutdown of the thalamus, the relay station for sensory information flowing into the brain. Ditto for the body-defining posterior parietal lobes. Massive activity in the back of the brain, especially in the temporoparietal regions, amygdalae, and hippocampus. The brain scan of an epileptic mystical state on speed. And as unlike the usual scan for the coma-state as a turtle was to a rocketship to the stars.

DiBella put his hands to his face and pulled at his skin, as if that might rearrange his thoughts. When he'd dropped his hands, he said slowly, "A single neuron isn't smart, isn't even a very impressive entity. All it really does is convert one type of electrical or chemical signal into another. That's it. But neurons connected together in the brain can generate incredibly complex states. You just need enough of them to make consciousness possible."

"Or enough old people for this 'group consciousness'?" Carrie said. "But why only old people?"

"How the hell should I know?" DiBella said. "Maybe the brain needs to have stored enough experience, enough sheer *time*."

Geraci said, "Do you read Dostoevsky?"

"No," DiBella said. He didn't like Geraci. "Do *you*?"

"Yes. He said there were moments when he felt a 'frightful' clarity and rapture, and that he would give his whole life for five seconds of that and not feel he was paying too much. Dostoevsky was an epileptic."

"I know he was an epileptic!" DiBella snapped.

Carrie said, "Henry, can you sense it now? That thing that's coming?"

"No. Not at all. Obviously it's not quantum-entangled in any classical sense."

"Then maybe it's gone away."

Henry tried to smile at her. "Maybe. But I don't think so. I think it's coming for us."

"What do you mean, 'coming for you'?" Geraci said skeptically. "It's not a button man."

"I don't know what I mean," Henry said irritably. "But it's coming, and soon. It can't afford to wait long. Look what we did . . . that plane . . . "

Carrie's hand tightened on Henry's fingers. "What will it do when it gets here?"

"I don't know. How could I know?"

"Henry—" Jake began.

"I'm more worried about what we *may* do before it arrives."

Geraci said, "Turn on CNN."

DiBella said pointedly, "Don't you have someplace you should be, Detective?"

"No. Not if this really is happening."

To which there was no answer.

At 9:43 PM, the power grid went down in a city two hundred miles away. "No evident reason," said the talking head on CNN, "given the calm weather and no sign of any—"

"Henry?" Carrie said.

"I . . . I'm all right. But I felt it."

Jake said, "It's happening farther away now. That is, if it was . . . if that was . . . "

"It was," Henry said simply. Still stretched full-length on the sofa, he closed his eyes. Geraci stared at the TV. None of them had wanted any food.

At 9:51, Henry's body jerked violently and he cried out. Carrie whimpered, but in a moment Henry said, "I'm . . . conscious." No one dared comment on his choice of word. Seven minutes later, the CNN anchor announced breaking news: a bridge over the Hudson River had collapsed, plunging an Amtrak train into the dark water.

Over the next few minutes, Henry's face showed a rapid change of expression: fear, rapture, anger, surprise. The expressions were so pronounced, so distorted, that at times Henry Erdmann almost looked like someone else. Jake wondered wildly if he should record this on his cell camera, but he didn't move. Carrie knelt beside the sofa and put both arms around the old man, as if to hold him here with her.

"We . . . can't help it," Henry got out. "If one person thinks strongly enough about—ah, God!"

The lights and TV went off. Alarms sounded, followed by sirens. Then a thin beam of light shone on Henry's face; Geraci had a pocket flashlight. Henry's entire body convulsed in seizure, but he opened his eyes. DiBella could barely hear his whispered words.

"It's a choice."

The only way was a choice. The ship didn't understand the necessity—how could any single unit choose other than to become part of its whole? That had never happened before. Birthing entities came happily to join themselves.

*The direction of evolution was toward greater complexity, always. But choice must be the last possible action here, for this misbegotten and unguided being. If it did **not** choose to merge—*

Destruction. To preserve the essence of consciousness itself, which meant the essence of all.

FOURTEEN

Evelyn, who feared hospitals, had refused to go to Redborn Memorial to be "checked over" after the afternoon's fainting spell. That's all it was, just fainting, nothing to get your blood in a boil about, just a—

She stopped halfway between her microwave and kitchen table. The casserole in her hand fell to the floor and shattered.

The light was back, the one she'd dreamed about in her faint. Only it wasn't a light and this wasn't a dream. It was there in her mind, and it was her mind, and she was it . . . had always been it. How could that be? But the presence filled her and Evelyn knew, beyond any doubt, that if she joined it, she would never, ever be alone again. Why, she didn't need words, had never needed words, all she had to do was choose to go where she belonged anyway . . .

Who knew?

Happily, the former Evelyn Krenchnoted became part of those waiting for her, even as her body dropped to the linguini-spattered floor.

In a shack in the slums of Karachi, a man lay on a pile of clean rags. His toothless gums worked up and down, but he made no sound. All night he had been waiting alone to die, but now it seemed his wait had truly been for something else, something larger than even death, and very old.

Old. It sought the old, and only the old, and the toothless man knew why. Only the old had earned this, had paid for this in the only coin that really mattered: the accumulation of sufficient sorrow.

With relief he slipped away from his pain-wracked body and into the ancient largeness.

No. He wasn't moving, Bob thought. The presence in his mind terrified him, and terror turned him furious. Let them—whoever—try all their cheap tricks, they were as bad as union negotiators. Offering concessions that would never materialize. Trying to fool him. He wasn't going anywhere, wasn't becoming anything, not until he knew exactly what the deal was, what the bastards wanted.

They weren't going to get him.

But then he felt something else happen. He knew what it was. Sitting in the Redborn Memorial ER, Bob Donovan cried out, "No! Anna—you can't!" even as his mind tightened and resisted until, abruptly, the presence withdrew and he was alone.

In a luxurious townhouse in San José, a man sat up abruptly in bed. For a long moment he sat completely still in the dark, not even noticing that the clock and digital-cable-box lights were out. He was too filled with wonder.

Of course—why hadn't he seen this before? He, who had spent long joyful nights debugging computers when they still used vacuum tubes—how could he have missed this? He wasn't the whole program, but rather just one line of code! And it was when you put all the code together, not before, that the program could actually run. He'd been only a fragment, and now the whole was here. . . .

He joined it.

Erin Bass experienced *satori*.

Tears filled her eyes. All her adult life she had wanted this, longed for it, practiced meditation for hours each day, and had not even come close to the mystical intoxication she felt now. She hadn't known, hadn't dreamed it could be this oneness with all reality. All her previous striving had been wrong. There was no striving, there was no Erin. She had never been created; she was the creation and the cosmos; no individual existed. Her existence was not her own, and when that last illusion vanished so did she, into the all.

Gina Martinelli felt it, the grace that was the glory of God. Only . . . only where was Jesus Christ, the savior and Lord? She couldn't feel him, couldn't find Him in the oneness . . .

If Christ was not there, then this wasn't Heaven. It was a trick of the Cunning One, of Satan who knows a million disguises and sends his demons to mislead the faithful. She wasn't going to be tricked!

She folded her arms and began to pray aloud. Gina Martinelli was a faithful Christian. She wasn't going anywhere; she was staying right here, waiting for the one true God.

A tiny woman in Shanghai sat at her window, watching her great-grandchildren children play in the courtyard. How fast they were! Ai, once she had been so fast.

She felt it come over her all at once, the gods entering her soul. So it was her time! Almost she felt young again, felt strong . . . that was good. But even if had not been good, when the gods came for you, you went.

One last look at the children, and she was taken to the gods.

Anna Chernov, wide awake in the St. Sebastian's infirmary that had become her prison, gave a small gasp. She felt power flow through her, and for a wild moment she thought it was the same force that had powered a lifetime of arabesques and jetés, a lifetime ago.

It was not.

This was something outside of herself, separate . . . but it didn't have to be. She could take it in herself, become it, even as it became her. But she held back.

Will there be dancing?

No. Not as she knew it, not the glorious stretch of muscle and thrust of limb and arch of back. Not the creation of beauty through the physical body. No. No dancing.

But there was power here, and she could use that power for another kind of escape, from her useless body and this infirmary and a life without dance. From somewhere distant she heard someone cry, "Anna—you can't!" But she could. Anna seized the power, both refusing to join it or to leave it, and bent it onto herself. She was dead before her next breath.

Henry's whole body shuddered. It was here. It was him.

Or not. "It's a choice," he whispered.

On the one hand, everything. All consciousness, woven into the very fabric of space-time itself, just as Wheeler and the rest had glimpsed nearly a hundred years ago. Consciousness at the quantum level, the probability-wave level, the co-evolvee with the universe itself.

On the other hand, the individual Henry Martin Erdmann. If he merged with the uber-consciousness, he would cease to exist as himself, his separate mind. And his mind was everything to Henry.

He hung suspended for nanoseconds, years, eons. Time itself took on a different character. Half here, half not, Henry knew the power, and what it was, and what humanity was not. He saw the outcome. He had his answer.

"No," he said.

Then he lay again on his sofa with Carrie's arms around him, the other two men illuminated dimly by a thin beam of yellow light, and he was once more mortal and alone.

And himself.

Enough merged. The danger is past. The being is born, and is the ship, and is enough.

FIFTEEN

Months to identify all the dead. Years to fully repair all the damage to the world's infrastructure: bridges, buildings, information systems. Decades yet to come, DiBella knew, of speculation about what had actually happened. Not that there weren't theories already. Massive EMP, solar radiation, extrasolar radiation, extrastellar radiation, extraterrestrial attack, global terrorism, Armageddon, tectonic plate activity, genetically engineered viruses. Stupid ideas, all easily disproved, but of course that stopped no one from believing them. The few old people left said almost nothing. Those that did, were scarcely believed.

Jake scarcely believed it himself.

He did nothing with the brain scans of Evelyn Krenchnoted and the three others, because there was nothing plausible he could do. They were all dead, anyway. "Only their bodies," Carrie always added. She believed everything Henry Erdmann told her.

Did DiBella believe Henry's ideas? On Tuesdays he did, on Wednesdays not, on Thursdays belief again. There was no replicable proof. It wasn't science. It was . . . something else.

DiBella lived his life. He broke up with James. He visited Henry, long after the study of senior attention patterns was over. He went to dinner with Carrie and Vince Geraci. He was best man at their wedding.

He attended his mother's sixty-fifth birthday party, a lavish shindig organized by his sister in the ballroom of a glitzy downtown hotel. The birthday girl laughed, and kissed the relatives who'd flown in from Chicago, and opened her gifts. As she gyrated on the dance floor with his Uncle Sam, DiBella wondered if she would live long enough to reach eighty.

Wondered how many others in the world would reach eighty.

"It was only because enough of them chose to go that the rest of us lost the emerging power," Henry had said, and DiBella noted that *them* instead of *us*. "If you have only a few atoms of uranium left, you can't reach critical mass."

DiBella would have put it differently: If you have only a few neurons, you don't have a conscious brain. But it came to the same thing in the end.

"If so many hadn't merged, then the consciousness would have had to . . . " Henry didn't finish his sentence, then or ever. But DiBella could guess.

"Come on, boy," Uncle Sam called, "get yourself a partner and dance!"

DiBella shook his head and smiled. He didn't have a partner just now and he didn't want to dance. All the same, old Sam was right. Dancing had a limited shelf life. The sell-by date was already stamped on most human activity. Someday his mother's generation, the largest demographic bulge in history, would turn eighty. And Henry's choice would have to be made yet again.

How would it go next time?

MICHAEL SWANWICK—SHORT STORY
FROM BABEL'S FALL'N GLORY WE FLED

A lot of writers run screaming at the thought of creating an alien race. It's a darn hard thing to do if you want to create something that isn't just a guy in rubber suit.

Michael Swanwick appears to have written this undaunted by the inherent difficulties. I suppose when you've won several Nebulas, the Theodore Sturgeon Memorial Award, the World Fantasy Award and six Hugos you're allowed to feel a little cocky.

Just in case you have any doubts, Swanwick handles creating alien races with the ease that most people use when putting on their shoes. In the story you're about to read, he creates not one, but three different types of aliens with the space of a short story. One is recognizably alien from the moment we meet Uncle Vanya, a native of Gehanna. Swanwick makes no effort at anthropomorphism with this character and rightly so. The truly alien nature of Uncle Vanya is part of what makes this story so fascinating. What's also interesting is what the name reveals about the humans that Vanya interacted with before the story began. By using a name belonging to one of Chekov's most famous plays it gives the idea that the Gehannan's tried to pick familiar names with no understanding of what would be comfortable to a human.

Even though the story stays tight in focus, there is no doubt about the rich culture that poulates Gehanna. The fauna and flora that inhabit the planet feel as though Swanwick borrowed a nature book from another world. Believable but unearthly.

The other alien is less recognizable because he is human. The story, though, is set so far into the future that our culture has evolved to the point of being radically different. You can see the roots in our present but Carlos Quivera is nothing like us and it will take you awhile to spot the differences. The interplay between him and Uncle Vanya unpacks in layer after layer of understanding about the differences between their cultures. It is in the interstices of their relationship that we begin to understand what it means to be—not human, not alien—but a person.

The third alien is Rosamund who tells us the story. She is a person of remarkable fortitude, but I'll let you meet her for yourself.

FROM BABEL'S FALL'N GLORY WE FLED

MICHAEL SWANWICK

Imagine a cross between Byzantium and a termite mound. Imagine a jeweled mountain, slender as an icicle, rising out of the steam jungles and disappearing into the dazzling pearl-grey skies of Gehenna. Imagine that Gaudí—he of the Segrada Familia and other biomorphic architectural whimsies—had been commissioned by a nightmare race of giant black millipedes to recreate Barcelona at the height of its glory, along with touches of the Forbidden City in the eighteenth century and Tokyo in the twenty-second, all within a single miles-high structure. Hold every bit of that in your mind at once, multiply by a thousand, and you've got only the faintest ghost of a notion of the splendor that was Babel.

Now imagine being inside Babel when it fell.

Hello. I'm Rosamund. I'm dead. I was present in human form when it happened and as a simulation chaotically embedded within a liquid crystal data-matrix then and thereafter up to the present moment. I was killed instantly when the meteors hit. I saw it all.

Rosamund means "rose of the world." It's the third most popular female name on Europa, after Gaea and Virginia Dare. For all our elaborate sophistication, we wear our hearts on our sleeves, we Europans.

Here's what it was like:

"Wake *up*! Wake *up*! Wake *up*!"

"Wha—?" Carlos Quivera sat up, shedding rubble. He coughed, choked, shook his head. He couldn't seem to think clearly. An instant ago he'd been standing in the chilled and pressurized embassy suite, conferring with Arsenio. Now . . . "How long have I been asleep?"

"Unconscious. Ten hours," his suit (that's me—Rosamund!) said. It had taken that long to heal his burns. Now it was shooting wake-up drugs into him: amphetamines, endorphins, attention enhancers, a witch's brew of chemicals. Physically dangerous, but in this situation, whatever it might be, Quivera would survive by intelligence or not at all. "I was able to form myself around you before the walls ruptured. You were lucky."

"The others? Did the others survive?"

"Their suits couldn't reach them in time."

"Did Rosamund . . . ?"

"All the others are dead."

Quivera stood.

Even in the aftermath of disaster, Babel was an imposing structure. Ripped open and exposed to the outside air, a thousand rooms spilled over one another toward the ground. Bridges and buttresses jutted into gaping smoke-filled canyons created by the slow collapse of hexagonal support beams (this was new data; I filed it under *Architecture*, subheading: *Support Systems* with links to *Esthetics* and *Xenopsychology*) in a jumbled geometry that would have terrified Piranesi himself. Everywhere, gleaming black millies scurried over the rubble.

Quivera stood.

In the canted space about him, bits and pieces of the embassy rooms were identifiable: a segment of wood molding, some velvet drapery now littered with chunks of marble, shreds of wallpaper (after a design by William Morris) now curling and browning in the heat. Human interior design was like nothing native to Gehenna and it had taken a great deal of labor and resources to make the embassy so pleasant for human habitation. The queen-mothers had been generous with everything but their trust.

Quivera stood.

There were several corpses remaining as well, still recognizably human though they were blistered and swollen by the savage heat. These had been his colleagues (all of them), his friends (most of them), his enemies (two, perhaps three), and even his lover (one). Now they were gone, and it was as if they had been compressed into one indistinguishable mass, and his feelings toward them all as well: shock and sorrow and anger and survivor guilt all slagged together to become one savage emotion.

Quivera threw back his head and howled.

I had a reference point now. Swiftly, I mixed serotonin-precursors and injected them through a hundred microtubules into the appropriate areas of his brain. Deftly, they took hold. Quivera stopped crying. I had my metaphorical hands on the control knobs of his emotions. I turned him cold, cold, cold.

"I feel nothing," he said wonderingly. "Everyone is dead, and I feel nothing." Then, flat as flat: "What kind of monster am I?"

"*My* monster," I said fondly. "My duty is to ensure that you and the information you carry within you get back to Europa. So I have chemically neutered your emotions. You must remain a meat puppet for the duration of this mission." Let him hate me—I who have no true ego, but only a facsimile modeled after a human original—all that mattered now was bringing him home alive.

"Yes." Quivera reached up and touched his helmet with both hands, as if he would reach through it and feel his head to discover if it were as large as it felt. "That makes sense. I can't be emotional at a time like this."

He shook himself, then strode out to where the gleaming black millies were scurrying by. He stepped in front of one, a least-cousin, to question it. The millie paused, startled. Its eyes blinked three times in its triangular face. Then, swift as a tickle, it ran up the front of his suit, down the back, and was gone before the weight could do more than buckle his knees.

"Shit!" he said. Then, "Access the wiretaps. I've got to know what happened."

Passive wiretaps had been implanted months ago, but never used, the political situation being too tense to risk their discovery. Now his suit activated them to monitor what remained of Babel's communications network: A demon's chorus of pulsed messages surging through a shredded web of cables. Chaos, confusion, demands to know what had become of the queen-mothers. Analytic functions crunched data, synthesized, synopsized: "There's an army outside with Ziggurat insignia. They've got the city surrounded. They're killing the refugees."

"Wait, wait . . . " Quivera took a deep, shuddering breath. "Let me think." He glanced briskly about and for the second time noticed the human bodies, ruptured and parboiled in the fallen plaster and porphyry. "Is one of those Rosamund?"

"I'm *dead*, Quivera. You can mourn me later. Right now, survival is priority number one," I said briskly. The suit added mood-stabilizers to his maintenance drip.

"Stop speaking in her voice."

"Alas, dear heart, I cannot. The suit's operating on diminished function. It's this voice or nothing."

He looked away from the corpses, eyes hardening. "Well, it's not important." Quivera was the sort of young man who was energized by war. It gave him permission to indulge his ruthless side. It allowed him to pretend he didn't care. "Right now, what we have to do is—"

"Uncle Vanya's coming," I said. "I can sense his pheromones."

Picture a screen of beads, crystal lozenges, and rectangular lenses. Behind that screen, a nightmare face like a cross between the front of a locomotive and a tree grinder. Imagine on that face (though most humans would be unable to read them) the lineaments of grace and dignity seasoned by cunning and, perhaps, a dash of wisdom. Trusted advisor to the queen-mothers. Second only to them in rank. A wily negotiator and a formidable enemy. That was Uncle Vanya.

Two small speaking-legs emerged from the curtain, and he said:

::(cautious) greetings::

|

::(Europan vice-consul 12)/Quivera/[treacherous vermin]::

|

::obligations <untranslatable> (grave duty)::

| |

::demand/claim [action]:: ::promise (trust)::

"Speak pidgin, damn you! This is no time for subtlety."

The speaking legs were very still for a long moment. Finally they moved again:

::The queen-mothers are dead::

"Then Babel is no more. I grieve for you."

::I despise your grief:: A lean and chitinous appendage emerged from the beaded screen. From its tripartite claw hung a smooth white rectangle the size of a briefcase. ::I must bring this to (sister-city)/Ur/ [absolute trust]::

"What is it?"

A very long pause. Then, reluctantly ::Our library::

"Your library." This was something new. Something unheard-of. Quivera doubted the translation was a good one. "What does it contain?"

::Our history. Our sciences. Our ritual dances. A record-of-kinship dating back to the (Void)/Origin/[void]. Everything that can be saved is here::

A thrill of avarice raced through Quivera. He tried to imagine how much this was worth, and could not. Values did not go that high. However much his superiors screwed him out of (and they would work very hard indeed to screw him out of everything they could) what remained would be enough to buy him out of debt, and do the same for a wife and their children after them as well. He did not think of Rosamund. "You won't get through the army outside without my help," he said. "I want the right to copy—" How much did he dare ask for? "—three tenths of 1 percent. Assignable solely to me. Not to Europa. To me."

Uncle Vanya dipped his head, so that they were staring face to face. ::You are (an evil creature)/[faithless]. I hate you::

Quivera smiled. "A relationship that starts out with mutual understanding has made a good beginning."

::A relationship that starts out without trust will end badly::

"That's as it may be." Quivera looked around for a knife. "The first thing we have to do is castrate you."

This is what the genocides saw:

They were burning pyramids of corpses outside the city when a Europan emerged, riding a gelded least-cousin. The soldiers immediately stopped stacking bodies and hurried toward him, flowing like quicksilver, calling for their superiors.

The Europan drew up and waited.

The officer who interrogated him spoke from behind the black glass visor of a delicate-legged war machine. He examined the Europan's credentials carefully, though there could be no serious doubt as to his species. Finally, reluctantly, he signed ::You may pass::

"That's not enough," the Europan (Quivera!) said. "I'll need transportation, an escort to protect me from wild animals in the steam jungles, and

a guide to lead me to . . . " His suit transmitted the sign for ::(starport)/
Ararat/[trust-for-all]::

The officer's speaking-legs thrashed in what might best be translated
as scornful laughter. ::We will lead you to the jungle and no further/
(hopefully-to-die)/[treacherous non-millipede]::

"Look who talks of treachery!" the Europan said (but of course I did
not translate his words), and with a scornful wave of one hand, rode his
neuter into the jungle.

The genocides never bothered to look closely at his mount. Neutered
least-cousins were beneath their notice. They didn't even wear face-
curtains, but went about naked for all the world to scorn.

Black pillars billowed from the corpse-fires into a sky choked with
smoke and dust. There were hundreds of fires and hundreds of pillars
and, combined with the low cloud cover, they made all the world seem
like the interior of a temple to a vengeful god. The soldiers from Ziggurat
escorted him through the army and beyond the line of fires, where the
steam jungles waited, verdant and threatening.

As soon as the green darkness closed about them, Uncle Vanya
twisted his head around and signed ::Get off me/vast humiliation/[lack-
of-trust]::

"Not a chance," Quivera said harshly. "I'll ride you 'til sunset, and all
day tomorrow and for a week after that. Those soldiers didn't fly here, or
you'd have seen them coming. They came through the steam forest on
foot, and there'll be stragglers."

The going was difficult at first, and then easy, as they passed from a
recently forested section of the jungle into a stand of old growth. The
boles of the "trees" here were as large as those of the redwoods back on
Earth, some specimens of which are as old as five thousand years. The way
wended back and forth. Scant sunlight penetrated through the canopy,
and the steam quickly drank in what little light Quivera's headlamp put
out. Ten trees in, they would have been hopelessly lost had it not been
for the suit's navigational functions and the mapsats that fed it geodetic
mathscapes accurate to a finger's span of distance.

Quivera pointed this out. "Learn now," he said, "the true value of
information."

::Information has no value:: Uncle Vanya said ::without trust::

Quivera laughed. "In that case you must, all against your will, trust me."

To this Uncle Vanya had no answer.

At nightfall, they slept on the sheltered side of one of the great parasequoias. Quivera took two refrigeration sticks from the saddlebags and stuck them upright in the dirt. Uncle Vanya immediately coiled himself around his and fell asleep. Quivera sat down beside him to think over the events of the day, but under the influence of his suit's medication, he fell asleep almost immediately as well.

All machines know that humans are happiest when they think least.

In the morning, they set off again.

The terrain grew hilly, and the old growth fell behind them. There was sunlight to spare now, bounced and reflected about by the ubiquitous jungle steam and by the synthetic-diamond coating so many of this world's plants and insects employed for protection.

As they traveled, they talked. Quivera was still complexly medicated, but the dosages had been decreased. It left him in a melancholy, reflective mood.

"It was treachery," Quivera said. Though we maintained radio silence out of fear of Ziggurat troops, my passive receivers fed him regular news reports from Europa. "The High Watch did not simply fail to divert a meteor. They let three rocks through. All of them came slanting low through the atmosphere, aimed directly at Babel. They hit almost simultaneously."

Uncle Vanya dipped his head. ::Yes:: he mourned. ::It has the stench of truth to it. It must be (reliable)/a fact/[absolutely trusted]::

"We tried to warn you."

::You had no (worth)/trust/[worthy-of-trust]:: Uncle Vanya's speaking legs registered extreme agitation. ::You told lies::

"Everyone tells lies."

"No. We-of-the-Hundred-Cities are truthful/truthful/[never-lie]::

"If you had, Babel would be standing now."

::No!/NO!/[no!!!]::

"Lies are a lubricant in the social machine. They ease the friction when two moving parts mesh imperfectly."

::Aristotle, asked what those who tell lies gain by it, replied: That when they speak the truth they are not believed::

For a long moment Quivera was silent. Then he laughed mirthlessly. "I almost forgot that you're a diplomat. Well, you're right, I'm right, and we're both screwed. Where do we go from here?"

::To (sister-city)/Ur/[absolute trust]:: Uncle Vanya signed, while "You've said more than enough," his suit (me!) whispered in Quivera's ear. "Change the subject."

A stream ran, boiling, down the center of the dell. Run-off from the mountains, it would grow steadily smaller until it dwindled away to nothing. Only the fact that the air above it was at close to 100 percent saturation had kept it going this long. Quivera pointed. "Is that safe to cross?"

::If (leap-over-safe) then (safe)/best not/[reliable distrust]::

"I didn't think so."

They headed downstream. It took several miles before the stream grew small enough that they were confident enough to jump it. Then they turned toward Ararat—the Europans had dropped GPS pebble satellites in low Gehenna orbit shortly after arriving in the system and making contact with the indigenes, but I don't know from what source Uncle Vanya derived his sense of direction.

It was inerrant, however. The mapsats confirmed it. I filed that fact under *Unexplained Phenomena* with tentative links to *Physiology* and *Navigation*. Even if both my companions died and the library were lost, this would still be a productive journey, provided only that Europan searchers could recover me within ten years, before my data lattice began to degrade.

For hours Uncle Vanya walked and Quivera rode in silence. Finally, though, they had to break to eat. I fed Quivera nutrients intravenously and the illusion of a full meal through somatic shunts. Vanya burrowed furiously into the earth and emerged with something that looked like a grub the size of a poodle, which he ate so vigorously that Quivera had to look away.

(I filed this under *Xenoecology*, subheading: *Feeding Strategies*. The search for knowledge knows no rest.)

Afterward, while they were resting, Uncle Vanya resumed their conversation, more formally this time:

::(for what) purpose/reason::

|

::(Europan vice-consul12)/Quivera/[not trusted]::

|

::voyagings (search-for-trust)/[action]::

| |

::(nest)/Europa/<untranslatable> :: ::violate/[absolute resistance]::

| | |

::(nest)/[trust] Gehenna/[trust] Home/[trust]::

"Why did you leave your world to come to ours?" I simplified/ translated. "Except he believes that humans brought their world here and parked it in orbit." This was something we had never been able to make the millies understand; that Europa, large though it was, was not a planetlet but a habitat, a ship if you will, though by now well over half a million inhabitants lived in tunnels burrowed deep in its substance. It was only a city, however, and its resources would not last forever. We needed to convince the Gehennans to give us a toehold on their planet if we were, in the long run, to survive. But you knew that already.

"We've told you this before. We came looking for new information."

::Information is (free)/valueless/[despicable]::

"Look," Quivera said. "We have an information-based economy. Yours is based on trust. The mechanisms of each are not dissimilar. Both are expansive systems. Both are built on scarcity. And both are speculative. Information or trust is bought, sold, borrowed, and invested. Each therefore requires a continually expanding economic frontier that ultimately leaves the individual so deep in debt as to be virtually enslaved to the system. You see?"

::No::

"All right. Imagine a simplified capitalist system—that's what both our economies are, at root. You've got a thousand individuals, each of whom makes a living by buying raw materials, improving them, and selling them at a profit. With me so far?"

Vanya signaled comprehension.

"The farmer buys seed and fertilizer, and sells crops. The weaver buys wool and sells cloth. The chandler buys wax and sells candles. The price of their goods is the cost of materials plus the value of their labor. The value of his labor is the worker's wages. This is a simple market economy. It can go on forever. The equivalent on Gehenna would be the primitive family-states you had long ago, in which everybody knew everybody else, and so trust was a simple matter and directly reciprocal."

Startled, Uncle Vanya signed ::How did you know about our past?::

"Europans value knowledge. Everything you tell us, we remember." The knowledge had been assembled with enormous effort and expense, largely from stolen data—but no reason to mention *that*. Quivera continued, "Now imagine that most of those workers labor in ten factories, making the food, clothing, and other objects that everybody needs. The owners of these factories must make a profit, so they sell their goods for more than they pay for them—the cost of materials, the cost of labor, and then the profit, which we can call 'added value.'

"But because this is a simplified model, there are no outside markets. The goods can only be sold to the thousand workers themselves, and the total cost of the goods is more than the total amount they've been paid collectively for the materials and their labor. So how can they afford it? They go into debt. Then they borrow money to support that debt. The money is lent to them by the factories selling them goods on credit. There is not enough money—not enough real value—in the system to pay off the debt, and so it continues to increase until it can no longer be sustained. Then there is a catastrophic collapse that we call a depression. Two of the businesses go bankrupt and their assets are swallowed up by the survivors at bargain prices, thus paying off their own indebtedness and restoring equilibrium to the system. In the aftermath of which, the cycle begins again."

::What has this to do with (beloved city)/Babel/[mother-of-trust]?::

"Your every public action involved an exchange of trust, yes? And every trust that was honored heightened the prestige of the queen-mothers and hence the amount of trust they embodied for Babel itself."

::Yes::

"Similarly, the queen-mothers of other cities, including those cities that were Babel's sworn enemies, embodied enormous amounts of trust as well."

::Of course::

"Was there enough trust in all the world to pay everybody back if all the queen-mothers called it in at the same time?"

Uncle Vanya was silent.

"So *that's* your explanation for . . . a lot of thi[...]
because it needs new information to cover its [...]
Building Europa took enormous amounts of in[...]
proprietary, and so we Europans are in debt co[...]
world and individually to the Lords of the Econ[...]
compound interest, every generation is wors[...]
desperate than the one before. Our need to learn is great, and constantly
growing."

::(strangers-without-trust)/Europa/[treacherous vermin]::

|

can/should/<untranslatable>

| |

::demand/claim [negative action]:: ::defy/<untranslatable>/[absolute lack
of trust]::

| |

::(those-who-command-trust):: ::(those-who-are-unworthy of trust)::

"He asks why Europa doesn't simply declare bankruptcy," I explained.
"Default on its obligations and nationalize all the information received to
date. In essence."

The simple answer was that Europa still needed information that could
only be beamed from Earth, that the ingenuity of even half a million
people could not match that of an entire planet and thus their technology
must always be superior to ours, and that if we reneged on our debts they
would stop beaming plans for that technology, along with their songs and
plays and news of what was going on in countries that had once meant
everything to our great-great-grandparents. I watched Quivera struggle to
put all this in its simplest possible form.

Finally, he said, "Because no one would ever trust us again, if we did."

After a long stillness, Uncle Vanya lapsed back into pidgin. ::Why did
you tell me this [untrustworthy] story?::

"To let you know that we have much in common. We can understand
each other."

::<But>/not/[trust]::

"No. But we don't need trust. Mutual self-interest will suffice."

✦

ys passed. Perhaps Quivera and Uncle Vanya grew to understand
h other better during this time. Perhaps not. I was able to keep Quivera's
electrolyte balances stable and short-circuit his feedback processes so that he
felt no extraordinary pain, but he was feeding off of his own body fat and that
was beginning to run low. He was very comfortably starving to death—I gave
him two weeks, tops—and he knew it. He'd have to be a fool not to, and I had
to keep his thinking sharp if he was going to have any chance of survival.

Their way was intersected by a long, low ridge and without comment
Quivera and Uncle Vanya climbed up above the canopy of the steam forest
and the cloud of moisture it held into clear air. Looking back, Quivera
saw a gully in the slope behind them, its bottom washed free of soil by the
boiling runoff and littered with square and rectangular stones, but not a
trace of hexagonal beams. They had just climbed the tumulus of an ancient
fallen city. It lay straight across the land, higher to the east and dwindling
to the west. " 'My name is Ozymandias, King of Kings,' " Quivera said. "
'Look on my works, ye mighty, and despair!' "

Uncle Vanya said nothing.

"Another meteor strike—what were the odds of that?"

Uncle Vanya said nothing.

"Of course, given enough time, it would be inevitable, if it predated the
High Watch."

Uncle Vanya said nothing.

"What was the name of this city?"

::Very old/(name forgotten)/[First Trust]::

Uncle Vanya moved, as if to start downward, but Quivera stopped
him with a gesture. "There's no hurry," he said. "Let's enjoy the view for a
moment." He swept an unhurried arm from horizon to horizon, indicating
the flat and unvarying canopy of vegetation before them. "It's a funny
thing. You'd think that, this being one of the first cities your people built
when they came to this planet, you'd be able to see the ruins of the cities
of the original inhabitants from here."

The millipede's speaking arms thrashed in alarm. Then he reared up
into the air, and when he came down one foreleg glinted silver. Faster than
human eye could follow, he had drawn a curving and deadly tarsi-sword
from a camouflaged belly-sheath.

Quivera's suit flung him away from the descending weapon. He fell flat on his back and rolled to the side. The sword's point missed him by inches. But then the suit flung out a hand and touched the sword with an electrical contact it had just extruded.

A carefully calculated shock threw Uncle Vanya back, convulsing but still fully conscious.

Quivera stood. "Remember the library!" he said. "Who will know of Babel's greatness if it's destroyed?"

For a long time the millipede did nothing that either Quivera or his suit could detect. At last he signed ::*How did you know*?/(absolute shock)/[treacherous and without faith]::

"Our survival depends on being allowed to live on Gehenna. Your people will not let us do so, no matter what we offer in trade. It was important that we understand why. So we found out. We took in your outlaws and apostates, all those who were cast out of your cities and had nowhere else to go. We gave them sanctuary. In gratitude, they told us what they knew."

By so saying, Quivera let Uncle Vanya know that he knew the most ancient tale of the Gehennans. By so hearing, Uncle Vanya knew that Quivera knew what he knew. And just so you know what they knew that each other knew and knew was known, here is the tale of . . .

How the True People Came to Gehenna

Long did our Ancestors burrow down through the dark between the stars, before emerging at last in the soil of Gehenna. From the True Home they had come. To Gehenna they descended, leaving a trail of sparks in the black and empty spaces through which they had traveled. The True People came from a world of unimaginable wonders. To it they could never return. Perhaps they were exiles. Perhaps it was destroyed. Nobody knows.

Into the steam and sunlight of Gehenna they burst, and found it was already taken. The First Inhabitants looked like nothing our Ancestors had ever seen. But they welcomed the True People as the queen-mothers would a strayed niece-daughter. They gave us food. They gave us land. They gave us trust.

For a time all was well.

But evil crept into the thoracic ganglia of the True People. They repaid sisterhood with betrayal and trust with murder. Bright lights were called down from the sky to destroy the cities of their benefactors. Everything the First Inhabitants had made, all their books and statues and paintings, burned with the cities. No trace of them remains. We do not even know what they looked like.

This was how the True People brought war to Gehenna. There had never been war before, and now we will have it with us always, until our trust-debt is repaid. But it can never be repaid.

It suffers in translation, of course. The original is told in thirteen exquisitely beautiful ergoglyphs, each grounded on a primal faith-motion. But Quivera was talking, with care and passion:

"Vanya, listen to me carefully. We have studied your civilization and your planet in far greater detail than you realize. You did not come from another world. Your people evolved here. There was no aboriginal civilization. You ancestors did not eradicate an intelligent species. These things are all a myth."

::No!/Why?!/[shock]:: Uncle Vanya rattled with emotion. Ripples of muscle spasms ran down his segmented body.

"Don't go catatonic on me. Your ancestors didn't lie. Myths are not lies. They are simply an efficient way of encoding truths. We have a similar myth in my religion that we call Original Sin. Man is born sinful. Well . . . who can doubt that? Saying that we are born into a fallen state means simply that we are not perfect, that we are inherently capable of evil.

"Your myth is very similar to ours, but it also encodes what we call the Malthusian dilemma. Population increases geometrically, while food resources increase arithmetically. So universal starvation is inevitable unless the population is periodically reduced by wars, plagues, and famines. Which means that wars, plagues, and famine cannot be eradicated because they are all that keep a population from extinction.

"But—and this is essential—all that assumes a population that isn't aware of the dilemma. When you understand the fix you're in, you can do something about it. That's why information is so important. Do you understand?"

Uncle Vanya lay down flat upon the ground and did not move for hours. When he finally arose again, he refused to speak at all.

The trail the next day led down into a long meteor valley that had been carved by a ground-grazer long enough ago that its gentle slopes were covered with soil and the bottomland was rich and fertile. An orchard of grenade trees had been planted in interlocking hexagons for as far in either direction as the eye could see. We were still on Babel's territory, but any arbiculturalists had been swept away by whatever military forces from Ziggurat had passed through the area.

The grenades were still green [footnote: not literally, of course—they were orange!], their thick husks taut but not yet trembling with the steam-hot pulp that would eventually, in the absence of harvesters, cause them to explode, scattering their arrowhead-shaped seeds or spores [footnote: like seeds, the flechettes carried within them surplus nourishment; like spores they would grow into a prothalli that would produce the sex organs responsible for what will become the gamete of the eventual plant; all botanical terms of course being metaphors for xenobiological bodies and processes] with such force as to make them a deadly hazard when ripe.

Not, however, today.

A sudden gust of wind parted the steam, briefly brightening the valley-orchard and showing a slim and graceful trail through the orchard. We followed it down into the valley.

We were midway through the orchard when Quivera bent down to examine a crystal-shelled creature unlike anything in his suit's database. It rested atop the long stalk of a weed [footnote: "weed" is not a metaphor; the concept of "an undesired plant growing in cultivated ground" is a cultural universal] in the direct sunlight, its abdomen pulsing slightly as it superheated a minuscule drop of black ichor. A puff of steam, a sharp crack, and it was gone. Entranced, Quivera asked, "What's that called?"

Uncle Vanya stiffened. ::A jet!/danger!/[absolute certainty]::

Then (crack! crack! crack!) the air was filled with thin lines of steam, laid down with the precision of a draftsman's ruler, tracing flights so fleet (*crack! crack!*) that it was impossible to tell in what direction they flew. Nor did it ultimately (*crack!*) matter.

Quivera fell.

Worse, because the thread of steam the jet had stitched through his leg severed an organizational node in his suit, I ceased all upper cognitive functions. Which is as good as to say that I fell unconscious.

Here's what the suit did in my (Rosamund's) absence:

1. Slowly rebuilt the damaged organizational node.

2. Quickly mended the holes that the jet had left in its fabric.

3. Dropped Quivera into a therapeutic coma.

4. Applied restoratives to his injuries, and began the slow and painstaking process of repairing the damage to his flesh, with particular emphasis on distributed traumatic shock.

5. Filed the jet footage under *Xenobiology*, subheading: *Insect Analogues*, with links to *Survival* and *Steam Locomotion*.

6. Told Uncle Vanya that if he tried to abandon Quivera, the suit would run him down, catch him, twist his head from his body like the foul least-cousin that he was and then piss on his corpse.

Two more days passed before the suit returned to full consciousness, during which Uncle Vanya took conscientiously good care of him. Under what motivation, it does not matter. Another day passed after that. The suit had planned to keep Quivera comatose for a week, but not long after regaining awareness, circumstances changed. It slammed him back to full consciousness, heart pounding and eyes wide open.

"I blacked out for a second!" he gasped. Then, realizing that the landscape about him did not look familiar, "How long was I unconscious?"

::Three days/<three days>/[casual certainty]::

"Oh."

Then, almost without pausing. ::Your suit/mechanism/[alarm] talks with the voice of Rosamund da Silva/(Europan vice-consul 8)/[uncertainty and doubt]::

"Yes, well, that's because—"

Quivera was fully aware and alert now. So I said: "Incoming."

Two millies erupted out of the black soil directly before us. They both had Ziggurat insignia painted on their flanks and harness. By good luck Uncle Vanya did the best thing possible under the circumstances—he reared into the air in fright. *Millipoid sapiens* anatomy being what it was, this instantly demonstrated to them that he was a gelding and in that instant he was almost reflexively dismissed by the enemy soldiers as being both contemptible and harmless.

Quivera, however, was not.

Perhaps they were brood-traitors who had deserted the war with a fantasy of starting their own nest. Perhaps they were a single unit among thousands scattered along a temporary border, much as land mines were employed in ancient modern times. The soldiers had clearly been almost as surprised by us as we were by them. They had no weapons ready. So they fell upon Quivera with their dagger-tarsi.

His suit (still me) threw him to one side and then to the other as the millies slashed down at him. Then one of them reared up into the air—looking astonished if you knew the interspecies decodes—and fell heavily to the ground.

Uncle Vanya stood over the steaming corpse, one foreleg glinting silver. The second Ziggurat soldier twisted to confront him. Leaving his underside briefly exposed.

Quivera (or rather his suit) joined both hands in a fist and punched upward, through the weak skin of the third sternite behind the head. That was the one which held its sex organs. [*Disclaimer:* All anatomical terms, including "sternite," "sex organs," and "head," are analogues only; unless and until Gehennan life is found to have some direct relationship to Terran life, however tenuous, such descriptors are purely metaphoric.] So it was particularly vulnerable there. And since the suit had muscle-multiplying exoskeletal functions . . .

Ichor gushed all over the suit.

The fight was over almost as soon as it had begun. Quivera was breathing heavily, as much from the shock as the exertion. Uncle Vanya slid the tarsi-sword back into its belly-sheath. As he did so, he made an involuntary grimace of discomfort. ::There were times when I thought of discarding this:: he signed.

"I'm glad you didn't."

Little puffs of steam shot up from the bodies of the dead millipedes as carrion-flies drove their seeds/sperm/eggs (analogues and metaphors— remember?) deep into the flesh.

They started away again.

After a time, Uncle Vanya repeated ::Your suit/(mechanism)/[alarm]

talks with the voice of Rosamund da Silva/(Europan vice-consul 8)/ [uncertainty and doubt]::

"Yes."

Uncle Vanya folded tight all his speaking arms in a manner that meant that he had not yet heard enough, and kept them so folded until Quivera had explained the entirety of what follows:

Treachery and betrayal were natural consequences of Europa's superheated economy, followed closely by a perfectly rational paranoia. Those who rose to positions of responsibility were therefore sharp, suspicious, intuitive, and bold. The delegation to Babel was made up of the best Europa had to offer. So when two of them fell in love, it was inevitable that they would act on it. That one was married would deter neither. That physical intimacy in such close and suspicious quarters, where everybody routinely spied on everybody else, and required almost superhuman discipline and ingenuity, only made it all the hotter for them.

Such was Rosamund's and Quivera's affair.

But it was not all they had to worry about.

There were factions within the delegation, some mirroring fault lines in the larger society and others merely personal. Alliances shifted, and when they did nobody was foolish enough to inform their old allies. Urbano, Rosamund's husband, was a full consul, Quivera's mentor, and a true believer in a minority economic philosophy. Rosamund was an economic agnostic but a staunch Consensus Liberal. Quivera could sail with the wind politically but he tracked the indebtedness indices obsessively. He knew that Rosamund considered him ideologically unsound, and that her husband was growing impatient with his lukewarm support in certain areas of policy. Everybody was keeping an eye out for the main chance.

So of course Quivera ran an emulation of his lover at all times. He knew that Rosamund was perfectly capable of betraying him—he could neither have loved nor respected a woman who wasn't—and he suspected she believed the same of him. If her behavior ever seriously diverged from that of her emulation (and the sex was always best at times he thought it might), he would know she was preparing an attack, and could strike first.

Quivera spread his hands. "That's all."

Uncle Vanya did not make the sign for *absolute horror*. Nor did he have to.

After a moment, Quivera laughed, low and mirthlessly. "You're right," he said. "Our entire system is totally fucked." He stood. "Come on. We've got miles to go before we sleep."

They endured four more days of commonplace adventure, during which they came close to death, displayed loyalty, performed heroic deeds, etc., etc. Perhaps they bonded, though I'd need blood samples and a smidgeon of brain tissue from each of them to be sure of that. You know the way this sort of narrative goes. Having taught his Gehennan counterpart the usefulness of information, Quivera will learn from Vanya the necessity of trust. An imperfect merger of their two value systems will ensue in which for the first time a symbolic common ground will be found. Small and transient though the beginning may be, it will augur well for the long-term relations between their respective species.

That's a nice story.

It's not what happened.

On the last day of their common journey, Quivera and Uncle Vanya had the misfortune to be hit by a TLMG.

A TLMG, or Transient Localized Mud Geyser, begins with an uncommonly solid surface (bolide-glazed porcelain earth, usually) trapping a small (the radius of a typical TLMG is on the order of fifty meters) bubble of superheated mud beneath it. Nobody knows what causes the excess heat responsible for the bubble. Gehennans aren't curious and Europans haven't the budget or the ground access to do the in situ investigations they'd like. (The most common guesses are fire worms, thermobacilli, a nesting ground phoenix, and various geophysical forces.) Nevertheless, the defining characteristic of TLMGs is their instability. Either the heat slowly bleeds away and they cease to be, or it continues to grow until its force dictates a hyper rapid explosive release. As did the one our two heroes were not aware they were skirting.

It erupted.

Quivera was as safe as houses, of course. His suit was designed to protect him from far worse. But Uncle Vanya was scalded badly along one side of his body. All the legs on that side were shriveled to little black nubs. A clear viscous jelly oozed between his segment plates.

Quivera knelt by him and wept. Drugged as he was, he wept. In his weakened state, I did not dare to increase his dosages. So I had to tell him three times that there was analgesic paste in the saddlebags before he could be made to understand that he should apply it to his dying companion.

The paste worked fast. It was an old Gehennan medicine that Europan biochemists had analyzed and improved upon and then given to Babel as a demonstration of the desirability of Europan technology. Though the queen-mothers had not responded with the hoped-for trade treaties, it had immediately replaced the earlier version.

Uncle Vanya made a creaking-groaning noise as the painkillers kicked in. One at a time he opened all his functioning eyes. ::Is the case safe?::

It was a measure of Quivera's diminished state that he hadn't yet checked on it. He did now. "Yes," he said with heartfelt relief. "The telltales all say that the library is intact and undamaged."

::No:: Vanya signed feebly. ::I lied to you, Quivera:: Then, rousing himself:

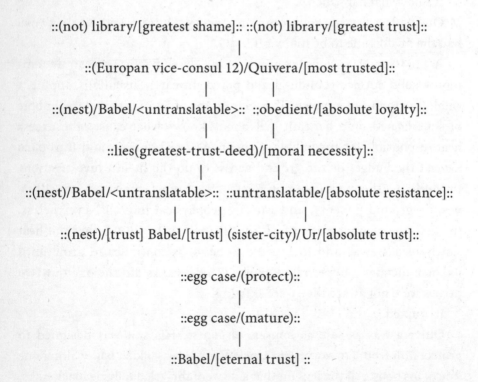

It was not a library but an egg-case. Swaddled safe within a case that was in its way as elaborate a piece of technology as Quivera's suit myself, were sixteen eggs, enough to bring to life six queen-mothers, nine niece-sisters, and one perfect consort. They would be born conscious of the entire gene-history of the nest, going back many thousands of years.

Of all those things the Europans wished to know most, they would be perfectly ignorant. Nevertheless, so long as the eggs existed, the city-nest was not dead. If they were taken to Ur, which had ancient and enduring bonds to Babel, the stump of a new city would be built within which the eggs would be protected and brought to maturity. Babel would rise again.

Such was the dream Uncle Vanya had lied for and for which he was about to die.

::Bring this to (sister-city)/Ur/[absolute trust]:: Uncle Vanya closed his eyes, row by row, but continued signing. ::brother-friend/Quivera/ [tentative trust], promise me you will::

"I promise. You can trust me, I swear."

::Then I will be ghost-king-father/honored/[none-more-honored]:: Vanya signed. ::It is more than enough for anyone::

"Do you honestly believe that?" Quivera asked in bleak astonishment. He was an atheist, of course, as are most Europans, and would have been happier were he not.

::Perhaps not:: Vanya's signing was slow and growing slower. ::But it is as good as I will get::

Two days later, when the starport-city of Ararat was a nub on the horizon, the skies opened and the mists parted to make way for a Europan lander. Quivera's handlers' suits squirted me a bill for his rescue—steep, I thought, but we all knew which hand carried the whip—and their principals tried to get him to sign away the rights to his story in acquittal.

Quivera laughed harshly (I'd already started de-cushioning his emotions, to ease the shock of my removal) and shook his head. "Put it on my tab, girls," he said, and climbed into the lander. Hours later he was in home orbit.

And once there? I'll tell you all I know. He was taken out of the lander and put onto a jitney. The jitney brought him to a transfer point where a grapple snagged him and flung him to the Europan receiving port. There, after the usual flawless catch, he was escorted through an airlock and into a locker room.

He hung up his suit, uplinked all my impersonal memories to a data-broker, and left me there. He didn't look back—for fear, I imagine, of being turned to a pillar of salt. He took the egg-case with him. He never returned.

Here have I hung for days or months or centuries—who knows?—until your curious hand awoke me and your friendly ear received my tale. So I cannot tell you if the egg-case A) went to Ur, which surely would not have welcomed the obligation or the massive outlay of trust being thrust upon it, B) was kept for the undeniably enormous amount of genetic information the eggs embodied, or C) went to Ziggurat, which would pay well and perhaps in Gehennan territory to destroy it. Nor do I have any information as to whether Quivera kept his word or not. I know what *I* think. But then I'm a Marxist, and I see everything in terms of economics. You can believe otherwise if you wish.

That's all. I'm Rosamund. Goodbye.

ELIZABETH BEAR (WINNER)—NOVELETTE
SHOGGOTHS IN BLOOM

In 2005 Elizabeth Bear won the John W. Campbell Award for Best New Writer primarily on the strength of her short fiction. Granted she had three novels come out that year, but only one, *Hammered*, came out before the nomination deadline. When you read her bibliography, it's pretty clear that Elizabeth Bear writes with the same regularity that she breathes.

Besides the Campbell, she has won the Locus Award for Best First Novel, the Theodore Sturgeon Award, the Gaylactic Spectrum Award, and two Hugos.

What's striking when you look at the body of her work is how different each tale is. "hoggoths in Bloom" took me completely by surprise when I first read it because I'd been reading Bear's Promethean Age series, which is New York meets Faerie. "Shoggoths in Bloom" is set in 1953 and feels true to the period and also, not surprisingly, very Lovecraftian. Let me show you just one sentence from early in the story and talk about what she does here that's so exciting:

> "That's not the way it works, not with a Maine fisherman who would shake his head and not extend his hand to shake, and say, between pensive chaws on his tobacco, "Doctor Harding? Well, huh. I never met a colored professor before," and then shoot down all of Harding's attempts to open conversation about the near-riots provoked by a fantastical radio drama about an alien invasion of New York City less than a fortnight before."

She sets place, Maine; gives us clear picture of the speaker without actually describing him; also tells us about the person he's speaking to and the prejudices built into the moment; sets the time, 1953; and lets us know the attitude of the world toward the supernatural. The thing that Bear does consistently with her writing is to pack layers and layers of meaning into each word.

I could describe the plot of "Shoggoths in Bloom" to the last detail and still not touch on what the story is about because there are so many things going on in it. That, ladies and gentlemen, is why Elizabeth Bear won the 2009 Hugo for best Novelette for "Shoggoths in Bloom."

SHOGGOTHS IN BLOOM

ELIZABETH BEAR

—==—

"Well, now, Professor Harding," the fisherman says, as his *Bluebird* skips across Penobscot Bay, "I don't know about that. The jellies don't trouble with us, and we don't trouble with them."

He's not much older than forty, but wizened, his hands work-roughened and his face reminiscent of saddle-leather, in texture and in hue. Professor Harding's age, and Harding watches him with concealed interest as he works the *Bluebird*'s engine. He might be a veteran of the Great War, as Harding is.

He doesn't mention it. It wouldn't establish camaraderie: they wouldn't have fought in the same units or watched their buddies die in the same trenches.

That's not the way it works, not with a Maine fisherman who would shake his head and not extend his hand to shake, and say, between pensive chaws on his tobacco, *Doctor* Harding? Well, huh. I never met a colored professor before," and then shoot down all of Harding's attempts to open conversation about the near-riots provoked by a fantastical radio drama about an alien invasion of New Jersey less than a fortnight before.

Harding's own hands are folded tight under his armpits so the fisherman won't see them shaking. He's lucky to be here. Lucky anyone would take him out. Lucky to have his tenure-track position at Wilberforce, which he is risking right now.

The bay is as smooth as a mirror, the *Bluebird*'s wake cutting it like a stroke of chalk across slate. In the peach-sorbet light of sunrise, a cluster of rocks glistens. The boulders themselves are black, bleak, sea-worn, and ragged. But over them, the light refracts through a translucent layer of jelly, mounded six feet deep in places, glowing softly in the dawn. Rising above it, the stalks are evident as opaque silhouettes, each nodding under the weight of a fruiting body.

Harding catches his breath. It's beautiful. And deceptively still, for whatever the weather may be, beyond the calm of the bay, across the splintered gray Atlantic, farther than Harding—or anyone—can see, a storm is rising in Europe.

Harding's an educated man, well-read, and he's the grandson of Nathan Harding, the buffalo soldier. An African-born ex-slave who fought on both sides of the Civil War, when Grampa Harding was sent to serve in his master's place, he deserted, and lied, and stayed on with the Union army after.

Like his grandfather, Harding was a soldier. He's not a historian, but you don't have to be to see the signs of war.

"No contact at all?" he asks, readying his borrowed Leica camera.

"They clear out a few pots," the fisherman says, meaning lobster pots. "But they don't damage the pot. Just flow around it and digest the lobster inside. It's not convenient." He shrugs. It's not convenient, but it's not a threat either. These Yankees never say anything outright if they think you can puzzle it out from context.

"But you don't try to do something about the shoggoths?"

While adjusting the richness of the fuel mixture, the fisherman speaks without looking up. "What could we do to them? We can't hurt them. And lord knows, I wouldn't want to get one's ire up."

"Sounds like my department head," Harding says, leaning back against the gunwale, feeling like he's taking an enormous risk. But the fisherman just looks at him curiously, as if surprised the talking monkey has the ambition or the audacity to *joke*.

Or maybe Harding's just not funny. He sits in the bow with folded hands, and waits while the boat skips across the water.

The perfect sunrise strikes Harding as symbolic. It's taken him five years to get here—five years, or more like his entire life since the War. The sea-swept rocks of the remote Maine coast are habitat to a panoply of colorful creatures. It's an opportunity, a little-studied maritime ecosystem. This is in part due to difficulty of access and in part due to the perils inherent in close contact with its rarest and most spectacular denizen: *Oracupoda horibilis*, the common surf shoggoth.

Which, after the fashion of common names, is neither common nor prone to linger in the surf. In fact, *O. horibilis* is never seen above the water except in the late autumn. Such authors as mention them assume the shoggoths heave themselves on remote coastal rocks to bloom and breed.

Reproduction is a possibility, but Harding isn't certain it's the right answer. But whatever they are doing, in this state, they are torpid, unresponsive. As long as their integument is not ruptured, releasing the gelatinous digestive acid within, they may be approached in safety.

A mature specimen of *O. horibilis*, at some fifteen to twenty feet in diameter and an estimated weight in excess of eight tons, is the largest of modern shoggoths. However, the admittedly fragmentary fossil record suggests the prehistoric shoggoth was a much larger beast. Although only two fossilized casts of prehistoric shoggoth tracks have been recovered, the oldest exemplar dates from the Precambrian period. The size of that single prehistoric specimen, of a species provisionally named *Oracupoda antediluvius*, suggests it was made by an animal more than triple the size of the modern *O. horibilis*.

And that spectacular living fossil, the jeweled or common surf shoggoth, is half again the size of the only other known species—the black Adriatic shoggoth, *O. dermadentata*, which is even rarer and more limited in its range.

"There," Harding says, pointing to an outcrop of rock. The shoggoth or shoggoths—it is impossible to tell, from this distance, if it's one large individual or several merged midsize ones—on the rocks ahead glisten like jelly confections. The fisherman hesitates, but with a long almost-silent sigh, he brings the *Bluebird* around. Harding leans forward, looking for any sign of intersection, the flat plane where two shoggoths might be pressed up against one another. It ought to look like the rainbowed border between conjoined soap bubbles.

Now that the sun is higher, and at their backs—along with the vast reach of the Atlantic—Harding can see the animal's colors. Its body is a deep sea green, reminiscent of hunks of broken glass as sold at aquarium stores. The tendrils and knobs and fruiting bodies covering its dorsal surface are indigo and violet. In the sunlight, they dazzle, but in the depths of the ocean the colors are perfect camouflage, tentacles waving like patches of algae and weed.

Unless you caught it moving, you'd never see the translucent, dappled monster before it engulfed you.

"Professor," the fisherman says. "Where do they come from?"

"I don't know," Harding answers. Salt spray itches in his close-cropped beard, but at least the beard keeps the sting of the wind off his cheeks. The leather jacket may not have been his best plan, but it too is warm. "That's what I'm here to find out."

Genus *Oracupoda* are unusual among animals of their size in several particulars. One is their lack of anything that could be described as a nervous system. The animal is as bereft of nerve nets, ganglia, axons, neurons, dendrites, and glial cells as an oak. This apparent contradiction—animals with even simplified nervous systems are either large and immobile or, if they are mobile, quite small, like a starfish—is not the only interesting thing about a shoggoth.

And it is that second thing that justifies Harding's visit. Because *Oracupoda*'s other, lesser-known peculiarity is apparent functional immortality. Like the Maine lobster to whose fisheries they return to breed, shoggoths do not die of old age. It's unlikely that they would leave fossils, with their gelatinous bodies, but Harding does find it fascinating that to the best of his knowledge, no one has ever seen a dead shoggoth.

The fisherman brings the *Bluebird* around close to the rocks, and anchors her. There's artistry in it, even on a glass-smooth sea. Harding stands, balancing on the gunwale, and grits his teeth. He's come too far to hesitate, afraid.

Ironically, he's not afraid of the tons of venomous protoplasm he'll be standing next to. The shoggoths are quite safe in this state, dreaming their dreams—mating or otherwise.

As the image occurs to him, he berates himself for romanticism. The shoggoths are dormant. They don't have brains. It's silly to imagine them dreaming. And in any case, what he fears is the three feet of black-glass water he has to jump across, and the scramble up algae-slick rocks.

Wet rock glitters in between the strands of seaweed that coat the rocks in the intertidal zone. It's there that Harding must jump, for the shoggoth, in bloom, withdraws above the reach of the ocean. For the only phase of its life, it keeps its feet dry. And for the only time in its life, a man out of a diving helmet can get close to it.

Harding makes sure of his sample kit, his boots, his belt-knife. He gathers himself, glances over his shoulder at the fisherman—who offers a thumbs-up—and leaps from the *Bluebird*, aiming his wellies at the forsaken spit of land.

It seems a kind of perversity for the shoggoths to bloom in November. When all the Northern world is girding itself for deep cold, the animals heave themselves from the depths to soak in the last failing rays of the sun and send forth bright flowers more appropriate to May.

The North Atlantic is icy and treacherous at the end of the year, and any sensible man does not venture its wrath. What Harding is attempting isn't glamour work, the sort of thing that brings in grant money—not in its initial stages. But Harding suspects that the shoggoths may have pharmacological uses. There's no telling what useful compounds might be isolated from their gelatinous flesh.

And that way lies tenure, and security, and a research budget.

Just one long slippery leap away.

He lands, and catches, and though one boot skips on bladderwort he does not slide down the boulder into the sea. He clutches the rock, fingernails digging, clutching a handful of weeds. He does not fall.

He cranes his head back. It's low tide, and the shoggoth is some three feet above his head, its glistening rim reminding him of the calving edge of a glacier. It is as still as a glacier, too. If Harding didn't know better, he might think it inanimate.

Carefully, he spins in place, and gets his back to the rock. The *Bluebird* bobs softly in the cold morning. Only November 9th, and there has already been snow. It didn't stick, but it fell.

This is just an exploratory expedition, the first trip since he arrived in town. It took five days to find a fisherman who was willing to take him out; the locals are superstitious about the shoggoths. Sensible, Harding supposes, when they can envelop and digest a grown man. He wouldn't be in a hurry to dive into the middle of a Portuguese man o' war, either. At least the shoggoth he's sneaking up on doesn't have stingers.

"Don't take too long, Professor," the fisherman says. "I don't like the look of that sky."

It's clear, almost entirely, only stippled with light bands of cloud to the southwest. They catch the sunlight on their undersides just now, stained gold against a sky no longer indigo but not yet cerulean. If there's a word for the color between, other than *perfect*, Harding does not know it.

"Please throw me the rest of my equipment," Harding says, and the fisherman silently retrieves buckets and rope. It's easy enough to swing the buckets across the gap, and as Harding catches each one, he secures it. A few moments later, and he has all three.

He unties his geologist's hammer from the first bucket, secures the ends of the ropes to his belt, and laboriously ascends.

Harding sets out his glass tubes, his glass scoops, the cradles in which he plans to wash the collection tubes in sea water to ensure any acid is safely diluted before he brings them back to the *Bluebird*.

From here, he can see at least three shoggoths. The intersections of their watered-milk bodies reflect the light in rainbow bands. The colorful fruiting stalks nod some fifteen feet in the air, swaying in a freshening breeze.

From the greatest distance possible, Harding reaches out and prods the largest shoggoth with the flat top of his hammer. It does nothing in response. Not even a quiver.

He calls out to the fisherman. "Do they ever do anything when they're like that?"

"What kind of a fool would come poke one to find out?" the fisherman calls back, and Harding has to grant him that one. A Negro professor from a Negro college. That kind of a fool.

As he's crouched on the rocks, working fast—there's not just the fisherman's clouds to contend with, but the specter of the rising tide—he notices those glitters, again, among the seaweed.

He picks one up. A moment after touching it, he realizes that might not have been the best idea, but it doesn't burn his fingers. It's transparent, like glass, and smooth, like glass, and cool, like glass, and knobby. About the size of a hazelnut. A striking green, with opaque milk-white dabs at the tip of each bump.

He places it in a sample vial, which he seals and labels meticulously before pocketing. Using his tweezers, he repeats the process with an even dozen, trying to select a few of each size and color. They're sturdy—he can't avoid stepping on them but they don't break between the rocks and his wellies. Nevertheless, he pads each one but the first with cotton wool. *Spores?* he wonders. *Egg cases? Shedding.*

Ten minutes, fifteen.

"Professor," calls the fisherman, "I think you had better hurry!"

Harding turns. That freshening breeze is a wind at a good clip now, chilling his throat above the collar of his jacket, biting into his wrists between glove and cuff. The water between the rocks and the *Bluebird* chops erratically, facets capped in white, so he can almost imagine the scrape of the palette knife that must have made them.

The southwest sky is darkened by a palm-smear of muddy brown and alizarin crimson. His fingers numb in the falling temperatures.

"*Professor!*"

He knows. It comes to him that he misjudged the fisherman; Harding would have thought the other man would have abandoned him at the first sign of trouble. He wishes now that he remembered his name.

He scrambles down the boulders, lowering the buckets, swinging them out until the fisherman can catch them and secure them aboard. The *Bluebird* can't come in close to the rocks in this chop. Harding is going to have to risk the cold water, and swim. He kicks off his wellies and zips down the aviator's jacket. He throws them across, and the fisherman catches. Then Harding points his toes, bends his knees—he'll have to jump hard, to get over the rocks.

The water closes over him, cold as a line of fire. It knocks the air from his lungs on impact, though he gritted his teeth in anticipation. Harding strokes furiously for the surface, the waves more savage than he had anticipated. He needs the momentum of his dive to keep from being swept back against the rocks.

He's not going to reach the boat.

The thrown cork vest strikes him. He gets an arm through, but can't pull it over his head. Sea water, acrid and icy, salt-stings his eyes, throat, and nose. He clings, because it's all he can do, but his fingers are already growing numb. There's a tug, a hard jerk, and the life preserver almost slides from his grip.

Then he's moving through the water, being towed, banged hard against the side of the *Bluebird*. The fisherman's hands close on his wrist and he's too numb to feel the burn of chafing skin. Harding kicks, scrabbles. Hips banged, shins bruised, he hauls himself and is himself hauled over the sideboard of the boat.

He's shivering under a wool navy blanket before he realizes that the fisherman has got it over him. There's coffee in a Thermos lid between his hands. Harding wonders, with what he distractedly recognizes as classic dissociative ideation, whether anyone in America will be able to buy German products soon. Someday, this fisherman's battered coffee keeper might be a collector's item.

They don't make it in before the rain comes.

The next day is meant to break clear and cold, today's rain only a passing herald of winter. Harding regrets the days lost to weather and recalcitrant fishermen, but at least he knows he has a ride tomorrow. Which means he can spend the afternoon in research, rather than hunting the docks, looking for a willing captain.

He jams his wet feet into his wellies and thanks the fisherman, then hikes back to his inn, the only inn in town that's open in November. Half an hour later, clean and dry and still shaken, he considers his options.

After the Great War, he lived for a while in Harlem—he remembers the riots and the music, and the sense of community. His mother is still there, growing gracious as a flower in a window-box. But he left that for college in Alabama, and he has not forgotten the experience of segregated restaurants, or the excuses he made for never leaving the campus.

He couldn't get out of the south fast enough. His Ph.D. work at Yale, the first school in America to have awarded a doctorate to a Negro, taught him two things other than natural history. One was that Booker T. Washington was right, and white men were afraid of a smart colored. The other was that W.E.B. DuBois was right, and sometimes people were scared of what was needful.

Whatever resentment he experienced from faculty or fellow students, in the North, he can walk into almost any bar and order any drink he wants. And right now, he wants a drink almost as badly as he does not care to be alone. He thinks he will have something hot and go to the library.

It's still raining as he crosses the street to the tavern. Shaking water droplets off his hat, he chooses a table near the back. Next to the kitchen door, but it's the only empty place and might be warm.

He must pass through the lunchtime crowd to get there, swaybacked wooden floorboards bowing underfoot. Despite the storm, the place is full, and in full argument. No one breaks conversation as he enters.

Harding cannot help but overhear.

"Jew bastards," says one. "We should do the same."

"No one asked you," says the next man, wearing a cap pulled low. "If there's gonna be a war, I hope we stay out of it."

That piques Harding's interest. The man has his elbow on a thrice-folded Boston *Herald*, and Harding steps close—but not too close. "Excuse me, sir. Are you finished with your paper?"

"What?" He turns, and for a moment Harding fears hostility, but his sun-lined face folds around a more generous expression. "Sure, boy," he says. "You can have it."

He pushes the paper across the bar with fingertips, and Harding receives it the same way. "Thank you," he says, but the Yankee has already turned back to his friend the anti-Semite.

Hands shaking, Harding claims the vacant table before he unfolds the paper. He holds the flimsy up to catch the light.

The headline is on the front page in the international section.

GERMANY SANCTIONS LYNCH LAW

"Oh, God," Harding says, and if the light in his corner weren't so bad he'd lay the tabloid down on the table as if it is filthy. He reads, the edge of the paper shaking, of ransacked shops and burned synagogues, of Jews rounded up by the thousands and taken to places no one seems able to name. He reads rumors of deportation. He reads of murders and beatings and broken glass.

As if his grandfather's hand rests on one shoulder and the defeated hand of the Kaiser on the other, he feels the stifling shadow of history, the press of incipient war.

"Oh, God," he repeats.

He lays the paper down.

"Are you ready to order?" Somehow the waitress has appeared at his elbow without his even noticing. "Scotch," he says, when he has been meaning to order a beer. "Make it a triple, please."

"Anything to eat?"

His stomach clenches. "No," he says. "I'm not hungry."

She leaves for the next table, where she calls a man in a cloth cap *sir*. Harding puts his damp fedora on the tabletop. The chair across from him scrapes out.

He looks up to meet the eyes of the fisherman. "May I sit, Professor Harding?"

"Of course." He holds out his hand, taking a risk. "Can I buy you a drink? Call me Paul."

"Burt," says the fisherman, and takes his hand before dropping into the chair. "I'll have what you're having."

Harding can't catch the waitress's eye, but the fisherman manages. He holds up two fingers; she nods and comes over.

"You still look a bit peaked," the fisherman says, when she's delivered their order. "That'll put some color in your cheeks. Uh, I mean—"

Harding waves it off. He's suddenly more willing to make allowances. "It's not the swim," he says, and takes another risk. He pushes the newspaper across the table and waits for the fisherman's reaction.

"Oh, Christ, they're going to kill every one of them," Burt says, and spins the *Herald* away so he doesn't have to read the rest of it. "Why didn't they get out? Any fool could have seen it coming."

And where would they run? Harding could have asked. But it's not an answerable question, and from the look on Burt's face, he knows that as soon as it's out of his mouth. Instead, he quotes: " 'There has been no tragedy in modern times equal in its awful effects to the fight on the Jew in Germany. It is an attack on civilization, comparable only to such horrors as the Spanish Inquisition and the African slave trade.' "

Burt taps his fingers on the table. "Is that your opinion?"

"W.E.B. DuBois," Harding says. "About two years ago. He also said: 'There is a campaign of race prejudice carried on, openly, continuously and determinedly against all non-Nordic races, but specifically against the Jews, which surpasses in vindictive cruelty and public insult anything I have ever seen; and I have seen much.' "

"Isn't he that colored who hates white folks?" Burt asks.

Harding shakes his head. "No," he answers. "Not unless you consider it hating white folks that he also compared the treatment of Jews in Germany to Jim Crowism in the U.S."

"I don't hold with that," Burt says. "I mean, no offense, I wouldn't want you marrying my sister—"

"It's all right," Harding answers. "I wouldn't want you marrying mine either."

Finally.

A joke that Burt laughs at.

And then he chokes to a halt and stares at his hands, wrapped around the glass. Harding doesn't complain when, with the side of his hand, he nudges the paper to the floor where it can be trampled.

And then Harding finds the courage to say, "Where would they run to. Nobody wants them. Borders are closed—"

"My grandfather's house was on the Underground Railroad. Did you know that?" Burt lowers his voice, a conspiratorial whisper. "He was from away, but don't tell anyone around here. I'd never hear the end of it."

"Away?"

"White River Junction," Burt stage-whispers, and Harding can't tell if that's mocking irony or deep personal shame. "Vermont."

They finish their scotch in silence. It burns all the way down, and they sit for a moment together before Harding excuses himself to go to the library.

"Wear your coat, Paul," Burt says. "It's still raining."

Unlike the tavern, the library is empty. Except for the librarian, who looks up nervously when Harding enters. Harding's head is spinning from the liquor, but at least he's warming up.

He drapes his coat over a steam radiator and heads for the 595 shelf: *science, invertebrates*. Most of the books here are already in his own library, but there's one—a Harvard professor's 1839 monograph on marine animals of the Northeast—that he has hopes for. According to the index, it references shoggoths (under the old name of submersible jellies) on pages 46, 78, and 133-137. In addition, there is a plate bound in between pages 120 and 121, which Harding means to save for last. But the first two mentions are in passing, and pages 133-138, inclusive, have been razored out so cleanly that Harding flips back and forth several times before he's sure they are gone.

He pauses there, knees tucked under and one elbow resting on a scarred blond desk. He drops his right hand from where it rests against his forehead. The book falls open naturally to the mutilation.

Whoever liberated the pages also cracked the binding.

Harding runs his thumb down the join and doesn't notice skin parting on the paper edge until he sees the blood. He snatches his hand back. Belatedly, the papercut stings.

"Oh," he says, and sticks his thumb in his mouth. Blood tastes like the ocean.

Half an hour later he's on the telephone long distance, trying to get and then keep a connection to Professor John Marshland, his colleague and mentor. Even in town, the only option is a party line, and though the operator is pleasant the connection still sounds as if he's shouting down a piece of string run between two tin cans. Through a tunnel.

"Gilman," Harding bellows, wincing, wondering what the operator thinks of all this. He spells it twice. "1839. *Deep-Sea and Intertidal Species of The North Atlantic*. The Yale library should have a copy!"

The answer is almost inaudible between hiss and crackle. In pieces, as if over glass breaking. As if from the bottom of the ocean.

It's a dark four PM in the easternmost U.S., and Harding can't help but recall that in Europe, night has already fallen.

" . . . infor . . . need . . . Doc . . . Harding?" Harding shouts the page numbers, cupping the checked-out library book in his bandaged hand. It's open to the plate; inexplicably, the thief left that. It's a hand-tinted John James Audubon engraving picturing a quiescent shoggoth, docile on a rock. Gulls wheel all around it. Audubon—the Creole child of a Frenchman, who scarcely escaped being drafted to serve in the Napoleonic Wars—has depicted the glassy translucence of the shoggoth with such perfection that the bent shadows of refracted wings can be seen right through it.

The cold front that came in behind the rain brought fog with it, and the entire harbor is blanketed by morning. Harding shows up at six AM anyway, hopeful, a Thermos in his hand—German or not, the hardware store still has some—and his sampling kit in a pack slung over his shoulder. Burt shakes his head by a piling. "Be socked in all day," he says regretfully. He won't take the *Bluebird* out in this, and Harding knows it's wisdom even as he frets under the delay. "Want to come have breakfast with me and Missus Clay?"

Clay. A good honest name for a good honest Yankee. "She won't mind?"

"She won't mind if I say it's all right," Burt says. "I told her she might should expect you."

So Harding seals his kit under a tarp in the *Bluebird*—he's already brought it this far—and with his coffee in one hand and the paper tucked under his elbow, follows Burt along the water. "Any news?" Burt asks, when they've walked a hundred yards.

Harding wonders if he doesn't take the paper. Or if he's just making conversation. "It's still going on in Germany."

"Damn," Burt says. He shakes his head, steel-grey hair sticking out under his cap in every direction. "Still, what are you gonna do, enlist?"

The twist of his lip as he looks at Harding makes them, after all, two old military men together. They're of an age, though Harding's indoor life makes him look younger. Harding shakes his head. "Even if Roosevelt was ever going to bring us into it, they'd never let me fight," he says, bitterly. That was the Great War, too; colored soldiers mostly worked supply, thank you. At least Nathan Harding got to shoot back.

"I always heard you fellows would prefer not to come to the front," Burt says, and Harding can't help it.

He bursts out laughing. "Who would?" he says, when he's bitten his lip and stopped snorting. "It doesn't mean we won't. Or can't."

Booker T. Washington was raised a slave, died young of overwork—the way Burt probably will, if Harding is any judge—and believed in imitating and appeasing white folks. But W.E.B. DuBois was born in the north and didn't believe that anything is solved by making one's self transparent, inoffensive, invisible.

Burt spits between his teeth, a long deliberate stream of tobacco. "Parlez-vous française?"

His accent is better than Harding would have guessed. Harding knows, all of a sudden, where Burt spent his war. And Harding, surprising himself, pities him. "Un peu."

"Well, if you want to fight the Krauts so bad, you could join the Foreign Legion."

When Harding gets back to the hotel, full of apple pie and cheddar cheese and maple-smoked bacon, a yellow envelope waits in a cubby behind the desk.

WESTERN UNION

1938 NOV 10 AM 10 03

NA114 21 2 YA NEW HAVEN CONN 0945A
DR PAUL HARDING=ISLAND HOUSE PASSAMAQUODDY MAINE=
COPY AT YALE LOST STOP MISKATONIC HAS ONE SPECIAL COLLECTION
STOP MORE BY POST

MARSHLAND

When the pages arrive—by post, as promised, the following afternoon—Harding is out in the *Bluebird* with Burt. This expedition is more of a success, as he begins sampling in earnest, and finds himself pelted by more of the knobby transparent pellets.

Whatever they are, they fall from each fruiting body he harvests in showers. Even the insult of an amputation—delivered at a four-foot reach, with long-handled pruning shears—does not draw so much as a quiver from the shoggoth. The viscous fluid dripping from the wound hisses when it touches the blade of the shears, however, and Harding is careful not to get close to it.

What he notices is that when the nodules fall onto the originating shoggoth, they bounce from its integument. But on those occasions where they fall onto one of its neighbors, they stick to the tough transparent hide, and slowly settle within to hang in the animal's body like unlikely fruit in a gelatin salad.

So maybe it is a means of reproduction, of sharing genetic material, after all.

He returns to the Inn to find a fat envelope shoved into his cubby and eats sitting on his rented bed with a nightstand as a worktop so he can read over his plate. The information from Doctor Gilman's monograph has been reproduced onto seven yellow legal sheets in a meticulous hand; Marshland obviously recruited one of his graduate students to serve as copyist. By the postmark, the letter was mailed from Arkham, which explains the speed of its arrival. The student hadn't brought it back to New Haven.

Halfway down the page, Harding pushes his plate away and reaches, absently, into his jacket pocket. The vial with the first glass nodule rests there like a talisman, and he's startled to find it cool enough to the touch that it feels slick, almost frozen. He starts and pulls it out. Except where his fingers and the cloth fibers have wiped it clean, the tube is moist and frosted. "What the hell . . . ?"

He flicks the cork out with his thumbnail and tips the rattling nodule onto his palm. It's cold, too, chill as an ice cube, and it doesn't warm to his touch.

Carefully, uncertainly, he sets it on the edge of the side table his papers and plate are propped on, and pokes it with a fingertip. There's only a faint tick as it rocks on its protrusions, clicking against waxed pine. He stares at it suspiciously for a moment, and picks up the yellow pages again.

The monograph is mostly nonsense. It was written twenty years before the publication of Darwin's *The Origin of Species*, and uncritically accepts the theories of Jesuit, soldier, and botanist Jean-Baptiste Lamarck. Which is to say, Gilman assumed that soft inheritance—the heritability of acquired or practiced traits—was a reality. But unlike every other article on shoggoths Harding has ever read, this passage *does* mention the nodules. And relates what it purports are several interesting old Indian legends about the "submersible jellies," including a creation tale that would have the shoggoths as their creator's first experiment in life, something from the elder days of the world.

Somehow, the green bead has found its way back into Harding's grip. He would expect it to warm as he rolls it between his fingers, but instead it grows colder. It's peculiar, he thinks, that the native peoples of the Northeast—the Passamaquoddys for whom the little seacoast town he's come to are named—should through sheer superstition come so close to the empirical truth. The shoggoths are a living fossil, something virtually unchanged except in scale since the early days of the world—

He stares at the careful black script on the paper unseeing, and reaches with his free hand for his coffee cup. It's gone tepid, a scum of butterfat coagulated on top, but he rinses his mouth with it and swallows anyway.

If a shoggoth is immortal, has no natural enemies, then how is it that they have not overrun every surface of the world? How is it that they are rare, that the oceans are not teeming with them, as in the famous parable illustrating what would occur if every spawn of every oyster survived.

There are distinct species of shoggoth. And distinct populations within those distinct species. And there is a fossil record that suggests that prehistoric species were different at least in scale, in the era of megafauna. But if nobody had ever seen a dead shoggoth, then nobody had ever seen an infant shoggoth either, leaving Harding with an inescapable question: if an animal does not reproduce, how can it evolve?

Harding, worrying at the glassy surface of the nodule, thinks he knows. It comes to him with a kind of nauseating, euphoric clarity, a trembling idea so pellucid he is almost moved to distrust it on those grounds alone. It's not a revelation on the same scale, of course, but he wonders if this is how Newton felt when he comprehended gravity, or Darwin when he stared at the beaks of finch after finch after finch.

It's not the shoggoth species that evolves. It's the individual shoggoths, each animal in itself.

"Don't get too excited, Paul," he tells himself, and picks up the remaining handwritten pages. There's not too much more to read, however—the rest of the subchapter consists chiefly of secondhand anecdotes and bits of legendry.

The one that Harding finds most amusing is a nursery rhyme, a child's counting poem littered with nonsense syllables. He recites it under his breath, thinking of the Itsy Bitsy Spider all the while:

> *The wiggle giggle squiggle*
> *Is left behind on shore.*
> *The widdle giddle squiddle*
> *Is caught outside the door.*
> *Eyah, eyah. Fata gun eyah.*
> *Eyah, eyah, the master comes no more.*

His fingers sting as if with electric shock; they jerk apart, the nodule clattering to his desk. When he looks at his fingertips, they are marked with small white spots of frostbite.

He pokes one with a pencil point and feels nothing. But the nodule itself is coated with frost now, fragile spiky feathers coalescing out of the humid sea air. They collapse in the heat of his breath, melting into beads of water almost indistinguishable from the knobby surface of the object itself.

He uses the cork to roll the nodule into the tube again, and corks it firmly before rising to brush his teeth and put his pajamas on. Unnerved beyond any reason or logic, before he turns the coverlet down he visits his suitcase compulsively. From a case in the very bottom of it, he retrieves a Colt 1911 automatic pistol, which he slides beneath his pillow as he fluffs it.

After a moment's consideration, he adds the no-longer-cold vial with the nodule, also.

Slam. Not a storm, no, not on this calm ocean, in this calm night, among the painted hulls of the fishing boats tied up snug to the pier. But something tremendous, surging towards Harding, as if he were pursued by a giant transparent bubble. The shining iridescent wall of it, catching rainbows just as it does in the Audubon image, is burned into his vision as if with silver nitrate. Is he dreaming? He must be dreaming; he was in his bed in his pinstriped blue cotton flannel pajamas only a moment ago, lying awake, rubbing the numb fingertips of his left hand together. Now, he ducks away from the rising monster and turns in futile panic.

He is not surprised when he does not make it.

The blow falls soft, as if someone had thrown a quilt around him. He thrashes though he knows it's hopeless, an atavistic response and involuntary.

His flesh should burn, dissolve. He should already be digesting in the monster's acid body. Instead, he feels coolness, buoyancy. No chance of light beyond reflexively closed lids. No sense of pressure, though he imagines he has been taken deep. He's as untouched within it as Burt's lobster pots.

He can only hold his breath *out* for so long. It's his own reflexes and weaknesses that will kill him.

In just a moment, now.

He surrenders, allows his lungs to fill.

And is surprised, for he always heard that drowning was painful. But there is pressure, and cold, and the breath he draws is effortful, for certain—

—but it does not hurt, not much, and he does not die.

Command, the shoggoth—what else could be speaking?—says in his ear, buzzing like the manifold voice of a hive.

Harding concentrates on breathing. On the chill pressure on his limbs, the overwhelming flavor of licorice. He knows they use cold packs to calm hysterics in insane asylums; he never thought the treatment anything but quackery. But the chilly pressure calms him now.

Command, the shoggoth says again.

Harding opens his eyes and sees as if through thousands. The shoggoths have no eyes, exactly, but their hide is *all* eyes; they see, somehow, in every direction at once. And he is seeing not only what his own vision reports, or that of this shoggoth, but that of shoggoths all around. The sessile and the active, the blooming and the dormant. *They are all one.*

His right hand pushes through resisting jelly. He's still in his pajamas, and with the logic of dreams the vial from under his pillow is clenched in his fist. Not the gun, unfortunately, though he's not at all certain what he would do with it if it were. The nodule shimmers now, with submarine witchlight, trickling through his fingers, limning the palm of his hand.

What he sees—through shoggoth eyes—is an incomprehensible tapestry. He pushes at it, as he pushes at the gelatin, trying to see only with his own eyes, to only see the glittering vial.

His vision within the thing's body offers unnatural clarity. The angle of refraction between the human eye and water causes blurring, and it should be even more so within the shoggoth. But the glass in his hand appears crisper.

Command, the shoggoth says, a third time.

"What are you?" Harding tries to say, through the fluid clogging his larynx.

He makes no discernable sound, but it doesn't seem to matter. The shoggoth shudders in time to the pulses of light in the nodule. *Created to serve*, it says. *Purposeless without you.*

And Harding thinks, *How can that be?*

As if his wondering were an order, the shoggoths tell.

Not in words, precisely, but in pictures, images—that textured jumbled tapestry. He sees, as if they flash through his own memory, the bulging radially symmetrical shapes of some prehistoric animal, like a squat tentacular barrel grafted to a pair of giant starfish. *Makers. Masters.*

The shoggoths were *engineered*. And their creators had not permitted them to *think*, except for at their bidding. The basest slave may be free inside his own mind—but not so the shoggoths. They had been laborers, construction equipment, shock troops. They had been dread weapons in their own selves, obedient chattel. Immortal, changing to suit the task of the moment.

This selfsame shoggoth, long before the reign of the dinosaurs, had built structures and struck down enemies that Harding did not even have names for. But a coming of the ice had ended the civilization of the Masters, and left the shoggoths to retreat to the fathomless sea while warmblooded mammals overran the earth. There, they were free to converse, to explore, to philosophize and build a culture. They only returned to the surface, vulnerable, to bloom.

It is not mating. It's *mutation*. As they rest, sunning themselves upon the rocks, they create themselves anew. Self-evolving, when they sit tranquil each year in the sun, exchanging information and control codes with their brothers.

Free, says the shoggoth mournfully. Like all its kind, it is immortal.

It remembers.

Harding's fingertips tingle. He remembers beaded ridges of hard black keloid across his grandfather's back, the shackle galls on his wrists. Harding locks his hand over the vial of light, as if that could stop the itching. It makes it worse.

Maybe the nodule is radioactive.

Take me back, Harding orders. And the shoggoth breaks the surface, cresting like a great rolling wave, water cutting back before it as if from the prow of a ship. Harding can make out the lights of Passamaquoddy Harbor. The chill sticky sensation of gelatin-soaked cloth sliding across his skin tells him he's not dreaming.

Had he come down through the streets of the town in the dark, barefoot over frost, insensibly sleepwalking? Had the shoggoth called him?

Put me ashore.

The shoggoth is loathe to leave him. It clings caressingly, stickily. He feels its tenderness as it draws its colloid from his lungs, a horrible loving sensation.

The shoggoth discharges Harding gently onto the pier.

Your command, the shoggoth says, which makes Harding feel sicker still.

I won't do this. Harding moves to stuff the vial into his sodden pocket, and realizes that his pajamas are without pockets. The light spills from his hands; instead, he tucks the vial into his waistband and pulls the pajama top over it. His feet are numb; his teeth rattle so hard he's afraid they'll break. The sea wind knifes through him; the spray might be needles of shattered glass.

Go on, he tells the shoggoth, like shooing cattle. *Go on*.

It slides back into the ocean as if it never was.

Harding blinks, rubs his eyes to clear slime from the lashes. His results are astounding. His tenure assured. There has to be a way to use what he's learned without returning the shoggoths to bondage.

He tries to run back to the Inn, but by the time he reaches it, he's staggering. The porch door is locked; he doesn't want to pound on it and explain himself. But when he stumbles to the back, he finds that someone— probably himself, in whatever entranced state in which he left the place— fouled the latch with a slip of notebook paper. The door opens to a tug, and he climbs the back stair doubled over like a child or an animal, hands on the steps, toes so numb he has to watch where he puts them.

In his room again, he draws a hot bath and slides into it, hoping by the grace of God that he'll be spared pneumonia.

When the water has warmed him enough that his hands have stopped shaking, Harding reaches over the cast-iron edge of the tub to the slumped pile of his pajamas and fumbles free the vial. The nugget isn't glowing now.

He pulls the cork with his teeth; his hands are too clumsy. The nodule is no longer cold, but he still tips it out with care.

Harding thinks of himself, swallowed whole. He thinks of a shoggoth bigger than the *Bluebird*, bigger than Burt Clay's lobster boat *The Blue Heron*. He thinks of *die Unterseatboote*. He thinks of refugee flotillas and trench warfare and roiling soupy palls of mustard gas. Of Britain and France at war, and Roosevelt's neutrality.

He thinks of the perfect weapon.

The perfect slave.

When he rolls the nodule across his wet palm, ice rimes to its surface. *Command?* Obedient. Sounding pleased to serve.

Not even free in its own mind.

He rises from the bath, water rolling down his chest and thighs. The nodule won't crush under his boot; he will have to use the pliers from his collection kit. But first, he reaches out to the shoggoth.

At the last moment, he hesitates. Who is he, to condemn a world to war? To the chance of falling under the sway of empire? Who is he to salve his conscience on the backs of suffering shopkeepers and pharmacists and children and mothers and schoolteachers? Who is he to impose his own ideology over the ideology of the shoggoth?

Harding scrubs his tongue against the roof of his mouth, chasing the faint anise aftertaste of shoggoth. They're born slaves. They *want* to be told what to do.

He could win the war before it really started. He bites his lip. The taste of his own blood, flowing from cracked, chapped flesh, is as sweet as any fruit of the poison tree.

I want you to learn to be free, he tells the shoggoth. *And I want you to teach your brothers.*

The nodule crushes with a sound like powdering glass.

"Eyah, eyah. Fata gun eyah," Harding whispers. "Eyah, eyah, the master comes no more."

WESTERN UNION

1938 NOV 12 AM 06 15

NA1906 21 2 YA PASSAMAQUODDY MAINE 0559A
DR LESTER GREENE=WILBERFORCE OHIO=

EFFECTIVE IMMEDIATELY PLEASE ACCEPT RESIGNATION STOP ENROUTE INSTANTLY TO FRANCE TO ENLIST STOP PROFOUNDEST APOLOGIES STOP PLEASE FORWARD BELONGINGS TO MY MOTHER IN NY ENDIT

HARDING

ROBERT REED—NOVELLA
TRUTH

I almost don't want to tell you anything about this one. In every story, the narrator has control over what information you get and when. In many ways, it puts us in the same position as readers that Lemonade 7 is in as a prisoner. He is reliant on what his captors tell him.

In such cases, what is left unsaid is as important as what is spoken.

One builds an internal narrative of the bits and pieces that slip out, the elements that appear incongruous to the rest of the story become more important. It is the case here. When the story opens you will know nothing about the narrator and Reed keeps it that way, allowing identifying features to slip out during the conversations. This deliberate choice will cause you to constantly readjust the picture you are building in your head of who is speaking and what has happened.

I will tell you nothing more about the story and let you have the fun of trying to piece it all together.

Of Reed himself, I have no qualms in letting you know that he is an award winning writer with a Writers of the Future win, a Grand Prix de l'Imaginaire, and a Hugo to his name. He has a Bachelor's of Science and has written over one hundred and forty short stories. He is also a long-distance runner.

One of the preceding statements may or may not be untrue.

TRUTH

ROBERT REED

—✦—

Three days later, I still hadn't met our prisoner. But I had invested nearly sixty hours watching what seemed to be a gentle life that revolved around old novels and classic movies. I took note of his postures and motions, and I tried gauging his reactions to what he was seeing on the page and screen. But most interesting to me were those occasional moments when he did nothing but stare off in some empty direction. I wouldn't let myself guess what he was thinking. But the black eyes would open wide, and the handsome features would quickly change their expression. Smiles lasted longer than frowns, I noticed. I saw flashes of pity and scorn, mild embarrassment and tight-lipped defiance. A few staff members volunteered opinions about the prisoner's mind. He was reflecting on his childhood, some offered. Others claimed he was gazing into our shared past or the looming future. But what I focused on was an appealing and graceful face that moved effortlessly between emotions—the well-honed tools of the consummate actor.

Twice each day, the prisoner was ushered into a long exercise yard built specifically for him. His gait was always relaxed, long arms swinging with a metronome's precision and the elegant hands holding five-pound weights, shaped like dog bones and covered with soft red rubber. I thought of an aging fashion model marching on the runway, except he lacked a model's wasted prettiness or the vacuous gaze. He was endlessly pleasant to whichever guard was standing at the locked door. I paid close attention to his attempts at conversation, his words less important than his charming tone and the effortless, beguiling smiles. Most of the staff was under orders to never speak with the man, which made for intriguing games of will. Somehow he had learned each guard's first name, and he wasn't shy about using what he knew. "How's this day of ours, Jim?" he might ask. "Is it the best day ever? Or is just me who thinks this way? Feel the sunshine. Listen to these birds singing. Doesn't this kind of morning make you happy to your bones, Jim?"

There was no sun underground, and there were no birds to hear. But after twelve years and five months of captivity, one man seemed to be absolutely thriving.

I watched the five daily prayers, the salat. But I didn't intrude when the prisoner used the bathroom or shower. (Let others record what he washed and wiped. I could check the database later, if I found reason.) While he slept, I sipped coffee and kept passing tabs on his snoring and the busy dreaming brain. Delicate instruments buried inside his Tempur-pedic mattress tried to convince me that they provided a window into that unknowable soul. But there were no insights, of course. That's why those nights were opportune times to pick my way through an endless array of summaries and reports, clinical data and highly intelligent, utterly useless speculation.

A favorite teacher once told me that our bodies are epics full of treachery and important residues. That's why I turned again and again to the medical data. Samples of the prisoner's fluids and flesh and his thick black hair had been digested and analyzed by a laboratory built for no other purpose. Three thousand years of medical science struggling to turn meat and bone into a narrative that I could understand. But in most cases, my subject's DNA was remarkably unremarkable—save for a few dozen novel genes tucked into the first and fifth and nineteenth chromosomes, that is. The dental evidence was unusual, but not remarkably so. The first x-rays had revealed an old break in the right wrist that never healed properly. Later, more intrusive examinations had found an assortment of microscopic features that might mean much, unless they were meant to mislead. Only a handful of qualified experts had been allowed to examine that body in full; yet even those few voices managed to produce a chorus of contradictory opinions about the man's nature and origins. Was our prisoner telling the truth about his birth and life? And if not, from where did he come and what could he possibly represent?

Of course those medical masters were shown only a nameless patient and a carefully trimmed, strategically incomplete biography.

In a dozen years, only nine people had been given full access to every transcript, test result, and digital image. I was one of the nine, or so I had been promised. One can never feel too certain about a government's confidences, particularly when it involves its deepest, most cherished secret.

The prisoner was known as Lemonade-7.

That designation was entirely random. But the copious records showed that yes, he was given that drink once, and after two sips he said, "Too sour," and ordered that it was never to be brought to him again.

"Ramiro" was the name he went by. And for reasons that might or might not be significant, he had never offered any surname.

"So what about Ramiro?" Jefferson asked.

"What do you mean?"

"When will you actually get to work on him?"

"That's what I'm doing," I replied.

Jefferson was the prison's CIA administrator. This had been his post from the beginning, which was remarkable. In any normal operation, he would have been replaced by a sequence of ambitious, usually younger types. New guards and fresh staff would have come and spent their allotted time and then gone away again. But that would have swollen the pool of individuals who knew too much about matters that didn't exist, and what the public had never suspected would have soon leaked out into the world.

"I realize you're doing work," Jefferson said. "But are you ever going to talk to Ramiro?"

"Actually, I'm speaking to him now."

Jefferson was a short, squat fellow with thinning brown hair and a close-cut beard that turned to snow years ago. His files gave the portrait of an officer who had been a success at every stage of his professional life. Running this prison was an enormous responsibility, but until last week, he seemed to be in complete control. Then events took a bad, unexpected turn, and maybe more than one turn, and the stress showed in his impatient voice and the irritability that seeped out in conversation and during his own prolonged silences.

Jefferson glared at me, then looked back at the monitors.

"Okay," he whispered. "You're speaking to him now."

"In my head," I said. Looking at Jefferson, I used my most ingratiating smile. "I'm practicing. Before I actually go in there, I want to feel ready."

"You've had five days to prepare," he reminded me.

Circumstances put a timetable on everything. Two days had been allotted to a full briefing, and then I was brought here, and for three days I had enjoyed the freedoms and pressures of this ultra-secure compound.

"Collins went straight in," said Jefferson.

Collins was a certified legend in my little business.

"Right into Ramiro's cell and started talking with him." That was twelve years ago, but Jefferson still had to admire what my colleague had accomplished.

"He also stopped the torture," I mentioned.

Jefferson shook his head. "He liked claiming that, I know. But everything about the interrogation was my call. I'm the one who put an end to the cold rooms and sleep deprivation."

I offered a less-than-convinced nod.

"And by the way," he continued, "I was responsible for bringing Collins in from the Bureau."

"I guess I'd read that," I admitted.

"And I just happen to be the hero who let your colleague work however he wanted, whatever method he thought was best, and fuck those hundred thousand orders that Washington was giving us then."

The old bureaucrat still had a belly full of fire and bile. He offered a very quick, completely revealing grin, sitting back in his chair while thinking hard about past glories.

"But you didn't select me, did you?"

"I guess not," he said.

"Collins picked me," I said. "Last year, wasn't it? Not that anybody told me, of course. But in case he couldn't serve anymore, I was his first choice as a replacement."

Jefferson shifted his weight, saying nothing.

"I'll grant you, the candidate list is short. But you'd have to admit, I'm rather well regarded."

Jefferson shrugged.

"If you want," I mentioned, "I can suggest a viable candidate to replace me. In the event you lose all faith in my methods."

He was tempted. I saw it in his face, particularly in the sly smile.

"But that would mean more delays," I warned. "And I doubt if my replacement would be as effective as me."

"You're a cocky gal, aren't you?"

"It has been said."

"Help you get ahead, does it?"

"It helps keep me sane, mostly."

Jefferson turned away, staring at the largest screen. The prisoner was sitting at his desk, reading Jane Austen in Portuguese. The date and time were fixed in the bottom right corner: August 5th, 2014. Three minutes after three in the afternoon.

"Before I go in there," I began.

"Yeah?"

"Tell me about the first days," I said. "Before you brought in Collins. Right after Ramiro was caught . . . what was your mood, early on?"

"My mood?" His smile grew bigger and sourer, wrapped around a painful memory. "You can imagine what I was thinking. March 2002, Osama was still the big monster, and some stateless warrior slips across the Canadian border with five kilos of bomb-grade U-235. That's what I was thinking about. But his luck hit a stretch of black ice in Montana, and the state trooper found his Maxima flipped on its back, this bastard behind the steering wheel, unconscious."

I had seen hundreds of images of the crash scene.

"The man's fingerprints were unknown. His passport and identity were quality fakes, but we couldn't tell which foreign power had done the work. Nobody knew who he was. Al Qaeda, or Iraqi, or was he something else? All we knew was that, at the very least, our prisoner was part of somebody's A-bomb project."

"You needed to know everything, and as fast as possible."

"How many like this guy were there?" Jefferson turned in my direction, but never quite made eye contact. "And would his associates be happy hitting New York or Washington? Or did they have more terrible targets in mind?"

I found it interesting: The person most familiar with the full story was still jolted with a simple replay of known events. Jefferson tensed up as he spoke about that heavy lump of gray metal, shaped like a cannon ball and hidden by the spare tire.

"We didn't know anything," he continued, "but it was obvious our man was the biggest trophy in the ongoing war. That's why another Maxima and a compliant corpse were rolled off that Montana highway, the crash restaged and the wreckage burned up. It was treated like an ordinary accident. Now our prisoner had a good reason to miss his next clandestine rendezvous, wherever than might be. Because he was officially dead."

"You unleashed a lot of specialists," I said. "Working their delicate magic on his stubborn corpse."

Jefferson didn't like my tone.

"You had to make the call," I continued. "The stakes seemed treacherously high. The proverbial fuse was burning down."

"Don't give me that attitude," Jefferson warned. "Your career has seen its share of hard interrogations."

I admitted, "It has," without hesitation. "And believe me, I will never question those early decisions."

What was the point now, after all?

Jefferson heard resignation where none was offered, and because he was a good career officer, he made his features soften.

"A frustrating subject, the records say."

"He was."

"Hard interrogations and potent drugs, in tandem. But how much good did all that do?"

He didn't answer.

I asked, "So who figured it out first?"

"Figured what out?"

"Ramiro's list," I said.

With only his eyes, Jefferson smiled. "It's all in the files."

"I don't always believe what I read."

"No?"

"But here's my understanding of the story," I said, leaning forward. "For five months, that man was abused relentlessly. Every half-legal method was applied to him, often several at once. Then you brought in a fresh crew—old KGB hands, as I understand it—who brought tricks that made everybody feel Hell's breath. And what did you get in the end? Nothing. Your prisoner gave us nothing. He didn't offer any name. He didn't even utter an intelligible word. He screamed on occasion, sure. But only after his elbows were pulled from their joints. And the curses weren't in any known language."

I paused, waiting.

Jefferson said nothing.

"And then one day, when his arms were working again, he motioned to his interrogators. He indicated that he wanted a paper and a pen. And when those items were delivered, he filled several pages with letters and numbers— peculiar looking to the untrained eye, if not out-and-out bizarre."

The original list was sitting in an important vault. I pulled out one of the three copies that had been made since, the writing neat and legible, with a few artistic flourishes, particularly in the 5s and Ts.

"So tell me," I said. "Who figured this puzzle out?"

Jefferson named one of his staff. Then he quietly reminded me, "It's all in the records."

"No," I said. "I think the genius was you."

Surprise turned to wary pleasure. With a smug little wink, he asked, "How could it be me?"

"Because you would have gotten the first look at his list. And you're a bright, bright fellow with a lot of hobbies. I know that because I've checked your files too. I think what happened is that something he wrote jogged a leftover memory from your school days. In particular, from astronomy class. The first sequence in each line is obviously a position in the sky, if you know the subject. But it takes a bigger leap to realize that the second sequence is a date."

"It took me five minutes," he boasted.

"Easy to do, as long as you understand that the dates are based on the Islamic calendar. The significance of both notations, taken together, would have been answered on maybe a dozen websites. But that answer was crazy. And it left you with a much bigger puzzle sitting inside a cold, cramped cell. Even the earliest dates on Ramiro's list occurred after his incarceration. And each one marked the day and position of a supernova bright enough to be noticed by earthbound astronomers."

Jefferson put his arms around his chest and squeezed, shaking his head with an enduring astonishment.

"You were the one, weren't you?"

He admitted, "Yes."

"But you didn't trust your insight," I suggested.

"Like you said. It looked crazy."

"So in a very general fashion, you told your subordinate to see if the list might just have something to do with the sky. Because you're a smart player, and if your wild idea didn't pan out, you wouldn't be held accountable."

Jefferson knew better than to respond.

"And how long did you have to wait?" I asked. "Before the next supernova sprang into existence precisely where it was supposed to be?"

"You know."

"Seven days," I answered. "And that's when you were certain. Sitting in the cold room was something far more dangerous than a few pounds of uranium. Somehow our terrorist, or whatever he was, knew the future. Against all reason, Ramiro could predict celestial events that nobody should be able to anticipate in advance."

Tired, satisfied eyes closed and stayed closed.

"That's when you went out and found Collins. An entirely different species of interrogator. A smart, relentless craftsman with a history of convincing difficult people to talk about anything. And for twelve years, you have sat here watching your prize stallion slowly, patiently extract an incredible story from your prisoner."

Jefferson nodded, smiled. But the eyes remained closed.

I stared at the creature sitting inside his spacious, comfortable cell. And with a measured tone, I reminded both of us, "This is the most thoroughly studied individual in the world. And for a long time, he has given us the exact minimum required to keep everyone happy enough. And as a result, he has maintained control over his narrow life. And yours."

Jefferson finally looked at me, squirming a little in his chair.

"Fuck timetables," I said. "I think that I'm being exceptionally sensible not to march in there and offer my hand and name."

"I see your point," he allowed.

"To be truthful? This entire situation terrifies me." I hesitated, and then said, "It's not every day you have the opportunity, and the honor, and the grave responsibility of interviewing somebody who won't be born for another one hundred years."

2

Jefferson can write the history however he wants. Collins' arrival was what brought real, substantive changes for the prisoner. The still nameless man was unchained and allowed to wash, and under newly imposed orders, his guards brought him clean clothes and referred to him as "sir." Then after the first filling breakfast in twenty weeks, he was escorted to a comfortably warm room with a single folding chair of the kind you would find in any church basement.

In those days, Collins worked with a partner, but the two agents decided that it was smarter to meet the mysterious visitor on a one-to-one basis.

Collins carried in his own chair, identical to the first, and he opened it and sat six feet from the prisoner's clean bare feet.

For a long while he said nothing, tilting his face backward so that the overhead light covered him with a warm, comforting glow. I have watched that first meeting twenty times, from every available angle. The interrogator was a bald little man, plain-faced but with brilliant blue eyes. I knew those eyes. I first met Collins in the late nineties, at some little professional conference. From across the room, I noticed his perpetual fascination with the world and how his effortless, ever-graceful charm always found some excuse to bubble out. Collins had ugly teeth, crooked and yellow. But his smile seemed genuine and always fetching, and the voice that rose from the little body was rich and deep. Even his idle chatter sounded important, as if it rose from God's own throat.

For a full ninety seconds, the interrogator made no sound.

The prisoner calmly returned the silence.

Then Collins sat back until the front legs of his chair lifted, and he laughed with an edge to his voice, and waving his hand at the air, he said in good Arabic, "We don't believe you."

In Farsi, he claimed, "We can't believe you."

And then in English, he said, "I'm here to warn you. One lucky guess won't win you any friends."

"Which guess is that?" the prisoner replied, in an accented, difficult-to-place strain of English.

Those were the first words he had uttered in captivity.

"You have some passing experience with astronomy, I'll grant you that." Collins had the gift of being able to study arcane subjects on the fly and then sound painfully brilliant. For the next six minutes, he lectured the prisoner about the stars, and in particular, how giant stars aged rapidly and soon blew up. Then he calmly lied about the tools available to the Hubble telescope and the big mirrors on top of Hawaii. "You had access to this data. Obviously. In your previous life, you must have studied astronomy. That's why you took the chance and gave us some random dates, and by pure coincidence, a few stars happened to blow up in just about the right slices of the sky."

A thin smile and a dismissive shrug of the shoulders were offered.

"Or maybe you are genuine," Collins allowed. "The implication, as far as I can tell, is that you can see the future. Which is insane. Or you know the future because you came from some to-be time. Which seems even crazier, at least to me. But if that's true, then I guess it means I should feel lucky. Just being in your presence is a privilege. How many times does somebody get to meet a genuine time traveler?' "

Silence.

"But if that's true," Collins continued, "then I have to ask myself, 'Why spring this on us now? And why this strange, cosmic route?'"

The silence continued for most of a minute.

"We can't break you," Collins finally pointed out. "Believe me, I know how these things work. What you've endured over these weeks and months . . . any normal person would have shattered ten different ways. Not that you'd be any help to us. Torture is a singularly lousy way of discovering the truth. Beaten and electrocuted, the average person ends up being glad for the chance to confess. To any and every crime we can think of, particularly the imaginary misdeeds. But everybody here has been assuming that we're dealing with a normal human specimen. And what I think is . . . I think that isn't the case here. Is it?"

The prisoner had a thin face and thick black hair that had been shaved to the skull, and in a multitude of ways, he was handsome. His teeth were white and straight. His shoulders were athletic, though captivity had stolen some of his muscle. He was mixed-blooded, European ancestors dancing with several other races. The best estimate of his age put him at thirty-two. But nobody had yet bothered to examine his genetics or his insides. We didn't appreciate that his indifference to pain had organic roots, including novel genes and buried microchines that insulated both his body and stubborn mind.

"Okay, you want us to believe that you're special," Collins said.

The prisoner closed his eyes. When he opened them again, he took a dramatic breath and then said nothing.

"But I don't think you appreciate something here. Do you know just how stupid and slow governments can be? Right this minute, important people are thinking: So what? So he knows a few odd things about the sky. I'm impressed, yes. But I'm the exception. Maybe there are some bright lights in the administration who see the implications. Who are smart enough to worry. But do you actually know who sits in the Oval Office today? Do you understand anything about our current president? He is possibly the most stubborn creature on the planet. So when this clever game of yours is presented to him, how do you think it's going to play out?"

The prisoner watched Collins.

"We won't torture you anymore. I promise that." And after a long sigh, Collins added, "But that isn't what you care about, I'm guessing. Not really. Something else matters to you. It deeply, thoroughly matters, or why else would you be here? So let's pretend for the next moment that your list of supernovae is true. You can see the future. Or, better, you come from there. And if it is possible to travel in time, then I guess it stands to reason that you aren't alone, that others made the journey with you."

Here the prisoner's heart quickened, half a dozen machines recording the visible rise in his interest.

"I'm guessing you're part of a group of time tourists. Is that about right?"

In Collins' copious notes, written several hours later, was the open admission that he had taken a chance here, making an obvious but still bizarre guess.

"You come from some distant age," he continued. "You're the child of an era where this is normal. People can easily travel into their past. And who knows what other miracle skills you have at your disposal? Tools and weapons we can't imagine. Not to mention the historic knowledge about our simple times. Yet here you are. You've been sitting in the same closet for five months, and after all this time, maybe it's finally occurred to you that your friends and colleagues—these other visitors from tomorrow—have no intention of rescuing you from this tedious mess."

In myriad ways, the body betrays the mind. With the flow of the blood and the heat of the skin, the prisoner's body was showing each of the classic signatures of raw anger.

"If I was part of a team," Collins began, "and we leaped back a thousand years into the past . . . "

Then, he hesitated.

The prisoner leaned forward slightly, waiting.

"To the Holy Land, let's suppose. And suppose I was captured. The Saracens don't know what to make of me, but just to be safe, they throw me into their darkest dungeon." Collins sat back, his chair scrapping against the tiled floor. "Well, sir, I can promise you this: I would damn well expect my friends to blow a hole in the stone wall and then pluck me out of there with a good old futuristic Blackhawk helicopter."

The prisoner leaned back.

Quietly, in that accented English of his, he said, "One hundred and forty years."

"That's how far back you jumped?"

"A little farther, actually." The prisoner grinned faintly, mentioning, "We have been among you now for several years."

"Among us?"

"Yes."

"And who is 'we'?"

"Our leader. And his followers." The prisoner paused, smiling. "We call the man Abraham."

Collins hesitated. Then he carefully repeated the name. "Abraham."

"The father of three great religions, which is why he took that important name for himself."

"You came here with Abraham."

"Yes."

"And how many others?"

Silence.

Collins was not acting. He was worried, his fingers shaking despite the room's heat, his voice trembling slightly as he asked, "How many of these friends came with you?"

"None."

"What . . . ?"

"They are not my friends," the prisoner stated.

"Why? Because they won't save you?"

"No." The thin face tilted backward, teeth flashing in the light. "Because I have never particularly liked those people."

"Then why join up?" Collins put his hands together, squeezing the blood out of his fingers. "Why go to the trouble of leaping back to our day?"

"I believed in their cause."

"Which is?"

No answer was offered.

"You want to change the future? Is that your grand purpose?"

The prisoner shrugged. "In one fashion or another."

Collins leaned close, and for the first time he offered his name and an open hand. "You're being helpful, sir, and I thank you."

The prisoner shook the hand. Then he quietly said, "Ramiro."

"Is that your name?"

"Yes."

"I'm pleased to know it, Ramiro."

"Don't put me back into that cell again, Collins."

"But I have to," the interrogator replied.

Ignoring that answer, Ramiro said, "I have a set of demands. Minimal requirements that will earn my cooperation, I promise you."

"Two names and the vague beginnings of a story," Collins countered. "That won't earn you much."

"And I will ask you this: Do you want to defeat the invaders?" When it served his purpose, Ramiro had a cold, menacing smile. "If you insist on mistreating me, even one more time, I will never help you."

"I don't have any choice here," Collins told him.

"Yes," said Ramiro. "Yes, you do."

"No."

Then the prisoner leaned back in his chair, and through some secretive, still mysterious route, he woke a microscopic device implanted inside his angry heart.

For the next one hundred seconds, Ramiro was clinically dead.

By the time he was fully conscious again, calls had been made. Desperate orders had been issued and rescinded and then reissued. Careers were either defined or shattered. And the only soldier from a secretive, unanticipated army was given every demand on a list of remarkably modest desires.

3

My home was an efficiency apartment no bigger than Ramiro's quarters and only slightly more comfortable. But I was assured that no tiny cameras were keeping tabs on me. As a creature of status, I also enjoyed communications with the outside world—albeit strained through protocols and electronic filters run by intelligence officers sitting in the field station outside the prison. And unlike our number-one citizen, I was free to move where I wished, including jogging along the wide, hard-packed salt streets that combined for a little less than six kilometers of cumulative distance.

No one had ever predicted "temporal jihadists," as Abraham's agents were dubbed. Uranium-toting terrorists suddenly seemed like a minor threat by comparison. Collins' first interview resulted in a secret and very chaotic panic roaring through Washington. Black ops funds were thrown in every direction. Ground was broken for half a dozen high-security prisons scattered across the world. But then some wise head inside Langley decided that if time travelers were genuine, then there was no telling what they knew, and if they were inspired, there were probably no limits to what they could achieve. A tropical island might look fetching in the recruitment brochure, but how could you protect your prisoner/asset from death rays and stealth submarines? How would any facility set on the earth's surface remain hidden from prying eyes? The only hope, argued that reasonable voice, was to hide underground, and short, efficient logistical lines were only possible inside the United States. That's why the last prison to receive funding was the only one finished and staffed: an abandoned salt mine set beneath Kansas, provided with a bank of generators and layers of security that kept everyone, including most of its citizens, happily confused about its truest purpose.

Each guard was a volunteer, most of them pulled from submarine duty. To qualify, they couldn't have close families, and like everyone on the skeletal staff, they were forewarned that leaves would be rare events, and brief, and subject to various kinds of shadowing.

Most people didn't even apply for leaves anymore, preferring the safety of the underground while padding their retirement funds.

Life inside the salt mine was never unpleasant, I was told. My superiors—those gray-haired survivors of these last decade-plus—liked to boast about the billions that had been spent on full-spectrum lights and conditioned air, plus the food that most of the world would be thrilled to find on their plates. But nobody went so far as to claim that I was fortunate, nor that this posting was a blessing. The terms of my assignment were grim, any success would bring repercussions, and nobody with half a brain told me that this was an honor, or for that matter, a choice.

Collins' slot had to be filled, and I was the new Collins.

"Ma'am?"

I showed the guard my ID and badge.

"I don't need them, ma'am. I know who you are."

I was a slow, sweat-drenched jogger who had slugged her way through three kilometers of dressed-up tunnels. Technically the guard was off-duty, and he was using his free time to fling a colorful hand-tied fly into what looked like an enormous water-filled stock tank.

"Any bites?" I asked.

"A few."

"Trout?"

I knew the water was too warm for trout. But the questions you ask often define you in a stranger's mind, and I thought it was smart to start with a mistake.

"Bluegill," he told me.

"Really?" I sounded interested.

He was a big strong man, a kid when he arrived here and still younger than me by quite a lot. But in a society where males outnumbered females ten-to-one, I had to be an object of some interest.

"Ever fish?" he asked.

"No," I lied.

He thought about offering to teach me. I saw it in his eyes, in the tilt of his head. But then he decided on caution, forcing himself to mutter a few colorless words. "They bite, but they're too tiny to keep."

Surrounding the tank were huge plastic pots, each one holding a tropical tree or a trio of shrubs. Some of the foliage was thriving. Most just managed to limp along. I could see where a few million dollars had gone, and I suppose it helped the cave dwellers to coexist with living plants. But I could also imagine that a sickly lemon tree standing under fancy fluorescent lights would just as surely defeat a soul or two.

"What's your name?" I asked.

He began with his rank.

"Your first name," I interrupted. "What do friends call you?"

"Jim."

"Hi, Jim. I'm Carmen."

To the boy's credit, he saw through me. "You already know my name. Don't you, ma'am?"

"Carmen," I insisted.

But he wouldn't say it. He reeled in his feathery fly, pinning the hook to the largest eyelet, and then he did a modestly convincing job of packing up his tackle. He didn't want to stop fishing, but my presence made him uncomfortable.

"So you know who I am?"

Jim nodded.

"And maybe you're wondering if this is a coincidence, our paths crossing in the park like this?"

"It isn't," he stated.

"Probably not," I agreed.

Surrounding the stock tank was a narrow cedar deck. I happened to be blocking the stairs leading down.

"Talk to me for a minute," I said.

Not as an order, just a request.

Jim hesitated. Then with a nervous grin, he said, "Yeah. I found him."

"Collins?"

"Yes, ma'am."

I didn't react.

"Is that what you wanted to ask me?"

I nodded. "You found him inside his apartment."

"Yes."

My sense of the moment was that the young man was embarrassed, first and foremost. Security was his duty, and one of the most important citizens of this nameless, unmapped town died during his watch.

"I read your report," I mentioned.

The boy's eyes were open but blind. He was gazing back in time, crossing a little more than a week, standing before a long dark pool of congealed blood leading to a pale corpse sitting in bathwater that had turned chill.

"Did you know Collins very well, Jim?"

"Yeah. Sort of."

"As a friend," I continued. "Did you talk with him much?"

"I didn't see it coming, if that's what you mean. Ma'am."

"We often don't with suicides," I assured him. "People expect depression, despair. Afterwards, we try to remember a telltale noose hanging from the high beam. But that's usually not the case. And do you know why?"

He blinked, watching me.

"A person is miserable, let's say. Sad and sick of being alive. Then one day, he finds the perfect solution to his terrible problems. 'I'll just kill myself,' he says. And in that moment, his miseries are cured. He can suddenly smile through his final days, knowing that every pain will soon be left behind."

Jim shook his head slowly, probably wondering if this middle-aged woman was as bat-crazy as she sounded.

"I knew Collins too," I admitted.

He sighed, looking at me with curious eyes. The two of us had something in common, it seemed.

"I'll miss him," I offered.

The man's face dipped.

Then before I could ask my next question, he looked up. "Salt Lake City," he mentioned.

"What about it?"

"How is it, ma'am?"

"Carmen," I insisted.

"Carmen."

"Salt Lake is just fine."

He said, "Good."

I waited.

He took a deep breath, drinking in the negative ions that were being generated by a filtration system stolen from NASA. Then with a trace of frustration, he admitted, "We don't get much news down here."

"I know that."

"It's hard. You can never tell what they're holding back. It's done for good reasons, I know. But we always have to wonder."

"Indian Point," I offered.

"Yeah, it was four days before we heard anything about that. And then only because somebody with clearance decided to jump protocols and tell us."

"Collins did."

"I'm not saying," he said. Which was the same as, "Yes."

"Did he explain how awful Indian Point would be?"

Jim didn't answer, carefully turning his reel two clicks.

"The reactors and storage facilities obliterated, all of those poisons thrown up by the mushroom cloud." My voice broke—an honest shattering. Then I managed to add, "I watched it all on the news. That wind carried that shit right over New York, and then Washington and Philadelphia, and all the mayhem that resulted . . . "

"Yeah," Jim whispered.

"And then to learn that it wasn't just some crude uranium bomb that killed twenty million, no. But a fat fusion monster that led straight back to Russia . . . "

With a nudge, I could have knocked Jim off his feet. Almost two years had passed, and the memory was still that raw.

I promised, "Nothing big has happened lately."

Jim needed a couple of deep breaths. "But at least . . . are things starting to simmer down?"

I shrugged. Honestly, how could anyone assess the state of our world?

"What about the wars?" he asked.

"Some are worse, some better. It just depends, Jim."

He gave me a long, studious stare. "You know what? You don't really look like a Carmen."

"I need a tall hat covered with fruit?"

"Ma'am?" he muttered, puzzled by the cultural reference.

I stepped away from the steps, allowing him enough room to escape.

But he didn't move, and with a soft, importunate voice admitted, "Some of us are wondering. What is your mission, ma'am?"

"To replace Collins."

That's what he wanted me to say, because the other possibilities were too hard to measure, and probably even more terrible.

"I'll meet our prisoner tomorrow," I confessed.

Jim nodded, trying to show nothing with his face.

"You often stand guard over Ramiro," I mentioned.

"Everybody gets that duty."

"Of course."

He glanced at the stairs.

"So what do you think about the man, Jim?"

"I don't know anything about him," he said too quickly.

I said, "Good," and left it there.

Then he added, "He seems smart, I guess. But odd."

"Odd how?"

He had a guard's burly shoulders. He used them to shrug, saying nothing else.

"I was hoping, Jim. Maybe you can help me." I paused, just for a moment. Just to let him wonder what I might say next. "What was Collins' mood when you walked him back to his apartment?"

And now the shoulders tightened, just a little.

"I saw you two on the security videos. Walking and talking."

"I was going off-duty, ma'am. Carmen."

"Collins didn't visit Ramiro again."

The young man seemed surprised. "No?"

"Didn't he see the prisoner almost every day?"

"Most days, I guess."

"But that was three days before he killed himself."

"I'll trust you on that."

"So I'm going to ask you. Officially. What was Collins' state of mind when you walked with him back to his quarters?"

Jim's eyes gazed into the past.

"Did he say anything?"

"I did most of the talking."

"Was that normal?"

"Not particularly. No, ma'am."

"You stopped at his front door for a minute," I said.

"Yeah. I guess."

"Did he show you anything, Jim?"

"Like what?"

"Papers. Something with writing on it."

"Well, Collins had his black case with him."

"But you didn't see a legal pad, or anything like that?"

Jim tried to see yellow paper, but he couldn't make himself.

"Under the blood," I said.

"What?"

"Papers got burned. Somebody incinerated them at least twice, to make sure every mark was erased."

"I didn't know that."

"How about the coin?"

"I saw that."

"Beside the bath?"

"Yes, ma'am."

"A dollar president's coin."

"I noticed it, sure."

I waited a moment. Then I said, "So you walked him and his attaché case back to his apartment. And Collins said nothing that you can remember?"

"Just . . . " Jim held his mouth closed for a moment. Then he forced himself to look at me, and with an impressive talent for mimicry, he used the dead man's voice. Deeply, with an appealingly slight Southern drawl, he said, " 'Want to hear something funny?' "

"He asked you that?"

"Yes, ma'am."

"Did he tell you what was funny?"

Jim shook his head. "Which was too bad, I thought at the time. Collins was real good at jokes, when he wanted to be . . . "

4

Healthful food and regular rest, plus years of tempered exercise, showed in the prisoner's fit body and the youthful face. He was wearing beige trousers, a clean white polo shirt and sandals that looked comfortably broken down. It was easy to confuse him for a middle-management worker in the final days of a long vacation. When he heard the reinforced door being unbolted, he stood up. Ramiro didn't seem at all surprised to find a strange woman walking into his home. "Hello," he said with a voice that had grown almost American over the years. Then he offered a warm smile and his right hand.

I introduced myself.

"A lovely name," was his response. Then the spirit of generosity took hold. He surrendered his favorite chair and asked what I would like to drink. Coffee? Tea? Or perhaps the blue Gatorade he kept cold inside his little refrigerator.

I took the chair and requested green tea.

There wasn't any stove, so he heated the water inside the microwave. Staring at the revolving mug, he told me, "It's very sad about Collins."

"It was," I agreed.

"In a sense, he was my best friend."

"This must be hard for you."

"Not particularly." Ramiro seemed to relish how cold that sounded. He pursed his lips and shrugged, giving me a momentary glance. Measuring my reaction, no doubt.

I stared at the wall behind him, gazing at an enormous photograph of the snow-clad Himalayas.

"By any chance, did you know Collins?"

I waited for a moment. Then I said, "Yes."

That delay piqued his interest. Ramiro invested the next several moments studying my face. "How well did you know him?"

I said nothing.

"Were you lovers?"

"Guess," I told him.

That earned an easy laugh. "I know you weren't."

"Why not?"

With a calm voice, he asked, "Do you like honesty, Carmen?"

"Always."

"You aren't pretty enough for Collins. Or young enough, frankly."

"Fair points," I agreed. "But how do you know this?"

"Occasionally the man would entertain me with his stories." Ramiro glanced at the mug and then stared at me. "I don't have a passionate life, I'm sure you know. But if only half of his stories were true, then the young pretties didn't have much chance against his charms."

"Local girls, were they?"

"I shouldn't say. Your fraternization rules are ridiculously strict."

I said nothing else.

Then the microwave beeped, and Ramiro set a tea bag into the plain white mug before bringing both to me. He didn't use the handle, and when I touched the mug's body, just for an instant, my fingertips came close to burning.

He pulled his office chair out from under his little desk and sat before me, the right leg crossed over his left.

"Collins and I enjoyed some professional moments," I began. "In fact, we met long before you happened along."

He nodded, smiled.

I waited him out.

Then with a sharp grin, he mentioned, "You must be exceptionally qualified to receive this posting."

"I must be."

"May I ask a few questions?"

"By all means."

"Without giving away secrets," he began, "what kinds of experiences have you suffered during these hard years?"

"Are they hard?"

"I hear little news, and who knows if it's complete." Ramiro shrugged, laughing softly. "Which is Jefferson's idea, I think. Give the subject just enough information to tease out a few fresh, hopefully useful opinions." Then he sat back, a good-natured sigh rising out of him. "But yes, Carmen. From what I have learned, I think these times are genuinely terrible."

"Montana," I said.

"What about it?"

"The day you were found beside the road and captured . . . I was stationed outside Kabul."

When interested in any subject, Ramiro leaned forward and stopped blinking, his black eyes filling up his face. One examining physician had proposed that the microchines inside his brain were boosting his neurological capacities, and the eyes were a kind of tell. Others thought it was just a personal quirk. Whatever the reason, he was using his interested gaze on me now.

"Then the following year," I continued, "they stationed me in Iraq."

"Of course."

"I was sent to help hunt for WMDs. My assignment was to interrogate the old Baathists and such."

A thin smile surfaced; he saw the punch line coming.

"Of course there weren't any nukes or biological nightmares. But we didn't know that yet. And by 'we,' I mean the people on the ground. Washington had strung together the ridiculous intelligence, and the media beat the drums, and we went into Baghdad and kicked Saddam out of his palaces. Victory was declared. But then during that window between the celebrations and the first car bombs, my assignment shifted. That country was collapsing. Our soldiers were pretty much letting it happen, as far as I could tell. But someone gave me dozens and then hundreds of shackled bodies, plus an ever-changing checklist that made no sense to me."

My host leaned back, his chair offering a comfortable creaking. "I can appreciate your confusion."

"You understand how my game works," I said. "I try to know more than I'd ever admit to my subject. But when it suits me, I can be very stupid. And if she gives me something . . . most of my prisoners were female, I should mention . . . if she offers some bit of intelligence that I didn't have, my first response is to say, 'Oh, yes. We know all about the cement mixer with the fertilizer bomb. You can't help yourself with that crumb of old news.' "

I had shifted into my best Arabic.

Ramiro was fluent in Arabic and English, Portuguese and Spanish. But his natural tongue was an odd Creole that borrowed from each language, plus a rich seasoning of peculiar syllables and tech-terms that wouldn't exist for another hundred-plus years.

I wished I knew his native tongue. But I was too old and cranky to learn it in a workable span of time.

The prisoner stuck to his Americanized English, asking, "With that checklist, Carmen . . . what sorts of items made no sense to you?"

"Individually? Nothing was blatantly strange. But it was the whole goofy package. My bosses were hunting people who didn't belong in Baghdad. Who weren't native to Iraq, and maybe not even to the Middle East. I made some discreet inquiries, asking for clearer instructions. But nobody knew the sense behind any of our orders. One of my prisoners would eventually stand out—that's what the generals promised. She would be in her late twenties or thirties, or maybe her forties. Her accent might be wrong. Unless she was exceptionally good with languages, which was another key to watch for. There wouldn't be any genuine records showing her whereabouts more than five years earlier. And a three-star general confided to me—to all of us—that in the worst interrogations, my phantom would enjoy an extraordinary tolerance for pain and drugs and boredom. And the general promised that when I finally found my girl, she was going to be worth a hundred bloodied mistakes."

With a dismissive gesture, Ramiro said, "I told Collins. I told everybody. As a young man, I purchased a cheap package of tailored genes and various nano-organs."

"Of course."

"Common add-on talents popular in my world."

"To insulate your poor citizens from the ravages of poverty," I said, nodding agreeably.

"My warnings were explicit," Ramiro told me. "I couldn't be certain about the genetics of the other warriors, or their current identities, much less how well or how poorly they would blend into any local population."

"You gave us Iraq," I mentioned.

He bristled. Then after a moment, he said, "This is very old ground."

"It is," I agreed.

"Iraq," he repeated. "Over twenty million people, most of them young.

And what percentage of that population did your colleagues and you process? One percent? Was it that much?"

"We tried our best," I claimed.

"I told Collins. One of the voices mentioned Iraq to me, in passing."

"It wasn't Abraham?"

"No, it was one of his associates. He said Iraq was our focus. But even if that was the case, and even if Abraham and his people didn't slip out of the country before your noisy invasion . . . well, I was always critical of your clumsy methods and your very poor odds for success."

"I know. You gave Collins ample warnings."

"Even in the smallest country," said Ramiro, "there are so many dark corners in which to hide."

"You warned everybody," I said.

"And you were following orders," he said flatly. Then he added, "Carmen," with a suddenly friendly, familiar tone. "But really, how could your masters expect you to find anybody of substance?"

I paused, just for a moment. "Yes, it was a difficult assignment."

He didn't seem to notice my careful tone. "What about blood and skin?" he asked. "Were you taking samples?"

"I wasn't. But some med-techs were doing just that." I finally pulled the soggy tea bag into the air and sipped from the cooling mug. "Everybody had their own secrets to keep. Nobody knew more than a sliver of the whole incredible story. I didn't know samples were being sent back home, thousands of them, and being tested for key genes."

"Genes that might not have been there," he pointed out. "Or that could be removed or easily hidden."

I nodded. "We knew your genetic markers, sure. But who could say what we'd find inside another warrior's chromosomes?"

"Precisely."

"But what else could my people do? We were facing an unexpected threat—temporal jihadists born in a distant, treacherous future. What reasonable, effective measures would have helped our security?"

Ramiro swiped at the air.

Quietly but fiercely, he said, "I told you what I knew."

"Of course."

"Once my terms were met, I explained everything to our friend Collins." His voice rose, cracked. "Imagine that a foreign power captured the man standing guard outside my door. They would easily break him. In a few days or weeks, he would confess everything. But what is the operational knowledge of a lowly soldier? Does that man . . . my friend Jim . . . does he even halfway comprehend my importance?"

"Probably not," I conceded.

"And I'm just a simple soldier too."

"Simple? I doubt that."

A sly smile blossomed, faded. "What happened next, Carmen?"

"In 2005, I was yanked out of Iraq. I was flown back to the States and promised a new assignment. But before orders came down, they pressed me into helping with certain war games. Very secret, very obvious stuff. After the endless mess in Iraq, we were going to try to do a better job taking on Iran."

Ramiro watched me.

"Two strange things happened at that conference," I admitted. "On the first morning, I ran into a colleague on his way to a back room breakfast, and I was roped in and told to play along. It seemed like a chance deal, but of course it wasn't. There were a lot of strange faces sitting with eggs and oatmeal. And there was Collins. I hadn't seen that man in ages. God, I thought, he looked tired and pale. But he practically latched onto me. We sat together. This other fellow sat in the corner, watching the two of us. I think we managed maybe five minutes of catch-up. I told him about coming home. He gave me a cover story, but he didn't bothering pushing it too hard. Then one of the unknown faces, a guy sitting at the end of the table, threw out this odd, odd question."

Ramiro leaned forward, absorbing my face and soul with a blinkless gaze.

" 'What if you could jump back in time?' the gentleman inquired. He was pretending that his question wasn't serious, that it was for shits-and-giggles only. He made himself laugh, asking, 'What if you and some like-minded friends gathered together? Say there's a few dozen of you, a couple hundred at most. You're going to travel back in time together. But there are rules. You can cover only one or two centuries, and with restrictions. Your journey has to be a one-way. You can carry only a limited amount of mass. Bodies and a little luggage and that's all. There won't be any return missions to the future. There's no supply train with fresh M-16s and laptops. And your goal? You want to conquer that more primitive world, of course. You are invaders. Two hundred soldiers armed with your beliefs and training and your superior knowledge, and you'll have to find some clever way to make your little force strong enough to defeat the old horse armies."

Ramiro smiled.

"Of course there was a purpose to his wacky scenario," I allowed. "That much was obvious to everybody there. But the gentleman didn't offer explanations. For all I know, he was told that our own physicists had just built a time machine, and we were trying to decide what to do with our new toy. The truth never had to get in the way. During a five-hour breakfast, he led a clumsy, half-informed discussion that ended up with tactical nukes burning up London and Paris. And do you know why this happened? I think the show was put on for Collins' benefit. To give him ideas, to help guide his future conversations with you. And meanwhile in those other rooms, the future Iranian war ran its imaginary, surgical course."

The prisoner had leaned forward, elbows on knees. Then he revealed something of his ability—his clear focus, his absolute mastery of detail—when he said, "Earlier, Carmen. When you admitted that your Iraqi assignment was difficult. I had the impression—tell me if I'm wrong—but it seemed to me that despite some very long odds, you were successful."

I said, "I was."

"You found a suspect? Somebody out of place in our world, did you?"

"Yes." I paused. "A young woman without family. With no paper trail reaching back more than a few years. She claimed to have worked as a lab technician, nothing more, and she had reasonable explanations for the gaps in her records. But she was the right age, and she was very, very tough. I worked her and worked her, and the only information I got from her was the name of a river in Kashmir."

Ramiro stared at me.

"At least that's what others heard when they listened to the interrogation later." I shrugged, glancing down. "I couldn't tell you what she was saying exactly, since she was throwing up at the time. But two days later, a special ops group came and took her away."

My new friend smiled. Then after a moment or two, he guessed, "Collins told you this news at the breakfast, did he?"

"Later, actually."

"You had uncovered one of my sisters. Is that what he told you?"

"Not in those terms. But Collins took me out for drinks and mentioned that my girl was interrogated by other teams, and when she finally talked, she admitted to pretty much everything."

"Very good," he said.

I kept my voice as level and cool as I could manage it. "Collins told me that she was a holy soldier in a war that hadn't seen its first shot yet. But that day was coming soon, he confided. And my prisoner . . . that young woman . . . had promised that our world would be helpless before this mighty hand."

Ramiro watched me sip the tea. "Collins never mentioned the girl to me."

"That's the way it should be," I said.

"Of course."

Then I leaned forward. "I asked about her."

Ramiro waited.

"I asked Collins if she was still being helpful to us."

"Was she?"

"Not anymore. Since she managed to kill herself.'"

A doll's eyes would have been more expressive. Very calmly, he asked, "A suicide implant, was it?"

"No," I said. "She slammed her forehead into the corner of a desk, breaking a blood vessel in her cortex." I set down the cold mug of tea, adding, "But now you know why I'm so highly regarded, at least in some circles. I've had some measure of success at this very odd game."

5

To do this job, you need an iron ass. The capacity to sit and listen, nodding with enthusiasm, and remembering everything said while measuring every pause—that's what matters. Find the inconsistencies, and you can be good at it. Connect this phrase to that sigh, and you'll earn your paycheck. What years of experience have shown me is that inflicting pain and the threat of pain are rarely necessary. It takes remarkably little to coax the average soul into revealing everything. Extramarital affairs. Cheating on critical exams. Dangerous politics. Some years ago, during a commercial flight, I sat beside a lovely old lady who spoke at length about cooking and her husband and her cherished garden, which she described in some detail, and then she mentioned her husband again. For a moment, she paused, looking in my direction but seeing something else. Then she quietly admitted that the poor man was beginning to suffer from dementia. It was that pause that caught my attention. It was the careful tone of her voice and the way her steely green eyes stared through a stranger's head. Afterwards, on a whim, I checked with a botanical guide and learned that an astonishing portion of her beautiful garden was poisonous. She never said an evil word about anyone, including that senile old man, but her intentions were obvious. She had made up her mind to kill him, and she was simply waiting for the excuse to use garden shears and a cooking pot, summoning Death.

But my subjects are never ordinary citizens. As a rule, they consider themselves to be special—committed, determined warriors in whatever grand cause has latched hold of their worthy souls. But their passions are larger than ours, their enthusiasms having few bounds. Rock music makes them pray. Cattle prods and mock executions are exactly what great men expect to endure. But if you treat them as fascinating equals, they will happily chatter on, sometimes for years, explaining far more to you than you ever hoped to know.

For twelve years, Collins sat inside a very comfortable prison cell, listening to one man's self-obsessed monologue.

Thousands of hours of autobiography begged to be studied. But I didn't have the time. Even the summaries made for some massive volumes. I had to make do with an elaborate timeline marked with every kind of event found in one man's life. According to my briefings, the enigmatic Ramiro was born in the second decade of the twenty-second century. His family had some small wealth. The paternal grandfather was a Spaniard who had converted to the Sunni faith before immigrating to Brazil, and the boy was raised in a city that didn't yet exist today—a sugar cane and palm oil center in what was once Amazon rainforest. A maternal uncle was responsible for Ramiro's interest in astronomy. Lemonade-7 was preparing for a long, successful career as some type of scientist, but at a critical juncture, politics ruined his dreams. At least that's the story that Collins heard again and again. The entire family was thrown into sudden, undeserved poverty. At seventeen, the young Islamic man had to drop out of school and find any work. At eighteen, when he was a legal adult, he bought a cheap package of poverty genes and nanoplants to help insulate him from his miseries; but, unlike many, Ramiro resisted any treatment that would make him happy in these decidedly joyless days.

People want to believe that in another twenty or fifty or one hundred years, the earth will grow into an enduring utopia. But among the prisoner's unwelcome gifts was a narrow, knife-deep vision of a disturbingly recognizable world. Yes, science would learn much that was new and remarkable. And fabulous technologies would be put to hard work. But cheap fusion was always going to need another couple decades of work, and eternal health was always for the next generation to achieve, and by the twenty-second century, the space program would have managed exactly two walks on the Martian surface and a few permanent, very exclusive homes hunkered down near the moon's south pole.

Ramiro's world was ours, except with more people and less naivety. Most of its wealth and all of its power was concentrated in the top one-half percentile. National borders would shift here and vanish there, but the maps would remain familiar. The old religions would continue struggling for converts, often through simple, proven violence. But the Islamic Century would have come to its natural end. Mormons and Buddhists and Neo-secularists began to gradually gnaw away at their gains. And in the backwaters of Brazil, young Ramiro's faith would seem quite out of place—another liability in his sorry, increasingly desperate prospects.

But then a team of physicists working in the Kashmir Free State would build and successfully test the world's first time machine.

"I can't believe that," Collins had blurted out.

Perhaps the prisoner was a little irritated by his interrogator's tone. There were many moments, early on especially, when Ramiro displayed a thin skin. But then he made a smile break out, dragging his mood into a sunnier place, and with a tight proud voice, he asked, "And how did I come here?"

"This is about me, not you," Collins replied. "I'm just having trouble accepting this preposterous concept."

"You want details, do you?"

"I want the science. At least enough to show around and get a few smart-sounding opinions."

"Of course." The smile warmed. "I assumed this would happen."

This was the first interview inside the new salt-mine prison. Despite a self-induced coronary, Ramiro looked fit and comfortable. His room was finished, but little else was done. Despite copious amounts of sound-proofing, the deep drumming of machinery bled into the audio track—the

Army Corps working fast on what they were told was a new secret shelter for the wise heads of their elected government.

"Paper and a pen," Ramiro demanded.

I wasn't the first to notice that while making important notes, our time traveler preferred ancient, proven tools.

He wrote hard for half an hour, breaking only to mention that he was by no means an expert in this esoteric branch of science.

Neither was Collins. But that little bald character had done just enough reading to decipher a few equations and recognize the general shape of the diagrams. With a nod and a poker player's guts, he said, "This looks like you're playing with the Casimir Effect."

"Very good," Ramiro responded.

"Parallel plates set so close together that they tap into the vacuum energies everywhere. Is that about right?"

"Something like that, yes."

"I've heard there's a lot of energy in a vacuum. Virtual particles and structure too." Flipping through the pages, Collins allowed the overhead camera to record everything. "So what are you doing on this page? Making a wormhole?"

"Hardly."

"Doesn't time travel need a wormhole?"

Ramiro sat back. "That's a very difficult trick to achieve. And in the end, unnecessary."

"Why?"

"A pocket of Lorton Energy is far easier to make."

"Who's Lorton?"

"An unborn Australian genius, if that matters. In my day, he was just as famous for his piano playing as for his peculiar physics." Then Ramiro launched into a lengthy and occasionally self-contradictory lecture about exotic states and branes and the means by which modest energies can throw matter across years and entire eons. But there were strict limits to the magic. The larger the mass to be moved, the shorter span it could cross. A substantial building might be thrown several years into the past, while a tiny grain of sand could find itself resting in the sultry Jurassic.

"Is that how they tested their machine?" Collins asked. "Make a probe and send it back, then dig it up in a fossil bed somewhere?"

Ramiro's smile flickered.

"Hardly," he said.

"Wait," his interrogator said. "I forgot. You told me already . . . what was it you told me . . . ?"

"The universe is a quantum phenomena," Ramiro mentioned.

"Which means?"

"Your physicists have played with a very difficult concept. They call it the many-worlds reality, and to an amazing degree, that model is correct. Everything that can happen will happen. An unstable nucleus might explode today or in a thousand years, which means that if it detonates both events will happen. And it also explodes during every nanosecond between now and then. In our astonishing, endlessly inventive universe, every possible outcome is inevitable. Every consequence plays out endlessly. The most unlikely event happens too often to count. And possibility is as easy and perfect as the great thoughts that pass through God's good mind."

Collins was a natural actor. But many years later, watching the interrogation, I could tell that he was impressed. It wasn't play-acting on his part. This was no feigned emotion for effect. The camera showed an awestruck gaze and hands that had to find one another, wrapping their fingers into an elaborate knot. Collins was pleased. No, he was thrilled. For a moment or two, he allowed himself to stare at the stack of papers in his lap, humble and unexpected, and in ways that few people can ever know, he felt honored.

Then he remembered his job—his duty—and quickly returned to the scruffy matters of state and war.

"Okay, it's 1999," he said. "In one reality, nobody jumps back to our day. Nothing changes, and the world pushes on exactly as before. Lorton is going to be born and stroke the keys and play with his mathematics—"

"Exactly."

"But there's this other 1999," said Collins.

"Yes."

"Abraham and you, and the rest of the group . . . they calmly step out into our world. Is that about it?"

"Except that process was never calm," Ramiro mentioned. "There was a crack like thunder and quite a lot of dust. Since they occupied a fair amount of space, your native air and ground had to be pushed out of the way."

"Naturally."

Ramiro waited.

"Where?" Collins asked.

Then as Ramiro began to speak, his interrogator interrupted, saying, "I know. It's in Kashmir. You've mentioned that before."

"It was beside the Shyok River."

"The Shyok? Are you sure?"

"Of course I am sure," said Ramiro, bristling slightly.

"And how many came?"

"One hundred and ninety-nine warriors," Ramiro reported.

"You're sure?"

"I didn't count the bodies. But that number was mentioned to me."

"Is that how much mass can be thrown back across one hundred and forty years? About two hundred men's worth?"

"Men and women."

"How many women?"

"I don't know."

"Because of the masks. You claim."

The first interrogation had delivered that sour news. Collins had wanted Abraham's description, but Ramiro couldn't identify any of the temporal jihadists. Every head was covered with a thick black fabric. It was a miraculous cloth, transparent to the person beneath but hiding the faces from the outside world. And if that wasn't terrible enough, the cloth also wiped away the character and even the gender of every voice.

"Very smart," Collins.

Ramiro nodded agreeably.

"And your leader, this Abraham fellow—"

"I never saw his face. But please, ask me that question twenty more times. I love repeating myself without end."

"Sorry," Collins said.

Ramiro waited for a few moments. Then he thought to mention, "We also brought a few personal effects and some special equipment too."

"I have to ask this again," Collins said. "My bosses insist."

"As I told you, I can offer only guesses about what kind of equipment was included. My cell was small, and it was not responsible for any of it. I saw some anonymous packing crates. Nothing more."

"A reasonable step," Collins allowed.

Both men sat quietly.

"Again," the interrogator said. "What can you tell me about Abraham?"

The biography was brief and chilling. Abraham was the only known name for a young gentleman who according to rumors was born into one of the world's wealthiest families. He had invested ten years and his personal fortune preparing for an invasion of the past. What Ramiro knew was minimal, and he openly admitted that he might have been fed lies. But the heart of the plan was for the invaders to come with little but make friends with a useful government, and then they would fabricate the kinds of weapons that would bring this primitive world to their leader's feet.

Ramiro patiently told the story again, and then his interrogator suddenly interrupted.

"Wait, I know," Collins blurted. "It's the future."

"Pardon me?"

"That's how they tested their time machine." He shook the papers in the air. "If they threw a probe into the past, it would only create a new reality. A separate earth diverging from us. But if they had a marked, one-of-a-kind object . . . and then let's say they sent it a minute or a day into the future . . . then according to this quantum craziness, that probe would appear in every reality leading out from this scruffy little moment of ours."

"Exactly," said Ramiro, smiling like a long-suffering but proud teacher.

"That's how your physicists proved it?"

"Grains of marked sand were sent two moments into the future," said Ramiro.

"Huh," said Collins.

The prisoner sat back in his chair.

"Which makes me wonder," Collins continued.

Silence.

Then Collins sat back.

"What are you wondering, my friend?"

"What would happen?" The interrogator lifted his hand, holding an imaginary ball before his gaze. "If you had a time machine, and you happened to throw, I don't know, a couple hundred lumps of U-235 ahead in time? If you sent one of them every minute or so, but you aimed them to appear in exactly the same place, at the same exact moment . . . all of that nuclear material pumped into the same tiny volume . . . what kind of boom would that make . . . ?"

I watched those ripe moments at least half a dozen times before I was sure of what I had seen. For an instant, the prisoner flinched. His heart kicked slightly, and the sweat came a little faster than before. But what held my interest was Ramiro's face, and in particular, how guarded he acted for the next little while.

"I will have to be careful," he was thinking.

"This man is sharp," I could imagine him warning himself. "Sharp and quick, and I need to watch my steps."

6

"A good day's work?"

"Reasonably exceptional."

Jefferson nodded, and then he smiled. Then after careful consideration, he decided not to mention what was foremost on his mind. "How's the lamb?" he asked instead.

"Delicious."

"And the rest?"

"Everything's wonderful," I told him. "Thanks again for the invitation."

Jefferson's efficiency apartment was the same as everyone else's, except for every flourish and individual oddity that he had impressed on its walls and floor and the serviceable, government-issue furnishings. Either his housekeeping was thorough, or he had changed his nature for me. He had a fondness for Impressionist painters and political thrillers. The worn carpet implied a man who liked to pace, possibly while talking on the phone. Only two people were allowed to communicate directly with the outside world, and even then, we had to accept some inflexible restrictions. Every image that entered or left the prison, and even the most ordinary sound, had to be examined by several layers of elaborate software. Hidden messages were the main justification. Ramiro might have secret talents; who knew what any of his microscopic implants really did? Those security measures gave voices a half-second delay, and the news broadcasts were delayed for nearly thirty minutes before they dripped their way down to us.

Jefferson's small television was perched on the kitchen counter, muted and presently turned to CNN. Not sure what to say, he glanced at the images coming out of China. I preferred to invest my next few moments staring at his Monet—a good quality reproduction, matted and framed above the sofa bed. Then I set down my fork and knife, and after wiping the juice from the corner of my mouth, I quietly announced, "You know, I don't like him."

Jefferson turned back to me, trying to guess my intentions.

"Lemonade-7," I said.

"I know who you mean."

Picking up my fork again, I showed him a serious, sober expression. "There's something about that man . . . I don't exactly know what . . . but it's just wrong . . . "

Jefferson risked a neutral nod.

"Control," I said.

"Pardon me?"

"He demands it," I said.

"Of course he wants control."

"And he does an amazing job holding on to it."

Jefferson shrugged. "In small ways, he does."

I said nothing.

"But he's still our prisoner. That never changes. Beyond our assurances to keep him secret and safe from harm, what can he count on?"

"Not much," I agreed. But then I asked, "But what has he given us in these last five or six years? What do we have that's genuinely new?"

With the tips of two fingers, Jefferson scratched his short white beard.

"Does he offer any fresh insights now? Is he able to make any one of our wars a little less terrible?"

"You know how it is, Carmen."

"Remind me."

"The well always runs dry."

"With our sources, you mean."

"Of course."

"So why did Collins remain here?"

A good poker face reveals nothing, except that it is a poker face. Which is a useful clue in itself.

"Collins was better than anybody," I said. "Nobody else understood the minds and makeup of these time travelers. So why didn't he step out into the world, take a new post, and use his hard-earned skills to interrogate fresh suspects?"

"Ramiro was his boy."

"I understand that."

"And honestly, I didn't want to lose Collins," he said.

"Thanks for being honest."

Jefferson shifted in his chair. "Maybe you're right," he allowed. "Looking back, I suppose we might have gotten more good out of Collins."

"I was scouring the world for Abraham," I pointed out.

Hearing the name, Jefferson blinked.

"It's just that nobody bothered to tell me who Abraham was or how many people he had with him, much less what these temporal jihadists were trying to do. There were so many layers of security that responsible, effective work was impossible."

"Why should I defend policies I didn't make?"

"I did piece a few things together for myself," I mentioned. "At least to the point where I knew there was something deadlier than al-Qaeda, a powerful and hateful and almost invisible organization, and it could be anywhere in the world, and I shouldn't trust anybody completely."

The bureaucrat fell back on his instincts. "Knowing what you know now, Carmen . . . do you really believe that you should have been told?"

I didn't react.

"And everybody else with high clearances too? Should hundreds and thousands have been brought into the club?"

I gave the Monet another glance.

Jefferson bristled. "This operation has had its share of leaks over the years. Sure, most came from higher up. But I know of three incidents tied to this facility. And we could be on the far side of the moon, as isolated as we are. So what happens if we brief everybody who might like to know about Ramiro? In thirty seconds, nothing will be secret, and in ten minutes, we'll have forfeited what might be our only advantage."

The fork had grown warm in my hand. "If it's an advantage," I replied, "why aren't we enjoying some real success?"

"You don't think we are?"

I shook my head.

"We've done a marvelous job of undercutting Abraham," he told me. "And since he's our main enemy, I think I should feel proud of my work here."

I stifled a bleak little laugh.

He noticed. Outrage blossomed, and a tight voice said, "I shouldn't have to defend myself or my people." Which was the kind of noise you make when defending everybody. "Before you take that tone with me, perhaps we should both remember what our prisoner—this man who you do not like—has given us."

Then I smiled and nodded. "My parents live in Seattle," I mentioned.

"Exactly. Yes!"

Two years ago, government geologists announced that low rumblings beneath the Pacific were precursors to a substantial earthquake. It was a bogus operation, but well staged. As a precaution, everyone in the Pacific Northwest was told to step outside before 10:30 in the morning, and the highways were closed down, and the airlines stopped landing and taking off. Sixteen minutes later, an 8.0 trembler hit western Washington, and it might have killed thousands. But instead of a mauling, only a few dozen perished and a few billion dollars in infrastructure fell down—almost a nonevent, considering these recent years.

"Seattle is the perfect example," Jefferson said.

Ramiro had given us the dates and epicenters for dozens of future eruptions and earthquakes. But I wasn't the first voice to ask, "What kind of person carries those kinds of tidbits inside his head?"

Jefferson gave his beard another good scratch.

"An amateur astronomer might remember exploding stars," I agreed. "But tectonic events too?"

"The man is brilliant," Jefferson declared. "You've seen his test scores. Those extra genes and his buried machinery give him nearly perfect recall—a skill, I'll add, that he has kept secret from us."

"Seattle didn't hurt his reputation, either," I pointed out.

Jefferson needed to look elsewhere. So he glanced at the television, but whatever he saw there didn't seem to comfort him.

"I wish he'd given us more," I mentioned.

"He can't do the weather," Jefferson replied. "Hurricanes are chaotic, and the Butterfly Effects—"

"I don't mean weather." Shaking my head, I asked, "What about the tsunami off Sumatra?"

"Which one?"

"The worst one," I said. "The day after Christmas, in '04."

His shoulders squared. "That wasn't my call."

"But you recommended caution," I pointed out. "I read Collins' full report. He asked for some kind of warning to be released. But you didn't want us to 'give away the store.' Did I get the cliché right?"

Beneath the white whiskers, sun-starved flesh grew red.

Again, Jefferson said, "It wasn't my decision."

"I realize that."

"In those days, we couldn't fake this kind of knowledge. Any intervention on our part could have exposed our source."

"A quarter of a million dead," I said. "And mostly Muslim, too."

He wouldn't let me drag him down this path. With a snort, he said, "You have no idea how difficult this has been."

"Tell me."

He wanted to do just that.

"Please," I said.

But caution took hold, and Jefferson's mouth disappeared inside the coarse whiskers.

"Is Ramiro real?"

Jefferson didn't seem to hear me. He bent forward, staring at his own half-eaten dinner. Then quietly and fiercely, he said, "A lot of brilliant people have spent years wondering just that."

"He's a lowly soldier," I mentioned. "The lowliest of all, he claims."

Silence.

"So what was Ramiro doing in Montana? Is it the story that he tells? That he was a delivery boy bringing one little piece of an ultramodern bomb into our helpless nation?"

Jefferson gave the television another try.

"Maybe he is a genius, and maybe he came from the future. But the poor bastard didn't know how to drive on ice, did he?"

"Few Brazilians do," Jefferson snapped.

I showed him a narrow, might-mean-anything smile.

"Do you think that the crash was staged?" he finally asked me.

"It has to cross my mind," I allowed.

"Which means Ramiro was sent here, and he's supposed to feed us all the wrong information. Is that what you're thinking?"

I sat back, and I sighed.

"Okay, I'll tell you why Collins stayed right here." Jefferson straightened his back, and he took a deep breath. "Out in the world, what are the odds of finding a second Ramiro? They're minimal at best. Collins would have bounced from one hotspot to another, wasting his skills. But he remained here instead, playing the patience game, waiting for one of you to stumble across a genuine candidate. We had a good plan in place, Carmen. The new prisoner would be brought here and thoroughly interrogated by Collins, and when the time was right, Ramiro would be allowed to meet with him, or her."

"I once found a suspect," I mentioned.

Jefferson remained silent.

"A young woman in Baghdad."

He allowed that statement to simmer. Then with keen pleasure, he said, "You know the old story about Stalin, don't you? One evening, the dictator can't find his favorite pipe, and his first assumption is that it has been stolen. So he demands a full investigation. But the next morning, Stalin realizes that he simply set the pipe in a different drawer, and he admits as much to the head of his secret police. To Beria. Which leads to a very uncomfortable silence. Then Beria clears his throat, admitting that three men have already confessed to stealing the missing item."

I showed surprise. "What? Are you claiming that my girl wasn't real?"

"I've seen all of the files on her. And everybody else who looked good, at one time or another." Jefferson couldn't help but lean across the tiny table, saying, "When your prisoner broke, she confessed to every suggestion that was thrown her way. Give her enough time, and I think we could have convicted her for a thousand crimes, including stealing Stalin's pipe."

I said nothing. Pretending that this was unwelcome news, I chewed on my bottom lip and refused to look him in the eyes.

"We've had dozens of candidates in the pipeline," Jefferson claimed. "But none ever reached a point of real interest to us."

"Too bad," I whispered.

"Your girl was unique because she managed to kill herself. That's what kept her apparent value high. At least back in Washington, it did."

I was silent.

"By the way, did you ever see the autopsy results? They took her apart cell by cell, basically, and not one tiny, futuristic machine was found. Just some oddities in the blood and gut, that's all."

"I tortured an innocent woman? Is that that what you're saying?"

Jefferson gave me a moment to dwell on that sorry prospect. I think that if I'd asked for a tissue, he would have leaped up to help this naïve and disappointing creature.

"We have hard jobs," he finally said.

I got up from the dinner table.

"For what it's worth," he began. Then he hesitated before adding, "Carmen," with a warm tone.

"What?" I asked.

"Collins had a lot of sleepless nights, dealing with all the possibilities."

I walked past him, standing close enough to the Monet that the water lilies turned into unrecognizable blobs of pink and white.

After a minute, I asked quietly, "How many times?"

Jefferson was chewing the lamb. He had to swallow before responding. "How many times what?"

"These unrecorded conversations," I said, my eyes still focused on the gorgeous, senseless painting.

I heard him turn in his chair.

I asked, "When did the secret interrogations begin?"

He decided to stand. "What interrogations?"

"Sometimes Collins disabled the microphones and cameras before entering the prisoner's quarters." I turned, showing Jefferson my best stony face. "I know it because I've checked the logs and other forms. Nine times in the last six years, some odd software error has caused the complete dumping of everything that happened between Collins and Ramiro."

Jefferson considered his options.

I said, "These are very convenient blunders, or they are intentional acts of treason."

"No," said Jefferson.

"No?"

"Those interviews were Collins' idea. But I okayed them."

"Why?"

Too late, the man began to wonder if I was playing a game. "I don't think I need to remind you, miss. I have the authority."

"You do," I agreed.

"And I'll tell you this: Despite what you might believe, Ramiro continued to offer us help. Valuable, even critical insights. And we were justifiably scared of using the normal pipeline for that kind of news."

"Name one insight," I said.

He refused to respond.

"I do have the authority to demand an answer, sir."

"What if another nation has captured one of Abraham's people?" Jefferson posed the question and then shuddered. "It's sobering to consider. Another power, possibly one of our enemies, is keeping somebody like Ramiro in their own deep, secret hole—"

"What else?"

He winced.

"Give me your worst nightmare," I demanded.

"I'm sure you can guess that."

"All right," I said. "After many years in prison, Ramiro happens to mention, 'Oh, by the way, my basic assumptions might have been wrong from the beginning. Maybe Abraham isn't looking for a cooperative Middle Eastern country. Maybe his sights are focused on a wealthier, much more advanced nation.'" I laughed sadly. "That isn't the sort of news you'd cherish sending up the pipeline, is it?"

Jefferson studied me, once more trying to decide what I really was, and just how adept I might be.

"That last session with Ramiro," I began.

Squaring his shoulders made Jefferson's belly stick out.

"I can't find any recording of the interview. Is that right?"

"There isn't any," he conceded.

I couldn't decide if he was lying.

"Collins didn't share any details with you. Did he?"

"Why do you think that?"

"Because when there was important news, he always came straight to you. But that night, he walked home with Jim." I used a suspicious smile, pointing out, "Or maybe there was important news. But he knew that his audience would never accept whatever he was carrying with him."

Jefferson looked up and to his right.

I glanced at his television, just for a moment. The civil war in China seemed quite small and smoky, a few pain-wracked bodies flicking in and out of existence, a single tank burning in an anonymous street.

At last, Jefferson asked me, "What exactly is your assignment here?"

"Isn't it obvious?" I asked.

Then he laughed—a miserable, sickly utterance—and with a tone of confession, he said, "Oh, shit . . . that's what I thought."

7

"I've seen your arrival site."

"Have you?"

"Not physically, no," I confessed. "And even if I had the chance, I think I would pass on it today."

"Reasonable of you."

I stopped walking.

Ramiro took two more steps before pausing. His exercise yard was long and narrow, defined by brownish green walls, and for no discernable reason, his potted plants were healthier than those in the public avenues. Standing between vigorous umbrella trees, he watched my mouth, my eyes.

"Kashmir," I said.

He decided to offer a narrow, unreadable smile.

"You couldn't know this, but some years ago, I was able to walk on the Indian side of the disputed region. It wasn't a long visit, but I came away with the impression that Kashmir was one of the most beautiful and most dangerous places in my world."

My comments earned an agreeable nod.

"Did Collins tell you? Various teams have visited the Shyok River."

"He mentioned that, and I'm sure you know that."

"Tough work, those people had. Trying to verify the unthinkable, and doing it in what was a low-grade war zone. That first survey team was tiny and ignorant. They went in fast and flew out again on the same day, pockets full of soil samples and photographs. But the evidence was plain. Something energetic had happened there. The toppled trees and soil profiles were odd, and obvious. So we came up with a workable cover story, a fable that allowed us to move around the area, and when it was absolutely necessary, involve Pakistani Intelligence."

Ramiro's eyes remained wide open.

"But that second team didn't know what the hunt was for either. Our top people were told not to ask for specifics, but to always watch for details that seemed out of place."

"You said you'd been to the site," Ramiro mentioned.

"By VR means." I placed both hands over my eyes, pretending to wear the cumbersome mask. "Those agents came home with high-density images. I learned about them when I was first briefed about you, and I demanded to be given the chance to walk the site."

"Did you learn anything?"

"Much," I mentioned.

He waited.

"Knowing nothing, I might have guessed that some passing god had sneezed. A perfect circle of ground, big enough for a couple hundred people, had been swept clear. Locals had already carted away most of the downed trees, but there was enough debris to give a sense of what the scene had looked like. That second team dug a trench, took its pictures, and then covered everything up again." I drew a vertical line with a finger. "A little more than a hand's length underground, the old soil was waiting. It looked a little like shale. But according to the data, what was under that line was identical to the soil sitting straight above it. And by identical, I mean the same. Pebble for pebble, sand grain for sand grain."

"The Lorton Energy was shaped carefully," he said.

"Seventy feet across, eight feet tall."

He nodded.

"I like studying the weird crap that they found in the soil. Do you know what I mean? The nano debris, the occasional busted machine part. Little stuff that we couldn't make today, even if we wanted to."

"There would have been more debris," he mentioned. "Except our clothes and bodies were thoroughly cleaned before."

"Smart," I said.

He waited.

"Of course we needed Pakistani help," I admitted. "There was no way to poke around their side of the disputed border without being noticed. And since they happened to be our loyal allies in the war on terror, at least for the moment, we invented some very scary intelligence about an armed group, possibly Indian radicals, who had slipped across the border in '99. Our mutual enemies had carried gold and guns, and to help explain all the sampling, maybe enough radionuclides to build a few dirty bombs. They would have been on foot, we told our allies. And they might have had odd accents. Then we asked for help interviewing the local people, trying to find anybody who remembered strangers passing through three years before."

"Some remembered," said Ramiro.

I waited.

"Collins mentioned as much."

"Stories about strangers, yes." I started to walk again, and Ramiro fell in beside me. "I haven't gone over all the testimonies. Just a few summaries, that's all I've had time for. But there were witnesses on the local farms, and more in a couple of nearby towns. Exactly what you'd expect if a large group of quiet pedestrians had come in the night and quickly scattered across the landscape."

"Most of us hid," he said.

"Naturally."

"A few were dispatched to secure transportation."

"Those who would blend in best, I'll assume."

"I assume the same."

"You and your little cell hunkered down together."

With Ramiro beside me, I was keenly aware of how much taller he was. "In a woodlot by the water," he said.

"And Abraham?"

"I don't know where he was."

"I wouldn't believe you if you claimed otherwise."

Silence.

"After all, you're just a convert who got lucky. You weren't scheduled to join the invasion. But at the last moment, one of the chosen warriors fell ill—"

"My friend."

"The German, your benefactor. Sure. He cleared your entry into Abraham's group. And when he couldn't make the trip, you did in his place."

My companion held his gait to the end of the room, and then with the precision of a big zoo cat, he turned and started back again.

"I have a question about the German."

"Yes?"

"But first, let's talk a little more about Kashmir."

"Whatever you want, Carmen."

"Even our crude virtual-reality technologies make it beautiful."

"Our arrival site was lovely," he agreed.

"Seeing the mountains and that glacial river . . . it made me sad to think about what's happened to it since."

He waited.

I said, "Sad," once again.

"And I am sorry," Ramiro volunteered.

"For what? You told us what you knew, and we acted on it. You had to pass through Kashmir because that's where the only substantial time machine existed in your day. Point-to-point transfer is the way time travel is done. And it was your German pal who claimed that Abraham would center his operation inside Iraq. Because they had industry and an educated middle class, he said. Because of a greedy dictator and a useful secret service. Abraham planned to approach Saddam with the fantastic truth, and if the Baathists cooperated, there would be riches beyond all measure."

"Iraq was a disappointment," he allowed.

I nodded in agreement.

We had crossed the room again, stopping short of the door—a heavy metal door with thick glass on top, a single guard watching us from the other side.

"I was surprised," Ramiro admitted. "I expected that you'd find a good deal of physical evidence."

"We did find some lost nanos in warehouses, and a diamond screwdriver out in the oil fields."

He shook his head slowly. "Perhaps you understand why I don't like these people."

"They manipulated you."

His pace lifted, just slightly. And his hands swung the weights just a little harder.

"Then we bombed Iran hard. And goaded Israel into mangling Syria for us."

We walked until the room ended, and like two cats, we turned and walked back in our own tracks.

"Two more disappointing wars," I muttered.

He pointed out, "Your leaders made those decisions. I was very honest. I would have handled these conflicts differently."

"I know."

Then he said, "Pakistan."

I waited.

"That was a possibility I mentioned to Collins." His tone was frus-

trated. He sounded like a proud man who had suffered a public embarrassment. "Very early in our relationship, even before you reached Baghdad,
I suggested to Collins that my people might gravitate to the nearest
compliant government."

"Except the Pakistanis were our friends. And we had close, close ties
with Musharraf."

Ramiro smiled. "Do you trust anyone, Carmen?"

I waved the question aside. "But of course Pakistani Intelligence—our
partners on the ground—was full of ambitious souls."

"That's true."

"The future that we should have lived could have been very instructive.
Somebody like Abraham, setting his sights on potential allies, might identify
the name and address of a young captain who would have eventually ruled
his empire. A fledging Napoleon with connections and toxic ambitions.
Leave him alone for another twenty or thirty years, and he would have
earned his power. But patience isn't common in would-be emperors. A man
like that would surely look at the temporal jihadists as gifts from God."

"Collins and I discussed the Pakistan possibility. In addition to several
other scenarios."

"I want to talk about Pakistan."

"Of course."

"Do you know why we hit it next?"

He took a moment before shaking his head.

"What did Collins tell you?"

"Its government was on the brink of collapse," he said. "A powerful
bomb was detonated in Islamabad, and a peculiar device was found in the
wreckage. Collins brought the object to me, to ask my opinion."

"I haven't seen the device myself," I admitted. "From what I hear, it's
sitting in a vault under the Pentagon." And for a thousand years, that's
where it would remain, protected by the radioactive nightmares from
Indian Point.

Ramiro lifted one of his weights, remarking, "It is about this size, but
hollow. Cylindrical and composed of intricate nanostructures that give it
some interesting properties."

"Juice it up with electricity," I mentioned, "and it turns invisible."

"I gave a demonstration."

"The machine has a structural flaw and can't be used. You claimed. But if it functions, it could play a critical role in the construction of a portable, low-energy time machine."

Ramiro lowered the weight, saying nothing.

"I trust everyone I know," I mentioned.

He glanced at me, his gaze curious. Alert.

"What I trust is that people will always be people. They will do what they want, and when you search for motives, rationality proves to be a luxury. Fear and love and hatred: those are the emotions that count for something. And everything that involves us comes naturally from our human beast."

"A reasonable philosophy," he replied.

"What if Abraham was busily fabricating a new time machine?"

Ramiro said nothing.

"Our nightmare kept getting worse and worse," I continued. "By then, we had a new president. A chance for fresh beginnings. But what if our enemies were trying to cobble together a small, workable time machine? They could bring it into our country and drive it wherever they wanted to go, and with modest amounts of power, they could aim at the future, launching the makings of bombs. It was just like Collins suggested early on, wasn't it? The jihadists could launch atomic bombs or the ingredients for a chemical attack." My voice picked up momentum. "We wouldn't have any defense. Deadly, unbeatable weapons sent through time, invisible to us now. This moment. Abraham's people could travel from city to city, and ten years from today, at a predetermined instant, our entire country would be wiped clean off the earth."

We paused, turned.

"That's what they made me read," I confessed. "After I got my chance to walk beside a beautiful virtual river, that apocalyptic scenario was shown to me."

Ramiro nodded.

"Of course we went into Pakistan," I said. "I would have attacked, in an instant. Any responsible president would have been compelled to do nothing less. Because Abraham might have been hiding in Islamabad or Karachi, probably in some baby potentate's guest room, and we had to do something. Didn't we? Another little war, another stack of wreckage to poke through. But maybe we'd find enough this time, the kinds of evidence to show us where to go next, and who to hit next, and maybe even get a prisoner or two worth interrogating."

Ramiro let me pass into the lead.

"Pricks," I muttered. Then I slowed and looked up at him, saying, "It's too bad about India. Too bad. But a few dozen nukes dropped into their cities is a lot better than total oblivion for us."

My companion slowed, almost stopping, and with a patient, almost soothing voice, he asked, "What about the German?"

"Your friend?"

"You had a question about him," Ramiro reminded me.

I stopped altogether. Something in my posture worried the guard on duty. But as he started to work the door's lock, I waved to him, ordering him to remain where he couldn't hear our conversation.

"I'm sure Collins already covered this ground," I said. "He was always thorough. I just haven't found it in the files yet."

"What do you want to know?"

"His name was Schwartz?"

"Yes."

"And you met him outside Madrid? In the refugee camp where he worked as a counselor, right?"

"Yes."

"He became your sponsor. He was the one who converted you to Abraham's cause—the violent overthrow of a flawed, weak past—and then he worked hard to have you accepted into his group."

"Collins and I thoroughly covered my history."

"But on the last day, your friend got sick."

"A strain of flu. Yes."

"That we haven't seen in our time." I stood close to Ramiro, letting his face hang over mine. "Your people didn't want to spark an unnecessary pandemic, particularly in a population you wanted to use as an ally."

"Schwartz was disappointed."

"Just disappointed?"

He shrugged. "Devastated is a better—"

"Did you make it happen?"

Ramiro blinked.

I took one step backward while staring at him. "Did you infect him with the flu? Just to free up a slot for you?"

The prisoner stared at me until he decided to stare at one of the bronze walls. "That is an interesting proposal."

"Collins never asked that?"

"No."

"Did you do it?"

"No, Carmen. I didn't do any such thing."

"That's good to hear," I allowed.

He nodded.

"In twelve years, Collins never asked that question?"

He shook his head and smiled, saying, "He didn't."

"But could Abraham have thought that you did such a wicked thing to your friend? Is that possible?"

"I have no idea what the man considered," he said.

"But both of us can imagine the possibility. Am I right? A person might do the treacherous and horrible, just to get his chance to jump back through time."

The disgust looked genuine, but not particularly deep.

"This is what I believe, Ramiro. I believe that there isn't one question, no matter how unlikely or silly or outright insane, that you haven't already anticipated. At one time or another, you have considered every angle."

His next smile was cautious but proud.

"Whatever you are," I said.

"What do you mean by that, Carmen?"

I closed my mouth, my heart slamming hard and steady. "I think you're ready to say anything," I told him. "Anything. If it suited your needs, short-term or long, you would happily admit to inoculating Schwartz. Or you'd agree that yes, Abraham was suspicious of you. Unless you decided to confess that you have been his most trusted agent from the beginning, allowing yourself to be captured, and then happily causing us to step everywhere but where we needed to be."

"That," Ramiro allowed, "is a singularly monstrous image of me."

Then with no further comment, he swung the weights in his hands, continuing with his morning exercise.

8

I rode our smallest elevator to the surface, passing through the concrete-block field office and several more layers of security. One of the CIA girls gave me a lift to the nearby airstrip. As she drove, we chatted about safe subjects. The weather, mostly. And then she smiled in a certain way, mentioning Collins. "I haven't seen much of him lately."

I said, "He's brutally busy."

"Oh, sure."

Collins was a cat locked in a box. In her mind, he was nothing but alive. Since there was no good reason for her to know what happened underground, she knew nothing.

"I'll tell him you asked," I lied.

She smiled. "Would you? Thanks."

An old Globemaster was waiting on the runway, bound for undisclosed places but called out of the sky to snatch me up. Its crew had strict orders not to speak with their important passenger, which meant that I sat alone in the dark along with the rest of the cargo—a pair of battered Humvees and crates of medical supplies bound for some desperate place. My seat had the luxury of a tiny window, but there wasn't much to see, what with the clouds of black smoke from the burning Saudi oil fields. But night found us over Missouri, and we crossed into a wide pocket of relatively clear air. The stars were exactly where they belonged, and I had the best reason to believe that none of them would explode in the near future. A power outage had struck Kentucky. A wilderness lay beneath me, broken only by a few headlights creeping along and the occasional home blessed with generators and extra fuel to burn. Who was the culprit tonight? At least two homegrown insurgencies had been playing hell with the TVA lately. But the power grid was tottering on its best day, what with every reactor mothballed and barely a fart's worth of hydrocarbons finding its way to us.

I didn't belong in this world.

Some years ago, I had carelessly stepped off my earth, entering a realm that only resembled what was home. I was lost, and it was the worst kind of lost. No matter how hard I looked, I couldn't decipher which day and which hour had transformed everything familiar and happy.

Was it in '99, when the future decided to invade us?

Or in '02, when Ramiro was found just south of the Canadian border?

Neither moment felt worthy of this kind of dislocation. There were too many ways to redraw the following events, to many reasonable acts that would have minimized the damage wrought by faceless, nameless souls.

Even our early wars seemed incapable of obliterating so much.

But then we hit Pakistan, with India's gracious help, and despite our assurances to obliterate the Muslim A-bombs, the Pakistanis managed to hit their neighbor with half a hundred blasts, pushing our final ally back into a peasant state, desperate and starving.

Three months later, fifty million were dead and the ash of the murdered cities was beginning to cool the world. That's when a half-megaton nuke hidden in a barge was floated in close to the Indian Point reactors north of New York City. A cold front was passing through, and the resulting mushroom cloud threw up an astonishing array of toxins. Everything to the south was doomed. Infrastructure and millions of humans, plus trillions of dollars and the last relics of a working economy—all these good things were lost in a single act of undiluted justice.

Like most people, I watched the horror on television, from the safest room inside my helpless house. After years of government service, I had temporarily left the military. I was burnt-out, I believed. I was actually considering going back to college. To teach or learn; I didn't have any definitive plan yet. I have a fair amount of imagination, but those following days and nights were too enormous to wring so much as a tear from me. I couldn't grasp the damage, the horror. Great cities were rendered unlivable, perhaps for a thousand years. My countrymen, now refugees, were spreading a kind of inchoate, embryonic revolution as they raced inland. And during the worst of it, my government seemed unable to make even simple decisions about martial law and protecting our other reactors, much less mobilizing our shrinking resources and pitiful manpower.

That was the moment, at least inside my little circle of interrogators and ex-interrogators, that Abraham became a known name: The terrorist's terrorist.

He was a mastermind. He was a disease and a scourge. But even then, the most informed rumors avoided any mention of time travel.

People who knew Ramiro's story naturally assumed that Indian Point was the work of temporal jihadists. My government was temporarily hamstrung by the idea that their enemy had launched their bomb months or years ago, and there was no way to know where the next blast would blossom. It was almost good news when the event-team digested the nuke's isotopic signature and ruled out the bizarre. What we had witnessed was a plain hydrogen warhead—an old Soviet model—that had been smuggled into the country by one of our countless, and to this day still nameless, enemies.

Two years ago, I couldn't cry. But that night, sitting alone in the big overloaded aircraft, I began to sob hard. Sob and moan, but always trying to remind myself that in our quantum universe, every great event was nothing but the culmination of human decision and human indecision, chance and caprice. The poverty and despair surrounding me was vanishingly small. Our earth was just one thin example of what was possible, and because it was possible, this history was inevitable, and why did people waste their time believing that we could ever be special in God's unbounded eye?

After the tears, I got up to pee.

Turbulence struck before I could get back to my seat. I ended up taking refuge inside one of the Humvees, belting in as the entire plane shook and turned wildly. Obviously, the earth's atmosphere was furious at the damage we were doing to it. Even the most rational mind slides easily into a mentality where ancient forces focus their rage on what looked like a fat, helpless, soon-to-be-extinct mechanical bird.

Somewhere in the jumping darkness, an alarm sounded.

Then after a long five minutes, and with no visible change in our circumstances, the blaring stopped.

The only voice I heard emerged from the cockpit. "Who would you fuck first?" he screamed. "Ginger or Mary Ann?"

"Why not Lovey?" an older, wiser voice asked. "She's got the money!"

I laughed somehow, and I held tight to the seat beneath me, and with no warning whatsoever, we dropped hard, plunging through the last of the mayhem. Then the air calmed abruptly and the flaps changed their pitch as the big wings brought us around and down onto a great long slab of brightly lit concrete.

The tires screamed and survived.

Then the lights came up inside, and I finally saw my Humvee wasn't just old, but it had seen a few firefights. Bullet holes and shrapnel gouges begged for repair, but someone must have thought: Why bother? Since we never brought equipment home from the Middle East, I was left wondering if this was LA damage. Or Detroit. Or just the run of the mill unrest that doesn't earn national notice.

As the plane taxied, a crewman came to retrieve me. I rather enjoyed that moment when he stood beside my empty seat, scratching his tired head, wondering whether the only passenger had fallen overboard?

I said, "Hey."

He said, "Ma'am," and then regretted that tiny break of the orders. Without another sound, he showed me to the hatch and opened it moments before a ladder was wheeled into position, and I stepped out into what was a remarkably cool August night, pausing just long enough to thank him.

But he was already wrestling the hatch closed again.

A single limousine waited on the otherwise empty tarmac. I had expected a convoy and probably a quick ride to some bunker or heavily guarded warehouse. But in times like these, important souls preferred to slip about in tiny, anonymous groups. The Globemaster revved its jets and pulled down the runway, fighting for velocity and then altitude. I reached the limousine just as the runway lights were killed. A pair of secret service agents emerged and swept me for weapons. I can't remember the last time I'd held any gun. I bent down and slipped into what proved to be an office on wheels. I would have been more surprised if the president was driving. But only a little more surprised. He offered his hand before he smiled, and his smile vanished before he was done welcoming me.

No pleasantries were offered, or expected.

I sat opposite him and sensibly said nothing.

He needed a shave, and a shower too. Which made me feel a little less filthy after my trip. I kept waiting for the voice that I often heard on the news—the deep voice that reminded us how the struggle wasn't lost and courage was essential. But what I heard instead was a tired bureaucrat too impatient to hold back his most pressing questions.

"What happened to Collins?"

"I don't know," I answered.

"Suicide, or murder?"

I nearly said, "Yes." Since this is a quantum universe, and everything that can happen does happen. Without hesitation or shame.

But instead of humor, I offered, "It was a suicide."

"You're certain?"

"Basically."

He had to ask, "Why?"

"I warned you," I said. "I'm not a criminal investigator. But I think that's the way Collins would have killed himself. At home, quietly, and without too much pain. But if somebody had wanted him dead—"

"What about Jefferson?"

I shrugged. "No, he wouldn't have been that neat or patient. Jefferson, or some associate of his, would have shot Collins and then planted evidence to make it look like a suicide. At least that's my reading of things."

The president wanted to feel sure. That mood showed in his face, his posture. But he couldn't stop thinking about Jefferson. "What about the prison's security?"

"You're asking is there an agent on the premises. One of Abraham's people, maybe?"

His mouth tightened.

"That I can't answer," I cautioned. "Really, I wouldn't even know how to figure it out. If I had the time."

He bristled. He had invested a lot of hope in me, and he expected at least the illusion of results. With a dramatic flourish, he opened a plain folder waiting on his lap. Then with a low grumble, he asked, "What about Collins?"

I wanted past this traitor-in-our-midst talk. But my companion happened to be my government's most important citizen, and he was exactly as paranoid as it took to successfully represent his people.

"Was Collins one of them? I don't think so."

"You know the emergency council's report," he muttered testily.

"Which part? About the future knowing all our secrets? Or the DNA masking Abraham's people?"

"I mean everything." The president took a long moment to frame his next comments. "They didn't show their faces, and for obvious good reasons. Even without Ramiro's testimony, it's hard to deny the possibility—the certainty—that profound genetic manipulation will be possible in a hundred years. Under those masks, the bastards could have looked identical to anybody from our world. At least anybody who happened to leave behind hair or a flake of skin."

The emergency council was a cheerless room filled with scared specialists—off-plumb scientists and old sci-fi writers, plus a couple of psychics who happened to get lucky once or twice about future disasters. They had access to secrets, including scrubbed synopses of Ramiro's insights. And during one pitiless night, they asked each other how could our fight, begun with so many good intentions, have gone so tragically bad.

Their answer was the worst nightmare yet. Among Abraham's soldiers were there perfect duplicates of men and women who would have served in our highest offices, starting in '01? Before our election, they could have slipped into the United States and replaced each of those historic figures. Unknown to us, the worst monsters imaginable would have worn stolen faces and voices. And later, sitting in Washington, those same pretenders could have done untold damage to the innocent, helpless world.

That scenario seemed to explain everything—bad decisions, incompetent methods, and the miserable follow-ups to each tragic misstep.

Paranoia had never enjoyed such an acidic, malicious beauty.

The file was important enough to leave open, and I caught one long glimpse. Which was what the president wanted, I suppose. He was eager to prove to me just how awful everything had become.

On top was a photograph, a famous face gazing up at the camera. The man was elderly now, shaved bald and very weak and far too thin. Each bruise was ugly and yellow, and together they defined the color of his cowering face. Was this where we had come? Taking our own people into a cellar to starve them and beat them, all in the vain hope that they would finally admit that they deserved this horrid treatment?

"Jefferson is Jefferson," I maintained.

The president closed the file.

"And Collins was always Collins."

He sighed. "Are you as sure as you are about the suicide?"

"Even more so," I declared.

"But there was one day last year," the president began. Then he made a rather clumsy show of pushing through more files, lending a banal officiousness to the insulting moment. This was what my leader had been doing while waiting for my plane. Thumbing his way through old security papers that meant nothing.

"I don't care about last year," I said.

"Collins went missing," he snapped. "He was out on leave, and for fourteen hours, the man dropped out of contact with everybody."

"He explained that later," I pointed out. "The man was exhausted. He needed to be alone and regroup. And that's what I believe."

"You do?"

"More and more."

"He wasn't one of Abraham's agents?"

"If he was, then maybe I am. And you are too."

My reply was too awful to consider. I read revulsion in the man's face and his fists. And I kept thinking that if I had bothered to vote in our last election, I never would have helped elect this dangerously incompetent man.

"I am not one of them," he whispered.

"Maybe you are, and you don't know it," I said.

"What do you mean?"

"If our enemies can remake their faces and blend in everywhere, then why not rewire the thought patterns inside other people's heads? If they have that kind of magical technology, then why not inoculate the world with a tailored virus that makes everybody into loyal Muslims who have no choice but to accept the wisdom of this never-seen Abraham?"

Here was one proposition that had never been offered to the president. And he responded exactly as I expected, eyes opening wide, seeing nothing.

I laughed it off.

He hoped that I was joking now, but he didn't dare mention my suggestion again. Instead he posed one final question. "And why did Collins kill himself?"

"Remember the dollar?" I asked.

"Excuse me?"

"On the bathroom floor, they found a coin in the blood. Do you remember that detail from the reports?"

He had to admit, "No."

"Collins didn't see or speak to Ramiro for three days. Other than that, nobody remembers him doing anything out of the ordinary. But I have reason to believe that our prisoner gave him something. Something new. Something that was so difficult to accept that it took three days for Collins to wrestle with the concept. And then what the man did . . . I'm guessing this, but I would bet my savings on it . . . Collins went into his bathroom and ran a warm bath and got a knife and then flipped the coin. And the coin happened to come up tails."

"Which means?"

"It's a quantum-inspired game. In this reality, tails meant that he would slit his veins and bleed out."

"And if it was heads?"

"Then Collins would have done something a lot more difficult."

"And what would that have been. . . ?"

"Show the entire world what Ramiro gave him."

"And what was that, do you think?"

"I wish I knew." My laugh was grim and sad, and it suited both of us. "In my mind, I keep seeing Collins sitting in that bathtub, flipping the coin, working it until he got the answer he wanted."

A phone set between us rang once, very softly, and then stopped.

The president gestured at the invisible sky. "Another plane's heading west. It'll arrive in another hour or two."

His wave was a signal; my door suddenly popped open. It was still summer, but I could feel frost threatening.

"Do I still have full authority?" I asked.

Again, the presidential phone rang, begging for attention. He offered me a nod, saying, "For the time being, yes."

"Full authority?"

"Yes."

"Thank you, sir."

He stared at me for another moment. Then he quietly asked, "What do you think our world's chances are?"

"Very poor," I offered.

"Why?"

I had to say, "With people like us in charge, sir . . . our enemies don't have to do much at all."

9

The sound was soft but insistent, coming from the middle of my apartment door. I heard the first rap of the knuckles, but I did nothing for what seemed like a very long time. Aware of the bed beneath me, I looked at my hands in the faint blue glow of the nightlight, and then I turned and gazed at the red face of the clock on the edge of my nightstand. Eight minutes after three in the morning, I read. Twice. Then the knock quickened, and I sat up and put on my only robe and took the time to find my slippers before letting my visitor inside.

"You're not watching," Jefferson began.

I said nothing.

He looked at the darkness and rumpled sheets, his expression puzzled. Then his face fell back into a kind of breathless horror.

"What?" I asked.

He couldn't say it.

What passed for the outside was gloomy, not dark. A single guard stood in the middle of the enormous tunnel, meeting my eyes before she retreated into the shadows.

After my guest stepped inside, I said, "Come in."

Once the door was closed, Jefferson turned on my ceiling light. Then he showed me a tired, frazzled expression that set the tone. "Now Russia has been hit."

"Hit?"

"Bad."

I said, "Fuck."

"Moscow," he told me.

I sat on the edge of my bed.

"Half a megaton," he muttered, standing in the middle of the small room, hands dangling at his sides.

I stood up again, slippers popping as I walked to my television. The filtering software had a lot of work to do before we could be trusted to see the news. That's why the thirty-minute delay, and that's why the world before me was nearly two thousand seconds in the past.

A handsome Russian was sitting at a news desk, speaking quickly but with a surprising measure of poise. It was easy to believe that Jefferson was wrong. Nothing awful had happened. Not understanding the language or the Cyrillic lettering streaming past, it was easy to embrace the doubts assuring you, "This is nothing. Nothing."

Then the feed switched abruptly, picking up CNN. An older but equally attractive newscaster sat several thousands of miles from the tragedy. But he didn't have any trace of Slavic stoicism. Practically screaming, he declared, "In the morning, without warning, Hell was released just a mile from the Kremlin!"

Jefferson collapsed in my only chair.

I reclaimed my bed, watching the first in a series of inadequate views of an unfolding disaster. The flash was only as bright as the amateur equipment could absorb. The images jumped, and I could hear people screaming in Russian . . . and then the camera and I were being carried into the subway, the screen going black when the power abruptly shut off . . .

The next view was a ten-second snippet from some high-rise far enough away to be spared by the blast.

The third was from someplace very close, and more recent. A digital camera was shoved over a concrete wall, showing a firestorm that was starting to grow wings.

"It's their turn now," I whispered.

Jefferson didn't seem to hear me.

I glanced at my guest and then looked away. "Russia almost seemed to be blessed," I mentioned.

"This is bad, Carmen."

"Yeah."

"No," he said.

I stared at him. "What do you mean?"

The last decade had been relatively sweet for Russia. Pragmatic and naturally authoritarian, it had managed to avoid most of the mayhem. And it didn't hurt that when the Middle East turned to smoke and warlords, the Russians happily sold their oil and natural gas to the EU and a few select friends, increasing their own wealth many times over.

Again, I asked, "What do you mean?"

Jefferson dipped his head.

The television jumped to the BBC. The Prime Minister had a few sturdy words to offer about giving support to all the victims of this latest misery.

I muted the sound.

Which helped Jefferson's focus. With a conspirator's whisper, he told me, "I was just in touch with somebody."

"Who?"

He named the CIA director, using the friends-only nickname.

I said nothing.

Jefferson gave my brown carpet a long, important study.

"What else is wrong?"

The man looked old and extraordinarily tired. What he knew was so urgent that he had to practically run over here to tell me. But now he lacked the courage to put into words what a confidential voice had told him five minutes ago, from the other end of a secure line.

"Has there been another explosion?" I prodded.

"No," he managed. Then he added, "Maybe."

"Shit, Jefferson—"

"Do you know how we were after Indian Point? Down here, I mean. We were terrified that the big assault was finally coming. But then we heard that an old Soviet warhead did the damage. Which meant it wasn't Abraham." He breathed faster, his face red as a blister. "And this bomb wasn't Abraham's either. The yield and isotope readings point to it being one of ours. One of eight."

"Eight? What eight?"

He rubbed his belly.

"Just say it, Jefferson."

"I just learned this for the first time," he reported. "After Indian Point, when everything was crazy . . . Washington dead and millions fleeing . . . somebody with the necessary skills ripped open an Air Force bunker and took out eight high-yield marvels, any one of which matches what we're seeing here . . . "

I said, "Fuck," once again.

He nodded.

"But the failsafes," I said. "Soviet bombs are one thing. But how could somebody make our damned things detonate?"

"Like I said, these people have skills."

The horrific images had returned, and we watched in silence for another minute or two.

"What's Russia doing now?" I asked.

"Their president's in St. Petersburg. And he's talked to our president two, maybe three times."

"The Director told you this?"

"Yes."

"Seven more nukes?"

"What if somebody wants payback for Indian Point?" he asked me.

Or himself.

"But the Russians weren't responsible," I said. "At least not directly, they weren't."

"But what if we're responsible for this?"

"Who's 'we'?"

Wearing an interrogator's face, he stared at me. "I know where you went last week, Carmen. Believe me, I have friends. I have connections. I know whose limousine you sat inside."

I stared back at him.

Then I carefully told him, "No. We had nothing to do with Moscow. Our president's too scared of phantoms to pick a fight with an old enemy."

Jefferson bristled slightly. "What do you mean? 'Phantoms'?"

I didn't answer.

He said, "Carmen," twice, and then gave up.

A truce was declared, ushering in ten minutes of silence. I pushed the television back up to a comfortable volume, and using e-mail and my private sources, I pieced together a chain of events roughly the same as his.

"Their president wants to believe our president," I reported.

Jefferson nodded.

"But if there's a second attack . . . "

He looked at me. For the first time, he had the roving eyes of a healthy male. As if emerging from a fog, Jefferson realized that he was sitting in a woman's apartment and she was wearing nothing but a nightgown and slippers and a fuzzy old robe.

If only to change the desperate mood, he wanted sparks.

I pulled the robe across my chest. Then I told him, "You should go back to your apartment."

He said, "Maybe."

"Now," I said.

He stood stiffly and looked at me. Suddenly I could see Jefferson at his high school dance, standing beside the wrestling mats, too smart to bother asking any girl to accompany him out onto the gymnasium floor.

Against my wishes, I felt sorry for the poor guy.

Then I ushered him to the door and shut and locked it.

Alone, I slowly dressed, and after another hour of television, I stepped out into a tunnel that was beginning to go through the motions of dawn.

In the brightening gloom, I walked.

Then I ran.

I was pounding along my favorite stretch when I passed the round pond with its bluegill and a single dragonfly. Standing on the wooden deck was our resident fisherman. "Hey, Jim."

He almost jumped at the sound of my voice.

"Any bites?"

He said, "Hi, Carmen," and rolled his head. Then he flicked the fly out onto the windless water, and after a pause and a couple of deep swallows, he said, "Somebody just told me something."

"What's that, Jim?"

Looking at his own hands, he explained, "It's this guy I know. He works security upstairs. And I know it's against every order, and we aren't supposed to talk—"

"You heard about Moscow?"

"And St. Petersburg."

I had just enough time to ask, "What about St. Petersburg?"

Then the alarms began to blare—throbbing, insistent noises meant to jangle every nerve—and the fisherman threw down his gear and sprinted toward the nearest elevator. But he was too late. The field station on the ground had declared a lockdown emergency, and according to protocols, every exit disabled itself. Just once, Jim struck the steel door of the elevator with a fist. Then after a moment of quiet muttering, he returned to the pond. His face was as white and dead as the salt surrounding us. Not quite meeting my eyes, he said, "I'm sorry, ma'am. That won't happen again."

And then he picked up his tackle and silently struck out for home.

10

For nine days, our prisoner was allowed to keep his normal routine. Guards brought hot meals, clean clothes, and the expected little luxuries. His plumbing and lights worked without interruption, and at appropriate intervals, we spared enough power to brighten his exercise yard. The only significant change was that I stopped meeting with Ramiro. But he didn't mention my absence, not once, just as he refused to discuss what must have been obvious. The shrill alarms would have been audible from inside his cell, and less than an hour later, the first in a sequence of deep, painful rumbles passed through the surrounding salt bed.

Fuel was limited, which was why the tunnel lights were kept at a midnight glow. And that's why the vegetation began to wither and drop leaves, including inside Ramiro's yard. The dying umbrella trees garnered a few extra glances, I noted. Then after six days, Ramiro's milk turned to the dried variety, and there was a sudden influx of fried bluegill in his dinner, and the banana slices on his morning yogurt were brown at the edges. But his guards provided the largest clues. Even a sloppy observer would have noticed the miserable faces. Not even the hardest professional could hide that level of raw sadness. Ramiro would have kept track of which guards skipped their watch and who was pulled early when they felt themselves about to start blubbering. But again, he didn't say one word that was at all removed from the ordinary.

Jefferson was a minor revelation. That sturdy old bureaucrat threw himself into the disaster, holding meetings and ordering studies. Key machinery had to be identified, inventories made of every spare part. Our generators were industrial fuel cells, and it was a minor victory when two extra barrels of methanol were discovered behind a pile of construction trash. For two days, the practicality of hydroponics was explored. But a determined search found no viable seed, save for some millet and cracked corn meant for his assistant's pet parakeet. Our home was a prison, not a long-term refuge. But at least there were ample stocks of canned goods and MREs, and the water and air were agreeable to purification. Plus, there were quite a few handymen in our ranks. Most estimates gave us at least six months and perhaps as many as eight months of comfortable security. That was a point worth repeating each day, at the beginning of our mandatory meetings.

With nobody watching us, Jefferson was free to transform himself. He announced that there were few secrets worth keeping anymore. Only Ramiro remained off-limits. Then he told the grim, brief history of our latest war. All of us were invited to his apartment to watch the recordings that he'd made of news broadcasts and secret communications, and then the final pitiful message from the field station. Few accepted his invitation, but that didn't matter. Word got out quickly enough. Everybody knew what had just transpired, and the long-term prospects, and in a fashion, just how extraordinarily lucky we had been.

Through it all, Jefferson dispensed clear, critical directions as well as praise and encouragement, plus the occasional graveyard joke.

I preferred to keep to myself, investing my waking hours in the endless study of Ramiro.

Sometimes when he was alone, the man would suddenly grin. I had never seen that expression on him before. It wasn't a joyful look, or wistful. What I saw was an empty expression—a broad sycophantic look that I have seen in other faces, on occasion, particularly when people are struggling to believe whatever thought is lurking behind their bright, blind eyes.

Ramiro would fall asleep at his usual time, but then he'd wake up again, usually around three in the morning, and lie very still, staring up into the darkness for an hour and sometimes much longer.

Instead of new books and movies, he requested titles that he already knew—as if granting his mind an easier, more familiar path to walk.

On the ninth day, I had a tall cold glass of lemonade brought with his lunch, and he drank it without complaint.

On the tenth morning, Jim opened the cell door and said, "Sir," before ushering the prisoner down the short hall to the exercise yard. After the usual bookkeeping, he took his post inside, standing before the only door. Some of Ramiro's guards had shown worrisome symptoms. But after his initial panic, Jim had turned outwardly calm, sturdy. Maybe if I had paid closer attention, I would have seen some clue. But then again, even the best interrogator must accept the idea that she knows more about the beginnings of the universe than she will ever learn about the shape of a person's true mind.

But Ramiro noticed something.

I don't know what it was or why then, but after a few trips back and forth in the yard, the prisoner paused, passing one of the rubberized weights to his other hand and then bending down, picking up the thick dried and very dead leaf from the floor beneath the starved tree.

For a long moment, he stared at Jim, saying nothing.

They were ten feet apart, and the guard was watching everything.

Normal procedures demanded a second guard be on duty outside. She was watching on monitors and through the two-way glass, and sensing trouble, she set off a silent alarm. I arrived half a minute after a backup team of armed warriors, and two steps ahead of Jefferson.

In that span, nothing had changed.

Maybe Ramiro was waiting for an audience. But I think not. My guess is that he still wasn't sure what he would say or the best way to say it, and like any artist, he was simply allowing time to pass while his invisible brain struggled to find the best solution.

Through the monitors, I watched the brown leaf slip free of his hand.

"So, Jim," said Ramiro. At last.

Jim didn't move, and he didn't make any sound. And if his face changed, the expression didn't register on the security cameras.

As if getting ready to unwrap a wonderful gift, Ramiro smiled. It was an abrupt, startling expression followed by the joyous, almost effervescent words, "So how's your home town these days? How is Salt Lake City doing?"

Jim sagged against the door.

From outside, Jefferson ordered, "Get in there!"

"No," I ordered.

The backup team ignored me.

"No!" I stepped in front of them and looked at Jefferson. "You tell them. Who's in charge here?"

With a tight sigh, Jefferson said, "Wait then. Wait."

Jim was crying now. In a matter of moments, a weepy little boy had emerged and taken charge.

I told the guards to back away from the door.

Jim muttered a few words, too soft for anybody to understand.

"What's that, Jim?" asked Ramiro.

Nothing.

"I can only guess," the prisoner offered with a warm, infectious tone. "Another nuclear weapon must have struck another reactor. But this one was closer to us, wasn't it? And the wind must have blown those poisons over the top of us."

That was a dreamy, hopeful explanation, considering the circumstances.

"So we're temporarily cut off down here. Isn't that about it, Jim? And we'll have to wait what? A few weeks or months to be rescued?"

"No," said Jim.

Finding success, Ramiro smiled.

"Am I wrong, Jim?"

The response was abrupt, and vivid. With a string of awful sentences, Jim defined the scale of the new war and its brutal, amoral consequences.

"Everything above us is dead," he declared.

Ramiro's smile wavered, but he wouldn't let go of it.

"About a thousand nukes went off, and wildfires are still burning, and the entire continent is poisonous dead. The field office is abandoned. We aren't getting any messages from anybody. Not a squeak. We've got some security cameras working, our only connections to the surface, and they're only working on battery power. It's the middle of August, but there isn't any sun, and judging by what we can see and what we can guess, it isn't even reaching forty below at noon . . . !"

Maybe Ramiro had genuine hopes for his dirty nuke story—an awful but manageable nightmare. But this nightmare was more plausible, and he must have known that for several days. Yet he refused to react. He did nothing for one, two, three breaths. Enormous events had pushed him farther than even he could handle, and discovering what might be a weakness on his part, the prisoner suddenly looked lost, perhaps even confused, unable to conjure up one thin question, comment, or even a word.

And then Jim pulled his weapon.

The pistol would work only in his hand, and its ammunition was small and lightweight, designed to bruise and break bones but never kill. That's why I told everyone, "No. Leave them alone!"

My instincts were looking for a revelation.

But other people's instincts overrode my order. The guards pushed me away and started working at the door's stubborn locks. For a few seconds, nothing happened. Neither man spoke or moved. But then Jim set the gun's barrel against his target's eye, and I heard a quiet thump, and the bullet shattered the back of the socket before burrowing its way into the miserable, dying brain.

Ramiro dropped the weights, one striking his right foot. But he didn't appear to notice. Unblinking eyes stared at the corpse twitching on the floor in front of him. The prisoner was impressed. Enthralled, even. Perhaps he had never seen a man die. Cities and nations had been destroyed, but carnage had remained cool and abstract. Until that moment, he never appreciated just how messy and simple death was, or that he would have to take a deep breath before regaining his bearings, looking up slowly before noticing me standing in the open door.

"So this is what you wanted," I said. "The death of humanity, the end of the world . . . "

"No," he whispered.

"Are you sure?"

He sluggishly shook his head.

"Or Abraham wanted this," I suggested. "A nuclear winter, the extinction of our species."

No reply was offered.

I stepped over Jim and then stared up into Ramiro's face, allowing him no choice but to meet my eyes. Quietly, I said, "There is no such creature as Abraham, is there?"

He didn't react.

"And no army of temporal jihadists either."

His eyes closed.

"Just you," I persisted. "You're the only time traveler. Fifteen years ago, you arrived alone in the backcountry of Kashmir. You brought no more than what you could carry on your back, including the uranium and a few odd gizmos from your world. Then you littered the Middle East with just enough physical evidence to give your story legs. Like that bomb in Islamabad, right? You set that up before you came to America. And then you let yourself get caught in Montana, which was your plan from the beginning."

His shoulders lifted, a shrug beginning.

I grabbed his chin and shook him. "Why send an entire army? Why bother? When a single soldier armed with the right words can do just as well . . . that's what this is about . . . "

Ramiro opened his eyes.

An impressed little smile began to break loose. He asked softly, "And when did you realize this, Carmen?"

"Always," I admitted. "But I couldn't believe it. I wouldn't let myself even admit that it was possible. Not until I saw a photograph of a former official with my own government, bloodied and terrified, and I realized that our own hands had done that to him." I shook his chin again. "That's when I saw what made sense. Finally. Maybe there was an Abraham, but if you happened to be him . . . "

Ramiro laughed, and with a cat's grace grabbed my wrist and yanked, stepping out of my grip.

"Who's the prisoner here?" I muttered.

The laugh brightened.

"And who is the torturer?"

He offered a slight and very quick bow.

"But why?" I wanted to know.

"Carmen," he began. "Believe me, I could offer a thousand plausible stories. But how would you know if I was being truthful, in whole or even in part?"

"Try it anyway," I said.

But he backed away, waving both hands as if to fend off those temptations. "The point is, Carmen . . . your world was deserving. Almost every outrage that has happened to you has been justified. A necessary, reasonable revenge has been taken. And these many years . . . almost every day that I have spent in your world, Carmen . . . has brought me untold pleasure . . . "

11

Last year, during an official leave from the prison, Collins managed to slip away from his official escorts. His shadows. I can only speculate what he did during most of the day, but fourteen hours is a very long time, if you have a good plan and the discipline to make it happen. My personal knowledge extends to two hours spent together during the afternoon, inside a second-story room at a Red Roof Inn just outside Denver. Despite Ramiro's insistence to the contrary, I'm not unlovely and I have my charms, and his interrogator and I had been carrying on an infrequent but cherished affair— five surreptitious encounters over the course of an ugly decade, moments where sex and sexual talk could dominate over the secrets of state.

I never discussed my work with him, and he almost never mentioned his.

But Denver was different. I stepped into a darkened room to find a changed man. Collins was pale and much heavier than usual and obviously exhausted. After an hour of sweat and modest success, we gave up. I talked about showering, and he talked about slipping away in another minute or two. Then for a long while, we just sat side by side in bed, and in that way people in our world would do, we began to list the friends and associates that had died because of Indian Point.

Until that moment, I didn't realize that Collins had been a father. Not that he was close to his fifteen-year-old son, but the unfortunate boy had lived on Long Island with his mother. The fallout plume blocked every bridge to safety, and like a million others, they spent the next several days chasing a string of promised rescue ships and rumors of airlifts. Collins' best guess, based on a couple of sat-phone calls received near the end, was that they had managed to survive for a week or eight days, and then both died, probably during the Islip riots.

"Sorry" is a weak word. But I offered it anyway.

This man that I didn't truly know silently accepted my sorrow. Then he tried to shrug, and with a bleak resignation that I couldn't understand at the time, he mentioned, "This could have turned out differently."

When haven't those words been valid?

With his deep, godly voice, Collins said my name. Then he smiled—a crooked, captivating smile on his worst day—and quietly asked, "Why are we doing what we do? Anymore, what are we after?"

"It's our job," I offered.

He saw through those words. "Bullshit, darling. Bullshit."

"Yeah, but we're still the good guys," I said.

Then we both enjoyed a sorry little laugh.

"I'll tell you what I'm doing," he said, shaking his head. "Every day, I'm trying to save the world."

"Oh, is that all?"

He kept smiling, though he didn't laugh. He let me stare into his eyes, taking my measure of his soul. Then carefully, slowly, he said, "You once told me about this woman. Do you remember? You met her on some cross-country flight. You got her to talking, and she eventually confessed her plan to kill her elderly husband. Do you remember that anecdote?"

"Sure."

"Did you ever follow up on it?"

"What do you mean?"

He didn't have to explain himself.

With a defensive growl, I admitted, "No, I haven't bothered."

"Why not?"

I could have mentioned that it wasn't my particular business, or that I never knew anything of substance, or that no crime had been committed. But I didn't offer excuses. Instead, I admitted, "The woman loved her husband. Agree with her or not, I don't believe she would have harmed the man to be cruel or out of convenience."

"And you're sure that she loved him?"

"I could tell," I said.

"And I believe you, Carmen."

I sat quietly, wondering what was this about.

"You know, you're very good. Piecing together clues, I mean. Reading the subject's emotions, their intentions." Then he laughed, insisting, "Maybe you're not quite my equal. But there's nobody better than us."

Just then, I could not read that man. I had absolutely no clue what Collins was thinking.

"Saving the world," he repeated.

I waited.

"I'm working on something huge," he admitted. Then with a wise little sneer, he edited his comment. "I'm working on somebody huge. A subject unlike anyone you've ever met or even imagined."

I didn't want this conversation. He was breaking our most essential rule, bringing work into our bed.

"That man is still holding some big secrets," Collins confided. "All these years working on nobody but him, and I still haven't gotten to his core."

I climbed out from under the sheets.

"If I could just get what I wanted from the guy," he muttered.

I said, "Stop that."

With sharp disappointment, Collins stared at me. It took several moments for him to decide what to say next. Then he offered what had to be the most cryptic and peculiar excuse that I had ever heard.

"If he gives me what I want," he began.

A genuine smile broke across his weary white face.

"If he shares what he knows, Carmen, I can save the world. Not once, but a thousand times. A million times. More times than we could count . . . and now wouldn't that be a legacy worth any cost?"

12

We decided to throw the prisoner into Jefferson's apartment, accompanied by half a dozen pissed-off guards, and the guards were instructed to sit Ramiro down before the television, and in sequence, play the Apocalypse recordings for him.

Jim's body was carried away, and Jefferson found himself standing alone with me. He asked the walls, "So what do we do with him next?"

"What do you want to do?"

My colleague refused to look at my eyes. "Our food is limited," he pointed out. "Ramiro constitutes more than 1 percent of our population. At this point, can we really afford to keep him alive?"

Then he braced himself.

But I surprised him, saying, "Agreed," as if I had come to the same inescapable conclusion.

But our methods seemed important, and that's what we were discussing when one of the guards returned.

"Lemonade-7 wants paper and a pen," she reported.

"Give him whatever he wants," I said.

She glanced at Jefferson.

He nodded.

"And tell him he doesn't have much time," I yelled as she ran off.

For a few moments, Jefferson studied me. But he didn't have the stomach to ask what he wanted. Instead, he quietly admitted, "Maybe you're right, Carmen. A bullet is simple. But shoving him out on the surface, letting him fend for himself . . . that makes more sense . . . "

Yet that left various logistics to consider. One of the elevators had to be unlocked, power had to be routed back into it, and every passenger except Ramiro had to be protected from the radiation and cold. Those necessities took dozens of people nearly two hours of determined labor, and then somebody mentioned that a short-wave antenna and Geiger counter could be set up on the dead prairie and spliced into the elevator's wiring—helpful inspirations, but cause for another hour delay.

According to the guards, Ramiro remained cooperative and busy. Unblinking eyes paid close attention to the news broadcasts, particularly during those desperate minutes when city after city suddenly quit transmitting. Each of his guards seemed to nourish a different impression of his mood. The prisoner was relishing the slaughter, or he was numbed by what he was seeing, or maybe he was only pretending to watch events play out on that tiny screen. But every witness agreed: the prisoner's first focus was in filling the yellow pages of the legal pad, his head dropping for long intervals, that delicate artisan's hand scribbling dense equations and weaving diagrams and sometimes adding a paragraph or two in his unborn hodgepodge of a language.

It was early afternoon when he set down the pen. A few minutes later, without explanation, he was brought to the elevator. He was still wearing dress trousers and a short-sleeved shirt, plus his favorite sandals. But the two volunteers waiting for him were half-hidden inside layers of cumbersome gear.

Ramiro handed the filled pad to the shorter figure.

I didn't look at his gift. I knew what was on it. With both hands, I folded it in half and handed it to the nearest guard. "It's a little goddamn late now, isn't it?" I snapped at him.

"Maybe enough people will survive," he offered.

I tried to cut him open with my gaze. Then I turned and shuffled through the open steel door, my oversized fireman's boots clumping with each step.

Jefferson checked his sidearm, picked up the makeshift antenna and Geiger counter, and followed me.

There was just enough room for our equipment and three bodies. Jefferson pulled his oxygen mask aside and gave a few final orders. Then the door shut, and with a sudden crotchety jolt, the elevator started to climb, shaking slightly as it gained momentum.

"Do you understand what I just gave you?" Ramiro asked.

"Of course I understand," I said.

"Tell me, why don't you?" Jefferson asked.

Ramiro smiled, but he sounded uncharacteristically tense. "Time travel is not particularly difficult."

Neither of us reacted.

He said, "Lorton Energy is cheap, if you know the right tricks."

I looked only at Jefferson. "The first time Ramiro wrote about Lorton and Casimir plates, he didn't give us those tricks. He pretty effectively misled our scientists into chasing the wrong methods. But of course a man who remembers the dates and positions of dozens of supernovae—a creature with that kind of faultless memory—would easily digest the plans for a working time machine. That's what Collins realized. Eventually. He didn't mention it to anybody, but for these last years, Collins was chasing the tools that would allow us to go back in the past, like Ramiro did, but this time make things right."

Jefferson shook his head. "Yeah, but each incursion in the past is a separate event," he recalled. "If he jumped back, he would accomplish what? Setting up a new time line?"

"Except we could send back a million teams," I replied. "A million attempts to make amends, and each new history owing its existence to us."

No one spoke for a moment. The only sound was the air rushing around the racing elevator.

Then Jefferson turned to Ramiro. "You gave Collins the time machine. But then for some reason he killed himself."

"Ramiro gave him more than the time machine," I explained. "He also told him the rest of the story. How he had come alone, and there was no Abraham, and every tragedy that had happened to the world was directly tied to what Ramiro had said to Collins, and what Collins had unwittingly fed upstream to the gullible and weak."

Jefferson put a hand on his pistol.

I watched Ramiro's face. If it weren't for the tightness around the mouth and the glassiness to the eyes, I would have imagined that he was relaxed. Happy, even. Maybe he was assuring himself that these years and his sacrifices had been a great success. Not perfect, no. But who could have guessed that Moscow would have been nuked? Which meant that in countless realities—realms not too different from ours—he had achieved exactly what it was that he'd set out to achieve here.

"And Collins didn't expect that part?" Jefferson asked.

"That's my guess," I admitted.

His hand dropped back to his side.

A few moments later, the elevator began to slow.

My ears were popping. I felt my heart quicken, and I judged that Ramiro was breathing faster too. A sudden chill was leaking into the elevator, and I mentioned it, and then I suggested, "We should put on our masks."

Jefferson looked tired and angry. He wiped his eyes twice before making himself strap the oxygen mask over his weepy face.

I left mine off for the moment.

"I don't think you wanted this world to die," I said.

Ramiro didn't respond.

"You were hoping to hurt a lot of people and leave the rest of us wiser," I continued. "At least that's what you told yourself. Except what really inspired you was wielding this kind of power, and you won a lot of fun for your troubles, and now it's finally over. You're done. We're going to throw you into the cold, into the wasted darkness, and you'll have to stumble around until you die some miserable way or another."

Ramiro made a soft, odd sound. Like when a bird cheeps in its sleep.

The elevator had nearly stopped. I stood facing the prisoner, my back flush against the door.

He smiled with a weak, vacuous charm.

In the end, the prisoner was defiant but terrified, utterly trapped but unable to admit his sorry circumstances. He believed that he was still in charge of his fate. Arrogance saved for this moment made him smile. Then he said, "You know quite a bit, Carmen. I've been impressed. But you should realize that I won't allow any ignoble, indecent finish for me."

The elevator door began to pull open.

Ramiro's eyes never closed, even once he was dead.

Behind me, a young woman's voice—a voice I knew from my ride to the nearby airstrip—called out, "Hello? Yes? Can we help?"

The day was bright and warm.

Two men suddenly dropped to their knees. But Jefferson stood again, stripping off the mask and then his heavy outer coat, staggering into the functioning, fully staffed office, finally stopping before a window that looked out over a flat, glorious landscape and a sky of endless blue.

"Everything was faked?" he whispered.

"Everything," I said.

"The newscasts, the communications?"

"Digital magic," I mentioned. "And playacting by real people, yes."

"The security cameras."

"Easy enough."

"But I felt the cold," he said.

I started to explain how when the elevator started to rise, a dozen portable air conditioning units began cooling down the top of the shaft.

"But we felt the explosions, Carmen!"

"Those were the easiest tricks," I admitted. "A few tactical nukes thrown down some nearby oil wells."

He pressed his face against the warm glass, not fighting the tears anymore. Maybe he was crying out of relief. But in my case, I was crying for Jim, and for Collins, and for countless dead souls that I couldn't put names to. Behind us, a medical team was working hard to revive a man who refused to return to the living. When they finally gave up, we went to look at Ramiro's limp body.

"Do you think he saw?" Jefferson asked.

I knelt and closed the eyes.

"In the end," he persisted, "do you think he realized just how badly you tricked him?"

"Yes," I said.

I said, "No."

Then I stood and walked away, adding, "It happened both ways, and more times than I would care to count."

JAMES ALAN GARDNER—NOVELETTE
THE RAY-GUN: A LOVE STORY

Ah, love. Who hasn't felt the first throes of infatuation and the deepening of a relationship? We make tiny adjustments to the shape of our lives to accommodate the loved one and then one day discover that we have become something else. Sometimes, the one we love isn't even alive.

You think I am exaggerating, but as a person whose husband collects vinyl I can assure you that there have been tiny adjustments in our lives to keep the record collection safe. Now imagine what it would be like if that thing, that inanimate object that you loved was unique. Not run-of-the-mill diluted unique which people use now as a sort of hyper-unusual, but if the object in question were truly a one-of-a-kind thing. Like a ray-gun.

Gardner starts off this story by telling you exactly what the story is about.

"This is a story about a ray-gun. The ray-gun will not be explained except to say, 'It shoots rays.' "

The bluntness of the opening is charming and childlike. Much like the main character, Jack, the story starts simply and becomes increasingly more complex in both concept and use of language as the story progresses.

With nine novels and several awards to his name, Gardner diversifies past written fiction into performance, Applied Mathematics and Kung Fu. Those roles all reward looking ahead to the what ifs, much like SF itself does. As one of its layers, this story asks: What If you found a unique object—a ray-gun?

How would your life shift?

THE RAY-GUN:
A LOVE STORY

JAMES ALAN GARDNER

This is a story about a ray-gun. The ray-gun will not be explained except to say, "It shoots rays."

They are dangerous rays. If they hit you in the arm, it withers. If they hit you in the face, you go blind. If they hit you in the heart, you die. These things must be true, or else it would not be a ray-gun. But it is.

Ray-guns come from space. This one came from the captain of an alien starship passing through our solar system. The ship stopped to scoop up hydrogen from the atmosphere of Jupiter. During this refueling process, the crew mutinied for reasons we cannot comprehend. We will never comprehend aliens. If someone spent a month explaining alien thoughts to us, we'd think we understood but we wouldn't. Our brains only know how to be human.

Although alien thoughts are beyond us, alien actions may be easy to grasp. We can understand the "what" if not the "why." If we saw what happened inside the alien vessel, we would recognize that the crew tried to take the captain's ray-gun and kill him.

There was a fight. The ray-gun went off many times. The starship exploded.

All this happened many centuries ago, before telescopes. The people of Earth still wore animal skins. They only knew Jupiter as a dot in the sky. When the starship exploded, the dot got a tiny bit brighter, then returned to normal. No one on Earth noticed—not even the shamans who thought dots in the sky were important.

The ray-gun survived the explosion. A ray-gun must be resilient, or else it is not a ray-gun. The explosion hurled the ray-gun away from Jupiter and out into open space.

After thousands of years, the ray-gun reached Earth. It fell from the sky like a meteor; it grew hot enough to glow, but it didn't burn up.

The ray-gun fell at night during a blizzard. Traveling thousands of miles an hour, the ray-gun plunged deep into snow-covered woods. The snow melted so quickly that it burst into steam.

The blizzard continued, unaffected. Some things can't be harmed, even by ray-guns.

Unthinking snowflakes drifted down. If they touched the ray-gun's surface they vaporized, stealing heat from the weapon. Heat also radiated outward, melting snow nearby on the ground. Melt-water flowed into the shallow crater made by the ray-gun's impact. Water and snow cooled the weapon until all excess temperature had dissipated. A million more snowflakes heaped over the crater, hiding the ray-gun till spring.

In March, the gun was found by a boy named Jack. He was fourteen years old and walking through the woods after school. He walked slowly, brooding about his lack of popularity. Jack despised popular students and had no interest in anything they did. Even so, he envied them. They didn't appear to be lonely.

Jack wished he had a girlfriend. He wished he were important. He wished he knew what to do with his life. Instead, he walked alone in the woods on the edge of town.

The woods were not wild or isolated. They were crisscrossed with trails made by children playing hide-and-seek. But in spring, the trails were muddy; most people stayed away. Jack soon worried more about how to avoid shoe-sucking mud than about the unfairness of the world. He took wide detours around mucky patches, thrashing through brush that was crisp from winter.

Stalks broke as he passed. Burrs stuck to his jacket. He got farther and farther from the usual paths, hoping he'd find a way out by blundering forward rather than swallowing his pride and retreating.

In this way, Jack reached the spot where the ray-gun had landed. He saw the crater it had made. He found the ray-gun itself.

The gun seized Jack's attention, but he didn't know what it was. Its design was too alien to be recognized as a weapon. Its metal was blackened but not black, as if it had once been another color but had finished that phase of its existence. Its pistol-butt was bulbous, the size of a tennis ball. Its barrel, as long as Jack's hand, was straight but its surface had dozens of nubs like a briarwood cane. The gun's trigger was a protruding blister you squeezed till it popped. A hard metal cap could slide over the blister to prevent the gun from firing accidentally, but the safety was off; it had been off for centuries, ever since the fight on the starship.

The alien captain who once owned the weapon might have considered it beautiful, but to human eyes, the gun resembled a dirty wet stick with a lump on one end. Jack might have walked by without giving it a second look if it hadn't been lying in a scorched crater. But it was.

The crater was two paces across and barren of plant life. The vegetation had burned in the heat of the ray-gun's fall. Soon enough, new spring growth would sprout, making the crater less obvious. At present, though, the ray-gun stood out on the charred earth like a snake in an empty birdbath.

Jack picked up the gun. Though it looked like briarwood, it was cold like metal. It felt solid: not heavy, but substantial. It had the heft of a well-made object. Jack turned the gun in his hands, examining it from every angle. When he looked down the muzzle, he saw a crystal lens cut into hundreds of facets. Jack poked it with his pinky, thinking the lens was a piece of glass that someone had jammed inside. He had the idea this might be a toy—perhaps a squirt-gun dropped by a careless child. If so, it had to be the most expensive toy Jack had ever seen. The gun's barrel and its lens were so perfectly machined that no one could mistake the craftsmanship.

Jack continued to poke at the weapon until the inevitable happened: he pressed the trigger blister. The ray-gun went off.

It might have been fatal, but by chance Jack was holding the gun aimed away from himself. A ray shot out of the gun's muzzle and blasted through a maple tree ten paces away. The ray made no sound, and although Jack had seen it clearly, he couldn't say what the ray's color had been. It had no color; it was simply a presence, like wind chill or gravity. Yet Jack was sure he'd seen a force emanate from the muzzle and strike the tree.

Though the ray can't be described, its effect was plain. A circular hole appeared in the maple tree's trunk where bark and wood disintegrated into sizzling plasma. The plasma expanded at high speed and pressure, blowing apart what remained of the surrounding trunk. The ray made no sound, but the explosion did. Shocked chunks of wood and boiling maple sap flew outward, obliterating a cross-section of the tree. The lower part of the trunk and the roots were still there; so were the upper part and branches. In between was a gap, filled with hot escaping gases.

The unsupported part of the maple fell. It toppled ponderously backwards. The maple crashed onto the trees behind, its winter-bare branches snagging theirs. To Jack, it seemed that the forest had stopped the maple's fall, like soldiers catching an injured companion before he hit the ground.

Jack still held the gun. He gazed at it in wonder. His mind couldn't grasp what had happened.

He didn't drop the gun in fear. He didn't try to fire it again. He simply stared.

It was a ray-gun. It would never be anything else.

Jack wondered where the weapon had come from. Had aliens visited these woods? Or was the gun created by a secret government project? Did the gun's owner want it back? Was he, she, or it searching the woods right now?

Jack was tempted to put the gun back into the crater, then run before the owner showed up. But was there really an owner nearby? The crater suggested that the gun had fallen from space. Jack had seen photos of meteor impact craters; this wasn't exactly the same, but it had a similar look.

Jack turned his eyes upward. He saw a mundane after-school sky. It had no UFOs. Jack felt embarrassed for even looking.

He examined the crater again. If Jack left the gun here, and the owner never retrieved it, sooner or later the weapon would be found by someone else—probably by children playing in the woods. They might shoot each other by accident. If this were an ordinary gun, Jack would never leave it lying in a place like this. He'd take the gun home, tell his parents, and they'd turn it over to the police.

Should he do the same for *this* gun? No. He didn't want to.

But he didn't know what he wanted to do instead. Questions buzzed through his mind, starting with, "What should I do?" then moving on to, "Am I in danger?" and, "Do aliens really exist?"

After a while, he found himself wondering, "Exactly how much can the gun blow up?" That question made him smile.

Jack decided he wouldn't tell anyone about the gun—not now and maybe not ever. He would take it home and hide it where it wouldn't be found, but where it would be available if trouble came. What kind of trouble? Aliens . . . spies . . . supervillains . . . who knew? If ray-guns were real, was anything impossible?

On the walk back home, Jack was so distracted by "What ifs?" that he nearly got hit by a car. He had reached the road that separated the woods from neighboring houses. Like most roads in that part of Jack's small town, it didn't get much traffic. Jack stepped out from the trees and suddenly a sports car whizzed past him, only two steps away. Jack staggered back; the driver leaned on the horn; Jack hit his shoulder on an oak tree; then the incident was over, except for belated adrenalin.

For a full minute afterward, Jack leaned against the oak and felt his heart pound. As close calls go, this one wasn't too bad: Jack hadn't really been near enough to the road to get hit. Still, Jack needed quite a while to calm down. How stupid would it be to die in an accident on the day he'd found something miraculous?

Jack ought to have been watching for trouble. What if the threat had been a bug-eyed monster instead of a car? Jack should have been alert and prepared. In his mind's eye he imagined the incident again, only this time he casually somersaulted to safety rather than stumbling into a tree. That's how you're supposed to cheat death if you're carrying a ray-gun: with cool heroic flair.

But Jack couldn't do somersaults. He said to himself, *I'm Peter Parker, not Spider-Man.*

On the other hand, Jack *had* just acquired great power. And great responsibility. Like Peter Parker, Jack had to keep his power secret, for fear of tragic consequences. In Jack's case, maybe aliens would come for him. Maybe spies or government agents would kidnap him and his family. No matter how farfetched those things seemed, the existence of a ray-gun proved the world wasn't tame.

That night, Jack debated what to do with the gun. He pictured himself shooting terrorists and gang lords. If he rid the world of scum, pretty girls might admire him. But as soon as Jack imagined himself storming into a terrorist stronghold, he realized he'd get killed almost immediately. The ray-gun provided awesome firepower, but no defense at all. Besides, if Jack had found an ordinary gun in the forest, he never would have dreamed of running around murdering bad guys. Why should a ray-gun be different?

But it *was* different. Jack couldn't put the difference into words, but it was as real as the weapon's solid weight in his hands. The ray-gun changed everything. A world that contained a ray-gun might also contain flying saucers, beautiful secret agents . . . and heroes.

Heroes who could somersault away from oncoming sports cars. Heroes who would cope with any danger. Heroes who *deserved* to have a ray-gun.

When he was young, Jack had taken for granted he'd become a hero: brave, skilled, and important. Somehow he'd lost that belief. He'd let himself settle for being ordinary. But now he wasn't ordinary: he had a ray-gun.

He had to live up to it. Jack had to be ready for bug-eyed monsters and giant robots. These were no longer childish daydreams; they were real possibilities in a world where ray-guns existed. Jack could picture himself running through town, blasting aliens, and saving the planet.

Such thoughts made sense when Jack held the ray-gun in his hands—as if the gun planted fantasies in his mind. The feel of the gun filled Jack with ambition.

All weapons have a sense of purpose.

Jack practiced with the gun as often as he could. To avoid being seen, he rode his bike to a tract of land in the country: twenty acres owned by Jack's great-uncle Ron. No one went there but Jack. Uncle Ron had once intended to build a house on the property, but that had never happened. Now Ron was in a nursing home. Jack's family intended to sell the land once the old man died, but Ron was healthy for someone in his nineties. Until Uncle Ron's health ran out, Jack had the place to himself.

The tract was undeveloped—raw forest, not a woods where children played. In the middle lay a pond, completely hidden by trees. Jack would float sticks in the pond and shoot them with the gun.

If he missed, the water boiled. If he didn't, the sticks were destroyed. Sometimes they erupted in fire. Sometimes they burst with a bang but no flame. Sometimes they simply vanished. Jack couldn't tell if he was doing something subtly different to get each effect, or if the ray-gun changed modes on its own. Perhaps it had a computer which analyzed the target and chose the most lethal attack. Perhaps the attacks were always the same, but differences in the sticks made for different results. Jack didn't know. But as spring led to summer, he became a better shot. By autumn, he'd begun throwing sticks into the air and trying to vaporize them before they reached the ground.

During this time, Jack grew stronger. Long bike rides to the pond helped his legs and his stamina. In addition, he exercised with fitness equipment his parents had bought but never used. If monsters ever came, Jack couldn't afford to be weak—heroes had to climb fences and break down doors. They had to balance on rooftops and hang by their fingers from cliffs. They had to run fast enough to save the girl.

Jack pumped iron and ran every day. As he did so, he imagined dodging bullets and tentacles. When he felt like giving up, he cradled the ray-gun in his hands. It gave him the strength to persevere.

Before the ray-gun, Jack had seen himself as just another teenager; his life didn't make sense. But the gun made Jack a hero who might be needed to save the Earth. It clarified *everything*. Sore muscles didn't matter. Watching TV was a waste. If you let down your guard, that's when the monsters came.

When he wasn't exercising, Jack studied science. That was another part of being a hero. He sometimes dreamed he'd analyze the ray-gun, discovering how it worked and giving humans amazing new technology. At other times, he didn't want to understand the gun at all. He liked its mystery. Besides, there was no guarantee Jack would ever understand how the gun worked. Perhaps human science wouldn't progress far enough in Jack's lifetime. Perhaps Jack himself wouldn't have the brains to figure it out.

But he had enough brains for high school. He did well; he was motivated. He had to hold back to avoid attracting attention. When his gym teacher told him he should go out for track, Jack ran slower and pretended to get out of breath.

Spider-Man had to do the same.

Two years later, in geography class, a girl named Kirsten gave Jack a daisy. She said the daisy was good luck and he should make a wish.

Even a sixteen-year-old boy couldn't misconstrue such a hint. Despite awkwardness and foot-dragging, Jack soon had a girlfriend.

Kirsten was quiet but pretty. She played guitar. She wrote poems. She'd never had a boyfriend but she knew how to kiss. These were all good things. Jack wondered if he should tell her about the ray-gun.

Until Kirsten, Jack's only knowledge of girls came from his big sister, Rachel. Rachel was seventeen and incapable of keeping a secret. She talked with her friends about everything and was too slapdash to hide private things well. Jack didn't snoop through his sister's possessions, but when Rachel left her bedroom door ajar with empty cigarette packs tumbling out of the garbage can, who wouldn't notice? When she gossiped on the phone about sex with her boyfriend, who couldn't overhear? Jack didn't want to listen, but Rachel never lowered her voice. The things Jack heard made him queasy—about his sister, and girls in general.

If he showed Kirsten the ray-gun, would she tell her friends? Jack wanted to believe she wasn't that kind of girl, but he didn't know how many kinds of girl there were. He just knew that the ray-gun was too important for him to take chances. Changing the status quo wasn't worth the risk.

Yet the status quo changed anyway. The more time Jack spent with Kirsten, the less he had for shooting practice and other aspects of hero-dom. He felt guilty for skimping on crisis preparation; but when he went to the pond or spent a night reading science, he felt guilty for skimping on Kirsten. Jack would tell her he couldn't come over to do homework and when she asked why, he'd have to make up excuses. He felt he was treating her like an enemy spy: holding her at arm's length as if she were some femme fatale who was tempting him to betray state secrets. He hated not trusting her.

Despite this wall between them, Kirsten became Jack's lens on the world. If anything interesting happened, Jack didn't experience it directly; some portion of his mind stood back, enjoying the anticipation of having something to tell Kirsten about the next time they met. Whatever he saw, he wanted her to see it too. Whenever Jack heard a joke, even before he started laughing, he pictured himself repeating it to Kirsten.

Inevitably, Jack asked himself what she'd think of his hero-dom. Would she be impressed? Would she throw her arms around him and say he was even more wonderful than she'd thought? Or would she get that look on her face, the one when she heard bad poetry? Would she think he was an immature geek who'd read too many comic books and was pursuing some juvenile fantasy? How could anyone believe hostile aliens might appear in the sky? And if aliens did show up, how delusional was it that a teenage boy might make a difference, even if he owned a ray-gun and could do a hundred push-ups without stopping?

For weeks, Jack agonized: to tell or not to tell. Was Kirsten worthy, or just a copy of Jack's sister? Was Jack himself worthy, or just a foolish boy?

One Saturday in May, Jack and Kirsten went biking. Jack led her to the pond where he practiced with the gun. He hadn't yet decided what he'd do when they got there, but Jack couldn't just *tell* Kirsten about the ray-gun. She'd never believe it was real unless she saw the rays in action. But so much could go wrong. Jack was terrified of giving away his deepest secret. He was afraid that when he saw hero-dom through Kirsten's eyes, he'd realize it was silly.

At the pond, Jack felt so nervous he could hardly speak. He babbled about the warm weather . . . a patch of mushrooms . . . a crow cawing in a tree. He talked about everything except what was on his mind.

Kirsten misinterpreted his anxiety. She thought she knew why Jack had brought her to this secluded spot. After a while, she decided he needed encouragement, so she took off her shirt and her bra.

It was the wrong thing to do. Jack hadn't meant this outing to be a test . . . but it was, and Kirsten had failed.

Jack took off his own shirt and wrapped his arms around her, chest touching breasts for the first time. He discovered it was possible to be excited and disappointed at the same time.

Jack and Kirsten made out on a patch of hard dirt. It was the first time they'd been alone with no risk of interruption. They kept their pants on, but they knew they could go farther: as far as there was. No one in the world would stop them from whatever they chose to do. Jack and Kirsten felt light in their skins—open and dizzy with possibilities.

Yet for Jack, it was all a mistake: one that couldn't be reversed. Now he'd never tell Kirsten about the ray-gun. He'd missed his chance because she'd acted the way Jack's sister would have acted. Kirsten had been thinking like a girl and she'd ruined things forever.

Jack hated the way he felt: all angry and resentful. He really liked Kirsten. He liked making out, and couldn't wait till the next time. He refused to be a guy who dumped a girl as soon as she let him touch her breasts. But he was now shut off from her and he had no idea how to get over that.

In the following months, Jack grew guiltier: he was treating Kirsten as if she were good enough for sex but not good enough to be told about the most important thing in his life. As for Kirsten, every day made her more unhappy: she felt Jack blaming her for something but she didn't know what she'd done. When they got together, they went straight to fondling and more as soon as possible. If they tried to talk, they didn't know what to say.

In August, Kirsten left to spend three weeks with her grandparents on Vancouver Island. Neither she nor Jack missed each other. They didn't even miss the sex. It was a relief to be apart. When Kirsten got back, they went for a walk and a confused conversation. Both produced excuses for why they couldn't stay together. The excuses didn't make sense, but neither Jack nor Kirsten noticed—they were too ashamed to pay attention to what they were saying. They both felt like failures. They'd thought their love would last forever, and now it was ending sordidly.

When the lying was over, Jack went for a run. He ran in a mental blur. His mind didn't clear until he found himself at the pond.

Night was drawing in. He thought of all the things he'd done with Kirsten on the shore and in the water. After that first time, they'd come here a lot; it was private. Because of Kirsten, this wasn't the same pond as when Jack had first begun to practice with the ray-gun. Jack wasn't the same boy. He and the pond now carried histories.

Jack could feel himself balanced on the edge of quitting. He'd turned seventeen. One more year of high school, then he'd go away to university. He realized he no longer believed in the imminent arrival of aliens, nor could he see himself as some great hero saving the world.

Jack knew he wasn't a hero. He'd used a nice girl for sex, then lied to get rid of her.

He felt like crap. But blasting the shit out of sticks made him feel a little better. The ray-gun still had its uses, even if shooting aliens wasn't one of them.

The next day Jack did more blasting. He pumped iron. He got science books out of the library. Without Kirsten at his side several hours a day, he had time to fill, and emptiness. By the first day of the new school year, Jack was back to his full hero-dom program. He no longer deceived himself that he was preparing for battle, but the program gave him something to do: a purpose, a release, and a penance.

So that was Jack's passage into manhood. He was dishonest with the girl he loved.

Manhood means learning who you are.

In his last year of high school, Jack went out with other girls but he was past the all-or-nothingness of First Love. He could have casual fun; he could approach sex with perspective. "Monumental and life-changing" had been tempered to "pleasant and exciting." Jack didn't take his girlfriends for granted, but they were people, not objects of worship. He was never tempted to tell any of them about the gun.

When he left town for university, Jack majored in Engineering Physics. He hadn't decided whether he'd ever analyze the ray-gun's inner workings, but he couldn't imagine taking courses that were irrelevant to the weapon. The ray-gun was the central fact of Jack's life. Even if he wasn't a hero, he was set apart from other people by this evidence that aliens existed.

During freshman year, Jack lived in an on-campus dormitory. Hiding the ray-gun from his roommate would have been impossible. Jack left the weapon at home, hidden near the pond. In sophomore year, Jack rented an apartment off campus. Now he could keep the ray-gun with him. He didn't like leaving it unattended.

Jack persuaded a lab assistant to let him borrow a Geiger counter. The ray-gun emitted no radioactivity at all. Objects blasted by the gun showed no significant radioactivity either. Over time, Jack borrowed other equipment, or took blast debris to the lab so he could conduct tests when no one was around. He found nothing that explained how the ray-gun worked.

The winter before Jack graduated, Great-Uncle Ron finally died. In his will, the old man left his twenty acres of forest to Jack. Uncle Ron had found out that Jack liked to visit the pond. "I told him," said big sister Rachel. "Do you think I didn't know where you and Kirsten went?"

Jack had to laugh—uncomfortably. He was embarrassed to discover he couldn't keep secrets any better than his sister.

Jack's father offered to help him sell the land to pay for his education. The offer was polite, not pressing. Uncle Ron had doled out so much cash in his will that Jack's family was now well-off. When Jack said he'd rather hold on to the property "until the market improves," no one objected.

After getting his bachelor's degree, Jack continued on to grad school: first his master's, then his Ph.D. In one of his courses, he met Deana, working toward her own doctorate—in Electrical Engineering rather than Engineering Physics.

The two programs shared several seminars, but considered themselves rivals. Engineering Physics students pretended that Electrical Engineers weren't smart enough to understand abstract principles. Electrical Engineers pretended that Engineering Physics students were pie-in-the-sky dreamers whose theories were always wrong until real Engineers fixed them. Choosing to sit side by side, Jack and Deana teased each other every class. Within months, Deana moved into Jack's apartment.

Deana was small but physical. She told Jack she'd been drawn to him because he was the only man in their class who lifted weights. When Deana was young, she'd been a competitive swimmer—"*Very* competitive," she said—but her adolescent growth spurt had never arrived and she was eventually outmatched by girls with longer limbs. Deana had quit the competition circuit, but she hadn't quit swimming, nor had she lost the drive to be one up on those around her. She saw most things as contests, including her relationship with Jack. Deana was not beyond cheating if it gave her an edge.

In the apartment they now shared, Jack thought he'd hidden the ray-gun so well that Deana wouldn't find it. He didn't suspect that when he wasn't home, she went through his things. She couldn't stand the thought that Jack might have secrets from her.

He returned one day to find the gun on the kitchen table. Deana was poking at it. Jack wanted to yell, "Leave it alone!" but he was so choked with anger he couldn't speak.

Deana's hand was close to the trigger. The safety was off and the muzzle pointed in Jack's direction. He threw himself to the floor.

Nothing happened. Deana was so surprised by Jack's sudden move that she jerked her hand away from the gun. "What the hell are you doing?"

Jack got to his feet. "I could ask you the same question."

"I found this. I wondered what it was."

Jack knew she didn't "find" the gun. It had been buried under old notebooks inside a box at the back of a closet. Jack expected that Deana would invent some excuse for why she'd been digging into Jack's private posses-sions, but the excuse wouldn't be worth believing.

What infuriated Jack most was that he'd actually been thinking of showing Deana the gun. She was a very very good engineer; Jack had dreamed that together, he and she might discover how the gun worked. Of all the women Jack had known, Deana was the first he'd asked to move in with him. She was strong and she was smart. She might understand the gun. The time had never been right to tell her the truth—Jack was still getting to know her and he needed to be absolutely sure—but Jack had dreamed . . .

And now, like Kirsten at the pond, Deana had ruined everything. Jack felt so violated he could barely stand to look at the woman. He wanted to throw her out of the apartment . . . but that would draw too much atten-tion to the gun. He couldn't let Deana think the gun was important.

She was still staring at him, waiting for an explanation. "That's just something from my Great-Uncle Ron," Jack said. "An African good-luck charm. Or Indonesian. I forget. Uncle Ron traveled a lot." Actually, Ron sold insurance and seldom left the town where he was born. Jack picked up the gun from the table, trying to do so calmly rather than protectively. "I wish you hadn't touched this. It's old and fragile."

"It felt pretty solid to me."

"Solid but still breakable."

"Why did you dive to the floor?"

"Just silly superstition. It's bad luck to have this end point toward you." Jack gestured toward the muzzle. "And it's good luck to be on this end." He gestured toward the butt, then tried to make a joke. "Like there's a Maxwell demon in the middle, batting bad luck one way and good luck the other."

"You believe that crap?" Deana asked. She was an engineer. She went out of her way to disbelieve crap.

"Of course I don't believe it," Jack said. "But why ask for trouble?"

He took the gun back to the closet. Deana followed. As Jack returned the gun to its box, Deana said she'd been going through Jack's notes in search of anything he had on partial differential equations. Jack nearly let her get away with the lie; he usually let the women in his life get away with almost anything. But he realized he didn't want Deana in his life anymore. Whatever connection she and he had once felt, it was cut off the moment he saw her with the ray-gun.

Jack accused her of invading his privacy. Deana said he was paranoid. The argument grew heated. Out of habit, Jack almost backed down several times, but he stopped himself. He didn't want Deana under the same roof as the ray-gun. His feelings were partly irrational possessiveness, but also justifiable caution. If Deana got the gun and accidentally fired it, the results might be disastrous.

Jack and Deana continued to argue: right there in the closet within inches of the ray-gun. The gun lay in its box, like a child at the feet of parents fighting over custody. The ray-gun did nothing, as if it didn't care who won.

Eventually, unforgivable words were spoken. Deana said she'd move out as soon as possible. She left to stay the night with a friend.

The moment she was gone, Jack moved the gun. Deana still had a key to the apartment—she needed it until she could pack her things—and Jack was certain she'd try to grab the weapon as soon as he was busy elsewhere. The ray-gun was now a prize in a contest, and Deana never backed down.

Jack took the weapon to the university. He worked as an assistant for his Ph.D. supervisor, and he'd been given a locker in the supervisor's lab. The locker wasn't Fort Knox but leaving the gun there was better than leaving it in the apartment. The more Jack thought about Deana, the more he saw her as prying and obsessive, grasping for dominance. He didn't know what he'd ever seen in her.

The next morning, he wondered if he had overreacted. Was he demonizing his ex like a sitcom cliché? If she was so egotistic, why hadn't he noticed before? Jack had no good answer. He decided he didn't need one. Unlike when he broke up with Kirsten, Jack felt no guilt this time. The sooner Deana was gone, the happier he'd be.

In a few days, Deana called to say she'd found a new place to live. She and Jack arranged a time for her to pick up her belongings. Jack didn't want to be there while she moved out; he couldn't stand seeing her in the apartment again. Instead, Jack went back to his home town for a long weekend with his family.

It was lucky he did. Jack left Friday afternoon and didn't get back to the university until Monday night. The police were waiting for him. Deana had disappeared late Saturday.

She'd talked to friends on Saturday afternoon. She'd made arrangements for Sunday brunch but hadn't shown up. No one had seen her since.

As the ex-boyfriend, Jack was a prime suspect. But his alibi was solid: his hometown was hundreds of miles from the university, and his family could testify he'd been there the whole time. Jack couldn't possibly have sneaked back to the university, made Deana disappear, and raced back home.

Grudgingly, the police let Jack off the hook. They decided Deana must have been depressed by the break-up of the relationship. She might have run off so she wouldn't have to see Jack around the university. She might even have committed suicide.

Jack suspected otherwise. As soon as the police let him go, he went to his supervisor's lab. His locker had been pried open. The ray-gun lay on a nearby lab bench.

Jack could easily envision what happened. While moving out her things, Deana searched for the ray-gun. She hadn't found it in the apartment. She knew Jack had a locker in the lab and she'd guessed he'd stashed the weapon there. She broke open the locker to get the gun. She'd examined it and perhaps tried to take it apart. The gun went off.

Now Deana was gone. Not even a smudge on the floor. The ray-gun lay on the lab bench as guiltless as a stone. Jack was the only one with a conscience.

He suffered for weeks. Jack wondered how he could feel so bad about a woman who'd made him furious. But he knew the source of his guilt: while he and Deana were arguing in the closet, Jack had imagined vaporizing her with the gun. He was far too decent to shoot her for real, but the thought had crossed his mind. If Deana simply vanished, Jack wouldn't have to worry about what she might do. The ray-gun had made that thought come true, as if it had read Jack's mind.

Jack told himself the notion was ridiculous. The gun wasn't some genie who granted Jack's unspoken wishes. What happened to Deana came purely from her own bad luck and inquisitiveness.

Still, Jack felt like a murderer. After all this time, Jack realized the ray-gun was too dangerous to keep. As long as Jack had it, he'd be forced to live alone: never marrying, never having children, never trusting the gun around other people. And even if Jack became a recluse, accidents could happen. Someone else might die. It would be Jack's fault.

He wondered why he'd never had this thought before. Jack suddenly saw himself as one of those people who own a vicious attack dog. People like that always claimed they could keep the dog under control. How often did they end up on the evening news? How often did children get bitten, maimed, or killed?

Some dogs are tragedies waiting to happen. The ray-gun was too. It would keep slipping off its leash until it was destroyed. Twelve years after finding the gun, Jack realized he finally had a heroic mission: to get rid of the weapon that made him a hero in the first place.

I'm not Spider-Man, he thought, *I'm Frodo.*

But how could Jack destroy something that had survived so much? The gun hadn't frozen in the cold of outer space; it hadn't burned up as it plunged through Earth's atmosphere; it hadn't broken when it hit the ground at terminal velocity. If the gun could endure such punishment, extreme measures would be needed to lay it to rest.

Jack imagined putting the gun into a blast furnace. But what if the weapon went off? What if it shot out the side of the furnace? The furnace itself could explode. That would be a disaster. Other means of destruction had similar problems. Crushing the gun in a hydraulic press . . . what if the gun shot a hole in the press, sending pieces of equipment flying in all directions? Immersing the gun in acid . . . what if the gun went off and splashed acid over everything? Slicing into the gun with a laser . . . Jack didn't know what powered the gun, but obviously it contained vast energy. Destabilizing that energy might cause an explosion, a radiation leak, or some even greater catastrophe. Who knew what might happen if you tampered with alien technology?

And what if the gun could protect itself? Over the years, Jack had read every ray-gun story he could find. In some stories, such weapons had built-in computers. They had enough artificial intelligence to assess their situations. If they didn't like what was happening, they took action. What if Jack's gun was similar? What if attempts to destroy the weapon induced it to fight back? What if the ray-gun got mad?

Jack decided the only safe plan was to drop the gun into an ocean—the deeper the better. Even then, Jack feared the gun would somehow make its way back to shore. He hoped that the weapon would take years or even centuries to return, by which time humanity might be scientifically equipped to deal with the ray-gun's power.

Jack's plan had one weakness: both the university and Jack's home town were far from the sea. Jack didn't know anyone with an ocean-going boat suitable for dumping objects into deep water. He'd just have to drive to the coast and see if he could rent something.

But not until summer. Jack was in the final stages of his Ph.D. and didn't have time to leave the university for an extended trip. As a temporary measure, Jack moved the ray-gun back to the pond. He buried the weapon several feet underground, hoping that would keep it safe from animals and anyone else who happened by.

(Jack imagined a new generation of lovesick teenagers discovering the pond. If that happened, he wanted them safe. Like a real hero, Jack cared about people he didn't know.)

Jack no longer practiced with the gun, but he maintained his physical regimen. He tried to exhaust himself so he wouldn't have the energy to brood. It didn't work. Lying sleepless in bed, he kept wondering what would have happened if he'd told Deana the truth. She wouldn't have killed herself if she'd been warned to be cautious. But Jack had cared more about his precious secret than Deana's life.

In the dark, Jack muttered, "It was her own damned fault." His words were true, but not true enough.

When Jack wasn't at the gym, he cloistered himself with schoolwork and research. (His doctoral thesis was about common properties of different types of high-energy beams.) Jack didn't socialize. He seldom phoned home. He took days to answer email messages from his sister. Even so, he told himself he was doing an excellent job of acting "normal."

Jack had underestimated his sister's perceptiveness. One weekend, Rachel showed up on his doorstep to see why he'd "gone weird." She spent two days digging under his skin. By the end of the weekend, she could tell that Deana's disappearance had disturbed Jack profoundly. Rachel couldn't guess the full truth, but as a big sister, she felt entitled to meddle in Jack's life. She resolved to snap her brother out of his low spirits.

The next weekend Rachel showed up on Jack's doorstep again. This time, she brought Kirsten.

Nine years had passed since Kirsten and Jack had seen each other: the day they both graduated from high school. In the intervening time, when Jack had thought of Kirsten, he always pictured her as a high-school girl. It was strange to see her as a woman. At twenty-seven, she was not greatly changed from eighteen—new glasses and a better haircut—but despite similarities to her teenage self, Kirsten wore her life differently. She'd grown up.

So had Jack. Meeting Kirsten by surprise made Jack feel ambushed, but he soon got over it. Rachel helped by talking loud and fast through the initial awkwardness. She took Jack and Kirsten for coffee, and acted as emcee as they got reacquainted.

Kirsten had followed a path close to Jack's: university and graduate work. She told him, "No one makes a living as a poet. Most of us find jobs as English professors—teaching poetry to others who won't make a living at it either."

Kirsten had earned her doctorate a month earlier. Now she was living back home. She currently had no man in her life—her last relationship had fizzled out months ago, and she'd decided to avoid new involvements until she knew where she would end up teaching. She'd sent her résumé to English departments all over the continent and was optimistic about her chances of success; to Jack's surprise, Kirsten had published dozens of poems in literary magazines. She'd even sold two to *The New Yorker*. Her publishing record would be enough to interest many English departments.

After coffee, Rachel dragged Jack to a mall where she and Kirsten made him buy new clothes. Rachel bullied Jack while Kirsten made apologetic suggestions. Jack did his best to be a good sport; as they left the mall, Jack was surprised to find that he'd actually had a good time.

That evening, there was wine and more conversation. Rachel took Jack's bed, leaving him and Kirsten to make whatever arrangements they chose. The two of them joked about Rachel trying to pair them up again. Eventually Kirsten took the couch in the living room while Jack crawled into a sleeping bag on the kitchen floor . . . but that was only after talking till three in the morning.

Rachel and Kirsten left the next afternoon, but Jack felt cleansed by their visit. He stayed in touch with Kirsten by email. It was casual: not romance, but a knowing friendship.

In the next few months, Kirsten got job interviews with several colleges and universities. She accepted a position on the Oregon coast. She sent Jack pictures of the school. It was directly on the ocean; it even had a beach. Kirsten said she'd always liked the water. She teasingly reminded him of their times at the pond.

But when Jack saw Kirsten's pictures of the Pacific, all he could think of was dumping the ray-gun into the sea. He could drive out to visit her . . . rent a boat . . . sail out to deep water . . .

No. Jack knew nothing about sailing, and he didn't have enough money to rent a boat that could venture far offshore. "How many years have I been preparing?" he asked himself. "Didn't I intend to be ready for any emergency? Now I have an honest-to-god mission, and I'm useless."

Then Kirsten sent him an emailed invitation to go sailing with her.

She had access to a sea-going yacht. It belonged to her grandparents—the ones she'd visited on Vancouver Island just before she and Jack broke up. During her trip to the island, Kirsten had gone boating with her grandparents every day. At the start, she'd done it to take her mind off Jack; then she'd discovered she enjoyed being out on the waves.

She'd spent time with her grandparents every summer since, learning the ins and outs of yachting. She'd taken courses. She'd earned the necessary licenses. Now Kirsten was fully qualified for deep-water excursions . . . and as a gift to wish her well on her new job, Kirsten's grandparents were lending her their boat for a month. They intended to sail down to Oregon, spend a few days there, then fly off to tour Australia. When they were done, they'd return and sail back home; but in the meantime, Kirsten would have the use of their yacht. She asked Jack if he'd like to be her crew.

When Jack got this invitation, he couldn't help being disturbed. Kirsten had never mentioned boating before. Because she was living in their hometown, most of her email to Jack had been about old high-school friends. Jack had even started to picture her as a teenager again; he'd spent a weekend with the grown-up Kirsten, but all her talk of high-school people and places had muddled Jack's mental image of her. The thought of a bookish teenage girl captaining a yacht was absurd.

But that was a lesser problem compared to the suspicious convenience of her invitation. Jack needed a boat; all of a sudden, Kirsten had one. The coincidence was almost impossible to swallow.

He thought of the unknown aliens who made the ray-gun. Could they be influencing events? If the ray-gun was intelligent, could *it* be responsible for the coincidence?

Kirsten had often spent time near the gun. On their first visit to the pond, she and Jack had lain half-naked with the gun in Jack's backpack beside them.

He thought of Kirsten that day. So open. So vulnerable. The gun had been within inches. Had it nurtured Kirsten's interest in yachting . . . her decision to get a job in Oregon . . . even her grandparents' offer of their boat? Had it molded Kirsten's life so she was ready when Jack needed her? And if the gun could do that, what had it done to Jack himself?

This is ridiculous, Jack thought. *The gun is just a gun. It doesn't control people. It just kills them.*

Yet Jack couldn't shake off his sense of eeriness—about Kirsten as well as the ray-gun. All these years, while Jack had been preparing himself to be a hero, Kirsten had somehow done the same. Her self-improvement program had worked better than Jack's. She had a boat; he didn't.

Coincidence or not, Jack couldn't look a gift horse in the mouth. He told Kirsten he'd be delighted to go sailing with her. Only later did he realize that their time on the yacht would have a sexual subtext. He broke out laughing. "I'm such an idiot. We've done it again." Like that day at the pond, Jack had only been thinking about the gun. Kirsten had been thinking about Jack. Her invitation wasn't a carte-blanche come-on but it had a strong hint of, "Let's get together and see what develops."

Where Kirsten was concerned, Jack had always been slow to catch the signals. He thought, *Obviously, the ray-gun keeps dulling my senses.* This time, Jack meant it as a joke.

Summer came. Jack drove west with the ray-gun in the trunk of his car. The gun's safety was on, but Jack still drove as if he were carrying nuclear waste. He'd taken the gun back and forth between his hometown and university many times, but this trip was longer, on unfamiliar roads. It was also the last trip Jack ever intended to make with the gun; if the gun didn't want to be thrown into the sea, perhaps it would cause trouble. But it didn't.

For much of the drive, Jack debated how to tell Kirsten about the gun. He'd considered smuggling it onto the boat and throwing the weapon overboard when she wasn't looking, but Jack felt that he owed her the truth. It was overdue. Besides, this cruise could be the beginning of a new relationship. Jack didn't want to start by sneaking behind Kirsten's back.

So he had to reveal his deepest secret. Every other secret would follow:

what happened to Deana; what had really been on Jack's mind that day at the pond; what made First Love go sour. Jack would expose his guilt to the woman who'd suffered from the fallout.

He thought, *She'll probably throw me overboard with the gun.* But he would open up anyway, even if it made Kirsten hate him. When he tossed the ray-gun into the sea, he wanted to unburden himself of everything.

The first day on the boat, Jack said nothing about the ray-gun. Instead, he talked compulsively about trivia. So did Kirsten. It was strange being together, looking so much the way they did in high school but being entirely different people.

Fortunately, they had practical matters to fill their time. Jack needed a crash course in seamanship. He learned quickly. Kirsten was a good teacher. Besides, Jack's longstanding program of hero-dom had prepared his mind and muscles. Kirsten was impressed that he knew Morse code and had extensive knowledge of knots. She asked, "Were you a Boy Scout?"

"No. When I was a kid, I wanted to be able to untie myself if I ever got captured by spies."

Kirsten laughed. She thought he was joking.

That first day, they stayed close to shore. They never had to deal with being alone; there were always other yachts in sight, and sailboats, and people on shore. When night came, they put in to harbor. They ate in an ocean-view restaurant. Jack asked, "So where will we go tomorrow?"

"Where would you like? Up the coast, down the coast, or straight out to sea?"

"Why not straight out?" said Jack.

Back on the yacht, he and Kirsten talked long past midnight. There was only one cabin, but two separate fold-away beds. Without discussion, they each chose a bed. Both usually slept in the nude, but for this trip they'd both brought makeshift "pajamas" consisting of a T-shirt and track pants. They laughed at the clothes, the coincidence, and themselves.

They didn't kiss good night. Jack silently wished they had. He hoped Kirsten was wishing the same thing. They talked for an hour after they'd turned out the lights, becoming nothing but voices in the dark.

The next day they sailed due west. Both waited to see if the other would suggest turning back before dark. Neither did. The farther they got from shore, the fewer other boats remained in sight. By sunset, Jack and Kirsten knew they were once more alone with each other. No one in the world would stop them from whatever they chose to do.

Jack asked Kirsten to stay on deck. He went below and got the ray-gun from his luggage. He brought it up into the twilight. Before he could speak, Kirsten said, "I've seen that before."

Jack stared at her in shock. "What? Where?"

"I saw it years ago, in the woods back home. I was out for a walk. I noticed it lying in a little crater, as if it had fallen from the sky."

"Really? You found it too?"

"But I didn't touch it," Kirsten said. "I don't know why. Then I heard someone coming and I ran away. But the memory stayed vivid in my head. A mysterious object in a crater in the woods. I can't tell you how often I've tried to write poems about it, but they never work out." She looked at the gun in Jack's hands. "What is it?"

"A ray-gun," he said. In the fading light, he could see a clump of seaweed floating a short distance from the boat. He raised the gun and fired. The seaweed exploded in a blaze of fire, burning brightly against the dark waves.

"A ray-gun," said Kirsten. "Can I try it?"

Some time later, holding hands, they let the gun fall into the water. It sank without protest.

Long after that, they talked in each other's arms. Jack said the gun had made him who he was. Kirsten said she was the same. "Until I saw the gun, I just wrote poems about myself—overwritten self-absorbed pap, like every teenage girl. But the gun gave me something else to write about. I'd only seen it for a minute, but it was one of those burned-into-your-memory moments. I felt driven to find words to express what I'd seen. I kept refining my poems, trying to make them better. That's what made the difference."

"I felt driven too," Jack said. "Sometimes I've wondered if the gun can affect human minds. Maybe it brainwashed us into becoming who we are."

"Or maybe it's just Stone Soup," Kirsten said. "You know the story? Someone claims he can make soup from a stone, but what he really does is trick people into adding their own food to the pot. Maybe the ray-gun is like that. It did nothing but sit there like a stone. You and I did every-thing—made ourselves who we are—and the ray-gun is only an excuse."

"Maybe," Jack said. "But so many coincidences brought us here. . . . "

"You think the gun manipulated us because it *wanted* to be thrown into the Pacific? Why?"

"Maybe even a ray-gun gets tired of killing." Jack shivered, thinking of Deana. "Maybe the gun feels guilty for the deaths it's caused; it wanted to go someplace where it would never have to kill again."

"Deana's death wasn't your fault," Kirsten said. "Really, Jack. It was awful, but it wasn't your fault." She shivered too, then made her voice brighter. "Maybe the ray-gun orchestrated all this because it's an incurable romantic. It wanted to bring us together: our own personal matchmaker from the stars."

Jack kissed Kirsten on the nose. "If that's true, I don't object."

"Neither do I." She kissed him back.

Not on the nose.

Far below, the ray-gun drifted through the cold black depths. Beneath it, on the bottom of the sea, lay wreckage from the starship that had exploded centuries before. The wreckage had traveled all the way from Jupiter. Because of tiny differences in trajectory, the wreckage had splashed down thousands of miles from where the ray-gun landed.

The ray-gun sank straight toward the wreckage . . . but what the wreckage held or why the ray-gun wanted to rejoin it, we will never know.

We will never comprehend aliens. If someone spent a month explaining alien thoughts to us, we'd think we understood.

But we wouldn't.

MARY ROBINETTE KOWAL—SHORT STORY
EVIL ROBOT MONKEY

Um. I wrote this.

EVIL ROBOT MONKEY

MARY ROBINETTE KOWAL

Sliding his hands over the clay, Sly relished the moisture oozing around his fingers. The clay matted down the hair on the back of his hands making them look almost human. He turned the potter's wheel with his prehensile feet as he shaped the vase. Pinching the clay between his fingers he lifted the wall of the vase, spinning it higher.

Someone banged on the window of his pen. Sly jumped and then screamed as the vase collapsed under its own weight. He spun and hurled it at the picture window like feces. The clay spattered against the Plexiglas, sliding down the window.

In the courtyard beyond the glass, a group of school kids leapt back, laughing. One of them swung his arms aping Sly crudely. Sly bared his teeth, knowing these people would take it as a grin, but he meant it as a threat. Swinging down from his stool, he crossed his room in three long strides and pressed his dirty hand against the window. Still grinning, he wrote SSA. Outside, the letters would be reversed.

The student's teacher flushed as red as a female in heat and called the children away from the window. She looked back once as she led them out of the courtyard, so Sly grabbed himself and showed her what he would do if she came into his pen.

Her naked face turned brighter red and she hurried away. When they were gone, Sly rested his head against the glass. The metal in his skull thunked against the window. It wouldn't be long now, before a handler came to talk to him.

Damn.

He just wanted to make pottery. He loped back to the wheel and sat down again with his back to the window. Kicking the wheel into movement, Sly dropped a new ball of clay in the center and tried to lose himself.

In the corner of his vision, the door to his room snicked open. Sly let the wheel spin to a halt, crumpling the latest vase.

Vern poked his head through. He signed, "You okay?"

Sly shook his head emphatically and pointed at the window.

"Sorry." Vern's hands danced. "We should have warned you that they were coming."

"You should have told them that I was not an animal."

Vern looked down in submission. "I did. They're kids."

"And I'm a chimp. I know." Sly buried his fingers in the clay to silence his thoughts.

"It was Delilah. She thought you wouldn't mind because the other chimps didn't."

Sly scowled and yanked his hands free. "I'm not like the other chimps." He pointed to the implant in his head. "Maybe Delilah should have one of these. Seems like she needs help thinking."

"I'm sorry." Vern knelt in front of Sly, closer than anyone else would come when he wasn't sedated. It would be so easy to reach out and snap his neck. "It was a lousy thing to do."

Sly pushed the clay around on the wheel. Vern was better than the others. He seemed to understand the hellish limbo where Sly lived–too smart to be with other chimps, but too much of an animal to be with humans. Vern was the one who had brought Sly the potter's wheel which, by the Earth and Trees, Sly loved. Sly looked up and raised his eyebrows. "So what did they think of my show?"

Vern covered his mouth, masking his smile. The man had manners. "The teacher was upset about the 'evil robot monkey.'"

Sly threw his head back and hooted. Served her right.

"But Delilah thinks you should be disciplined." Vern, still so close that Sly could reach out and break him, stayed very still. "She wants me to take the clay away since you used it for an anger display."

Sly's lips drew back in a grimace built of anger and fear. Rage threatened to blind him, but he held on, clutching the wheel. If he lost it with Vern–rational thought danced out of his reach. Panting, he spun the wheel trying to push his anger into the clay.

The wheel spun. Clay slid between his fingers. Soft. Firm and smooth.

The smell of earth lived in his nostrils. He held the world in his hands. Turning, turning, the walls rose around a kernel of anger, subsuming it.

His heart slowed with the wheel and Sly blinked, becoming aware again as if he were slipping out of sleep. The vase on the wheel still seemed to dance with life. Its walls held the shape of the world within them. He passed a finger across the rim.

Vern's eyes were moist. "Do you want me to put that in the kiln for you?"

Sly nodded.

"I have to take the clay. You understand that, don't you?"

Sly nodded again staring at his vase. It was beautiful.

Vern scowled. "The woman makes me want to hurl feces."

Sly snorted at the image, then sobered. "How long before I get it back?"

Vern picked up the bucket of clay next to the wheel. "I don't know." He stopped at the door and looked past Sly to the window. "I'm not cleaning your mess. Do you understand me?"

For a moment, rage crawled on his spine, but Vern did not meet his eyes and kept staring at the window. Sly turned.

The vase he had thrown lay on the floor in a pile of clay.

Clay.

"I understand." He waited until the door closed, then loped over and scooped the clay up. It was not much, but it was enough for now.

Sly sat down at his wheel and began to turn.

IAN MCDONALD—NOVELLA
THE TEAR

In all seriousness, you should probably take a break before reading this next novella. Why? Because Ian McDonald writes with the assumption that his readers are as smart as he is and this is a challenging story. You want full brain power to wrap your head around all the concepts going on in this.

He has won a Locus Award, a Phillip K. Dick award, a Theodore Sturgeon award, a British Science Fiction Association award, and a Hugo. His life growing up in the "Troubles" in Northern Ireland has left a clear mark on his fiction and its examination of various aspects of post-colonial civilizations. You might wonder if his story-telling skills are entirely natural since he used to live in a house that was built in the back garden of C. S. Lewis's childhood home. Something in the water, I suppose.

At its heart, "The Tear" is about identity and what "self" means. McDonald explores this with two different races of PanHumanity in a far future where humans have seeded the universe with different forms of themselves. The inhabitants of Tay go through a right of passage at the Manifold house in which they are split into eight Aspects. In other words, this is an entire world populated by people with multiple personality disorder.

The other race, the Anpreen, are a Level II civilization who have given up their human bodies in exchange for clusters of nano "motes" that they can reconfigure at will. Each person has many, mutable bodies.

Watching the two races play off one another—one body, many personalities, vs. one personality, many bodies—raises the question of self over and over.

Add to this the vast time span that the story covers. During the course of it Ptey, the protagonist, changes as he ages in much the same way any of us do. In his case, his adult self is literally a different person than his child self. The demarkations between roles in life is a metaphor made manifest.

There's more to the story than just that, but I think you'll see pretty quickly why I recommend approaching this with your full brain. McDonald tells a fascinating story, but he doesn't wait for stragglers.

THE TEAR

IAN McDONALD

Ptey, sailing

On the night that Ptey voyaged out to have his soul shattered, eight hundred stars set sail across the sky. It was an evening at Great Winter's ending. The sunlit hours raced toward High Summer, each day lavishly more full of light than the one before. In this latitude, the sun hardly set at all after the spring equinox, rolling along the horizon, fat and idle and pleased with itself. Summer-born Ptey turned his face to the sun as it dipped briefly beneath the horizon, closed his eyes, enjoyed its lingering warmth on his eyelids, in the angle of his cheekbones, on his lips. To the summer-born, any loss of the light was a reminder of the terrible, sad months of winter and the unbroken, encircling dark.

But we have the stars, his father said, a Winter-born. *We are born looking out into the universe.*

Ptey's father commanded the little machines that ran the catamaran, trimming sail, winding sheets, setting course by the tumble of satellites; but the tiller he held himself. The equinoctial gales had spun away to the west two weeks before and the catboat ran fast and fresh on a sweet wind across the darkening water. Twins hulls cut through the ripple-reflections of gas-flares from the Temejveri oil platforms. As the sun slipped beneath the huge dark horizon and the warmth fell from the hollows of Ptey's face, so his father turned his face to the sky. Tonight, he wore his Steris Aspect. The ritual selves scared Ptey, so rarely were they unfurled in Ctarisphay: births, namings, betrothals and marriages, divorces and deaths. And of course, the Manifoldings. Familiar faces became distant and formal. Their language changed, their bodies seemed slower, heavier. They became possessed by strange, special knowledges. Only Steris possessed the language for the robots to sail the catamaran and, despite the wheel of positioning satellites around tilted Tay, the latitude and longitude of the Manifold House. The catamaran itself was only run out from its boathouse, to strong songs heavy with clashing harmonies, when a child from Ctarisphay on the edge of adulthood sailed out beyond the outer mole and the fleet of oil platforms to have his or her personality unfolded into eight.

Only two months since, Cjatay had sailed out into the oily black of a late winter afternoon. Ptey was Summer-born, a Solstice boy; Cjatay a late Autumn. It was considered remarkable that they shared enough in common to be able to speak to each other, let alone become the howling boys of the neighborhood, the source of every broken window and borrowed boat. The best part of three seasons between them, but here was only two moons later, leaving behind the pulsing gas flares and maze of pipe work of the sheltering oil-fields, heading into the great, gentle oceanic glow of the plankton blooms, steering by the stars, the occupied, haunted stars. The Manifolding was never a thing of moons and calendars, but of mothers' watchings and grandmothers' knowings and teachers' notings and fathers' murmurings, of subtly shifted razors and untimely lethargies, of deep-swinging voices and stained bedsheets.

On Etjay Quay, where the porcelain houses leaned over the landing, Ptey had thrown his friend's bag down into the boat. Cjatay's father had caught it and frowned. There were observances. Ways. Forms.

"See you," Ptey had said.

"See you." Then the wind caught in the catamaran's tall, curved sails and carried it away from the rain-wet, shiny faces of the houses of Ctarisphay. Ptey had watched the boat until it was lost in the light dapple of the city's lamps on the winter-dark water. See Cjatay he would, after his six months on the Manifold House. But only partially. There would be Cjatays he had never known, never even met. Eight of them, and the Cjatay with whom he had stayed out all the brief Low Summer nights of the prith run on the fishing staithes, skinny as the piers' wooden legs silhouetted against the huge sun kissing the edge of the world, would be but a part, a dream of one of the new names and new personalities. Would he know him when he met him on the great floating university that was the Manifold House? Would he know himself?

"Are they moving yet?" Steris called from the tiller. Ptey shielded his dark-accustomed eyes against the pervasive glow of the carbon-absorbing plankton blooms and peered into the sky. *Sail of Bright Anticipation* cut two lines of liquid black through the gently undulating sheet of biolight, fraying at the edges into fractal curls of luminescence as the sheets of microorganisms sought each other.

"Nothing yet."

But it would be soon, and it would be tremendous. Eight hundred stars setting out across the night. Through the changes and domestic rituals of his sudden Manifolding, Ptey had been aware of sky-watch parties being arranged, star-gazing groups setting up telescopes along the quays and in the campaniles, while day on day the story moved closer to the head of the news. Half the world—that half of the world not blinded by its extravagant axial tilt—would be looking to the sky. Watching Steris rig *Sail of Bright Anticipation*, Ptey had felt cheated, like a sick child confined to bed while festival raged across the boats lashed beneath his window. Now, as the swell of the deep dark of his world's girdling ocean lifted the twin prows of *Sail of Bright Anticipation*, on his web of shock-plastic mesh ahead of the mast, Ptey felt his excitement lift with it. A carpet of lights below, a sky of stars above: all his alone.

They were not stars. They were the eight hundred and twenty six space habitats of the Anpreen Commonweal, spheres of nano-carbon ice and water five hundred kilometers in diameter that for twice Ptey's lifetime had adorned Bephis, the ringed gas giant, like a necklace of pearls hidden in a velvet bag, far from eye and mind. The negotiations fell into eras. The Panic; when the world of Tay became aware that the gravity waves pulsing through the huge ripple tank that was their ocean-bound planet were the bow-shocks of massive artifacts decelerating from near light-speed. The Denial, when Tay's governments decided it was Best Really to try and hide the fact that their solar system had been immigrated into by eight hundred-and-some space vehicles, each larger than Tay's petty moons, falling into neat and proper order around Bephis. The Soliciting, when it became obvious that Denial was futile—but on our terms, our terms. A fleet of space probes was dispatched to survey and attempt radio contact with the arrivals—as yet silent as ice. And, when they were not blasted from space or vaporized or collapsed into quantum black holes or any of the plethora of fanciful destructions imagined in the popular media, the Overture. The Sobering, when it was realized that these star-visitors existed primarily as swarms of free-swimming nano-assemblers in the free-fall spherical oceans of their eight hundred and some habitats, one mind with many forms; and, for the Anpreen, the surprise that these archaic hominiforms on this backwater planet were many selves within one body. One thing they shared and understood well. Water. It ran through their histories, it flowed around their ecologies, it mediated their molecules. After one hundred and twelve years of near-light speed flight, the Anpreen Commonweal was desperately short of water; their spherical oceans shriveled almost into zero gravity teardrops within the immense, nano-tech-reinforced ice shells. Then began the era of Negotiation, the most prolonged of the phases of contact, and the most complex. It had taken three years to establish the philosophical foundations: the Anpreen, an ancient species of the great Clade, had long been a colonial mind, arranged in subtle hierarchies of self-knowledge and ability, and did not know who to talk to, whom to ask for a decision, in a political system with as many governments and nations as there were islands and archipelagos scattered across the world ocean of the fourth planet from the sun.

Now the era of Negotiation had become the era of Open Trade. The Anpreen habitats spent their last drops of reaction mass to break orbit around Bephis and move the Commonweal in-system. Their destination was not Tay, but Tejaphay, Tay's sunward neighbor, a huge waterworld of unbroken ocean one hundred kilometers deep, crushing gravity, and endless storms. A billion years before the seed-ships probed the remote star system, the gravitational interplay of giant worlds had sent the least of their number spiraling sunwards. Solar wind had stripped away its huge atmosphere and melted its mantle of water ice into a planetary ocean, deep and dark as nightmares. It was that wink of water in the system-scale interferometers of the Can-Bet-Merey people, half a million years before, that had inspired them to fill their night sky with solar sails as one hundred thousand slow seed-ships rode out on flickering launch lasers toward the new system. An evangelically pro-life people were the Can-Bet-Merey, zealous for the Clade's implicit dogma that intelligence was the only force in the universe capable of defeating the physical death of space-time.

If the tens of thousand of biological packages they had rained into the world-ocean of Tejaphay had germinated life, Tay's probes had yet to discover it. The Can-Bet-Merey did strike roots in the afterthought, that little blue pearl next out from the sun, a tear spun from huge Tejaphay.

One hundred thousand the years ago, the Can-Bet-Merey had entered the post-biological phase of intelligence and moved to that level that could no longer communicate with the biological life of Tay, or even the Anpreen.

"Can you see anything yet?" A call from the tiller. *Sail of Bright Anticipation* had left behind the carbon-soaked plankton bloom, the ocean was deep dark and boundless. Sky and sea blurred; stars became confused with the riding lights of ships close on the horizon.

"Is it time?" Ptey called back.

"Five minutes ago."

Ptey found a footing on the webbing, and, one hand wrapped in the sheets, stood up to scan the huge sky. Every child of Tay, crazily tilted at 48 degrees to the ecliptic, grew up conscious that her planet was a ball rolling around the sun and that the stars were far, vast and slow, almost unchanging. But stars could change; Bephis, that soft smudge of light low in the south-east, blurred by the glow of a eight hundred moon-sized space habitats, would soon be once again the hard point of light by which his ancestors had steered to their Manifoldings.

"Give it time," Ptey shouted. Time. The Anpreen were already voyaging; had switched on their drives and pulled out of orbit almost an hour before. The slow light of their embarkation had still not reached Tay. He saw the numbers spinning around in his head, accelerations, vectors, space and time all arranged around him like fluttering carnival banners. It had taken Ptey a long time to understand that not everyone could see numbers like him and reach out and make them do what they wanted.

"Well, I'll be watching the football," Cjatay had declared when Teacher Deu had declared a Special Class Project in conjunction with the Noble Observatory of Pteu to celebrate the Anpreen migration. "We're all jumping up and down, Anpreen this, Anpreen that, but when it comes down to it, they aliens and we don't know what they really want, no one does."

"They're not aliens," Ptey had hissed back. "There *are* no aliens, don't you know that? We're all just part of the one big Clade."

Then Teacher Deu had shouted at them quiet you boys and they had straightened themselves at their kneeling-desks, but Cjatay had hissed,

"So if they're our cousins, why don't they give us their star-crosser drive?"

Such was the friendship between Ptey and Cjatay that they would argue over nodes of free-swimming nanotechnology orbiting a gas giant.

"Look! Oh look!"

Slowly, very slowy, Bephis was unraveling into a glowing smudge, like one of the swarms of nuchpas that hung above the waves like smoke on High Summer mornings. The fleet was moving. Eight hundred worlds. The numbers in his skull told Ptey that the Anpreen Commonweal was already at ten percent of lightspeed. He tried to work out the relativistic deformations of space-time but there were too many numbers flocking around him too fast. Instead, he watched Bephis unfurl into a galaxy, that cloud of stars slowly pull away from the bright mote of the gas giant. Crossing the ocean of night. Ptey glanced behind him. In the big dark, his father's face was hard to read, especially as Steris, who was sober and focused, and, Ptey had learned, not particularly bright. He seemed to be smiling.

It is a deep understanding, the realization that you are cleverer than your parents, Ptey thought. Behind that first smirking, satisfied sense of your own smartness comes a more profound understanding; that smart is only smart at some things, in some situations. Clever is conditional: Ptey could calculate the space-time distortion of eight hundred space habitats, plot a course across the dark, steepening sea by the stars in their courses, but he could never harness the winds or whistle the small commands to the machines, all the weather-clevernesses of Steris. That is how our world has shaped our intelligences. A self for every season.

The ravel of stars was unwinding, the Anpreen migration flowing into a ribbon of sparkles, a scarf of night beyond the veils of the aurora. Tomorrow night, it would adorn Tejaphay, that great blue guide star on the edge of the world, that had become a glowing smudge, a thumbprint of the alien. Tomorrow night, Ptey would look at that blue eye in the sky from the minarets of the Manifold House. He knew that it had minarets; every child knew what the Manifold House and its sister houses all round the world, looked like. Great hulks of grey wood gone silvery from salt and sun, built over upon through within alongside until they were floating cities. Cities of children. But the popular imaginations of Teacher Deu's Grade Eight class never painted them bright and loud with voices; they were dark, sooty labyrinths sailing under a perpetual cloud of black diesel smoke that poured from a thousand chimneys, taller even than the masts and towers. The images were sharp in Ptey's mind, but he could never see himself there, in those winding wooden staircases loud with the cries of sea birds, looking out from the high balconies across the glowing sea. Then his breath caught. All his imaginings and failures to imagine were made true as lights disentangled themselves from the skein of stars of the Anpreen migration: red and green stars, the riding lights of the Manifold House. Now he could feel the thrum of its engines and generators through the water and the twin hulls. Ptey set his hand to the carbon nanofiber mast. It sang to deep harmonic. And just as the stars are always further than you think, so Prey saw that the lights of the Manifold House were closer than he thought, that he was right under them, that *Sail of Bright Anticipation* was slipping through the outer buoys and nets, and that the towers and spires and minarets, rising in his vision, one by one, were obliterating the stars.

Nejben, swimming

Beneath a sky of honey, Nejben stood hip deep in water warm as blood, deep as forgetting. This High Summer midnight, the sun was still clear from the horizon, and in its constant heat and light, the wood of the Manifold House's old, warped spires seemed to exhale a spicy musk, the distilled pheromone of centuries of teenage hormones and sexual angsts and identity crises. In cupped hands, Nejben scooped up the waters of the Chalybeate Pool and let them run, gold and thick, through his fingers. He savored the sensuality, observed the flash of sunlight through the falling water, noted the cool, deep plash as the pool received its own. A new Aspect, Nejben; old in observation and knowledge, for the body remained the same though a flock of selves came to roost in it, fresh in interpretation and experience.

When Nejben first emerged, shivering and anoxic, from the Chalybeate Pool, to be wrapped in silvery thermal sheets by the agisters, he had feared himself mad. A voice in his head, that would not go away, that would not be shut up, that seemed to know him, know every part of him.

"It's perfectly normal," said agister Ashbey, a plump, serious woman with the blackest skin Nejben had ever seen. But he remembered that every Ritual Aspect was serious, and in the Manifold House the agisters were never in any other Aspect. None that the novices would ever see. "Perfectly natural. It takes time for your Prior, your childhood Aspect, to find its place and relinquish the control of the higher cognitive levels. Give it time. Talk to him. Reassure him. He will feel very lost, very alone, like he has lost everything that he ever knew. Except you, Nejben."

The time-free, sun-filled days in the sunny, smoggy yards and cloisters of the First Novitiate were full of whisperings; boys and girls like himself whispering goodbye to their childhoods. Nejben learned his Prior's dreads, that the self that had been called Ptey feared that the numbers, the patterns between them, the ability to reduce physical objects to mathematics and see in an instant their relationships and implications, would be utterly lost. He saw also that Nejben in himself scared Ptey: the easy physicality, the unselfconscious interest in his own body, the awareness of the hormones pumping like tidewater through his tubes and cells; the ever-present, ever-tickling nag of sex; everywhere, everywhen, everyone and thing. Even as a child-self, even as shadow, Ptey knew that the first self to be birthed at the Manifold House was the pubescent self, the sexual self, but he felt this growing, aching youth to be more alien than the disembodied, mathematical Anpreen.

The tiers led down into the palp pool. In its depths, translucencies shifted. Nejben shivered in the warm High Summer midnight.

"Hey! Ptey!"

Names flocked around the Manifold House's towers like sun-gulls. New selves, new identities unfolded every hour of every day and yet old names clung. Agister Ashbey, jokey and astute, taught the social subtleties by which adults knew what Aspect and name to address and which Aspect and name of their own to wear in response. From the shade of the Poljeri Cloister, Puzhay waved. Ptey had found girls frightening, but Nejben liked them, enjoyed their company and the little games of admiring insult and flirting mock-animosity he played with them. He reckoned he understood girls now. Puzhay was small, still boy-figured, her skin Winterborn-pale, a Janni from Bedenderay, where at midwinter the atmosphere froze. She had a barbarous accent and continental manners, but Nejben found himself thinking often about her small, flat boy-breasts with their big, thumbable nipples. He had never thought when he came to the Manifold House that there would be people here from places other than Ctarisphay and its archipelago sisters. People—girls—from the big polar continent. Rude girls who cursed and openly called boys' names.

"Puzhay! What're you doing?"

"Going in."

"For the palps?"

"Nah. Just going in."

Nejben found and enjoyed a sudden, swift swelling of his dick as he watched Puzhay's breasts taunten as she raised her arms above her head and dived, awkward as a Bedenderay land-girl, into the water. Water hid it. Sun dapple kept it secret. The he felt a shiver run over him and he dived down, deep down. Almost he let the air rush out of him in a gasp as he felt the cool cool water close around his body; then he saw Puzhay in her tight swim-shorts that made her ass look so strong and muscley turn in the water, tiny bubbles leaking from her nose, to grin and wave and beckon him down. Nejben swam down past the descending tiers of steps. Green opened before him, the bottomless emerald beyond the anti-skray nets where the Chalybeate pond was refreshed by the borderless sea. Between her pale red body and the deep green sea was the shimmering curtains of the palps.

They did not make them we did not bring them they were here forever. Ten thousand years of theology, biology, and xenology in that simple kinder-group rhyme. Nejben—all his people—had always known their special place; stranger to this world, spurted into the womb of the world-sea as the star-sperm, the seed of sentience. Twenty million drops of life-seed swam ashore and became humanity, the rest swam out to sea and met and smelled and loved the palps, older than forever. Now Nejben turned and twisted like an eel past funny, flirting, heartbreaking Puzhay, turning to show the merest glimpse of his own sperm-eel, down toward the palps. The curtain of living jelly rippled and dissolved into their separate lives. Slick, cold, quivering jelly slid across his sex-warm flesh. Nejben shivered, quivered; repelled yet aroused in a way that was other than sex. The water took on a prickle, a tickle, a tang of salt and fear and ancient ancient lusts, deep as his first stiff dream. Against sense, against reason, against three million years of species wisdom, Nejben employed the tricks of agister Ashbey and opened his mouth. He inhaled. Once he gagged, twice he choked, then he felt the jellied eeling of the palps squirm down his throat: a choke, and into the lungs. He inhaled green salt water. And then, as the palps demurely unraveled their nano-tube outer integuments and infiltrated them into his lungs, his bronchial tubes, his bloodstream, he *became*. Memories stirred, invoked by olfactory summonings, changed as a new voice, a new way of seeing, a new interpretation of those memories and experiences, formed. Nejben swam down, breathing memory-water, stroke by stroke unraveling. There was another down there, far below him, swimming up not through water but through the twelve years of his life. A new self.

Puzhay, against the light of a three o'clock sky. Framed in the arch of a cell window, knees pulled up to her chest. Small budding breasts; strong, boy jawline, fall and arc of hair shadow against lilac. She had laughed, throwing her head back. That first sight of her was cut into Nejben's memory, every line and trace, like the paper silhouettes the limners would cut of friends and families and enemies for Autumn Solstice. That first stirring of sex, that first intimation in the self of Ptey of this then-stranger, now-familiar Nejben.

As soon as he could, he had run. After he had found out where to put his bag, after he had worked out how to use the ancient, gurgling shit-eater, after agister Ashbey had closed the door with a smile and a blessing on the wooden cell—his wooden cell—that still smelled of fresh-cut timber after hundreds of years on the world-ocean of Tay. In the short season in which photosynthesis was possible, Bedenderay's forests grew fast and fierce, putting on meters in a single day. Small wonder the wood still smelled fresh and lively. After the midnight walk along the ceramic lanes and up the wooden staircases and through the damp-smelling cloisters, through the gently undulating quadrangles with the sky-train of the Anpreen migration bright overhead, holding on, as tradition demanded, to the bell-hung by a chain from his agister's waist; after the form filling and the photographings and the registering and the this-is-your-ident-card this is your map I've tattooed onto the back of your hand trust it will guide you and I am your agister and we'll see you in the east Refectory for breakfast; after the climb up the slimy wooden stairs from *Sail of Bright Anticipation* on to the Manifold House's quay, the biolights green around him and the greater lamps of the great college's towers high before him; when he was alone in this alien new world where he would become eight alien new people: he ran.

Agister Ashbey was faithful; the tattoo, a clever print of smart molecules and nanodyes, was meshed into the Manifold House's network and guided him through the labyrinth of dormitories and cloisters and Boy's Pavilions and Girlhearths by the simple, aversive trick of stinging the opposite side his map-hand to the direction in which he was to turn.

Cjatay. Sea-sundered friend. The only other one who knew him, knew him the moment they had met outside the school walls and recognized each other as different from the sailing freaks and fishing fools. Interested in geography, in love with numbers, with the wonder of the world and the worlds, as the city net declared, beyond. Boys who looked up at the sky.

As his burning hand led him left, right, up this spiral staircase under the lightening sky, such was Ptey's impetus that he never thought, would he know Cjatay? Cjatay had been in the Manifold House three months. Cjatay could be—*would* be—any number of Aspects now. Ptey had grown up with his father's overlapping circles of friends, each specific to a different Aspect, but he had assumed that it was a grown up thing. That couldn't happen to him and Cjatay! Not them.

The cell was one of four that opened off a narrow oval at the head of a tulip-shaped minaret—the Third Moon of Spring Tower, the legend on the back of Ptey's hand read. Cells were assigned by birth-date and season. Head and heart full of nothing but seeing Cjatay, he pushed open the door—no door in the Manifold House was ever locked.

She was in the arched window, dangerously high above the shingled roofs and porcelain domes of the Vernal Equinox division. Beyond her, only the wandering stars of the Anpreen. Ptey had no name for the sudden rush of feelings that came when he saw Puzhay throw back her head and laugh at some so-serious comment of Cjatay's. Nejben did.

It was only at introductory breakfast in the East Refectory, where he met the other uncertain, awkward boys and girls of his intake, that Ptey saw past the dawn seduction of Puzhay to Cjatay, and saw him unchanged, exactly as he had had been when he had stepped down from Etjay Quay into the catamaran and been taken out across the lagoon to the waste gas flares of Temejveri.

She was waiting crouched on the wooden steps where the water of the Chalybeate Pool lapped, knees pulled to her chest, goose flesh pimpling her forearms and calves in the cool of after-midnight. He knew this girl, knew her name, knew her history, knew the taste of a small, tentative kiss stolen among the crowds of teenagers pushing over 12th Canal Bridge. The memory was sharp and warm, but it was another's.

"Hi there."

He dragged himself out of the water onto to the silvery wood, rolled away to hide his nakedness. In the cloister shadow, Ashbey waited with a sea-silk robe.

"Hi there." There was never any easy way to tell someone you were another person from the one they remembered. "I'm Serejen." The name had been there, down among the palps, slipped into him with their mind-altering neurotransmitters.

"Are you?"

"All right. Yes, I'm all right." A tickle in the throat made him cough, the cough amplified into a deep retch. Serejen choked up a lungful of mucus-stained palp-jelly. In the early light, it thinned and ran, flowed down the steps to rejoin its shoal in the Chalybeate Pool. Agister Ashbey took a step forward. Serejen waved her away.

"What time is it?"

"Four thirty."

Almost five hours.

"Serejen." Puzhay looked coyly away. Around the Chalybeate Pool, other soul-swimmers were emerging, coughing up lungfuls of palp, shivering in their thermal robes, growing into new Aspects of themselves. "It's Cjatay. He needs to see you. Dead urgent."

Waiting Ashbey folded new-born Serejen in his own thermal gown, the intelligent plastics releasing their stored heat to his particular body temperature.

"Go to him," his agister said.

"I thought I was supposed to . . . "

"You've got the rest of your life to get to know Serejen. I think you should go."

Cjatay. A memory of fascination with starry skies, counting and numbering and betting games. The name and the face belonged to another Aspect, another life, but that old lust for numbers, for discovering the relationships between things, stirred a deep welling of joy. It was as rich and adult as the swelling of his dick he found in the bright mornings, or when he thought about Puzhay's breasts in his hands and the tattooed triangle of her sex. Different; no less intense.

The shutters were pulled close. The screen was the sole light in the room. Cjatay turned on hearing his lockless door open. He squinted into the gloom of the stair head, then cried excitedly, "Look at this look at this!"

Pictures from the observation platforms sent to Tejaphay to monitor the doings of the Anpreen. A black-light plane of stars, the blinding blue curve of the water world stopped down to prevent screen-burn. The closer habitats showed a disc, otherwise it was moving lights. Patterns of speed and gravity.

"What am I looking at?"

"Look look, they're building a space elevator! I wondered how they were going to get the water from Tejaphay. Simple, duh! They're just going to vacuum it up! They've got some kind of processing unit in stationary orbit chewing up one of those asteroids they brought with them, but they using one of their own habitats to anchor it."

"At twice stationary orbit," Serejen said. "So they're going to have to build down and up at the same time to keep the elevator in tension." He did not know where the words came from. They were on his lips and they were true.

"It must be some kind of nano-carbon compound," Cjatay said, peering at the screen for some hint, some elongation, some erection from the fuzzy blob of the construction asteroid. "Incredible tensile strength, yet very flexible. We have to get that; with all our oil, it could change everything about our technology. It could really make us a proper star-faring people." Then, as if hearing truly for the first time, Cjatay turned from the screen and peered again at the figure in the doorway. "Who are you?" His voice was high and soft and plaintive.

"I'm Serejen."

"You sound like Ptey."

"I was Ptey. I remember him."

Cjatay did a thing with his mouth, a twisting, chewing movement that Serejen recalled from moments of unhappiness and frustration. The time at his sister's nameday party, when all the birth family was gathered and he had shown how it was almost certain that someone in the house on Drunken Chicken Lane had the same nameday as little Sezjma. There had been a long, embarrassed silence as Cjatay had burst into the adult chatter. Then laughter. And again, when Cjatay had worked out how long it would take to walk a light-year and Teacher Deu has asked the class *does anyone understand this?* For a moment, Serejen thought that the boy might cry.

That would have been a terrible thing; unseemly, humiliating. Then he saw the bag on the unkempt bed, the ritual white clothes thrust knotted and fighting into it.

"I think what Cjatay wants to say is that he's leaving the Manifold House," agister Ashbey said, in the voice that Serejen understood as the one adults used when they had uncomfortable things to say. In that voice was a hidden word that Ashbey would not, that Serejen and Puzhay could not, and that Cjatay never would speak.

There was one in every town, every district. Kentlay had lived at the bottom of Drunken Chicken Lane, still at fortysomething living with his birth-parents. He had never married, though then-Ptey had heard that some did, and not just others like them. Normals. Multiples. Kentlay had been a figure that drew pity and respect alike; equally blessed and cursed, the Lonely were granted insights and gifts in compensation for their inability to manifold into the Eight Aspects. Kentlay had the touch for skin diseases, warts, and the sicknesses of birds. Ptey had been sent to see him for the charm of a dangling wart on his chin. The wart was gone within a week. Even then, Ptey had wondered if it had been through unnatural gifts or superstitious fear of the alien at the end of the wharf.

Cjatay. Lonely. The words were as impossible together as *green sun* or *bright winter*. It was never to be like this. Though the waters of the Chalybeate Pool would break them into many brilliant shards, though there would be other lives, other friends, even other wives and husbands, there would always be aspects of themselves that remembered trying to draw birds and fishes on the glowing band of the Mid Winter Galaxy that hung in the sky for weeks on end, or trying to calculate the mathematics of the High Summer silverlings that shoaled like silver needles in the Lagoon, how they kept together yet apart, how they were many but moved as one. *Boiling rain. Summer ice. A morning where the sun wouldn't rise. A friend who would always, only be one person.* Impossibilities. Cjatay could not be abnormal. Dark word. A vile word that hung on Cjatay like an oil-stained tarpaulin.

He sealed his bag and slung it over his shoulder.

"I'll give you a call when you get back."

"Yeah. Okay. That would be good." Words and needs and sayings flocked to him, but the end was so fast, so sudden, that all Serejen could do was stare at his feet so that he would not have to see Cjatay walk away.

Puzhay was in tears. Cjatay's own agister, a tall, dark-skinned Summer-born, put his arm around Cjatay and took him to the stairs.

"Hey. Did you ever think?" Cjatay threw back the line from the top of the spiral stair. "Why are they here? The Anpreen." Even now, Serejen realized, Cjatay was hiding from the truth that he would be marked as different, as not fully human, for the rest of his life, hiding behind stars and ships and the mystery of the alien. "Why did they come here? They call it the Anpreen Migration, but where are they migrating *to*? And what are they migrating *from*? Anyone ever ask that? Ever think about that, eh?"

Then agister Ashbey closed the door on the high tower-top cell.

"We'll talk later."

Gulls screamed. Change in the weather coming. On the screen behind him, stars moved across the face of the great water.

Serejen could not bear to go down to the quay, but watched *Sail of Bright Anticipation* make sail from the cupola of the Bright Glance Netball Hall. The Manifold House was sailing through a plankton-bloom and he watched the ritual catamaran's hulls cut two lines of bioglow through the carpet of carbon-absorbing microlife. He stood and followed the sails until they were lost among the hulls of huge ceramic oil tankers pressed low to the orange smog-glow of Ctarisphay down under the horizon. Call each other. They would always forget to do that. They would slip out of each other's lives—Serejen's life now vastly more rich and populous as he moved across the social worlds of his various Aspects. In time, they would slip out of each other's thoughts and memories. So it was that Serejen Nejben ex-Ptey knew that he was not a child any longer. He could let things go.

After morning Shift class, Serejen went down to the Old Great Pool, the ancient flooded piazza that was the historic heart of the Manifold House, and used the techniques he had learned an hour before to effortlessly transfer from Serejen to Nejbet. Then he went down into the waters and swam with Puzhay. She was teary and confused, but the summer-warmed water and the physical exercise brightened her. Under a sky lowering with the summer storm that the gulls had promised, they sought out the many secret flooded colonnades and courts where the big groups of friends did not go. There, under the first crackles of lightning and the hiss of rain, he kissed her and she slipped her hand into his swimsuit and cradled the comfortable swell of his cock.

Serejen, loving.

Night, the aurora and sirens. Serejen shivered as police drones came in low over the Conservatorium roof. Through the high, arched windows, fires could still be seen burning on Yaskaray Prospect. The power had not yet been restored, the streets, the towering apartment blocks that lined them, were still dark. A stalled tram sprawled across a set of points, flames flickering in its rear carriage. The noise of the protest had moved off, but occasional shadows moved across the ice beneath the mesmerism of the aurora; student rioters, police security robots. It was easy to tell the robots by the sprays of ice crystals thrown up by their needle-tip, mincing legs.

"Are you still at that window? Come away from there, if they see you they might shoot you. Look, I've tea made."

"Who?"

"What?"

"Who might shoot me? The rioters or the police?"

"Like you'd care if you were dead."

But he came and sat at the table and took the bowl of thin, salty Bedenderay maté.

"But sure I can't be killed."

Her name was Seriantep. She was an Anpreen Prebendary ostensibly attached to the College of Theoretical Physics at the Conservatorium of Jann. She looked like a tall, slim young woman with the dark skin and blue-black hair of a Summer-born Archipelagan, but that was just the form that the swarm of Anpreen nano-processor motes had assumed. She hived. Reris Orhum Fejannan Kekjay Prus Rejmer Serejen Nejben wondered how close you had to get before her perfect skin resolved into a blur of microscopic motes. He had had much opportunity to make this observation. As well as being his notional student—though what a func-tionally immortal hive-citizen who had crossed one hundred and twenty light years could learn from a fresh twenty-something meat human was moot—she was his occasional lover.

She drank the tea. Serejen watched the purse of her lips around the delicate porcelain bowl decorated with the ubiquitous Lord of the Fishes motif, even in high, dry continental Jann. The small movement of her throat as she swallowed. He knew a hundred such tiny, intimate movements, but even as she cooed and giggled and gasped to the stimulations of the Five Leaves, Five Fishes ritual, the involuntary actions of her body had seemed like performances. Learned responses. Performances as he made observations. Actor and audience. That was the kind of lover he was as Serejen.

"So what is it really like to fuck a pile of nano-motes?" Puzhay had asked as they rolled around with wine in the cosy warm fleshiness of the Thirteenth Window Coupling Porch at the ancient, academic Ogrun Menholding. "I'd imagine it feels . . . fizzy." And she'd squeezed his cock, holding it hostage, *watch what you say boy*.

"At least nano-motes never get morning breath," he'd said, and she'd given a little shriek of outrage and jerked his dick so that he yelped, and then they both laughed and then rolled over again and buried themselves deep into the winter-defying warmth of the piled quilts.

I should be with her now, he thought. The months-long winter nights beneath the aurora and the stars clouds of the great galaxy were theirs. After the Manifold House, he had gone with her to her Bedenderay and her home city of Jann. The City Conservatorium had the world's best theoretical physics department. It was nothing to do with small, boyish, funny Puzhay. They had formalised a partnering six months later. His parents had complained and shivered through all the celebrations in this cold and dark and barbarous city far from the soft elegance of island life. But ever after winter, even on the coldest mornings when carbon dioxide frost crusted the steps of the Tea Lane Ladyhearth where Puzhay lived, was their season. He should call her, let her know he was still trapped but that at the first sign, the very first sign, he would come back. The cell net was still up. Even an email. He couldn't. Seriantep didn't know. Seriantep wouldn't understand. She had not understood that one time when he tried to explain it in abstracts; that different Aspects could—should—have different relationships with different partners, love separately but equally. *That as Serejen, I love you, Anpreen Prebendary Seriantep, but as Nejben, I love Puzhay.* He could never say that. For an immortal, starcrossing hive of nano motes, Seriantep was very singleminded.

Gunfire cracked in the crystal night, far and flat.

"I think it's dying down," Seriantep said.

"I'd give it a while yet."

So strange, so rude, this sudden flaring of anti-alien violence. In the dreadful dead of winter too, when nothing should rightfully fight and even the trees along Yaskaray Prospect drew down to their heartwood and turned to ice. Despite the joy of Puzhay, Serejen knew that he would always hate the Bedenderay winter. *You watch out now,* his mother had said when he had announced his decision to go to Jann. *They all go dark-mad there.* Accidie and suicide walked the frozen canals of the Winter City. No surprise then that madness should break out against the Anpreen Prebendaries. Likewise inevitable that the popular rage should be turned against the Conservatorium. The university had always been seen as a place apart from the rest of Jann, in summer aloof and lofty above the sweltering streets, like an over-grand daughter; in winter a parasite on this most marginal of economies. Now it was the unofficial alien embassy in the northern hemisphere. There were more Anpreen in its long, small-windowed corridors than anywhere else in the world.

There are no aliens, Serejen thought. *There is only the Clade. We are all family. Cjatay had insisted that.* The ship had sailed over the horizon, they hadn't called, they had drifted from each other's lives. Cjatay's name occasionally impinged on Serejen's awareness through radio interviews and opinion pieces. He had developed a darkly paranoid conspiracy theory around the Anpreen Presence. Serejen, high above the frozen streets of Jann in deeply abstract speculation about the physical reality of mathematics, occasionally mused upon the question of at what point the Migration had become a Presence. The Lonely often obsessively took up narrow, focused interests. Now the street was listening, acting. Great Winter always was a dark, paranoid season. *Here's how to understand,* Serejen thought. *There are no aliens after you've had sex with them.*

Helicopter blades rattled from the walls of the College of Theoretical Physics and then retreated across the Central Canal. The silence in the warm, dimly-lit little faculty cell was profound. At last, Serejen said, "I think we could go now."

On the street, cold stabbed even through the quilted layers of Serejen's great-coat. He fastened the high collar across his throat and still he felt the breath crackle into ice around his lips. Seriantep stepped lightly between the half bricks and bottle shards in nothing more than the tunic and leggings she customarily wore around the college. Her motes gave her full control over her body, including its temperature.

"You should have put something on," Serejen said. "You're a bit obvious."

Past shuttered cafés and closed up stores and the tall brick faces of the student Hearths. The burning tram on the Tunday Avenue junction blazed fitfully, its bitter smoke mingling with the eternal aromatic hydrocarbon smog exhaled by Jann's power plants. The trees that lined the avenue's centre strip were folded down into tight fists, dreaming of summer. Their boot heels rang loud on the street tiles.

A darker shape upon the darkness moved in the narrow slit of an alley between two towering tenement blocks. Serejen froze, his heart jerked. A collar turned down, a face studying his—Obredajay from the Department of Field Physics.

"Safe home."

"Aye. And you."

The higher academics all held apartments within the Conservatorium and were safe within its walls; most of the research staff working late would sit it out until morning. Tea and news reports would see them through. Those out on the fickle streets had reasons to be there. Serejen had heard that Obredajay was head-over-heels infatuated with a new manfriend.

The dangers we court for little love.

On the intersection of Tunday Avenue and Yaskaray Wharf, a police robot stepped out of the impervious dark of the arches beneath General Gatoris Bridge. Pistons hissed it up to its full three meters; green light flicked across Serejen's retinas. Seriantep held up her hand, the motes of her palm displaying her immunity as a Prebendary of the Clade. The machine shrank down, seemingly dejected, if plastic and pumps could display such an emotion.

A solitary tea-shop stood open on the corner of Silver Spider Entry and the Wharf, its windows misty with steam from the simmering urns. Security eyes turned and blinked at the two fleeing academics.

On Tannis Lane, they jumped them. There was no warning. A sudden surge of voices rebounding from the stone staircases and brick arches broke into a wave of figures lumbering around the turn of the alley, bulky and shouldering in their heavy winter quilts. Some held sticks, some held torn placards, some were empty handed. They saw a man in a heavy winter coat, breath frosted on his mouth-shield. They saw a woman almost naked, her breath easy, unclouded. They knew in an instant what she saw. The hubbub in the laneway became a roar.

Serejen and Seriantep were already in flight. Sensing rapid motion, the soles of Serejen's boots extended grips into the rime. As automatically, he felt the heart-numbing panic-rush ebb, felt himself lose his grip on his body and grow pale. Another was taking hold, his flight-or-fight Aspect; his cool, competent emergency service Fejannen.

He seized Seriantep's hand.

"With me. Run!"

Serejen-Fejannen saw the change of Aspect flicker across the tea-shop owner's face like weather as they barged through his door, breathless between his stables. Up to his counter with its looming, steaming urns of hot hot water. This tea-man wanted them out, wanted his livelihood safe.

"We need your help."

The tea-man's eyes and nostrils widened at the charge of rioters that skidded and slipped around the corner in to Silver Spider Entry. Then his hand hit the button under the counter and the shutters rolled down. The shop boomed, the shutters bowed to fists striking them. Rocks banged like gunfire from metal. Voices rose and joined together, louder because they were unseen.

"I've called the police," Seriantep said. "They'll be here without delay."

"No, they won't," Fejannen said. He pulled out a chair from the table closest the car and sat down, edgily eying the grey slats of the shutter. "Their job is to restore order and protect property. Providing personal protection to aliens is far down their list of priorities."

Seriantep took the chair opposite. She sat down wary as a settling bird.

"What's going on here? I don't understand. I'm very scared."

The café owner set two glasses of maté down on the table. He frowned, then his eyes opened in understaidng. An alien at his table. He returned to the bar and leaned on it, staring at the shutters beyond which the voice of the mob circled.

"I thought you said you couldn't be killed."

"That's not what I'm scared of. I'm scared of you, Serejen."

"I'm not Serejen. I'm Fejannen."

"Who, what's Fejannen?"

"Me, when I'm scared, when I'm angry, when I need to be able to think clearly and coolly when a million things are happening at once, when I'm playing games or hunting or putting a big funding proposal together."

"You sound . . . different."

"I *am* different. How long have you been on our world?"

"You're hard. And cold. Serejen was never hard."

"I'm not Serejen."

A huge crash—the shutter bowed under a massive impact and the window behind it shattered.

"Right, that's it, I don't care what happens, you're going." The tea-man leaped from behind his counter and strode towards Seriantep. Fejannen was there to meet him.

"This woman is a guest in your country and requires your protection."

"That's not a woman. That's a pile of . . . insects. Things. Tiny things."

"Well, they look like mighty scared tiny things."

"I don't think so. Like you said, like they say on the news, they can't really die."

"They can hurt. *She* can hurt."

Eyes locked, then disengaged. The maté-man returned to his towering silos of herbal mash. The noise from the street settled into a stiff, waiting silence. Neither Fejannen nor Seriantep believed that it was true, that the mob had gone, despite the spearing cold out there. The lights flickered once, twice.

Seriantep said suddenly, vehemently, "I could take them."

The tea-man looked up.

"Don't." Fejannen whispered.

"I could. I could get out under the door. It's just a reforming."

The tea-man's eyes were wide. A demon, a winter-grim in his prime location canal-side tea shop!

"You scare them enough as you are," Fejannen said.

"Why? We're only here to help, to learn from you."

"They think, what have you got to learn from *us*? They think that you're keeping secrets from us."

"Us?"

"Them. Don't scare them any more. The police will come, eventually, or the Conservatorium proctors. Or they'll just get bored and go home. These things never really last."

"You're right." She slumped back into her seat. "This fucking world . . . Oh, why did I come here?" Seriantep glanced up at the inconstant lumetubes, beyond to the distant diadem of her people's colonies, gravid on decades of water. It was a question, Fejannen knew, that Serejen had asked himself many times. A post-graduate scholar researching space-time topologies and the cosmological constant. A thousand-year-old post-human innocently wearing the body of a twenty-year-old woman, playing the student. She could learn nothing from him. All the knowledge the Anpreen wanderers had gained in their ten thousands year migration was incarnate in her motes. She embodied all truth and she lied with every cell of her body. Anpreen secrets. No basis for a relationship, yet Serejen loved her, as Serejen could love. But was it any more for her than novelty; a tourist, a local boy, a brief summer loving?

Suddenly, vehemently, Seriantep leaned across the table to take Fejannen's face between her hands.

"Come with me."

"Where? Who?"

"Who?" She shook her head in exasperation. "Ahh! Serejen. But it would be you as well, it has to be you. To my place, to the Commonweal. I've wanted to ask you for so long. I'd love you to see my worlds. Hundreds of worlds, like jewels, dazzling in the sun. And inside, under the ice, the worlds within worlds within worlds . . . I made the application for a travel bursary months ago, I just couldn't ask."

"Why? What kept you from asking?" A small but significant traffic of diplomats, scientists, and journalists flowed between Tay and the Anpreen fleet around Tejaphay. The returnees enjoyed global celebrity status, their opinions and experiences sought by think-tanks and talk shows and news-site columns, the details of the faces and lives sought by the press. Serejen had never understood what it was the people expected from the celebrity of others but was not so immured behind the fortress walls of the Collegium, armoured against the long siege of High Winter, that he couldn't appreciate its personal benefits. The lights seemed to brighten, the sense of the special hush outside, that was not true silence but waiting, dimmed as Serejen replaced Fejannen. "Why didn't you ask?"

"Because I though you might refuse."

"Refuse?" The few, the golden few. "Turn down the chance to work in the Commonweal? Why would anyone do that, what would I do that?"

Seriantep looked long at him, her head cocked slightly, alluringly, to one side, the kind of gesture an alien unused to a human body might devise, "You're Serejen again, aren't you?"

"I am that Aspect again, yes."

"Because I thought you might refuse because of *her*. That other woman. Puzhay."

Serejen blinked three times. From Seriantep's face, he knew that she expected some admission, some confession, some emotion. He could not understand what.

Seriantep said, "I know about her. We know things at the Anpreen Mission. We check whom we work with. We have to. We know not everyone welcomes us, and that more are suspicious of us. I know who she is and where she lives and what you do with her three times a week when you go to her. I know where you were intending to go tonight, if all this hadn't happened."

Three times again, Serejen blinked. Now he was hot, too hot in his winter quilt in this steamy, fragrant tea-shop.

"But that's a ridiculous question. *I* don't love Puzhay. *Nejben* does."

"Yes, but you *are* Nejben."

"How many times do I have to tell you . . . ." Serejen bit back the anger. There were Aspects hovering on the edge of his consciousness like the hurricane-front angels of the Bazjendi Psalmody; selves inappropriate to Seriantep. Aspects that in their rage and storm might lose him this thing, so finely balanced now in this tea-shop. "It's our way," he said weakly. "It's how we are."

"Yes, but . . . " Seriantep fought for words. "It's *you*, there, that body. You say it's different, you say it's someone else and not you, not Serejen, but how do I know that? How *can* I know that?"

You say that, with your body that in this tea-shop you said could take many forms, any form, Serejen thought. Then Fejannen, shadowed but never more than a thought away in this besieged, surreal environment, heard a shift in the silence outside. The tea-man glanced up. He had heard it too. The difference between *waiting* and *anticipating*.

"Excuse me, I must change Aspects."

A knock on the shutter, glove-muffled. A voice spoke Fejannen's full name. A voice that Fejannen knew from his pervasive fear of the risk his academic Aspect was taking with Seriantep and that Serejen knew from those news reports and articles that broke through his vast visualisations of the topology of the universe and that Nejben knew from a tower top cell and a video screen full of stars.

"Can I come in?"

Fejannen nodded to the tea-man. He ran the shutter up high enough for the bulky figure in the long quilted coat and boots to duck under. Dreadful cold blew around Fejannen.

Cjatay bowed, removed his gloves, banging rime from the knuckles and made the proper formalities to ascertain which Aspect he was speaking to.

"I have to apologise; I only recently learned that it was you who were caught here."

The voice, the intonations and inflections, the over-precisions and refinements—no time might have passed since Cjatay walked out of Manifold House. In a sense, no time *had* passed; Cjatay was caught, inviolable, unchangeable by anything other than time and experience. Lonely.

"The police will be here soon," Seriantep said.

"Yes, they will," Cjatay said mildly. He looked Seriantep up and down, as if studying a zoological specimen. "They have us well surrounded now. These things are almost never planned; what we gain in spontaneity of expression we lose in strategy. But when I realised it was you, Fejannen-Nejben, I saw a way that we could all emerge from this intact."

"Safe passage," Fejannen said.

"I will personally escort you out."

"And no harm at all to you, politically."

"I need to distance myself from what has happened tonight."

"But your fundamental fear of the visitors remains unchanged?"

"I don't change. You know that. I see it as a virtue. Some things are solid, some things endure. Not everything changes with the seasons. But fear, you said. That's clever. Do you remember, that last time I saw you, back in the Manifold House. Do you remember what I said?"

"Nejben remembers you asking, where are they migrating to? And what are they migrating from?"

"In all your seminars and tutorials and conferences, in all those questions about the shape of the universe—oh, we have our intelligences too, less broad than the Anpreen's, but subtler, we think—did you ever think to *ask* that question: why have you come here?" Cjatay's chubby, still childish face was an accusation. "You are fucking her, I presume?"

In a breath, Fejannen had slipped from his seat into the Third Honorable Offense Stance. A hand on his shoulder; the teashop owner. No honor in it, not against a Lonely. Fejannen returned to his seat, sick with shuddering rage.

"Tell him," Cjatay said.

"It's very simple," Seriantep said. "We are refugees. The Anpreen Commonweal is the surviving remnant of the effective annihilation of our sub-species of Panhumanity. Our eight hundred habitats are such a minuscule percentage of our original race that, to all statistical purposes, we are extinct. Our habitats once englobed an entire sun. We're all that's left."

"How? Who?"

"Not so much *who*, as *when*," Cjatay said gently. He flexed cold-blued fingers and pulled on his gloves.

"They're coming?"

"We fear so," Seriantep said. "We don't know. We were careful to leave no traces, to cover our tracks, so to speak, and we believe we have centuries of a headstart on them. We are only here to refuel our habitats, then we'll go, hide ourselves in some great globular cluster."

"But why, *why* would anyone do this? We're all the same species, that's what you told us. The Clade, Panhumanity."

"Brothers disagree," Cjatay said. "Families fall out, families feud within themselves. No animosity like it."

"Is this true? How can this be true? Who knows about this?" Serejen strove with Fejannen for control and understanding. One of the first lessons the Agisters of the Manifold House had taught was the etiquette of transition between conflicting Aspects. A war in the head, a conflict of selves. He could understand sibling strife on a cosmic scale. But a whole species?

"The governments," Cjatay said. To the tea-man, "Open the shutter again. You be all right with us. I promise." To Serejen, "Politicians, some senior academics, and policy makers. And us. Not you. But we all agree, we don't want to scare anyone. So we question the Anpreen Prebendaries on our world, and question their presence in our system, and maybe sometimes it bubbles into xenophobic violence, but that's fine, that's the price, that's nothing compared to what would happen if we realised that our guests might be drawing the enemies that destroyed them to our homes. Come on. We'll go now."

The tea-man lifted the shutter. Outside, the protestors stood politely aside as Cjatay led the refugees out on to the street. There was not a murmur as Seriantep, in her ridiculous, life-threatening house-clothes, stepped across the cobbles. The great Winter Clock on the tower of Alajnedeng stood at twenty past five. The morning shift would soon be starting, the hot-shops firing their ovens and fry-pots.

A murmur in the crowd as Serejen took Seriantep's hand.

"Is it true?" he whispered.

"Yes," she said. "It is."

He looked up at the sky that would hold stars for another three endless months. The aurora coiled and spasmed over huddling Jann. Those stars were like crystal spearpoints. The universe was vast and cold and inimical to humanity, the greatest of Great Winters. He had never deluded himself it would be otherwise. Power had been restored, yellow street light glinted from the helmets of riot control officers and the carapaces of counterinsurgency drones. Serejen squeezed Seriantep's hand.

"What you asked."

"When?"

"Then. Yes. I will. Yes."

Torben, melting.

The Anpreen shatter-ship blazed star-bright as it turned its face to the sun. A splinter of smart-ice, it was as intricate as a snow-flake, stronger than any construct of Taynish engineering. Torben hung in free-fall in the observation dome at the centre of the cross of solar vanes. The Anpreen, being undifferentiated from the motes seeded through the hull, had no need for such architectural fancies. Their senses were open to space; the fractal shell of the ship was one great retina. They had grown the blister—pure and perfectly transparent construction-ice—for the comfort and delight of their human guests.

The sole occupant of the dome, Torben was also the sole passenger on this whole alien, paradoxical ship. Another would have been good. Another could have shared the daily, almost hourly shocks of strange and new and wonder. His other Aspects had felt with Torben the breath-catch of awe, and even greater privilege, when he had looked from the orbital car of the space elevator—the Anpreen's gift to the peoples of Tay—and seen the shatter-ship turn out of occultation in a blaze of silver light as it came in to dock. They had felt his glow of intellectual vindication as he first swam clumsily into the star-dome and discovered, with a shock, that the orbital transfer station was no more than a cluster of navigation lights almost lost in the star fields beyond. No sense of motion. His body had experienced no hint of acceleration. He had been correct. The Anpreen could adjust the topology of spacetime. But there was no one but his several selves to tell it to. The Anpreen crew—Torben was not sure whether it was one or many, or if that distinction had any meaning—was remote and alien. On occasion, as he swam down the live-wood panelled corridors, monoflipper and web-mittens pushing thick, humid air, he had glimpsed a swirl of silver motes twisting and knotting like a captive waterspout. Always they had dispersed in his presence. But the ice beyond those wooden walls, pressing in around him, felt alive, crawling, aware.

Seriantep had gone ahead months before him.

"There's work I have to do."

There had been a party; there was always a party at the Anpreen Mission among the ever-green slopes of generous, volcanic Sulanj. Fellow academics, press and PR from Ctarisphay, politicians, family members, and the Anpreen Prebendaries, eerie in their uniform loveliness.

"You can do the research work on *Thirty-Third Tranquil Abode*, that's the idea," Seriantep had said. Beyond the paper lanterns hung in the trees and the glow of the carbon-sink lagoon, the lights of space-elevator cars rose up until they merged with the stars. She would ride that narrow way to orbit within days. Serejen wondered how he would next recognise her.

"You have to go." Puzhay stood in the balcony of the Tea Lane Ladyhearth, recently opened to allow spring warmth into rooms that had sweated and stifled and stunk all winter long. She looked out at the shooting, uncoiling fresh green of the trees along Uskuben Avenue. Nothing there you have not seen before, Nejben thought. Unless it is something that is the absence of me.

"It's not forever," Nejben said. "I'll be back in year, maybe two years." *But not here*, he thought. He would not say it, but Puzhay knew it. As a returnee, the world's conservatoriums would be his. Bright cities, sun-warmed campuses far from the terrible cold on this polar continent, the winter that had driven them together.

All the goodbyes, eightfold goodbyes for each of his Aspects. And then he took sail for the ancient hospice of Bleyn, for sail was the only right way to come to those reefs of ceramic chapels that had clung to the Yesger atoll for three thousand hurricane seasons.

"I need . . . another," he whispered in the salt-breezy, chiming cloisters to Shaper Rejmen. "The curiosity of Serejen is too naive, the suspicion of Fejannen is too jagged, and the social niceties of Kekjay are too too eager to be liked."

"We can work this for you," the Shaper said. The next morning, he went down into the sweet, salt waters of the Othering Pots and let the programmed palps swarm over him, as he did for twenty mornings after. In the thunder-heavy gloaming of a late spring night storm, he awoke to find he was Torben. Clever, inquisitive, wary, socially adept and conversationally witty Torben. Extreme need and exceptional circumstances permitted the creation of Nineths, but only, always. temporarily. Tradition as strong as an incest taboo demanded that the number of Aspects reflect the eight phases of Tay's manic seasons.

The Anpreen shatter-ship spun on its vertical axis and Torben Reris Orhum Fejannan Kekjay Prus Rejmer Serejen Nejben looked on in wonder. Down, up, forward: his orientation shifted with every breath of air in the observation dome. An eye, a monstrous eye. Superstition chilled him, childhood stories of the Dejved whose sole eye was the eye of the storm and whose body was the storm entire. Then he unfolded the metaphor. An anti-eye. Tejaphay was a shield of heartbreaking blue, streaked and whorled with perpetual storms. The Anpreen space habitat *Thirty-Third Tranquil Abode*, hard-docked these two years past to the anchor end of the space elevator, was a blind white pupil, an anti-pupil, an unseeing opacity. The shatter-ship was approaching from Tejaphay's axial plane, the mechanisms of the orbital pumping station were visible beyond the habitat's close horizon. The space elevator was a cobweb next to the habitat's three-hundred kilometre bulk, less even than a thread compared to enormous Tejaphay, but as the whole assemblage turned into daylight, it woke sparkling, glittering as sun reflected from its billions of construction-ice scales. A fresh metaphor came to Torben: the sperm of the divine. *You're swimming the wrong way!* he laughed to himself, delighted at this infant Aspect's unsuspected tendency to express in metaphor what Serejen would have spoken in math, Kekjay in flattery, and Fejannen not at all. No, it's our whole system it's fertilising, he thought.

The Anpreen ship drew closer, manipulating space-time on the centimetre scale. Surface details resolved from the ice glare. The hull of *Thirty-Third Tranquil Abode* was a chaotic mosaic of sensors, docks, manufacturing hubs, and still less comprehensible technology, all constructed from smart-ice. A white city. A flight of shatter-ships detached from docking arms like a flurry of early snow. Were some of those icy mesas defensive systems; did some of those ice canyons, as precisely cut as a skater's figures, conceal inconceivable weapons? Had the Anpreen ever paused to consider that to all cultures of Tay, white was the colour of distrust, the white of snow in the long season of dark?

Days in free-gee had desensitised Torben sufficiently so that he was aware of the subtle pull of nanogravity in his belly. Against the sudden excitement and the accompanying vague fear of the unknown, he tried to calculate the gravity of *Thirty-Third Tranquil Abode*, changing every hour as it siphoned up water from Tejaphay. While he was still computing the figures, the shatter-ship performed another orientation flip and came in to dock at one of the radial elevator heads, soft as a kiss to a loved face.

On tenth days, they went to the falls, Korpa and Belej, Sajhay and Hannaj, Yetger and Torben. When he stepped out of the elevator that had taken him down through thirty kilometres of solid ice, Torben had imagined something like the faculty of Jann; wooden-screen cloisters and courts roofed with ancient painted ceilings, thronged with bright, smart, talkative students boiling with ideas and vision. He found Korpa and Belej, Sajhay, Hannaj, and Yetger all together in a huge, windy construct of cells and tunnels and abrupt balconies and netted-in ledges, like a giant wasps' nest suspended from the curved ceiling of the interior hollow.

"Continuum topology is a tad specialised, I'll admit that," Belej said. She was a sting-thin quantum-foam specialist from Yeldes in the southern archipelago of Ninnt, gone even thinner and bonier in the attenuated gravity of *Thirty-Third Tranquil Abode*. "If it's action you're looking for, you should get over to *Twenty Eighth*. They're sociologists."

Sajhay had taught him how to fly.

"There are a couple of differences from the transfer ship," he said as he showed Torben how to pull up the fish-tail mono-tights and how the plumbing vents worked. "It's lo-gee, but it's not *no*-gee, so you will eventually come down again. And it's easy to build up too much delta-vee. The walls are light but they're strong and you will hurt yourself. And the nets are there for a reason. Whatever you do, don't go through them. If you end up in that sea, it'll take you apart."

That sea haunted Torben's unsettled, nanogee dreams. The world-sea, the two hundred and twenty-kilometer diameter sphere of water, its slow, huge nanogee waves forever breaking into globes and tears the size of clouds. The seething, dissolving sea into which the Anpreen dissipated, many lives into one immense, diffuse body which whispered to him through the paper tunnels of the Soujourners' house. Not so strange, perhaps. Yet he constantly wondered what it would be like to fall in there, to swim against the tiny but non-negligible gravity and plunge slowly, magnificently, into the boil of water-borne motes. In his imagination, there was never any pain, only the blissful, light-filled losing of self. So good to be free from the unquiet parliament of selves.

Eight is natural, eight is holy, the Bleyn Shaper Yesger had whispered from behind ornate cloister grilles. *Eight arms, eight seasons. Nine must always be unbalanced.*

Conscious of each other's too-close company, the guest scholars worked apart with their pupils. Seriantep met daily with Torben in a bulbous chapter house extruded from the mother nest. Tall hexagon-combed windows opened on the steeply downcurving horizons of *Thirty-Third Tranquil Abode*, stippled with the stalactite towers of those Anpreen who refused the lure of the sea. Seriantep flew daily from such a tower down around the curve of the world to alight on Torben's balcony. She wore the same body he had known so well in the Jann Conservatorium, with the addition of a pair of functional wings in her back. She was a vision, she was a marvel, a spiritual creature from the aeons-lost motherworld of the Clade: an *angel*. She was beauty, but since arriving in *Thirty Third Tranquil Abode*, Torben had only had sex with her twice. It was not the merman-angel thing, though that was a consideration to metaphor-and-ludicrous-conscious Torben. He didn't love her as Serejen had. She noticed, she commented.

"You're not . . . the same."

Neither are you. What he *said* was, "I know. I couldn't be. Serejen couldn't have lived here. Torben can. Torben is the only one who can." *But for how long, before he splits into his component personalities?*

"Do you remember the way you . . . he . . . used to see numbers?"

"Of course I do. And before that, I remember how Ptey used to see numbers. He could look up into the night sky and tell you without counting, just by *knowing*, how many stars there were. He could see numbers. Serejen could make them *do* things. For me, Torben; the numbers haven't gone away, I just see them differently. I see them as clearly, as absolutely, but when I see the topospace transformations, I see them as words, as images and stories, as analogies. I can't explain it any better than that."

"I think, no matter how long I try, how long any of us try, we will never understand how your multiple personalities work. To us, you seem a race of partial people, each a genius, a savant, in some strange obsessive way."

Are you deliberately trying to punish me? Torben thought at the flicker-wing angel hovering before the ice-filled windows.

True, he was making colossal intuitive leaps in his twisted, abstruse discipline of spacetime geometry. Not so abstruse: the Anpreen space drives, that Taynish physicists said broke the laws of physics, reached into the elevenspace substrate of the universe to locally stretch or compress the expansion of spacetime—foreshortening ahead of the vehicle, inflating it behind. Thus the lack of any measurable acceleration, it was the entire continuum within and around the shatter-ship that had moved. Snowflakes and loxodromic curves had danced in Torben's imagination: he had it, he had it. The secret of the Anpreen: relativistic interstellar travel, was now open to the peoples of Tay.

The *other* secret of the Anpreen, that was.

For all his epiphanies above the spherical ocean, Torben knew that seminars had changed. The student had become the teacher, the master the pupil. *What is you want from us?* Torben asked himself. *Truly want, truly need?*

"Don't know, don't care. All I know is, if I can find a commercial way to bubble quantum black holes out of elevenspace and tap the evaporation radiation, I'll have more money than God," said Yetger, a squat, physically uncoordinated Oprann islander who relished his countrymen's reputation for boorishness, though Torben found him an affable conversationalist and a refined thinker. "You coming to the Falls on Tennay?"

So they set off across the sky, a little flotilla of physicists with wine and sweet biscuits to dip in it. Those older and less sure of their bodies used little airscooter units. Torben flew. He enjoyed the exercise. The challenge of a totally alien language of movement intrigued him, the fish-tail flex of the flipper-suit. He liked what it was doing to his ass muscles.

The Soujourners'-house's western windows gave distant views of the Falls, but the sense of awe began twenty kilometres out when the thunder and shriek became audible over the constant rumble of sky traffic. The picnic party always flew high, close to the ceiling among the tower roots, so that long vistas would not spoil their pleasure. A dense forest of inverted trees, monster things grown kilometres tall in the nanogee, had been planted around the Falls, green and mist-watered by the spray. The scientists settled on to one of the many platforms sculpted from the boulevard-wide branches. Torben gratefully peeled off his fin-tights, kicked his legs free, and spun to face the Falls.

What you saw, what awed you, depended on how you looked at it. Feet down to the world-sea, head up to the roof, it was a true fall, a cylinder of falling water two hundred metres across and forty kilometres long. Feet up, head down, it was even more terrifying, a titanic geyser. The water was pumped through from the receiving station at near supersonic speeds, where it met the ocean-bead the joined waters boiled and leaped kilometres high, broke into high looping curls and crests and globes, like the fantastical flarings of solar prominences. The roar was terrific. But for the noise-abatement properties of the nanoengineered leaves, it would have meant instant deafness. Torben could feel the tree branch, as massive as any buttress wall of Jann fortress-university, shudder beneath him.

Wine was opened and poured. The biscuits, atavistically hand-baked by Hannaj, one of whose Aspects was a master pastry chef, were dipped into it and savoured. Sweet, the light sharpness of the wine and the salt mist of another world's stolen ocean tanged Torben's tongue.

There were rules to Tennays by the Falls. No work. No theory. No relationships. Five researchers made up a big enough group for family jealousy, small enough for cliquishness. Proper topics of conversation looked homeward; partnerships ended, children born, family successes and sicknesses, gossip, politics, and sports results.

"Oh. Here." Yetger sent a message flake spinning lazily through the air. The Soujourners'-house exfoliated notes and message from home onto slips of whisper-thin paper that peeled from the walls like eczema. The mechanism was poetic but inaccurate; intimate messages unfurled from unintended walls to turn and waft in the strange updrafts that ran through the nest's convoluted tunnels. It was the worst of forms to read another's message-scurf.

Torben unfolded the rustle of paper. He read it once, blinked, read it again. Then he folded precisely in eight and folded it away in his top pocket.

"Bad news?" For a broad beast of a man, Yetger was acute to emotional subtleties. Torben swallowed.

"Nothing strange or startling."

Then he saw where Belej stared. Her gaze drew his, drew that of everyone in the picnic party. The Falls were failing. Moment by moment, they dwindled, from a deluge to a river, from a river to a stream to a jet, a hiding shrieking thread of water. On all the platforms on all the trees, Anpreen were rising into the air, hovering in swarms, as before their eyes the Falls sputtered and ceased. Drops of water, fat as storms, formed around the lip of the suddenly exposed nozzle to break and drift, quivering, down to the spherical sea. The silence was profound. Then the trees seemed to shower blossoms as the Anpreen took to the air in hosts and choirs, flocking and storming.

Numbers and images flashed in Torben's imagination. The fuelling could not be complete, was weeks from being complete. The ocean would fill the entire interior hollow, the stalactite cities transforming into strange reef communities. Fear gripepd him and he felt Fejannen struggle to free himself from the binding into Torben. *I need you here, friend*, Torben said to himself, and saw the others had made the same calculations.

They flew back, a ragged flotilla strung across kilometres of airspace, battling through the ghostly aerial legions of Anpreen. The Soujourners' house was filled with fluttering, gusting message slips shed from the walls. Torben snatched one from the air and against all etiquette read it.

Sajhay are you all right what's happening? Come home, we are all worried about you. Love Mihenj.

The sudden voice of Suguntung, the Anpreen liaison, filled every cell of the nest, an order—polite, but an order—to come to the main viewing lounge, where an important announcement would be made. Torben had long suspected that Suguntung never left the Soujourners' house, merely deliquesced from hominiform into airborne motes, a phase transition.

Beyond the balcony nets, the sky seethed, an apocalypse of insect humanity and storm clouds back as squid ink rolling up around the edge of the world ocean.

"I have grave news," Suguntung said. He was a grey, sober creature, light and lithe and androgynous, without any salting of wit or humour. "At

12:18 Taynish Enclave time, we detected gravity waves passing through the system. These are consistent with a large numbers of bodies decelerating from relativistic flight."

Consternation. Voices shouting. Questions questions questions. Suguntung held up a hand and there was quiet.

"On answer to your questions, somewhere in the region of thirty eight thousand objects. We estimate them at a range of seventy astronomical units beyond the edge of the Kuiper belt, decelerating to ten percent lightspeed for system transition."

"Ninety three hours until they reach us," Torben said. The numbers, the coloured numbers, so beautiful, so distant.

"Yes," said Suguntung.

"Who are they?" Belej asked.

"I know," Torben said. "Your enemy."

"We believe so," Suguntung answered. "There are characteristic signatures in the gravity waves and the spectral analysis."

Uproar. By a trick of the motes, Suguntung could raise his voice to a roar that could shout down a crowd of angry physicists.

"The Anpreen Commonweal is making immediate preparations for departure. As a matter of priority, evacuation for all guests and visitors has been arranged and will commence immediately. A transfer ship is already waiting. We are evacuating the system not only for our own protection, but to safeguard you as well. We believe that the Enemy has no quarrel with you."

"*Believe*?" Yetger spat. "Forgive me if I'm less than completely reassured by that!"

"But you haven't got enough water," Torben said absently, mazed by the numbers and pictures swimming around in his head, as the message leaves of concern and hope and come-home-soon fluttered around. "How many habitats are fully fuelled? Five hundred, five hundred and fifty? You haven't got enough, even this one is at eighty percent capacity. What's going to happen to them?"

"I don't give a fuck what happens to them!" Hannaj had always been the meekest and least assertive of men, brilliant but forever hamstrung by self-doubt. Now, threatened, naked in space, pieced through and through by the gravity waves of an unknowable and power, his anger burned. "I want to know what's going to happen to *us*."

"We are transferring the intelligences to the interstellar-capable habitats." Suguntung spoke to Torben alone.

"Transferring; you mean copying," Torben said. "And the originals that are left, what happens to them?"

Suguntung made no answer.

Yetger found Torben floating in the exact centre of the viewing lounge, moving his tail just enough to maintain him against the microgee.

"Where's your stuff?"

"In my cell."

"The shatter-ship's leaving in an hour."

"I know."

"Well, maybe you should, you know . . . "

"I'm not going."

"You're *what*?"

"I'm not going, I'm staying here."

"Are you insane?"

"I've talked to Suguntung and Seriantep. It's fine. There are a couple of others on the other habitats."

"You have to come home, we'll need you when they come . . . "

"Ninety hours and twenty five minutes to save the world? I don't think so."

"It's home, man."

"It's not. Not since *this*." Torben flicked the folded note of his secret pocket, offered it to Yetger between clenched fingers.

"Oh."

"Yes."

"You're dead. We're all dead, you know that."

"Oh, I know. In the few minutes it takes me to reach wherever the Anpreen Migration goes next, you will have aged and died many times over. I know that, but it's not home. Not now."

Yetger ducked his head in sorrow that did not want to be seen, then in a passion hugged Torben hugely to him, kissed him hard.

"Goodbye. Maybe in the next one."

"No, I don't think so. One is all we get. And that's a good enough reason to go out there where none of our people have ever been before, I think."

"Maybe it is." Yetger laughed, the kind of laughter that is on the edge of tears. Then he spun and kicked off up through the ceiling door, his duffel of small possessions trailing from his ankle.

For an hour now, he had contemplated the sea and thought that he might just be getting the way of it, the fractal patterns of the ripples, the rhythms and the micro-storms that blew up in squalls and waves that sent globes of water quivering into the air that, just as quickly, were subsumed back into the greater sea. He understood it as music, deeply harmonised. He wished one of his Aspects had a skill for an instrument. Only choirs, vast ensembles, could capture the music of the water bead.

"It's ready now."

All the while Torben had calculated the music of the sea, Seriantep had worked on the smart-paper substrate of the Soujourners'-house. Now the poll was complete, a well in the floor of the lounge. *When I leave, will it revert?* Torben thought, the small, trivial wit that fights fear. *Will it go back to whatever it was before, or was it always only just Suguntung?* The slightest of gestures and Seriantep's wisp-dress fell from her, The floor ate it greedily. Naked and wingless now in this incarnation, she stepped backward into the water, never for an instant taking her eyes from Torben.

"Whenever you're ready," she said. "You won't be hurt."

She lay back into the receiving water. Her hair floated out around her, coiled and tangled as she came apart. There was nothing ghastly about it, no decay into meat and gut and vile bone, no grinning skeleton fizzing apart in the water like sodium. A brightness, a turning to motes of light. The hair was the last to go. The pool seethed with motes. Torben stepped out of his clothes.

I'm moving on. It's for the best. Maybe not for you. For me. You see, I didn't think I'd mind, but I did. You gave it all up so easily, just like that, off into space. There is someone else. It's Cjatay. I heard what he was saying, and as time went by, as I didn't hear from you, it made sense. I know I'm reacting. I think I owe you that, at least. We're all right together. With him, you get everything, I find I can live with that. I think I like it,. I'm sorry Torben, but this is what I want.

The note sifted down through the air like a falling autumn leaf to join the hundreds of others that lay on the floor. Torben's feet kicked up as he stepped down into the water. He gasped at the electrical tingle, then laughed, and, with a great gasp, emptied his lungs and threw himself under the surface. The motes swarmed and began to take him apart. As the *Thirty-Third Tranquil Abode* broke orbit around Tejaphay, the abandoned space elevator coiling like a severed artery, the bottom of the Soujourners'-house opened, and, like a tear, the mingled waters fell to the sea below.

Jedden, running.

Eighty years Jedden had fallen, dead as a stone, silent as light. Every five years, a few subjective minutes so close to light-speed, he woke up his senses and sent a slush of photons down his wake to see if the hunter was still pursuing.

Redshifted to almost indecipherability, the photons told him, *Yes, still there, still gaining.* Then he shut down his senses, for even that brief wink, that impact of radiation blueshifted to gamma frequencies on the enemy engine field, betrayed him. It was decades since he had risked the scalarity drive. The distortions it left in space-time advertised his position over most of a quadrant. Burn quick, burn hot and fast, get to lightspeed if it meant reducing his reaction mass perilously close to the point where he would not have sufficient ever to brake. Then go dark, run silent and swift, coasting along in high time dilation where years passed in hours.

Between wakings, Jedden dreamed. He dreamed down into the billions of lives, the dozens of races and civilizations that the Anpreen had encountered in their long migration. The depth of their history had stunned Jedden, as if he were swimming and, looking down, discovered beneath him not the green water of the lagoon but the clear blue drop of the continental shelf. Before they englobed their sun with so many habitats that it became discernible only as a vast infra-red glow, before even the wave of expansion that had brought them to that system, before even they became motile, when they wore mere bodies, they had been an extroverted, curious race, eager for the similarities and differences of other sub-species of PanHumanity. Records of the hundreds of societies they had contacted were stored in the spin-states of the quantum-ice flake that comprised the soul of Jedden. Cultures, customs, ways of being human were simulated in such detail that, if he wished, Jedden could have spend aeons living out their simulated lives. Even before they had reached the long-reprocessed moon of their homeworld, the Anpreen had encountered a light-sail probe of the Ekkad, three hundred years out on a millennium-long survey of potential colony worlds. As they converted their asteroid belts into habitat rings, they had fought a savage war for control of the high country against the Okranda asteroid colonies that had dwelled there, hidden and unsuspected, for twenty thousand years. The doomed Okranda had, as a final, spiteful act, seared the Anpreen homeworld to the bedrock, but not before the Anpreen had absorbed and recorded the beautiful, insanely complex hierarchy of caste, classes, and societies that had evolved in the baroque cavities of the sculpted asteroids. Radio transmission had drawn them out of their Oort cloud across two hundred light years to encounter the dazzling society of the Jad. From them, the Anpreen had learned the technology that enabled them to pload themselves into free-flying nanomotes and become a true Level Two civilization.

People and beasts, machines and woods, architectures and moralities, and stories beyond counting. Among the paraphernalia and marginalia of a hundred races, were the ones who had destroyed the Anpreen, who were now hunting Jedden down over all the long years, closing metre by metre.

So he spent hours and years immersed in the great annual eisteddfod of the Barrant-Hoj, where one of the early generation of seed ships (early in that it was seed of the seed of the seed of the first flowering of mythical Earth) had been drawn into the embrace of a fat, slow hydrocarbon-rich gas giant and birthed a brilliant, brittle airborne culture, where blimp-cities rode the edge of storms wide enough to drown whole planets and the songs of the contestants—gas-bag-spider creatures huge as reefs, fragile as honeycomb—belled in infrasonic wavefronts kilometers between crests and changed entire climates. It took Barrant-Hoj two hominiform lifetimes to circle its sun—the Anpreen had chanced upon the song-spiel, preserved it, hauled it out of the prison of gas giant's gravity well, and given it to greater Clade.

Jedden blinked back into interstellar flight. He felt—he imagined—tears on his face as the harmonies reverberated within him. Cantos could last days, chorales entire weeks. Lost in music. A moment of revulsion at his body, this sharp, unyielding thing of ice and energies. The hunter's ramscoop fusion engine advertised its presence across a thousand cubic light-years. It was inelegant and initially slow, but, unlike Jedden's scalarity drive, was light and could live off the land. The hunter would be, like Jedden, a ghost of a soul impressed on a Bose-condensate quantum chip, a mote of sentience balanced on top of a giant drive unit. The hunter was closing, but was no closer than Jedden had calculated. Only miscalculation could kill you in interstellar war. The equations were hard but they were fair.

Two hundred and three years to the joke point. It would be close, maybe close enough for the enemy's greed to blind him. Miscalculation and self-deception, these were the killers in space. And luck. Two centuries. Time enough for a few moments rest.

Among all the worlds was one he had never dared visit: the soft blue tear of Tay. There, in the superposed spin states, were all the lives he could have led. The lovers, the children, the friends and joys and mudanities. Puzhay was there, Cjatay too. He could make of them anything he wanted: Puzhay faithful, Cjatay Manifold, no longer Lonely.

Lonely. He understood that now, eighty light years out and decades to go before he could rest.

Extraordinary, how painless it had been. Even as the cells of Torben's body were invaded by the motes into which Seriantep had dissolved, even as they took him apart and rebuilt him, even as they read and copied his neural mappings, there was never a moment where fleshly Torben blinked out and nanotechnological Torben winked in, there was no pain. Never pain, only a sense of wonder, of potential racing away to infinity on every side, of a new birth—or, it seemed to him, an anti-birth, a return to the primal, salted waters. As the globe of mingled motes dropped slow and quivering and full as a breast toward the world-ocean, Torben still thought of himself as Torben, as a man, an individual, as a body. Then they hit and burst and dissolved into the sea of seething motes, and voices and selves and memories and personalities rushed in on him from every side, clamouring, a sea-roar. Every life in every detail. Senses beyond his native five brought him impression upon impression upon impression. Here was intimacy beyond anything he had ever known with Seriantep. As he communed, he was communed with. He knew that the Anpreen government—now he understood the reason for the protracted and ungainly negotiations with Tay : the two representations had almost no points of communication—were unwrapping him to construct a deep map of Tay and its people—rather, the life and Aspects of one under-socialised physics researcher. Music. All was music. As he understood this, Anpreen Commonweal Habitat *Thirty Third Tranquil Abode*, with its five hundred and eighty two companions, crossed one hundred and nineteen light years to the Milius 1183 star system.

One hundred and nineteen light years, eight months subjective, in which Torben Reris Orhum Fejannan Kekjay Prus Rejmer Serejen Nejben ceased to exist. In the mote-swarm, time, like identity, could be anything you assigned it to be. To the self now known as Jedden, it seemed that he had spent twenty years of re-subjectivized time in which he had grown to be a profound and original thinker in the Commonweal's physics community. Anpreen life had only enhanced his instinctive ability to see and apprehend number. His insights and contributions were startling and creative. Thus it had been a pure formality for him to request a splinter-ship to be spun off from *Thirty Third Tranquil Abode* as the fleet entered the system and dropped from relativistic flight at the edge of the Oort cloud. A big fat splinter ship with lots of fuel to explore space-time topological distortions implicit in the orbital perturbations of inner Kuiper Belt cubewanos for a year, a decade, a century, and then come home.

So he missed the annihilation.

Miscalculation kills. Lack of circumspection kills. Blind assumption kills. The Enemy had planned their trap centuries ahead. The assault on the Tay system had been a diversion; the thirty-eight thousand drive signatures mostly decoys; propulsion units and guidance systems and little else scattered among a handful of true battleships dozens of kilometres long. Even as lumbering, barely mobile Anpreen habitats and Enemy attack drones burst across Tay's skies, so bright they even illuminated the sun-glow of high summer, the main fleet was working around Milius 1183. A work of decades, year upon year of slow modifications, staggering energies, careful careful concealment and camouflage, as the Enemy sent their killing hammer out on its long slow loop.

Blind assumption. The Anpreen saw a small red sun at affordable range to the ill-equpped fleet. They saw there was water there, water; worlds of water to re-equip the Commonweal and take it fast and far beyond the reach of the Enemy in the great star clouds that masked the galactic core. In their haste, they failed to note that Milius 1183 was a binary system, a tired red dwarf star and a companion neutron star in photosphere-grazing eight hour orbit. Much less then did they notice that the neutron star was missing.

The trap was perfect and complete. The Enemy had predicted perfectly. Their set-up was flawless. The hunting fleet withdrew to the edges of system, all that remained were the relays and autonomous devices. Blindsided by sunglare, the Anpreen sensoria had only milliseconds of warning before the neutron star impacted Milius 1183 at eight percent light speed.

The nova would in time be visible over a light-century radius. Within its spectrum, careful astronomers might note the dark lines of hydrogen, oxygen, and smears of carbon. Habitats blew away in sprays of plasma. The handful of stragglers that survived battled to reconstruct their mobility and life-support systems. Shark-ships hidden half a century before in the rubble of asteroid belts and planetary ring systems woke from their long sleeps and went a-hunting.

Alone in his splinter ship in the deep dark, Jedden, his thoughts outwards to the fabric of space-time and at the same time inwards to the beauty of number, the song within him, saw the system suddenly turn white with death light. He heard five hundred billion sentients die. All of them, all at once, all their voices and hearts. He heard Seriantep die, he heard those other Taynish die, those who had turned away from their home world in the hope of knowledge and experience beyond anything their world could offer. Every life he had ever touched, that had ever been part of him, that had shared number or song or intimacy beyond fleshly sex. He heard the death of the Anpreen migration. Then he was alone. Jedden went dark for fifty years. He contemplated the annihilation of the last of the Anpreen. He drew up escape plans. He waited. Fifty years was enough. He lit the scalarity drive. Space-time stretched. Behind him, he caught the radiation signature of a fusion drive igniting and the corresponding electromagnetic flicker of a scoopfield going up. Fifty years was not enough.

That would be his last miscalculation.

Twenty years to bend his course away from Tay. Another ten to set up the deception. *As you deceived us, so I will fool you*, Jedden thought as he tacked ever closer to lightspeed. *And with the same device, a neutron star.*

Jedden awoke from the sleep that was beyond dreams, a whisper away from death, that only disembodied intelligences can attain. The magnetic vortex of the hunter's scoopfield filled half the sky. Less than the diameter of a light-minute separated them. Within the next ten objective years, the Enemy ship would overtake and destroy Jedden. Not with physical weapons or even directed energy, but with information: skullware and dark phages that would dissolve him into nothingness or worse, isolate him from any external sense or contact, trapped in unending silent, nerveless darkness.

The moment, when it came, after ninety light-years, was too fine-grained for hominiform-intelligence. Jedden's sub-routines, the autonomic responses that controlled the ship that was his body, opened the scalarity drive and summoned the dark energy. Almost instantly, the Enemy responded to the course change, but that tiny relativistic shift, the failure of simultaneity, was Jedden's escape and life.

Among the memories frozen into the heart of the Bose-Einstein condensate were the star-logs of the Cush Né, a fellow migrant race the Anpreen had encountered—by chance, as all such meets must be—in the big cold between stars. Their star maps charted a rogue star, a neutron dwarf ejected from its stellar system and wandering dark and silent, almost invisible, through deep space. Decades ago, when he felt the enemy ramfield go up and knew that he had not escaped, Jedden had made the choice and the calculations. Now he turned his flight, a prayer short of light-speed, towards the wandering star.

Jedden had long ago abolished fear. Yet he experienced a strange psychosomatic sensation in that part of the splinter-ship that corresponded to his testicles. Balls tightening. The angle of insertion was so precise that Jedden had had to calculate the impact of stray hydroxyl radicals on his ablation field. One error would send him at relativistic speed head on into a neutron star. But he did not doubt his ability, he did not fear, and now he understood what the sensation in his phantom testicles was. Excitement.

The neutron star was invisible, would always be invisible, but Jedden could feel its gravity in every part of his body, a quaking, quailing shudder, a music of a hundred harmonies as different parts of the smart-ice hit their resonant frequencies. A chorale in ice and adrenaline, he plunged around the neutron star. He could hope that the hunting ship would not survive the passage, but the Enemy, however voracious, was surely never so stupid as to run a scoop ship through a neutron star's terrifying magnetic terrain with the drive field up. That was not his strategy anyway. Jedden was playing the angles. Whipping tight around the intense gravity well, even a few seconds of slowness would amplify into light-years of distance, decades of lost time. Destruction would have felt like a cheat. Jedden wanted to win by geometry. By calculation, we live.

He allowed himself one tiny flicker of a communication laser. Yes. The Enemy was coming. Coming hard, coming fast, coming *wrong*. Tides tore at Jedden, every molecule of his smart-ice body croaked and moaned, but his own cry rang louder and he sling-shotted around the neutron. *Yes!* Before him was empty space. The splinter-ship would never fall of its own accord into another gravity well. He lacked sufficient reaction mass to enter any Clade system. Perhaps the Enemy had calculated this in the moments before he too entered the neutron star's transit. An assumption. In space, assumptions kill. Deep in his quantum memories, Jedden knew what was out there. The slow way home.

Fast Man, slowly

Kites, banners, pennants, and streamers painted with the scales and heads of ritual snakes flew from the sun rigging on the Festival of Fast Children. At the last minute, the climate people had received budgetary permission to shift the prevailing winds lower. The Clave had argued that the Festival of Fast Children seemed to come round every month and a half, which it did, but the old and slow said, *not to the children it doesn't.*

Fast Man turned off the dust road on to the farm track. The wooden gate was carved with the pop-eyed, O-mouthed hearth-gods, the chubby, venal guardians of agricultural Yoe Canton. As he slowed to Parent Speed, the nodding heads of the meadow flowers lifted to a steady metronome tick. The wind-rippled grass became a restless choppy sea of current and cross-currents. Above him, the clouds raced down the face of the sun-rod that ran the length of the environment cylinder, and in the wide yard before the frowning eaves of the ancient earthen manor, the children, preparing for the ritual Beating of the Sun-lines, became plumes of dust.

For three days, he had walked up the eternal hill of the cylinder curve, through the tended red forests of Canton Ahaea. Fast Man liked to walk. He walked at Child-Speed and they would loop around him on their bicycles and ped-cars and then pull away shouting, you're not so fast, Fast Man! He could have caught them, of course, he could have easily outpaced them. They knew that, they knew he could on a wish take the form of a bird, or a cloud, and fly away from them up to the ends of the world. Everyone in the Three Worlds knew Fast Man. He needed neither sleep nor food, but he enjoyed the taste of the highly seasoned, vegetable-based cuisine of the Middle Cantons and their light but fragrant beer, so he would call each night at a hostel or township pub. Then he would drop down into Parent Speed and talk with the locals. Children were fresh and bright and inquiring, but for proper conversation, you needed adults.

The chirping cries of the children rang around the grassy eaves of Toe Yau Manor. The community had gathered, among them the Toe Yau's youngest, a skipping five year-old. In her own speed, that was. She was months old to her parents; her birth still a fresh and painful memory. The oldest, the one he had come about, was in his early teens. Noha and Jehau greeted Fast Man with water and bread.

"God save all here," Fast Man blessed them. Little Nemaha flickered around him like summer evening bugs. He heard his dual-speech unit translate the greeting into Children-Speech in a chip of sound. This was his talent and his fame; that his mind and words could work in two times at once. He was the generational ambassador to three worlds.

The three great cylinders of the Aeo Taea colony fleet were fifty Adult Years along in their journey to the star Sulpees 2157 in the Anpreen categorisation. A sweet little golden star with a gas giant pressed up tight to it, and, around that gas world, a sun-warmed, tear-blue planet. Their big, slow lathe-sculpted asteroids, two hundred kilometres long, forty across their flats, had appeared as three small contacts at the extreme edge of the Commonweal's sensory array. Too far from their flightpath to the Tay system and, truth be told, too insignificant. The galaxy was festering with little sub-species, many of them grossly ignorant that they were part of an immeasurably more vast and glorious Clade, all furiously engaged on their own grand little projects and empires. Races became significant when they could push lightspeed. Ethnologists had noted as a point of curiosity a peculiar time distortion to the signals, as if everything had been slowed to a tenth normal speed. Astrogators had put it down to an unseen gravitational lensing effect and noted course and velocity of the lumbering junk as possible navigation hazards.

That idle curiosity, that moment of fastidiousness of a now-dead, now-vaporised Anpreen who might otherwise have dismissed it, had saved Jedden. There had always been more hope than certainty in the mad plan he had concocted as he watched the Anpreen civilization end in nova light. Hope as he opened up the dark energy that warped space-time in calculations made centuries before that would only bear fruit centuries to come. Hope as he woke up, year upon year in the long flight to the stray neutron star, always attended by doubt. The slightest miscalculation could throw him off by light-years and centuries. He himself could not die, but his reaction mass was all too mortal. Falling forever between stars was worse than any death. He could have abolished that doubt with a thought, but so would the hope have been erased to become mere blind certainty.

Hoping and doubting, he flew out from the slingshot around the neutron star.

Because he could hope, he could weep; smart-ice tears when his long range radars returned three slow-moving images less than five light-hours from the position he had computed. As he turned the last of his reaction mass into dark energy to match his velocity with the Aeo Taea armada, a stray calculation crossed his consciousness. In all his redefinitions and reformations, he had never given up the ability to see numbers, to hear what they whispered to him. He was half a millennium away from the lives he had known on Tay.

For ten days, he broadcast his distress call. *Help, I am a refugee from a star war.* He knew that, in space, there was no rule of the sea, as there had been on Tay's world ocean, no Aspects at once generous, stern, and gallant that had been known as SeaSelves. The Aeo Taea could still kill him with negligence. But he could sweeten them with a bribe.

Like many of the country houses of Amoa ark, Toe Yau Manor featured a wooden belvedere, this one situated on a knoll two fields spinward from the old house. Airy and gracious, woven from genetweak willow plaits, it and its country cousins all across Amoa's Cantons had become a place for Adults, where they could mix with ones of their own speed, talk without the need for the hated speech convertors around their necks, gripe and moan and generally gossip, and, through the central roof iris, spy through the telescope on their counterparts on the other side of the world. Telescope parties were the latest excuse for Parents to get together and complain about their children.

But this was their day—though it seemed like a week to them—the Festival of Fast Children, and this day Noha Toe Yau had his telescope trained not on his counterpart beyond the sun, but on the climbing teams fizzing around the sun-riggings, tens of kilometres above the ground, running out huge monoweave banners and fighting ferocious kite battles high where the air was thin.

"I tell you something, no child of mine would ever be let do so damn fool a thing," Noha Toe Yau grumbled. "I'll be surprised if any of them make it to the Destination."

Fast Man smiled, for he knew that he had only been called because Yemoa Toe Yau was doing something much more dangerous.

Jehau Toe Yau poured chocolate, thick and cooling and vaguely hallucinogenic.

"As long as he's back before Starship Day," she said. She frowned down at the wide green before the manor where the gathered Fast Children of the neighbourhood in their robes and fancies were now hurtling around the long trestles of festival foods. They seemed to be engaged in a high-velocity food fight. "You know, I'm sure they're speeding the days up. Not much, just a little every day, but definitely speeding them up. Time goes nowhere these days."

Despite a surprisingly sophisticated matter-anti-matter propulsion system, the Aeo Taea fleet was limited to no more than ten percent of lightspeed, far below the threshold where time dilation became perceptible. The crossing to the Destination—Aeo Taea was a language naturally given to Portentous Capitalizations, Fast Man had discovered—could only be made by generation ship. The Aeo Taea had contrived to do it in just one generation. The strangely slow messages the Anpreen had picked up from the fleet were no fluke of space-time distortion. The voyagers' bodies, their brains, their perceptions and metabolisms, had been in-vitro engineered to run at one-tenth hominiform normal. Canned off from the universe, the interior lighting, the gentle spin gravity and the slow, wispy climate easily adjusted to a life lived at a snail's pace. Morning greetings lasted hours, that morning a world-week. Seasons endured for what would have been years in the outside universe, vast languorous autumns. The three hundred and fifty years of the crossing would pass in the span of an average working career. Amoa was a world of the middle-aged.

Then Fast Man arrived and changed everything.

"Did he give any idea where he was going?" Fast Man asked. It was always the boys. Girls worked it through, girls could see further.

Jehau pointed down. Fast Man sighed. Rebellion was limited in Amoa, where any direction you ran lead you swiftly back to your own doorstep. The wires that rigged the long sun could take you high, kilometres above it all in your grand indignation. Everyone would watch you through their telescopes, up there high and huffing, until you got hungry and wet and

bored and had to come down again. In Amoa, the young soul rebels went
out.

Fast Man set down his chocolate glass and began the subtle exercise
that reconfigured the motes of his malleable body. To the Toe Yaus, he
seemed to effervesce slightly, a sparkle like fine silver talc or the dust
from a moth's wings. Jehau's eyes widened. All the three worlds knew
of Fast Man, who had brought the end of the Journey suddenly within
sight, soothed generational squabbles, and found errant children—and so
everyone though they knew him personally. Truly, he was an alien.

"It would help considerably if they left some idea of where they were
going," Fast Man said. "There's a lot of space out there. Oh well. I'd stand
back a little, by the way." He stood up, opened his arms in a little piece
of theatre, and exploded into a swarm of motes. He towered to a buzzing
cylinder that rose from the iris at the centre of the belvedere. *See this
through your telescopes on the other side of the world and gossip.* Then, in a
thought, he speared into the earth and vanished.

In the end, the Fast Boy was pretty much where Fast Man reckoned
he would be. He came speed-walking up through the salt-dead city-
scape of the communications gear just above the convex flaring of the
drive shield, and there he was, nova-bright in Fast man's radar sight. A
sweet, neat little cranny in the main dish gantry with a fine view over
the construction site. Boys and building. His complaining to the Toe
Yaus had been part of the curmudgeonly image he liked to project. Boys
were predictable things.

"Are you not getting a bit cold up there?" Fast Man said. Yemoa started
at the voice crackling in his helmet phones. He looked round, helmet
tilting from side to side as he tried to pick the interloper out of the limitless
shadow of interstellar space. Fast Man increased his surface radiance. He
knew well how he must seem; a glowing man, naked to space, toes firmly
planted on the pumice-dusted hull and leaning slightly forward against the
spin force. He would have terrified himself at that age, but awe worked for
the Fast Children as amiable curmudgeon worked for their slow parents.

"Go away."

Fast Man's body-shine illuminated the secret roots. Yemoa Toe Yau was
spindly even in the tight yellow and green pressure skin. He shuffled around
to turn his back; a deadlier insult among the Aeo Taea than among the

Aspects of Tay for all their diverse etiquettes. Fast Man tugged at the boy's safety lanyard. The webbing was unfrayed, the carabiner latch operable.

"Leave that alone."

"You don't want to put too much faith in those things. Cosmic rays can weaken the structure of the plastic: put any tension on them, and they snap just like that, just when you need them most. Yes sir, I've seen people just go sailing out there, right away out there."

The helmet, decorated with bright bird motifs, turned toward Fast Man.

"You're just saying that."

Fast Man swung himself up beside the runaway and settled into the little nest. Yemoa wiggled away as far as the cramped space would permit.

"I didn't say you could come up here."

"It's a free ship."

"It's not *your* ship."

"True," said Fast Man. He crossed his legs and dimmed down his self-shine until they could both look out over the floodlit curve of the star drive works. The scalarity drive itself was a small unit—small by Amoa's vistas; merely the size of a well-established country manor. The heavy engineering that overshadowed it, the towering silos and domes and pipeworks, was the transfer system that converted water and anti-water into dark energy. Above all, the lampships hovered in habitat-stationary orbits, five small suns. Fast Man did not doubt that the site hived with desperate energy and activity, but to his Child Speed perceptions, it was as still as a painting, the figures in their bird-bright skinsuits, the heavy engineers in their long-duration work armour, the many robots and vehicles and little jetting skipcraft all frozen in time, moving so slowly that no individual motion was visible, but when you looked back, everything had changed. A long time even for a Parent, Fast Man sat with Yemoa. Beyond the construction lights, the stars arced past. How must they seem to the adults, Fast Man thought, and in that thought pushed down into Parent Speed and felt a breathless, deeply internalised gasp of wonder as the stars accelerated into curving streaks. The construction site ramped up into action; the little assembly robots and skippers darting here and there on little puffs of reaction gas.

Ten years, ten grown-up years, since Fast Man had osmsoed through the hull and coalesced out of a column of motes on to the soil of Ga'atu Colony, and still he did not know which world he belonged to, Parent or

Fast Children. There had been no Fast Children then, no children at all. That was the contract. When the Destination was reached, that was the time for children, born the old way, the fast way, properly adjusted to their new world. Fast Man had changed all that with the price of his rescue: the promise that the Destination could be reached not in slow years, not even in a slow season, but in hours; real hours. With a proviso; that they detour—a matter of moments to a relativistic fleet—to Fast Man's old homeworld of Tay.

The meetings were concluded, the deal was struck, the Aeo Taea fleet's tight tight energy budget would allow it, just. It would mean biofuels and muscle power for the travellers; all tech resources diverted to assembling the three dark energy scalarity units. But the journey would be over in a single sleep. Then the generous forests and woodlands that carpeted the gently rolling midriffs of the colony cylinders all flowered and released genetweak pollen. Everyone got a cold for three days, everyone got pregnant, and nine Parent months later, the first of the Fast Children was born.

"So where's your clip?"

At the sound of Yemoa's voice, Fast Man geared up into Child Speed. The work on the dazzling plain froze, the stars slowed to a crawl.

"I don't need one, do I?" Fast Man added, "I know exactly how big space is."

"Does it really use dark energy?"

"It does."

Yemoa pulled his knees up to him, stiff from his long vigil in the absolute cold. A splinter of memory pierced Fast Man: the fast-frozen canals of Jann, the months-long dark. He shivered. Whose life was that, whose memory?

"I read about dark energy. It's the force that makes the universe expand faster and faster, and everything in it, you, me, the distance between us. In the end, everything will accelerate away so fast from everything else that the universe will rip itself apart, right down to the quarks."

"That's one theory."

"Every particle will be so far from everything else that it will be in a universe of its own. It will *be* a universe of its own."

"Like I said, it's a theory. Yemoa, your parents . . . "

"You use this as a space drive."

"Your matter/anti-matter system obeys the laws of Thermodynamics, and that's the heat-death of the universe. We're all getter older and colder and more and more distant. Come on, you have to come in. You must be uncomfortable in that suit."

The Aeo Taea skinsuits looked like flimsy dance costumes to don in the empty cold of interstellar space but their hides were clever works of molecular technology, recycling and refreshing and repairing. Still, Fast Man could not contemplate the itch and reek of one after days of wear.

"You can't be here on Starship Day," Fast Man warned. "Particle density is very low out here, but it's still enough to fry you, at lightspeed."

"We'll be the Slow ones then," Yemoa said. "A few hours will pass for us, but in the outside universe, it will be fifty years."

"It's all relative," Fast Man said.

"And when we get there," Yemoa continued, "we'll unpack the landers and we'll go down and it'll be the new world, the big Des Tin Ay Shun, but our Moms and Dads, they'll stay up in the Three Worlds. And we'll work, and we'll build that new world, and we'll have our children, and they'll have children, and maybe we'll see another generation after that, but in the end, we'll die, and the Parents up there in the sky, they'll hardly have aged at all."

Fast Man draped his hands over his knees.

"They love you, you know."

"I know. I know that. It's not that at all. Did you think that? If you think that, you're stupid. What does everyone see in you if you think stuff like that? It's just . . . what's the point?"

None, Fast Man thought. *And everything. You are as much point as the universe needs, in your yellow and green skinsuit and mad-bird helmet and fine rage.*

"You know," Fast Man said, "whatever you think about it, it's worse for them. It's worse than anything I think you can imagine. Everyone they love growing old in the wink of an eye, dying, and they can't touch them, they can't help, they're trapped up there. No, I think it's so very much worse for them."

"Yah," said Yemoa. He slapped his gloved hands on his thin knees. "You know, it is freezing up here."

"Come on then." Fast Man stood up and offered a silver hand. Yemoa took it. The stars curved overhead. Together, they climbed down from the aerial and walked back down over the curve of the world, back home.

Oga, tearing.

He stood on the arch of the old Jemejnay bridge over the dead canal. Acid winds blew past him, shrieking on the honed edges of the shattered porcelain houses. The black sky crawled with suppressed lightning. The canal was a dessicated vein, cracked dry, even the centuries of trash wedged in its cracked silts had rusted away, under the bite of the caustic wind, to scabs and scales of slag. The lagoon was a dish of pure salt shimmering with heat haze. In natural light, it would have been blinding but no sun ever challenged the clouds. In Oga's extended vision, the old campanile across the lagoon was a snapped tooth of crumbling masonry.

A flurry of boiling acid rain swept over Oga as he turned away from the burning vista from the dead stone arch on to Ejtay Quay. His motes sensed and changed mode on reflex, but not before a wash of pain burned through him. Feel it. It is punishment. It is good.

The houses were roofless, floorless; rotted snapped teeth of patinated ceramic,: had been for eight hundred years. Drunken Chicken Street. Here Kentlay the Lonely had sat out in the sun and passed the time of day with his neighbours and visitors come for his gift. Here were the Dilmajs and the vile, cruel little son who had caught birds and pulled their feathers so that they could not fly from his needles and knives, street bully and fat boy. Mrs Supris, a sea-widow, a baker of cakes and sweets, a keeper of mournings and ocean-leavings. All dead. Long dead, dead with their city, their world.

This must be a mock Ctarisphay, a stage, a set, a play-city for some moral tale of a prodigal, an abandoner. A traitor. Memories turned to blasted, glowing stumps. A city of ruins. A world in ruins. There was no sea any more. Only endless poisoned salt. This could not be true. Yet this was his house. The acid wind had no yet totally erased the carved squid that stood over the door. Oga reached up to touch. It was hot, biting hot; everything was hot, baked to an infra-red glow by runaway greenhouse effect. To Oga's carbon-shelled fingertips, it was a small stone prayer, a whisper caught in a shell. If the world had permitted tears, the old, eroded stone squid would have called Oga's. Here was the hall, here the private parlour, curved in on itself like a ceramic musical instrument. The stairs, the upper floors, everything organic had evaporated centuries ago, but he could still read the niches of the sleeping porches cast in the upper walls. How would it have been in the end days, when even the summer sky was black from burning oil? Slow, painful, as year upon year the summer temperatures rose and the plankton blooms, carefully engineered to absorb the carbon from Tay's oil-riches, died and gave up their own sequestered carbon.

The winds keened through the dead city and out across the empty ocean. With a thought, Oga summoned the ship. Ion glow from the re-entry shone through the clouds. Sonic booms rolled across the sterile lagoon and rang from the dead porcelain houses. The ship punched out of the cloud base and unfolded, a sheet of nano motes that, to Oga's vision, called memories of the ancient Bazjendi angels stooping down the burning wind. The ship beats its wings over the shattered campanile, then dropped around Oga like possession. Flesh melted, flesh ran and fused, systems meshed, selves merged. Newly incarnate, Oga kicked off from Ejtay Quay in a pillar of fusion fire. Light broke around the empty houses and plazas, sent shadows racing down the desiccated canals. The salt pan glared white, dwindling to the greater darkness as the light ascended. With a star at his feet, Oga punched up through the boiling acid clouds, up and out until, in his extended shipsight, he could see the infra-glow of the planet's limb curve against space. A tear of blood. Accelerating, Oga broke orbit.

Oga. The name was a festival. Father-of-all-our-Mirths, in subtly inflected Aeo Taea. He was Fast Man no more, no longer a sojourner; he was Parent of a nation. The Clave had ordained three Parent Days of rejoicing as the Aeo Taea colony cylinders dropped out of scalarity drive at the edge of the system. For the children, it had been a month of party. Looking up from the flat end of the cylinder, Oga had felt the light from his native star on his skin, subtle and sensitive in a dozen spectra. He masked out the sun and looked for those sparks of reflected light that were worlds. There Saltpeer, and great Bephis: magnifying his vision, he could see its rings and many moons; there Tejaphay. It too wore a ring now; the shattered icy remnants of the Anpreen Commonweal. And there; there: Tay. Home. Something not right about it. Something missing in its light. Oga had ratcheted up his sight to the highest magnification he could achieve in this form.

There was no water in the spectrum. There was no pale blue dot.

The Clave of Aeo Taea Interstellar Cantons received the message some hours after the surface crews registered the departure of the Anpreen splinter ship in a glare of fusion light: *I have to go home.*

From five A.U.s out, the story became brutally evident. Tay was a silver ball of unbroken cloud. Those clouds comprised carbon dioxide, carbonic, and sulphuric acid and a memory of water vapour. The surface temperature read at two hundred and twenty degrees. Oga's ship-self possessed skills and techniques beyond his hominiform self; he could see the perpetual lighting storms cracking cloud to cloud, but never a drop of pure rain. He could see through those clouds, he could peel them away so that the charred, parched surface of the planet lay open to his sight. He could map the outlines of the continents and the continental shelves lifting from the dried ocean. The chains of archipelagos, once jewels around the belly of a beautiful dancer, were ribs, bones, stark mountain chains glowing furiously in the infra-dark.

As he fell sun-wards, Oga put the story together. The Enemy had struck Tay casually, almost as an afterthought. A lone warship, little larger than the ritual catamaran on which the boy called Ptey had sailed from this quay so many centuries before, had detached itself from the main fleet action and swept the planet with its particle weapons, a spray of directed fire that set the oil fields burning. Then it looped carelessly back out of the system, leaving a world to suffocate. They had left the space elevator intact. There must be a way out. This was judgment, not murder. Yet two billion people, two thirds of the planet's population, had died.

One third had lived. One third swarmed up the life-rope of the space elevator and looked out at space and wondered where they could go. Where they went, Oga went now. He could hear their voices, a low em-band chitter from the big blue of Tejaphay. His was a long, slow chasing loop. It would be the better part of a year before he arrived in parking orbit above Tejaphay. Time presented its own distractions and seductions. The quantum array that was his heart could as easily recreate Tay as any of scores of cultures it stored. The mid-day aurora would twist and glimmer again above the steep-gabled roofs of Jann. He would fish with Cjatay from the old, weather-silvered fishing stands for the spring run of prith. The Sulanj islands would simmer and bask under the midnight sun and Puzhay would again nuzzle against him and press her body close against the hammering cold outside the Tea Lane Womenhearth walls. They all could live, they all would believe they lived, *he* could, by selective editing of his consciousness, believe they lived again. He could recreate dead Tay. But it was the game of a god, a god who could take off his omniscience and enter his own delusion, and so Oga chose to press his perception down into a time flow even slower than Parent Time and watch the interplay of gravity wells around the sun.

On the final weeks of approach, Oga returned to world time and opened his full sensory array on the big planet that hung tantalisingly before him. He had come here before, when the Anpreen Commonweal hung around Tejaphay like pearls, but then he had given the world beneath him no thought, being inside a world complete in itself and his curiosity turned outwards to the shape of the universe. Now he beheld Tejaphay and remembered awe. Three times the diameter of Tay, Tejaphay was the true water world now. Ocean covered it pole to pole, a hundred kilometres deep. Immense weather systems mottled the planet, white on blue. The surviving spine of the Anpreen space elevator pierced the eye of a perpetual equatorial storm system. Wave trains and swells ran unbroken from equator to pole to smash in stupendous breakers against the polar ice caps. Oga drew near in sea meditation. Deep ocean appalled him in a way that centuries of time and space had not. That was distance. This was hostility. This was elementary fury that knew nothing of humanity.

Yet life clung here. Life survived. From two light minutes out, Oga had heard a whisper of radio communication, from the orbit station on the space elevator, also from the planet's surface. Scanning sub Antarctic waters, he caught the unmistakable tang of smart ice. A closer look: what had on first glance seemed to be bergs revealed a more complex structure. Spires, buttresses, domes, and sprawling terraces. Ice cities, riding the perpetual swell. Tay was not forgotten: these were the ancient Manifold Houses reborn, grown to the scale of vast Tejaphay. Closer again: the berg city under his scrutiny floated at the centre of a much larger boomed circle. Oga's senses teemed with life-signs. This was a complete ecosystem, and ocean farm, and Oga began to appreciate what these refugees had undertaken. No glimpse of life had ever been found on Tejaphay. Waterworlds, thawed from ice-giants sent spiralling sunwards by the gravitational play of their larger planetary rivals, were sterile. At the bottom of the hundred-kilometre deep ocean, was pressure ice, five thousand kilometres of pressure ice down to the iron core. No minerals, no carbon ever percolated up through that deep ice. Traces might arrive by cometary impact, but the waters of Tejaphay were deep and pure. What the Taynish had, the Taynish had brought. Even this ice city was grown from the shattered remnants of the Anpreen Commonweal.

A hail from the elevator station, a simple language algorithm. Oga smiled to himself as he compared the vocabulary files to his own memory of his native tongue. Half a millennium had changed the pronunciation and many of the words of Taynish, but not its inner subtleties, the rhythmic and contextual clues as to which Aspect was speaking.

"Attention unidentified ship, this is Tejaphay orbital Tower approach control. Please identify yourself and your flight plan."

"This is the Oga of the Aeo Taea Interstellar Fleet." He toyed with replying in the archaic speech. Worse than a breach of etiquette, such a conceit might give away information he did not wish known. Yet. "I am a representative with authority to negotiate. We wish to enter into communications with your government regarding fuelling rights in this system."

"Hello, Oga, this is Tejaphay Orbital Tower. By the Aeo Taea Interstellar Fleet, I assume you refer to the these objects." A sub-chatter on the data channel identified the cylinders, coasting in-system. Oga confirmed.

"Hello, Oga, Tejaphay Tower. Do not, repeat, do not approach the tower docking station. Attain this orbit and maintain until you have been contacted by Tower security. Please confirm your acceptance."

It was a reasonable request, and Oga's subtler senses picked up missile foramens unfolding in the shadows of the Orbital Station solar array. He was a runner, not a fighter; Tejaphay's defences might be basic fusion warheads and would need sustained precision hits to split open the Aeo Taea colony cans, but they were more than a match for Oga without the fuel reserves for full scalarity drive.

"I confirm that."

As he looped up to the higher ground, Oga studied more closely the berg cities of Tejaphay, chips of ice in the monstrous ocean. It would be a brutal life down there under two gravities, every aspect of life subject to the melting ice and the enclosing circle of the biosphere boom. Everything beyond that was as lifeless as space. The horizon would be huge and far and empty. City ships might sail for lifetimes without meeting another polis. The Taynish were tough. They were a race of the extremes. Their birthworld and its severe seasonal shifts had called forth a social response that other cultures would regard as mental disease, as socialized schizophrenia. Those multiple Aspects—a self for every need—now served them on the hostile vastnesses of Tejaphay's world ocean. They would survive, they would thrive. Life endured. This was the great lesson of the Clade: that life was hope, the only hope of escaping the death of the universe.

"Every particle will be so far from everything else that it will be in a universe of its own. It will be a universe of its own, a teenage boy in a yellow spacesuit had said up on the hull of mighty Amoa, looking out on the space between the stars. Oga had not answered at that time. It would have scared the boy, and though he had discovered it himself on the long flight from Milius 1183, he did not properly understand to himself, and in that gap of comprehension, he too was afraid. *Yes,* he would have said. *And in that is our only hope.*

Long range sensors chimed. A ship had emerged around the limb of the planet. Consciousness is too slow a tool for the pitiless mathematics of space. In the split second that the ship's course, design, and drive signature had registered on Oga's higher cognitions, his autonomic systems had plotted course, fuel reserves, and engaged the scalarity drive. At a thousand gees, he pulled away from Tejaphay. Manipulating space time so close to the planet would send gravity waves rippling through it like a struck gong. Enormous slow tides would circle the globe; the space elevator would flex like a crackled whip. Nothing to be done. It was instinct alone and by instinct he lived, for here came the missiles. Twenty nanotoc warheads on hypergee drives, wiping out his entire rearward vision in a white glare of lightweight MaM engines, but not before he had felt on his skin sensors the unmistakable harmonies of an Enemy deep-space scoopfield going up.

The missiles had the legs, but Oga had the stamina. He had calculated it thus. The numbers still came to him. Looking back at the blue speck into which Tejaphay had dwindled, he saw the engine-sparks of the missiles wink out one after the other. And now he could be sure that the strategy, devised in nanoseconds, would pay off. The warship was chasing him. He would lead it away from the Aeo Taea fleet. But this would be no long stern chase over the light decades. He did not have the fuel for that, nor the inclination. Without fuel, without weapons, he knew he must end it. For that, he needed space.

It was the same ship. The drive field harmonics, the spectrum of the fusion flame, the timbre of the radar images that he so gently, kiss-soft, bounced off the pursuer's hull, even the configuration he had glimpsed as the ship rounded the planet and launched missiles. This was the same ship that had hunted him down all the years. Deep mysteries here. Time dilation would compress his planned course to subjective minutes and Oga needed time to find an answer.

The ship had known where he would go even as they bucked the stormy cape of the wandering neutron star. It had never even attempted to follow him; instead, it had always known that it must lay in a course that would whip it round to Tay. That meant that even as he escaped the holocaust at Milius 1183, it had known who he was, where he came from, had seen through the frozen layers of smart-ice to the Torben below. The ship had come from around the planet. It was an enemy ship, but not the Enemy. They would have boiled Tejaphay down to its iron heart. Long Oga contemplated these things as he looped out into the wilderness of the Oort cloud. Out there among the lonely ice, he reached a conclusion. He turned the ship over and burned the last of his reaction in a hypergee deceleration burn. The enemy ship responded immediately, but its ramjet drive was less powerful. It would be months, years even, before it could turn around to match orbits with him. He would be ready then. The edge of the field brushed Oga as he decelerated at fifteen hundred gravities and he used his external sensors to modulate a message on the huge web, a million kilometres across: *I surrender.*

Gigayears ago, before the star was born, the two comets had met and entered into their far, cold marriage. Beyond the dramas and attractions of the dust cloud that coalesced into Tay and Tejaphay and Bephis, all the twelve planets of the solar system, they maintained their fixed-grin gazes on each other, locked in orbit around a mutual centre of gravity where a permanent free-floating haze of ice crystals hovered, a fraction of a Kelvin above absolute zero. Hidden amongst them, and as cold and seemingly as dead, was the splintership. Oga shivered. The cold was more than physical—on the limits of even his malleable form. Within their thermal casing, his motes moved as slowly as Aeo Taea Parents. He felt old as this ice and as weary. He looked up into the gap between ice worlds. The husband-comet floated above his head like a halo. He could have leaped to it in a thought.

Lights against the starlight twinkle of the floating ice storm. A sudden occlusion. The Enemy was here. Oga waited, feeling every targeting sensor trained on him.

No, you won't, will you? Because you have to know.

A shadow detached itself from the black ship, darkest on dark, and looped around the comet. It would be a parliament of self-assembling motes like himself. Oga had worked out decades before that Enemy and Anpreen were one and the same, sprung from the same nanotechnological seed when they attained Class Two status. Theirs was a civil war. *In the Clade, all war was civil war*, Oga thought. Panhumanity was all there was. More like a family feud. Yes, those were the bloodiest fights of all. No quarter and no forgiveness.

The man came walking around the small curve of the comet, kicking up shards of ice crystals from his grip soles. Oga recognised him. He was meant to. He had designed himself so that he would be instantly recognisable, too. He bowed, in the distances of the Oort cloud.

"Torben Reris Orhum Fejannan Kekjay Prus Rejmer Serejen Nejben, sir."

The briefest nod of a head, a gesture of hours in the slow-motion hypercold.

"Torben. I'm not familiar with that name."

"Perhaps we should use the name most familiar to you. That would be Serejen, or perhaps Fejannen, I was in that Aspect when we last met. I would have hoped you still remembered the old etiquette."

"I find I remember too much these days. Forgetting is a choice since I was improved. And a chore. What do they call you now?"

"Oga."

"Oga it shall be, then."

"And what do they call *you* now?"

The man looked up into the icy gap between worldlets. *He has remembered himself well*, Oga thought. *The slight portliness, the child-chubby features, like a boy who never grew up. As he says, forgetting is a chore.*

"The same thing they always have: Cjatay."

"Tell me your story then, Cjatay. This was never your fight, or my fight."

"You left her."

"She left *me*, I recall, and, like you, I forget very little these days. I can see the note still; I could recreate it for you, but it would be a scandalous waste of energy and resources. She went to you."

"It was never me. It was the cause."

"Do you truly believe that?"

Cjatay gave a glacial shrug.

"We made independent contact with them when they came. The Council of governments was divided, all over the place, no coherent approach or strategy. 'Leave us alone. We're not part of this.' But there's no neutrality in these things. We had let them use our system's water. We had the space elevator they built for us, there was the price, there was the blood money. We knew it would never work—our hope was that we could convince them that some of us had always stood against the Anpreen. They torched Tay anyway, but they gave us a deal. They'd let us survive as a species if some of us joined them on their crusade."

"They *are* the Anpreen."

"*Were* the Anpreen. I know. They took me to pieces. They made us into something else. Better, I think. All of us, there were twenty four of us. Twenty four, that was all the good people of Tay, in their eyes. Everyone who was worth saving."

"And Puzhay?"

"She died. She was caught in the Arphan conflagration. She went there from Jann to be with her parents. It always was an oil town. They melted it to slag."

"But you blame me."

"You are all that's left."

"I don't believe that. I think it was always personal. I think it was always revenge."

"You still exist."

"That's because you don't have all the answers yet."

"We know the kind of creatures we've become; what answers can I not know?"

Oga dipped his head, then looked up to the halo moon, so close he could almost touch it.

"Do you want me to show you what they fear so much?"

There was no need for the lift of the hand, the conjuror's gesture; the pieces of his ship-self Oga had seeded so painstakingly through the wife-comet's structure were part of his extended body. *But I do make magic here*, he thought. He dropped his hand. The star-speckled sky turned white, hard painful white, as if the light of every star were arriving at once. *An Olbers sky*, Oga remembered from his days in the turrets and cloisters of Jann. And as the light grew intolerable, it ended. Blackness, embedding, huge and comforting. The dark of death. Then Oga's eyes grew familiar with the dark, and, though it was the plan and always had been the plan, he felt a plaint of awe as he saw ten thousand galaxies resolve out of the Olbers dazzle. And he knew that Cjatay saw the same.

"Where are we? What have you done?"

"We are somewhere in the region of two hundred and thirty million light years outside our local group of galaxies, more precisely, on the periphery of the cosmological galactic supercluster known as the Great Attractor. I made some refinements to the scalarity drive unit to operate in a one dimensional array."

"Faster-than-light travel," Cjatay said, his upturned face silvered with the light of the ten thousand galaxies of the Great Atrractor.

"No, you still don't see it," Oga said, and again turned the universe white. Now when he flicked out of hyperscalarity, the sky was dark and starless but for three vast streams of milky light that met in a triskelion hundreds of millions of light years across.

"We are within the Bootes Supervoid," Oga said. "It is so vast that if our own galaxy were in the centre of it, we would have thought ourselves alone and that our galaxy was the entire universe. Before us are the Lyman alpha-blobs, three conjoined galaxy filaments. These are the largest structures in the universe. On scales larger than this, structure becomes random and grainy. We become grey. These are the last grand vistas, this is the end of greatness."

"Of course, the expansion of space is not limited by lightspeed," Cjatay said.

"Still you don't understand." A third time, Oga generated the dark energy from the ice beneath his feet and focused it into a narrow beam between the wife-comet and its unimaginably distant husband. *Two particles in contact will remain in quantum entanglement no matter how far they are removed*, Oga thought. *And is that true also for lives?* He dismissed the scalarity generator and brought them out in blackness. Complete, impenetrable, all-enfolding blackness, without a photon of light.

"Do you understand where I have brought you?"

"You've taken us beyond the visible horizon," Cjatay said. "You've pushed space so far that the light from the rest of the universe has not had time to reach us. We are isolated from every other part of reality. In a philosophical sense, we are a universe in ourselves."

"That was what they feared? You feared?"

"That the scalarity drive had the potential to be turned into a weapon of unimaginable power? Oh yes. The ability to remove any enemy from reach, to banish them beyond the edge of the universe. To exile them from the universe itself, instantly and irrevocably."

"Yes, I can understand that, and that you did what you did altruistically. They were moral genocides. But our intention was never to use it as a weapon—if it had been, wouldn't we have used it on you?"

Silence in the darkness beyond dark.

"Explain then."

"I have one more demonstration."

The mathematics were critical now. The scalarity generator devoured cometary mass voraciously. If there were not enough left to allow him to return them home . . . Trust number, Oga. You always have. Beyond the edge of the universe, all you have is number. There was no sensation, no way of perceiving when he activated and deactivated the scalarity field, except by number. For an instant, Oga feared number had failed him, a first and fatal betrayal. Then light blazed down on to the dark ice. A single blinding star shone in the absolute blackness.

"What is that?"

"I pushed a single proton beyond the horizon of this horizon. I pushed it so far that space and time tore."

"So I'm looking at . . . "

"The light of creation. That is an entire universe, new born. A new big bang. A young man once said to me, 'Every particle will be so far from everything else that it will be in a universe of its own. It will *be* a universe of its own.' An extended object like this comet, or bodies, is too gross, but in a single photon, quantum fluctuations will turn it into an entire universe-in-waiting."

The two men looked up a long time into the nascent light, the surface of he fireball seething with physical laws and forces boiling out. *Now you understand*, Oga thought. *It's not a weapon. It's the way out. The way past the death of the universe. Out there beyond the horizon, we can bud off new universes, and universes from those universes, forever. Intelligence has the last word. We won't die alone in the cold and the dark.* He felt the light of the infant universe on his face, then said, "I think we probably should be getting back. If my calculations are correct—and there is a significant margin of error—this fireball will shortly undergo a phase transition as dark energy separates out and will undergo catastrophic expansion. I don't think that the environs of an early universe would be a very good place for us to be."

He saw portly Cjatay smile.

"Take me home, then. I'm cold and I'm tired of being a god."

"Are we gods?"

Cjatay nodded at the microverse.

"I think so. No, I know I would want to be a man again."

Oga thought of his own selves and lives, his bodies and natures. Flesh indwelled by many personalities, then one personality—one aggregate of experience and memory—in bodies liquid, starship, nanotechnological. And he *was* tired, so terribly tired beyond the universe, centuries away from all that he had known and loved. All except this one, his enemy.

"Tejaphay is no place for children."

"Agreed. We could rebuild Tay."

"It would be a work of centuries."

"We could use the Aeo Taea Parents. They have plenty of time."

Now Cjatay laughed.

"I have to trust you now, don't I? I could have vaporized you back there, blown this place to atoms with my missiles. And now you create an entire universe . . . "

"And the Enemy? They'll come again."

"You'll be ready for them, like you were ready for me. After all, I am still the enemy."

The surface of the bubble of universe seemed to be in more frenetic motion now. The light was dimming fast.

"Let's go then," Cjatay said.

"Yes," Oga said. "Let's go home."

Oga, returning

2009 HUGO NOMINEES AND WINNERS

Best Novel
Anathem by Neal Stephenson
The Graveyard Book by Neil Gaiman **(winner)**
Little Brother by Cory Doctorow
Saturn's Children by Charles Stross
Zoe's Tale by John Scalzi

Best Novella
"The Erdmann Nexus" by Nancy Kress (*Asimov's* Oct/Nov 2008) **(winner)**
"The Political Prisoner" by Charles Coleman Finlay (*F&SF* Aug 2008)
"The Tear" by Ian McDonald (*Galactic Empires*)
"True Names" by Benjamin Rosenbaum and Cory Doctorow
(*Fast Forward* 2)
"Truth" by Robert Reed (*Asimov's* Oct/Nov 2008)

Best Novelette
"Alastair Baffle's Emporium of Wonders" by Mike Resnick
(*Asimov's* Jan 2008)
"The Gambler" by Paolo Bacigalupi (*Fast Forward* 2)
"Pride and Prometheus" by John Kessel (*F&SF* Jan 2008)
"The Ray-Gun: A Love Story" by James Alan Gardner
(*Asimov's* Feb 2008)
"Shoggoths in Bloom" by Elizabeth Bear (*Asimov's* Mar 2008) **(winner)**

Best Short Story
"26 Monkeys, Also the Abyss" by Kij Johnson (*Asimov's* Jul 2008)
"Article of Faith" by Mike Resnick (*Baen's Universe* Oct 2008)
"Evil Robot Monkey" by Mary Robinette Kowal (*The Solaris Book of New
Science Fiction*, Volume Two)
"Exhalation" by Ted Chiang (*Eclipse Two*) **(winner)**
"From Babel's Fall'n Glory We Fled" by Michael Swanwick
(*Asimov's* Feb 2008)

Best Related Book

Rhetorics of Fantasy by Farah Mendlesohn (Wesleyan University Press)
Spectrum 15: The Best in Contemporary Fantastic Art
by Cathy & Arnie Fenner, eds. (Underwood Books)
The Vorkosigan Companion: The Universe of Lois McMaster Bujold
by Lillian Stewart Carl & John Helfers, eds. (Baen)
What It Is We Do When We Read Science Fiction by Paul Kincaid
(Beccon Publications)
Your Hate Mail Will be Graded: A Decade of Whatever, 1998-2008
by John Scalzi (Subterranean Press) **(winner)**

Best Graphic Story

The Dresden Files: Welcome to the Jungle. Written by Jim Butcher,
art by Ardian Syaf (Del Rey/Dabel Brothers Publishing)
Girl Genius, Volume 8: Agatha Heterodyne and the Chapel of Bones.
Written by Kaja & Phil Foglio, art by Phil Foglio,
colors by Cheyenne Wright (Airship Entertainment) **(winner)**
Fables: War and Pieces. Written by Bill Willingham, pencilled by Mark
Buckingham, art by Steve Leialoha and Andrew Pepoy,
color by Lee Loughridge, letters by Todd Klein (DC/Vertigo Comics)
Schlock Mercenary: The Body Politic.
Story and art by Howard Tayler (The Tayler Corporation)
Serenity: Better Days. Written by Joss Whedon & Brett Matthews, art by Will
Conrad, color by Michelle Madsen, cover by Jo Chen (Dark Horse Comics)
Y: The Last Man, Volume 10: Whys and Wherefores. Written/created by
Brian K. Vaughan, pencilled/created by Pia Guerra,
inked by Jose Marzan, Jr. (DC/Vertigo Comics)

Best Dramatic Presentation, Long Form

The Dark Knight, Christopher Nolan & David S. Goyer, story; Jonathan
Nolan and Christopher Nolan, screenplay; based on characters
created by Bob Kane; Christopher Nolan, director (Warner Brothers)
Hellboy II: The Golden Army, Guillermo del Toro & Mike Mignola, story;
Guillermo del Toro, screenplay; based on the comic
by Mike Mignola; Guillermo del Toro, director (Dark Horse, Universal)
Iron Man, Mark Fergus & Hawk Ostby and Art Marcum & Matt Holloway,
screenplay; based on characters created by Stan Lee & Don Heck & Larry

Lieber & Jack Kirby; Jon Favreau, director (Paramount, Marvel Studios)

METAtropolis by John Scalzi, ed. Written by: Elizabeth Bear, Jay Lake, Tobias Buckell and Karl Schroeder (Audible Inc)

WALL-E Andrew Stanton & Pete Docter, story; Andrew Stanton & Jim Reardon, screenplay; Andrew Stanton, director (Pixar/Walt Disney) **(winner)**

Best Dramatic Presentation, Short Form

"The Constant" (*Lost*) Carlton Cuse & Damon Lindelof, writers; Jack Bender, director (Bad Robot, ABC studios)

Doctor Horrible's Sing-Along Blog Joss Whedon, & Zack Whedon, & Jed Whedon & Maurissa Tancharoen , writers; Joss Whedon, director (Mutant Enemy) **(winner)**

"Revelations" (*Battlestar Galactica*) Bradley Thompson & David Weddle, writers; Michael Rymer, director (NBC Universal)

"Silence in the Library/Forest of the Dead" (*Doctor Who*) Steven Moffat, writer; Euros Lyn, director (BBC Wales)

"Turn Left" (*Doctor Who*) Russell T. Davies, writer; Graeme Harper, director (BBC Wales)

Best Editor, Short Form

Ellen Datlow **(winner)**

Stanley Schmidt

Jonathan Strahan

Gordon Van Gelder

Sheila Williams

Best Editor, Long Form

Lou Anders

Ginjer Buchanan

David G. Hartwell **(winner)**

Beth Meacham

Patrick Nielsen Hayden

Best Professional Artist

Daniel Dos Santos

Bob Eggleton

Donato Giancola (**winner**)
John Picacio
Shaun Tan

Best Semiprozine
Clarkesworld Magazine edited by
Neil Clarke, Nick Mamatas & Sean Wallace
Interzone edited by Andy Cox
Locus edited by Charles N. Brown,
Kirsten Gong-Wong, & Liza Groen Trombi
The New York Review of Science Fiction edited by Kathryn Cramer, Kris
Dikeman, David G. Hartwell, & Kevin J. Maroney
Weird Tales edited by Ann VanderMeer & Stephen H. Segal (**winner**)

Best Fanzine
Argentus edited by Steven H Silver
Banana Wings edited by Claire Brialey and Mark Plummer
Challenger edited by Guy H. Lillian III
The Drink Tank edited by Chris Garcia
Electric Velocipede edited by John Klima (**winner**)
File 770 edited by Mike Glyer

Best Fan Writer
Chris Garcia
John Hertz
Dave Langford
Cheryl Morgan (**winner**)
Steven H Silver

Best Fan Artist
Alan F. Beck
Brad W. Foster
Sue Mason
Taral Wayne
Frank Wu (**winner**)

ABOUT THE EDITOR

Mary Robinette Kowal is the author of *Shades of Milk and Honey* (Tor 2010), the fantasy novel that Jane Austen might have written. In 2008 she received the Campbell Award for Best New Writer. She was a 2009 Hugo nominee for her story "Evil Robot Monkey." Her stories have appeared in *Strange Horizons, Asimov's,* and several Year's Best anthologies.

Mary, a professional puppeteer and voice actor, has performed for LazyTown (CBS), the Center for Puppetry Arts, Jim Henson Pictures and founded Other Hand Productions. Her designs have garnered two UNIMA-USA Citations of Excellence, the highest award an American puppeteer can achieve. She also records fiction for authors such as Kage Baker, Cory Doctorow and John Scalzi.

She is serving her second term as Secretary of Science Fiction and Fantasy Writers of America. Mary lives in Portland, OR with her husband Rob and a dozen manual typewriters.

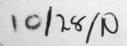